DRINK YOU

EXPLORE MEN OF THE HAMPTONS
BOOK THREE

LULA WHITE

ONGOING SERIES ADVISEMENT

THE SAG HARBOR COMMUNITY

If you are new to LW Books, *Drink You* is a continuation of an ongoing plot line. It contains references to prior events in the series.

This series is a spin-off of the *Sag Harbor Black Romances,* all of which span twelve books. While the *Sag Harbor* series could be read out of order, and this book provides a complete love story, it is highly suggested that you read *Explore Men of the Hamptons* in order.

Here's the order in which to get acquainted with this world. The events do not occur based on order of the books:

Brown Sugar This Christmas
Hot Chocolate This Winter
Flinging All Spring
Overheated for Summer
One Tasty Night FREE Novella
Explore You
Rouse Family Christmas
Christmas Down Under (FREE Download- website only)

Taste You
Drink You
See Through You
Find You

It all started with 3 childhood friends
Books 1-4

Maddy

LULA WHITE
BROWN SUGAR THIS
Christmas

Chrissy

LULA WHITE
HOT CHOCOLATE THIS
Winter

LULA WHITE
Summer

Adella

LULA WHITE
FLINGING ALL
Spring

The Old Hamptons Money

ELLIS/PAGE BLOODLINE

Maddy marries Jerrell
William
Marguerite

TOWNSEND COUSINS

Chrissy marries Sheldon
Cher marries Kevin
Neeraja marries Roland

ENGLISH FAMILY

Solomon marries Chaitra
Lonnie
Constance
Rachel
Martin
Adella marries Desmond
Ilyana

MIDDLETON SONS

Lion marries Kamila
Brendan
Kevin marries Cher

These Black families have thrived in New York since 1700s & 1800s.

The English family arrived in the 1970s & 80s during the real estate boom.

LULA WHITE

LULA WHITE

Explore Adventures is created by Keenan, Solomon, & Kevin

Taste You
LULA WHITE

New Hamptons Money, Books 5-12

ROUSE FAMILY

Roland marries Neeraja
Sheldon married Chrissy
(ex-wife is Eugenia)
Etta
Kamila marries Lion
Jerrell marries Maddy

These Black families arrived in New York after 2000.

MCLAIN FAMILY

Chaitra marries Solomon
Desmond married Adella
Keenan loves Eugenia

CONTENT WARNING, DISCLAIMER & COPYRIGHT

***This book contains strong language and medium-heat sex depictions.**

Trigger warning: pregnancy loss, cancer

This is a work of fiction. Sag Harbor is a real place and the author has included some of its actual neighborhoods, streets and history. However, all of the characters and plot are fictionalized as products of the author's creation, as well as most of the small businesses. (I.e., please do not go to Sag Harbor expecting to visit Little Italy restaurant.) Names of real businesses may be included from time to time, for benign purposes, and to lend authenticity. Any resemblance to actual persons, living or deceased, is entirely coincidental.

ISBN: 978-1-959784-06-7

DRINK YOU PLAYLIST

Hey Loves, I have a music playlist for most of the books in the series. These are the songs I think are most fitting for this couple. In my more intimate posts on Patreon, I share the songs I listened to on repeat and which songs defined some scenes. Lion and Kamilah are funny and fun, but also a little more mellow and chill with how they roll. Some of their music is international jazz, and soulful throwbacks from the seventies through the nineties, with a few relaxing exceptions.

On Spotify it's free to set up an account, open up the web player and listen for free. Here's Drink You on Spotify.

CONTENTS

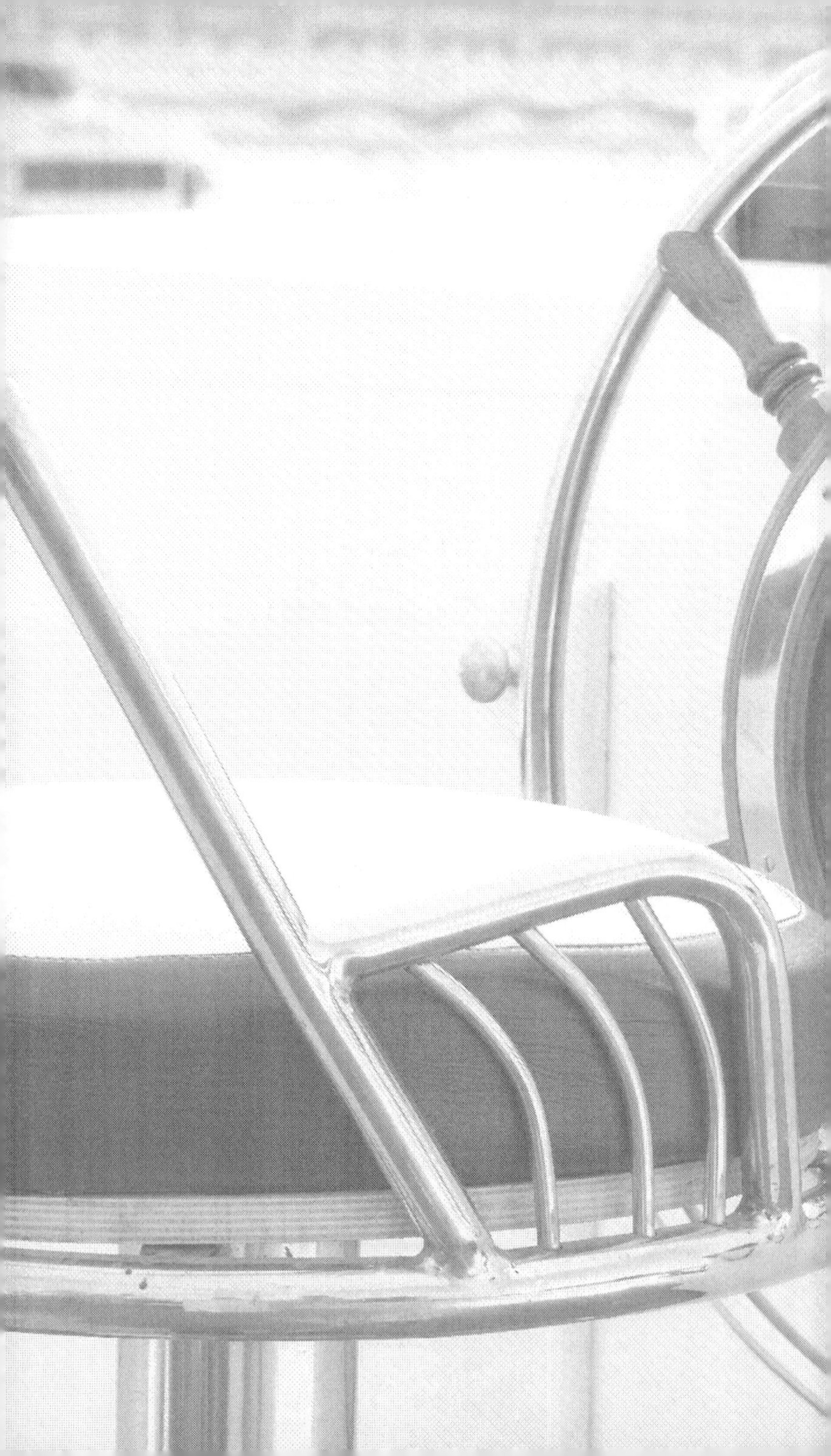

PROLOGUE

HOODWINKED

LION

My phone fumbles through my hands, and almost thuds to the floor. In my fury and confusion, I manage to catch it.

My palm vibrates from scores of text notifications from my family's lawyers, our press handlers, reputation damage team, and my sneaky links. Sitting atop them all is one from my brother, Kevin.

Kevin: *Stop tripping and answer the phone. We need to handle this.*

Not only do I ignore him, but I swipe off all the noise.

I need a minute, or maybe I need the last thirteen years.

Staring back at me is the entire board of directors for Houston PetroChem.

"You understand, don't you, Lion?" the company founder and chairman of the board asks.

What in the hell? Should I lie or tell the truth?

"What do you mean by 'not right now?' When exactly do

you think will be the 'appropriate time?'" With everything in me, it's a struggle to keep my calm and remain seated.

It's unclear what bullshit explanation they give since I already know the answer and have mentally checked out.

Ten minutes later, I raise my head from the cool, granite divider of the bathroom stall. I straighten my tie and make sure my "high yella" skin complexion no longer shows any beet-red hints of blood flow from humiliation.

"Lion! Congratulations!" one of my colleagues calls out. "Come throw a few passes! Let's pop a couple brewskis after work!"

"Not tonight, bruh. Got a plane to catch! You got it, though. Toss one back for me!" I push out fake energy from what's left of me, without turning around, in my haste for the exit.

Another colleague shouts, "What's a party without the Lion? You're a promoted man. This is it! We're going all the way!"

Even while I struggle with the "happy office Negro" pretense, I flee the company I've served for the past thirteen years. My legs can't take me out of here fast enough. "Yeah! All the w--" Angry energy's got me tripping over my own damn feet.

Every wave to the underlings in the hallways drains another ounce from my bottle of fakeness.

"How many chicks we got lined up this weekend, man? Whewww… what I wouldn't give to be you!" a young Black brother calls out, his grin as large and admiring as Texas.

My arms up in the air, no smart-ass retort comes to me. "Who knows? The sky is the limit!" I lie.

False braggadocio is what I wear on the elevator ride down my life to the basement level.

Finally, the safety of my Mercedes engulfs me, where I can loosen my tie from forming a corporate noose around my neck. But I still can't unleash. Even though this is a gated, limited-access parking deck, one of my colleagues might see me break down. A security camera somewhere might capture footage, which could do even more damage to my family.

Still reeling, I stare in the rearview mirror. Myriad inconvenient truths stare back at me.

President. *President.*

Not CEO.

My phone buzzes again. Kevin. I ignore it.

Chess pieces of my situation move through my mind as I move through Houston's afternoon traffic.

In the privacy and sanctity of my house, there's no time to stop and reel at what just happened. I've got to change into my traveling 'fit, confirm the cleaning service will come while I'm away, and check in with my frat who'll grab mail. On the way out, I lock up.

"Come on, King," I call to my French bulldog. "Time to go see Mommy." He seems to sense he won't see me for a minute and whines. "Don't look at me like that, dude, you'll have fun with Cedric."

For my last stop, the door flings open before I ring the doorbell. "Thanks for taking him."

"Whoa, whoa, what's going on?" Ashlyn asks upon seeing me still processing it all. "Boy," she says, rubbing King, "what's wrong with Dad? Am I actually witnessing what I think I am? Your face… wow, I wish I had seen this ten years ago."

"There is no face, Ash. Stop being drama." With some of King's toys and care products in my arm, I brush past her and into her house. Or rather, *our* old house.

"Liar." Her index finger shoots to the space between my eyebrows. "A whole crease, huh? So what is it? Your stocks aren't performing? Your link last night didn't go down on you? The head wasn't good as you hoped? One of them actually got pregnant?" My ex-wife cocks her head to the side with genuine curiosity.

"Lion! Hey there, buddy." Her husband enters from the game room. "I hear we're having company the next few weeks."

"Hey, Lion!" Ash's son greets me while trailing his father.

"Lamar. Cedric. Good to see you two. Fellas, thanks for taking care of my boy. I've got some family business to attend in New York. I owe you guys big. Barbecue on me when I get back!"

"You've got a couple skills on the grill, so I'm holding you to that. Safe travels, man!"

I watch him pat my ex-wife on the butt, and he heads back to the living room with my dog in tow. "Come on, King."

King tosses me a lonesome expression and another whine before I squat to hug him. "I'll be back, homie. I just need time to…"

What?

Resurrect my family's name from the dead?

And to bury my little brother for destroying us.

Despite my attitude, she won't let the issue go, and Ash trails me to the door. "You don't have to admit it. But I only see that crease when you're losing." She kisses her finger pads and places them on my forehead. "Tell Roberta I said hello. And tell Lionel his favorite white girl says he can keep fucking himself."

"That was unnecessary," I say on the way out.

"But dissing your asshole father still feels *so* good. King is in good hands until you get back. Cedric will love having him. Oh, and Lion?" She calls out as I head back to the chauffeured car waiting for me. "Whatever is going on, I hope this is a turning point for you."

She knows me too well.

An hour later, the chauffeur delivers me to the private hangar at the airport, and I'm home free. Shortly, I'll be en route to my beloved New York.

"Mr. Middleton! Has your father gotten off easy by escaping criminal indictment for bribery?"

Shit.

"No comment." I rush out of the car while the driver and concierge service remove my bags. "How did a fucking reporter sneak in here?"

"We have no idea, Mr. Middleton. We apologize for the inconvenience!" one of the workers says and security comes running.

The news reporter is insistent and clearly wants her story, so she shoves her phone toward me. "Did your father also bribe someone for your acceptance at Cornell, Mr. Middleton?"

The airport worker throws himself between us. "Ma'am, get back!"

I'm thankful this guy is a brother.

But this lady clearly has bills to pay, and I must be her next check. "Does your family have a right to keep the Costa Smeralda property in Italy, since your purchase did not amount to fair consideration? Or should you relinquish it to the government? Should your brother, Kevin, return his Harvard degree? What amends will your family make for taking coveted college spots from well-deserving kids who lack your money? Should your father be criminally prosecuted? And will he pay some form of restitution to society?" She continues shouting questions even as security guards carry her away.

The numerous apologies from airport staff turn to white noise behind me.

Aboard the chartered private flight, I sink a couple shots

of whiskey in preparation for takeoff. Liquor loosens the knots tying up my body, but not my mind. In it, the chess pieces of my life keep dancing across the landscape of my future, my family's future, and legacy.

"Mr. Middleton, your duck is prepared and ready for you, sir," one of the flight attendants aboard says, her breasts practically serving themselves on my knees. Along with it, she offers up a smile as easy and smooth as my whiskey. "Will you also be having dessert, Mr. Middleton?"

The loaded expression in her eyes, and breasts cascading, signals what she's really asking: Will I meet her in the bathroom as I have on other flights.

"Actually, Erin, I don't have the appetite this afternoon." I place the cover back on the meal and return it to her. Any other time, I'd be game, but I've been screwed enough for today.

Disappointment crash-lands on her downturned mouth. "Of course. Let us know if we can get you anything else."

Unbothered, I return to the mental chess game I can't stop playing the entire flight home. Which, no matter how many ways I approach it, only leads to one result.

The board of directors is playing me.

They're holding up my promotion and my life, because they intend to use me as bait.

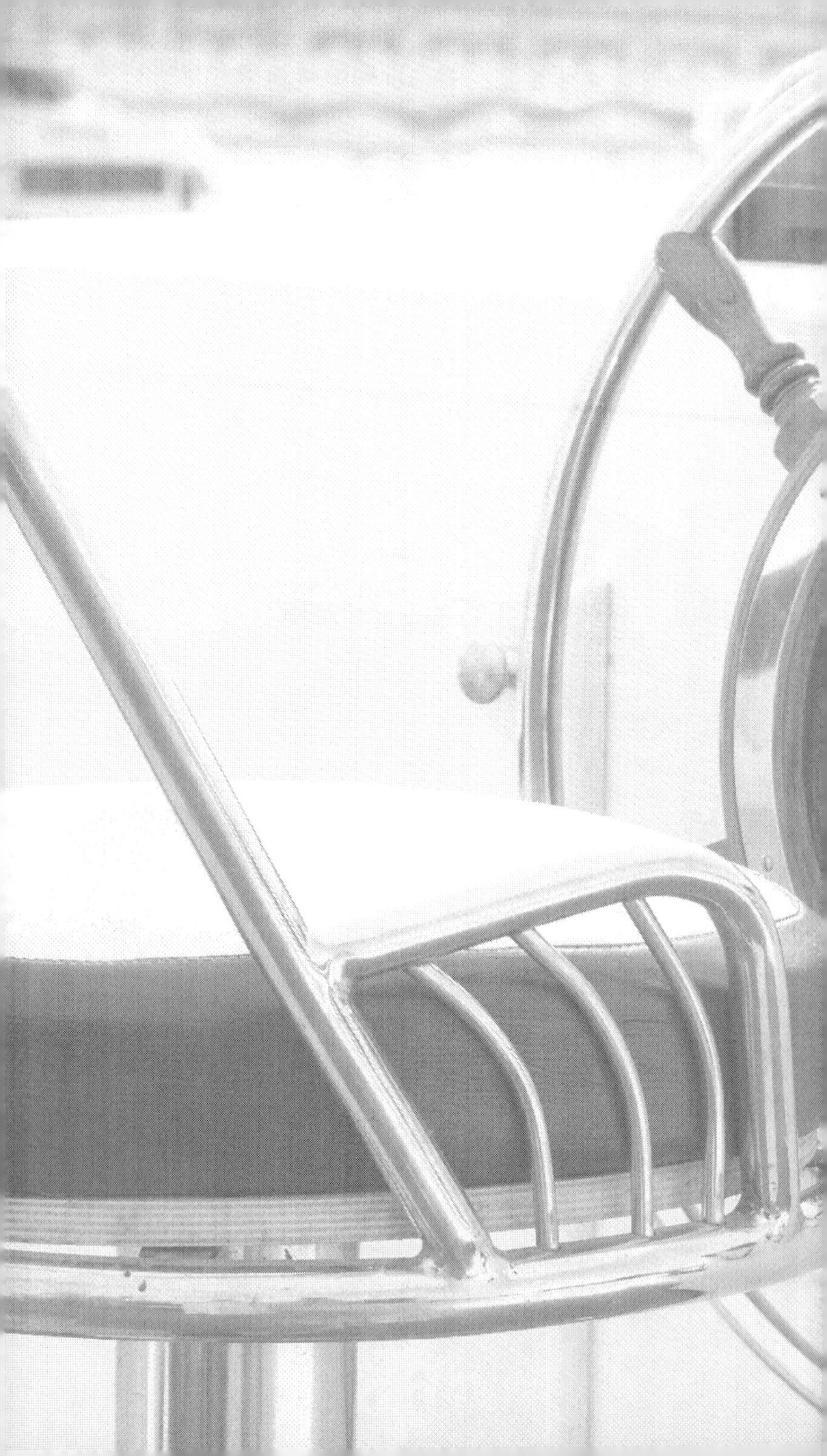

I DIDN'T THROW IT

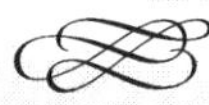

LION

Back in Southampton again, salty Atlantic air recharges my lungs.

I'm home.

Thankfully, my dad must be out with my nephew, and Mom must be shopping. Neither of my brothers have arrived yet from California or Maryland. I'm not ready to tell any of them what's happened when I'm still figuring it out myself.

Once I switch off airplane mode on my phone, multiple voicemails roll through.

My first callback is to my family's attorney.

"Lion! Finally, dude, I've been trying to call you all day. Look, the Boston city attorney wants another interview with your father. They call it just a friendly sit-down. But we know it's another fishing expedition. And then there are the authorities in Italy, and we've received more interrogatories from the IRS, but they won't come up with a damn thing, because *my* father, Percell Sr., made sure your dad's Italian deal was airtight twenty years ago!"

I swipe my hand down my face on the way into my Ferrari. "Percell, let me have some time with him first, all right? I need to explain all this to him. How about we do a conference call this weekend? I just flew into town and I'm headed to go support my friend."

Before I can hang up with him, the reputation management strategist beeps through on the other end.

"Toni."

"Lion, please tell me you're in New York. We need to scrap our plans for a charity golf tournament this fall. The handlers tested a rollout and are receiving blowback for dealing with your family. We'll have to come up with another way to drum up favorable press for your Dad and you."

"Blowback?" I stop myself from punching the steering wheel. "Dad's been supporting that charity since before I was born!"

"We need a new plan, Lion. This is not impossible. It just will not be as easy as we were hoping. Businesses and charities are understandably afraid of touching you guys right now, with all the investigations and bad news write-ups. But we'll forge ahead. Cynthia will shoot you an email with some times we can meet next week. For now, you and your dad relax and take a breather this weekend, and we'll regroup."

Regroup. Tuh.

I'm in the Hamptons for an extended period of time because my family needs a lifeline. Now.

Scrolling to the message from my longtime friend, Duncan Milsap, I pull up the location where he's having a political fundraiser.

As he runs to become the first Black US senator from New York, he needs me at his side and he couldn't have picked a better time. These next few weeks of helping him get his campaign off the ground are my perfect escape from Houston PetroChem. It is also an excuse to return to my father's side and be with him after almost a year of pain and embarrassment.

I stare at the address in my phone again. Slurp? What kind of name is that? That spot is definitely new.

On the quick drive the fourteen or so miles from East Hampton to Montauk with my window down, heavy ocean air slaps me from outside my window. Though we've got salt water in the Texas's Galveston Bay and beaches down in Houston, the Hamptons is where I tossed footballs as a young peanut head, ran barefoot in the fields for baseball, and sailed boats on the tranquil waters where my boys and I often slept under the stars. Nothing compares to the sexy high grass and hushed seclusion of the Hamptons.

With my hand dangling out of the window, I salute the numerous people who watched me grow up. Among them is my boy from yachting as a kid, one of the coolest guys around. He must not see me, so I blow my horn.

"Eh, Karl, what's good, man?" I yell, ready to shoot the shit and catch up.

Rather than face me, he directs his whole body until his back is turned to me, and greets someone else.

The hell? It takes a couple of misses for me to realize that quite a few of my running buddies aren't greeting me back.

Stung and somewhat vexed, I drive over a graveled parking area once I arrive in Montauk. Checking out the brick building, I recall this place was once an old tire warehouse. Now I'm greeted by a humble tavern setup that screams rural America, complete with shiny floors, polished wooden tables, and piles of French oak barrels stacked along a wall.

Am I at the right spot? A *brewery*? This is a far cry from the posh halls and vast, emerald-green hills of the Hamptons Country Club I was expecting for Duncan's political event.

Why would Duncan hold his inaugural fundraiser… *here?*

"Ayyyye!" several voices boom and whoop from the counter at the bar.

Streamers, party hats, campaign election signs, and other memorabilia decorate the tables in the eating area. All clearly marked "Milsap for Senate." Duncan hasn't arrived yet, and the event hasn't started, but his staffers are present and they break from a meeting to start signing in guests. I hate being early.

"Hey, Lion!" a chick calls out who I dated way back. Well, we didn't exactly date.

"Hey, Delia. Good to see you," I respond politely and turn my head so she doesn't come this way.

Two other women call for my attention. But they're not the people whose attention I want.

With a polite, dismissive wave, I approach the bar for a drink. There will be a lot of those over the next few days.

Damn. And here I was looking for a break. To let off some steam and vent to my friends who would actually understand. Now I have to keep up the pretense.

"Ohhh!" Cheers and laughter follow clapping and stomping.

A beer-drinking contest? At a fundraiser announcement? For United States senator? Duncan must be losing his mind.

With a keg of frustration already brewed in me, I'm never one to turn down a good kickback. A ruckus at the bar damn near rocks the entire block. I stand on my toes to see over all the heads, at who stands iun the center of the raucous circle. A beer slams down on the bar.

"Damn! She killed you again!"

I can't miss the sister in the middle.

"Oh no, no, no, sir." A real dime, she wags her small hands that are manicured, her nails short and sharp. "I don't take my payment in Venmo or MoneyCruncher. Cash only."

Her lovely palm slides out and stops in front of her competitor's face. Her athletic, slender arm connects to a tiny, tough, shapely frame. She's a slightly taller version of

Simone Biles or Gabrielle Douglass. Strong and firm, kissed with a carob-shaded complexion, she could easily have been carrying baskets of fruit on her head in the African sun.

A sense of recognition hits me—where one swears they've seen somebody before, but so much time has passed, the memory is lost in the fog of life.

The guy who slaps several hundred-dollar bills in her palm seems about to vomit.

No sooner than he's handed over ten bills, she folds them up. Rather than reaching for a purse, clutch, or pricey wallet, she shoves the wad down her orange spandex halter top. Packs it in alongside her girls and pushes together the entire package, makes sure it's nice and secure in there.

When I manage to uncork my gaze, every other hot-blooded male in the group is eyeballing the same event.

"Mind if I give it a shot?" one brother asks bravely.

With a deep inhale that forces her packages to rise in that strapless halter, she guzzles down a long swig of brew, swallows, sucks the foam off her lips. "Nah. I'm bored enough as it is."

Ha.

"You're standing in the middle of a pack of men in a brewery and you're bored?" I inquire. "Maybe you're just in the wrong location. I can suggest an activity more exciting." I couldn't help myself.

"Tuh." With a side-eye that the devil must have given her himself, she scans me for more than my sex potential. "I doubt it."

Now those eyes cut away from me. I have a response for her. I just haven't figured it out yet.

Somewhere in the distance, familiar voices laugh amid back-slapping. The attention of the group turns to the door, where my friend, Duncan, makes his entrance. Cheers fill the air as he glad-hands his way around the brewery. Tanja, that gorgeous wife of his, flanks him.

Finally, pressing all the priciest flesh on the East Coast, we move toward each other.

He looks over the crowd toward me.

I'm so glad to see this guy, one of the few true friends I might have left after all the scandal of the past year.

"Lion Middleton! You came! It's been a hot damn minute, bruh!"

"We definitely need to talk. Your style has changed, brother."

He grabs me and takes me into a bear hug, and then addresses all his staffers and millennial friends. "Changed? What's better than holding the Senate announcement at one of the hottest venues in New York? Everybody's talking about this place. It's dope." He pulls on my neck, lowers his voice. "And my campaign manager thought it would be good to capitalize on the hype behind this spot. Black men making big moves in the Hamptons. Thought you'd be happy about that, dude."

"Black men, huh?" I've been so laser-focused on the job and my promotion down in Texas that this Slurp thing snuck by me.

"Come on. Meet the new Black money in the Hamptons." His arm still clamped around my shoulder, he turns to a bunch of faces I've never seen. In fact, at least half of them are barely old enough to drink.

"Everybody," Duncan begins, "this is my guy, my longtime friend, Lion Middleton! He's a huge institution around here. You've probably heard of him and his incredible family. A big-shot oil executive down in Houston." Duncan's gaze darts around the crowd.

The laughter and smiles drop. A summer storm must be on the horizon judging by how the temperature in this place just plummeted from red-hot excitement to stone cold. I'm usually a pro in awkward situations like this, but a keg of embarrassment has got me feeling out of place in my own backyard.

Ever the political bullshitter, Duncan carries on like nothing is amiss. "Lion's family was one of the first African American families in these here Hamptons. Over a hundred years ago." He squeezes my shoulders. "They practically built Sag Harbor Hills, Azurest and Ninevah Beach. They were Black whalers and boaters. Some of the Middletons' boats still sail the oceans to this day!"

The uninterested faces of these newcomers stifle yawns and some of them whip out their cell phones. The little runts.

Thankfully, a handful of my friends from the old guard throw up a hand or cup their hands around their mouths. "Lion! The animal is here. Now we can get started."

But aside from my childhood crew, the newer generation is already checked out.

"Aren't you Kevin Middleton's brother?" one of them finally asks. Some young blood with his Afro-Mohawk dyed platinum blond.

"Oh!" one of the campaign staffers says. "Now I see how he looks familiar."

Well, damn, I'm not *that* old.

"Good to see you, dude. Let me handle business, and then, we can talk," Duncan says with a sympathetic pound on my arm. He moves to the center of the event for his formal announcement and speech.

At his side appears the she-devil who is responsible for my family's current strife. Madison Rouse.

The disgust of swallowing my own vomit has never been greater than it is this minute. My hands remain pinned in my pockets, despite the urge to go put her in her place. Her stare crosses mine and freezes, a deer caught in headlights. She knows why I'm here. After the game she and her little friend played last fall, she and I have unfinished business.

As I figure out how to approach her, a server carries a tray of brews by me. "Hello, sir. Which would you like? We have dark ale, pale ale, lager, wheat, stout—"

Any kind that'll get me fucked up. "Which one has the highest ABV?"

"The Slurp Hustler, sir. Thirty-nine-point-nine percent."

I grab that one. And on second thought, another one. "Thanks."

She appreciates the twenty I throw on her tray.

The first mug I take to the head and sink within a minute. No, I can't drain the last nine months that my family name has been in the doghouse, but at least I'm doing something with my hands beside wrapping them around Maddy's neck.

I'm not feeling this crowd with all these strange, new faces. And I'm not ready for the pity party my childhood friends across the room are sure to throw me. It was probably a bad idea to come to this event, but I promised Duncan. At this point, I need his support as much as he needs mine.

I'm not ignorant to how these election seasons work. Duncan only called me here to help him collect dollars from "old money" families like mine, who might be skeptical about voting for a young, fresh guy such as himself. He still needs endorsements from the old guard, types like my dad.

"All right, everybody, let's get started, and I want to introduce the man who will be New York's first Black United States Senator!" Another kid I don't recognize yammers from the microphone.

Duncan takes the stage.

I exit stage left. I'll hang out while he finishes his speech, since I have no stomach for political baloney. Especially not organized by Madison Rouse.

Strolling between the heavy, polished wooden tables, I

sneak away from the crowd and give myself a tour of this building I haven't visited since I was a kid. Before it was a tire warehouse, back in my grandfather's day, it was a shipyard worked by my ancestors who used their pay to fund my forefathers' education at colleges like Howard, Lincoln University, and Yale.

On my way down to the basement, a cereal aroma dominates the stairway and overpowers my sense of smell. Shiny, new steel fermentation vessels of beer greet me in the downstairs area. How things have changed. I suck down some of the brew that doesn't taste too bad at all. In fact, it's pretty damn good. As I meander around these massive silver tanks, I marvel at yet another milestone in the Black Hamptons, a Black-owned brewery.

Guzzling down my second beer, I want another, but I'm too lazy to go back upstairs and get it. But more than that, I'm not in the mood for a crowd that's not "my" people, i.e., old enough to remember Levert.

Besides, there's plenty of beer in these tanks.

There aren't too many handles and hoses at the bottom of the Brite machines. This shouldn't be too hard. I can just grab a little beer from one of these spigots. But when I unscrew one of the knobs, the shit spews in every direction.

"Urgh!" Foamy alcohol soaks my face and neck.

I retwist the cap, but it won't return to its position. Beer gushes on my hands.

Shit!

A hand overtakes mine and mashes downward while twisting the cap. The strong scent of rich, lemon-orange bergamot oil wafts into my nostrils and shakes up my tipsy state of mind.

"If you didn't know how to turn it off, why'd you touch it?" a no-nonsense voice chastises.

"I've been to a ton of breweries. I thought I had it."

"Only you didn't." A sturdy arm brushes across me.

Once I press the beer from my eyes, I capture my first close-up of her muscles twisting along her bare arms that are now soaked and glistening with beer. She's bent over, her avocado-sized breasts peeking at me from inside her halter.

She unscrews another cap and fills my mug.

My lust is interrupted when she straightens up and shoves the mug into my chest, sending more beer sloshing over the rim.

"Did you follow me down here?" I ask.

She pushes up the breasts in her halter where the one thousand dollars she collected earlier sits. I'm guessing this princess probably should have been born a man. She rests her hand against the tank. One of her stilettos kicks out in front of her, and she snaps the other hand on her hip. Her eyebrow cocks up. "You said some place more exciting."

What in the...?

"U-um." Not me stammering. "And you said you doubted there was any place more exciting." I suck down some beer.

"No," she responds, swinging her wicked, bone-straight bob. "I said I doubted *you* could suggest any place more exciting."

Her skin-tight pencil skirt wraps around her hips that can't be any wider than a svelte size four. I wonder just how high I could throw her shrimp-sized ass and catch. With one hand. Her medium-sized lips part a bit, as if waiting for me to speak so she can shoot me down with her next missile.

"What are you going to say? No?"

Is this some fucking joke?

After an excruciating day, I sip more beer and process this for a moment. "I might."

She shifts legs, and her head tips back some. Those honeyed eyes stare at me through slits, like she's daring me to. "All right then. Go ahead. Say no."

Not once does she blink.

Okay, so let me clear my head. Things are getting kind of hazy.

First of all, I have *definitely* seen her somewhere before. A long time ago. If only I could recall where. "Do we know each other?" I ask.

"Are you lollygagging?" she asks back.

Second, this is a trap.

But it's been a long ass day. Hell, a long year, and I've already passed up ass once today.

"How do you fit all that attitude into that miniscule body?"

"Don't worry about my attitude." Her gaze ventures to my crotch and makes me… *me*… feel naked. "Just worry about how I use it."

Still staring at me, she turns up her beer mug and takes devastatingly long, sexual swigs.

Fuck it. I'm tipsy. She is clearly tipsy. And her entire chest is soaking wet. I don't know what her motive was for following me down here. But I'm tired of watching her thin, graceful throat swallow something other than me, so I take her by the waist.

"Enough talking then. How *do* you use it?" I spin her to face the steel tank.

With all her cocky, arrogant self-assurance, I need to confirm she isn't a dude. Or worse, an undercover reporter.

"Just give me a minute to check if this is some bullshit." I inch my hands up her tight skirt, feeling her strong, athletic thighs. She's got a little meat along her lats and femur muscles that bricks me up more. A smooth thong greets me.

Over her shoulder, her stare matches mine while I round the curve of her smooth ass to her inner thighs. Damn, I'm hit with a rush of excitement at how they're slick.

Soon as I touch her feminine lips, where cream gushes, we both snatch air.

For the first time, she almost blinks. An arch curves her back that dips down to her poked-out ass. Through a slight part in her mouth, she sucks in and out. I'm stupefied at how my dick jumps to feel her wetness. She's more than a woman, and more than ready.

I roll her wet thong down her legs, slip my fingers around her opening.

"You going to play with it or fuck it?" Mystery Chick murmurs. Those eyes peer at me again. Piercing, unsmiling, with clear intention behind them that dares me to deny my erection.

Conducting a quick scan of these corners and walls for cameras, I unzip my pants.

Damn. I have no condom.

A genie couldn't produce a condom faster from the other side of her halter. So she clearly came here in need of a quick tryst, and I'm just as quick to oblige.

In my drunken urge to relieve this tension I brought all the way from Texas, I lift her skirt. In a weird, serendipitous moment, we both breathe in at the same time. And I enter her.

Her back shudders and she curls over a bit. Pressed against the tank, she grips the steel until her blood leaves her fingertips. The stiffness across her shoulders tells me she's adjusting to my size.

"Is all that exciting enough for you?"

Apparently, she wasn't expecting so much work tonight.

It's either our synergy or our shared itch that clasps us like magnets.

Not missing a beat, she powers through my size. Circles her ass around as I dive into her. Even through the condom, her cream splashes on my shaft. The sound of her wetness hardens me more. Excited, I push in deeper. Fuck letting her adjust. I'm not pulling it out but winding around and side to side. She's too juicy and muscular, and her cat is eating me.

That toned ass twists and bounces on me until I'm forced to sober up, pay attention, and fuck right. Still behind her, I ratchet up her leg and lock her to me, jam myself all the way in, and thrust toward her chest.

She grimaces with some pain. Curls those smooth lips while she's trying to withstand it. "Mmph."

"More excitement, you said. Right? I still don't know where it's at?" I wrap my fingers around that pretty throat. Even from behind her, I witness the shock along the profile of her face when I bounce her size-four ass on my lap. "You thought you were coming down here to play with a boy?"

"Grrr…" Her pussy grips my shaft like she wants to take it home with her.

"Still doubt me?" I whisper. The sight of her tight lips and her face toughing out what I know is my pressure, hardens my concrete erection.

Pounding, pushing back and forth, jerking, this woman gives it back to me. Not shy, unreserved, no pretense, she's not running. The energy…

Her ass eats me. I pound back, into her muscles throbbing and squishing while they suck me into her. But more than her body, I'm penetrating her strength and force.

Heated, gushing, her pussy quakes around my shaft. I smash my entire rough, hard-ass day into her. But she's a boss, and rides me like she doesn't want me walking out of here with my dick.

"Shit."

Hotter, faster, she whips her ass around until I'm in a trance. She might be in a trance too, and we're on the same telepathic trip. I swear I'm so plugged into her she's controlling every nerve in my wood. This ride is better than LSD.

Mystery Chick's head drops back, with fine, pressed strands of her hair falling across flawless shoulders. Her body convulses once she reaches the tip of her orgasmic wave. I lose myself in this unexpected honey exploding on me. My fingers in her hair, along her scalp, my dick buried in her energetic wetness, I'm lost.

Liquid pours from somewhere close, and sprays over us in a practically earth-shattering explosion that soaks us.

"Aah!" she shrieks, one of her legs still hooked around the back of my knee while she rides. My hands still jerk and bounce her hips so I can live in this juicy heaven just a few seconds longer. I don't want to pull out.

A couple more jerks, and the delirium sends the front of my head leaning on the back of hers, where I pause a moment.

Because when is the next time somebody'll swing on me like Jane in *Tarzan*?

"Get off me."

Only then do I realize the knob on the beer fermenter has spun around. One of us used it for leverage and now it squirts beer all over us.

I twist it in every direction to shut it off as soon as I can.

"Stop," she snaps, twisting in the opposite direction until it slows.

Noises fill up the stairwell above us. As best I can, I wipe off with my hand and wrestle my zipper back up. Mystery Chick maneuvers her skirt back over her ass.

"What's going on down here?" Someone demands to know, heels clacking down the stairs.

Tanja Milsap, Duncan's wife, folds her arms into one another. She is followed by several of Duncan's campaign staffers. Mystery Chick and Tanja hold a stare-down, like a brawl is about to go down. This shocks me, because normally, Tanja is the perfect hostess with everyone at Duncan's events.

Mystery Chick begins, "I was –"

"She tripped." I don't understand why I feel the need to protect this chick's honor. "It looks like... she shouldn't have come here in those crazy high heels. Wrong shoes. I saw her come down here, and I wanted to make sure she was good. And her heel twisted, and she fell into that tank."

I gesture to the vessel where her tiny ass just shined *my* tank.

The appall on Mystery Chick's face rips me a new one. "Yes. I can't imagine what must have gotten into silly, clumsy little me, who didn't know how to work these knobs." Her stank-face could be a weapon, and she definitely wants to destroy me. "Whatever would this damsel in distress have done without Mr. uh—"

"Middleton."

She's pissed. "Yes, Mr. Middleton here. My knight in shining armor when I didn't know what *I* was doing."

"Ha! That's funny," Maddy Rouse says. She also scrutinizes Mystery Chick, as if the two of them know one another. "We should all, um, head back upstairs then. The campaign event is that way. Not down here."

"Thank you," Mystery Chick says to me.

"You're welcome." I still reel from that whole trip around the planet. "The pleasure is mine."

She rolls her eyes. "I was being sarcastic. I didn't really mean that."

I swallow my indignation. Of course, this sexy wanna-be man has no decorum to speak of. "It was pleasurable for a minute anyway."

Everyone else has filtered back up the stairs.

But once Tanja reaches the middle flight, she does a one-eighty toward Mystery Chick and cuts her with a hard glare.

One long nail unfurls from Tanja's hand. "I have that same skirt. It's backwards. Must've gotten twisted around in the short time you tripped and fell."

The way they face off, these two women clearly must have military grade rifles around here somewhere.

"Did I miss something?" I ask.

Tanja's pivot puts the period on whatever silent exchange they just had. Mystery Chick straightens the skirt that is now a wet bandage clinging to her. She struts off.

No chitchat, no ask for a phone number or a follow-up. Which…

…I might not mind.

"I didn't catch your name," I call out after her.

She gives her skirt a final tug, ascending the stairs as if she's not soaking wet and we didn't just get caught freshly fucked. "I didn't throw it."

GROSS UNDERESTIMATION

KAMILAH

"Haha! You still can't catch me!" Through the gardens, I take off running from my nephews and niece.

"You go this way!" my oldest nephew, Jerome, directs the others. "Halle, you go that way!"

"You can go all the ways you want!" I brag. These times with them are probably the ones I enjoy most. At age thirty-six, I might be more out of breath than I was at thirty, but I'm still quick.

They spread out, and I jump over a cluster of tulips.

"Watch it!" my mother calls from the patio. "Don't be trampling all over my new flowers."

Past the gazebo, my parents' backyard extends outward, toward the beach, where I don't feel like running. So they all close in and I've got nowhere else to run. They come to tackle me, and Halle starts with the tickling.

"I got you, Auntie Kam!" Her cute, angelic face hovers over me.

"Yes, you… haha… finally managed to… tehe… catch me."

I laugh harder so she feels like she's really doing something in her effort to tickle me.

Her small fingers tapping and poking all over me give literal life. This is probably one of the best parts of summer—seeing them more now that school is out.

On a cool, early summer Saturday, we head back up to the new house my parents just bought a few months ago.

"Auntie, we're all going to Aunt Maddy's to play with William's kids. You coming, too?" Isaac asks and flings his arms around my waist.

"Why do these kids love to play with me like I'm one of them?" I ask their mother and my sister-in-law, Princess.

"Because you *are* one of them," my mother answers first, on her way to make some phone calls.

"Not this time," I say to Isaac. "But I will next time." After I push a kiss onto his forehead, he takes off to some other distraction.

I plunk down at the breakfast table on the portico, across from Princess. And suck in as much oxygen as I can. Yet, I'm still not breathing.

Last night was the first time all of us were together at the same time, my first instance being in the same room with both of *them*. I haven't seen *him* in fifteen years.

Now my sister-in-law eyeballs me hard. "You need to talk about it."

There's little comfort in my unfinished peach Bellini. I can't think about anything else, other than how fifteen long years fell on my head in one night. The tidal wave of flashbacks sweeps over me again. "You should have been there and seen her face, Princess."

That smirk of victory plastered all over Tanja still dismantles me. Still shoots a flame all the way down my esophagus.

Princess's eyes reflect my appall. "I'm so sorry, Kam." My

sister-in-law and de facto big sister reaches across my family's breakfast table to clutch my hand.

I manage to mutter, "I could've taken that lace-front wig and smothered her ass with it."

"Why did you even *go?"*

"Your husband. He wanted me to check out the brewery, this new spot, Slurp. I thought I was meeting a business client out here. When I got there, the place was full of all this political campaign decor. That's when I saw the signs and paraphernalia everywhere."

Princess shoots me a skeptical side-eye. "Girl, you haven't seen the news lately? You didn't know he was announcing?"

"P." I push my upper torso over the table, closer to her. "Look into these eyes." The mild, ocean air blows my hair that I clear from my face. "Are these the eyes of somebody who wanted to see the world's worst excuse for a man during my breezy summer? You know I don't keep up with politics."

Princess cracks up, but her burst of humor dissolves into ragged coughs, forcing her to take out a handkerchief.

"Are you all right?"

My sister-in-law is slightly off this morning. Like she's tired and has been overexerting herself.

"Girl, Roland needs to take you on a vacation or something. Maybe a trip will do you some good."

She shakes her head and waves me off. "No, I've just been a under the weather these last few weeks. This damn cold won't leave me alone. Plus my allergies are acting up. But back to you." She grabs my other hand. "Listen here. You live a fantastic life most people would kill for, girl. You're stronger than ever. And blessed. Stay focused on that."

I swirl my Bellini around in my champagne flute. "I know, P, but…"

"There is no 'but', Kam. You've been so happy and living in your own element all this time. It was just a momentary run-in. Don't let it steal your joy. Just tell Ro somebody else needs to come meet this client—"

Another bout of coughs rack her chest, her lungs whining and whistling as if they contain a broken engine.

"Sis! What is going on with you? You need to go and get that checked."

Her body jerks from the cough overtaking her otherwise thick, sturdy figure.

"My folks!" Roland enters the door in golf shorts and a golfing shirt. "P, come and take your kids."

P stifles her coughs.

"They're your kids too," she manages to croak. The lemon water next to her plate disappears into P's throat when she sucks it down.

"Yeah, but they're one-point-one percent more yours than mine." He shifts to me. "So, Kam, what did you think of Slurp last night? Lit, right?"

While P tries to control her outburst of gags, she silently urges me to speak my piece.

But this is a tough choice that has me squirming in my seat. I don't normally tell my big brother no. "I didn't like it, Ro. Why did you ask me to go there?" May as well cut to the chase.

"You love alcohol! In every possible form. Breweries, wineries, distilleries, all of that is your jam. And, Kevin Middleton and Solomon English have asked us to serve as their auditing consultants and help them shape up their financial systems and operations. They need us to spearhead the organization of their inventory and assets. Explore will need it for leverage as they grow. Particularly Taste Chocolatier and Slurp. They want a more formal corporate structure, and we're going to help them achieve it."

I roll my eyes. "Why can't Hamp do it?"

Roland jumps back in exaggerated fashion the way he

tends to do with his dramatics. "What do you mean? This project at Explore has Kam written all over it! That's why." He talks while stacking eggs and sausage inside a breakfast croissant and wrapping it all in aluminum foil.

"Why can't you do it? I'm sure you're the one they really wanted."

Now it's he and P who hold the suspicious silent exchange.

"My plate is full already. Plus, you're winding down the Stereo Street project and you've got Flower Haven under control."

"But give me something else. Let me audit Dream Stage. I would rather work with Chrissy and Maddy." I don't care if it's the next planet. I need to be *any*where, other than in this dreary community where I will surely cross paths with those same people again.

"First of all." Ro pauses to suck the food from his fingers.

"Baby, stop that," P chastises.

"My bad, bae."

I roll my eyes. "You can take the Negro out of the country, but not the country out of the Negro."

"And I am damn proud of my country roots," he shoots back while waving his greasy fingers at me. "But anyway, Chrissy and Maddy are our family members, and that's a potential ethics issue I'd rather avoid. And, Dream Stage has a lot of entertainment elements with Chrissy's singing and performances, so I'm giving that to an entertainment auditor. I don't understand what the problem is with you handling Slurp. Men, alcohol, parties. I thought you'd be over the moon. What is up with you?"

I gulp down another long swig of my Bellini to avoid the real answer. The real pain. And to hide my face so he doesn't uncover any hints of it. "I'm not into this whole Hamptons thing. The city is what's up, where my friends are. You know... Harlem? Brooklyn? *Black* people." That part is the straight truth.

My oldest brother still tries to read me as he pops fruit in his mouth and leans over the table to inspect me hard. "Or is this really about you and J still hating Kevin Middleton? And you just don't want to do work for him?" he asks, referencing our little brother, Jerrell, and his old rivalry against Maddy's childhood crush.

Though I'm still not that fond of Kevin Middleton, if he and Jerrell have made their peace, I'm good with that man.

No way am I about to tell Roland's nosy ass the real reason I want nothing to do with Slurp, or anybody even remotely connected to it. So for now, I will allow him to misinterpret the disgust on my face as being associated with the Middletons.

And that one particular Middleton—Lion—it had been a long time since I'd seen him. He didn't remember. But goodness, did he surprise me.

My legs are still vibrating.

"Grow up and get over it, Kam." Roland's voice snaps me back to the present. "Kevin and Sheldon are apparently moving on. Jerrell and Kevin are moving on. Kevin has specifically requested our division. It's what Sheldon wants. The Middletons practically run these Hamptons. Therefore, no is not an option."

With my whole attitude, I pour up another glass of Bellini. Not only do I have personal issues with being here, but generally speaking, my stomach churns at the thought of spending the next several days in these humid, boring marshes. "If I wanted to be in the country, Ro, I would just go home to the Boot. At least our cousins will keep things popping down there."

"But we need to make some money here. Sasha Static is not performing in Baton Rouge. She's coming to the

Hamptons, and Slurp doesn't have much time to get ready."

"I quit."

"Ha! The hell you do."

"Language, young man!" Our mother Verona Rouse is a gentle breeze in this humidity as she sneaks out of the house and onto the patio.

"My bad, Ma." Roland smacks food that leaves a grease stain on our mother's cheek when he kisses it. "Kam, you're not going anywhere. Nobody else will pay you as much as me for you to sneak from work in the middle of the day and go get your hair done or your mani-pedi's. And you love your Manolo Blahniks too much."

He drops to his wife. His hand slides under Princess's chin, tilts her face up, to which she lovingly responds. My brother's hand cups her throat as they exchange decades of sanctity in those few precious seconds of loaded kisses.

Damn.

Now that is the reason I'll probably never marry. Something about Roland and Princess is so syrupy and storybook that if I can't have it like that, I don't ever want it.

Since I've never experienced that one hundred percent vulnerable type of love, I've felt zero pressure to wed and birth children.

My brother rises from her and stretches over to me with his lips puckered. "Come here, baby, give big brother kisses."

I push out my middle finger. Onto his mouth. "There. Kiss that."

He takes out a stack of papers from his back pocket and plops them in front of me. "Here you go. Use the weekend to familiarize yourself. Maybe you can go over there before Monday and say hi."

I cock my neck. "And where are you going?"

"Golf. Gentlemen's lunch on the green. Apparently, this

Duncan Milsap dude is making the rounds for his campaign launch, and Sheldon wants me to come see what's up. Oh! And tonight, Maddy is having a fundraiser at her house. The men of Explore will be there, as well as some of our bank colleagues. You need to drop the attitude and bring your checkbook. The bank needs—"

All of his other words drone on as white noise.

There goes my oxygen again.

No.

Princess's eyes flare at me, and our shared panic ping-pongs across the table. She silently screams for me to *say* something.

"Ro—"

"And no more tripping down and falling in their fermenting cellar." He sucks his teeth and inspects me. "Yeah, I heard about that. Remember your professionalism, Kam."

"Heard about what?" Mama comes back in holding Jerrell's toddler, Chase.

"Nothing, Mama." My side-eye signals to Ro that he should shut up.

I am certain my sister-in-law, Maddy, probably told Ro what happened.

P shoots me a glare. "Tripping and falling? Uh-huh." Her suspicious eyebrow cocks up. "You didn't mention that part. You sure are quiet suddenly. So what did you *really* do?"

I scratch the back of my neck, slide some hair behind my ear, sip more bubbly, anything but connect with her eyes. "Nothing worth mentioning, girl."

"Uh-huh." P's not buying it. "If it wasn't worth mentioning, you would've mentioned it. And laughed about it until your stomach hurt. But you left that one out. And now those lips aren't moving." Over the rim of her lemon water, she squints.

"Hush, P." I reach for my little nephew. At nine months,

he's reached the stage where he's teething and grabbing hold of the chairs while he tries to stand. "Come here, Auntie's Baby."

Chase's chubby cheeks are so kissable. Maddy might be a lot of things—cocky, hard-ass, shrewd—but she and J put a perfect angel into this world with Chase. I sniff his baby powder and baby oil, nuzzle my nose against his soft, moisturized coils, feel his chubby flesh that wriggles in my arms, and I close my eyes.

Fifteen years.

My mother brings me back to the present and our family's new summer home when she reenters the portico. "It's well past time you had one of your own."

The truth spills from my gut. "I don't want kids, Ma."

My mother's lips pinch together with disapproval. "Don't say that. Kids are a blessing."

"My niece and nephews are a blessing, too."

At the thought of opening myself up like that again, the gears and pulleys of my respiratory system come to a screaming halt. Never.

"Kam." P comes over and reaches for the baby who now squirms to get away from me. "You're holding him too tight."

When Chase whimpers, the mother of three displays her parenting prowess and P easily soothes him before she sets him back on the ground to explore again.

"Chase, I'm sor—" I got lost in my own head.

Once Mama clears out, a concerned Princess leans toward me. "What did you—?"

My girlfriend, Ameera, texts me.

Ameera: ***What's popping, hon?***

Me: ***SOS. Please come to these sleepy Hamptons and rescue me. Too many folks with spouses and kids. I'll treat you to brunch. I'm stuck. We need to talk.***

Ameera: ***No need for brunch. Link me to brothas w/ bags.***

Me: ***No promises, but I'll try. Maddy's got a campaign fundraiser tonight. Dicks will likely be in there.***

Ameera: ***Bet.***

Even though Ameera is married, I know sometimes she steps out on her husband, and he does the same. That's likely why they get along so well.

P shoots me a concerned side-eye. After Etta ventures off to play with her kids, P comes for me again. "What did you do?"

Not even Princess can learn this.

I grossly underestimated Lion.

It doesn't matter, since he is a one-and-done. When I followed him down the stairs, the last thing I expected that prep school pretty boy to give me was a rumble in the jungle. His ferocious energy caught me off guard, and now my thigh muscles still feel aftershocks.

I'll manage. It's just a week.

How bad could this be? Explore is a relatively small company that'll only need simple business efficiency methods. I'll put their balance sheets, inventory, and business structure in order. And then I can move on with my life. Easy peasy.

BETWEEN US

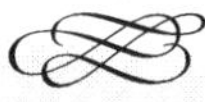

LION

I wake up and go to sleep thinking of how to help my father, and protect him so he can live out his life with the same peace he provided for me. For the past nine months, I've thought of nothing else.

And yet…

…on my way down the stairs, spontaneously, I bring the soft burgundy fabric to my nostrils. I'm thinking of something else, or somebody.

The bergamot aroma blesses my nostrils, my consciousness, my dick again.

A woman has never lingered on me.

Not even Ash.

I've had too much pussy. Of every type, color, and caliber. It's simply too readily available for a man in my position. Even among the so-called celebrities—actresses, singers, models—it's too easy. Since I never have to go without, sex is not a treat I have to crave.

But, for what must be the thirtieth time today, I return to last night, how her muscles rippled under her skin as her ass exercised on my dick and nearly brought me to my knees. How the foam and beer glazed her dusky, African desert skin.

I sniff her thong again. Since Mystery Chick refused to give me her name, I decided not to tell her she'd left it on the floor.

She was so cool and self-assured, maybe even dominant.

Until she crossed Tanja and froze up faster than a trapped rabbit. It must have thrown her off her game, along with Maddy's added scrutiny. How does she know those powerful political players in New York politics? Who is she? I asked a couple of my boys at the event, and they were clueless. And Duncan was so wrapped up in news interviews and donor huddles, he and I never got to talk privately.

But we will. I'll make sure of it. He owes me.

Just inside the foyer stands my father, bent over and grappling with bulky golfing bags.

"Big guy!" I call out and surprise him.

Stunned, he almost teeters over. In his arms are several golf bags filled with clubs. But he catches himself before I can reach him, seeming to grasp desperately for the table as if trying to catch his life. As if the clubs scattering all over the floor might signal his life falling apart.

For a fraction of a second, a flicker of agony crosses his face.

He masks it.

"On two!" he yells back and hauls out a football.

"Whatcha got?" My legs backing up, I trot onto the patio, draw my wrists together and open up my palms in receiving fashion.

Dad pulls the ball, twists his waist, hikes up a leg, and tosses it from the base of the stairs, across the living room, through the dining room, to me on the patio.

Perfect catch. I throw down the ball and dance a celebratory Dougie in a circle.

That hearty laughter from his gut is still strong, even if it wheezes some in his old age. No matter its strength, I'll never grow tired of it strengthening me, cheering me on, pushing me harder and higher.

"Old man," he calls me, "what are you doing scaring this young man? Huh?" he asks, a tired smile creeping along his lips. The proud gleam in his eye is no longer as bright as it was when I ran the football field as an All-American running back.

"I'm making sure that young man stays young. You're looking a little beat there, fella," I joke and yank him to me for a kiss on his forehead. He squeezes my waist.

The way we grip one another with extra pressure, just a few seconds more, is an entire conversation. The fading energy of his arms underscores what I've suspected for months. He needs me here. I kiss his head a couple more times.

"Beat, my foot. I'll show you beat."

Though he's growing weak, he'll keep up his tough-talk anyway. With stress straining his face that he must not want me to see, he returns to the golf equipment.

"Pop, let me help you with that." I assist with his set of golf clubs. "What are you doing with these? You love these clubs."

"The new Black Business Council is doing summer programs with the inner-city youth, where they learn how to play golf. And since I have several bags of clubs, I can donate a few. It's a Middleton family donation." The creases appear over his brow have deepened into ditches these past few months since our family fell into scandal. "There's going to be a lot more donating to charity and volunteering and whatnot... while we handle this here... *situation...*"

He falters a moment, and I race to grab him.

"Come on now, Dad, go easy. Let me carry these."

"I'm fine," he protests. But the twisted direction of his mouth, and deep wrinkles in his sixty-seven-year-old face, say otherwise.

"No, you're not." I take the golf bags from his arms and tote them the rest of the way to his car. "Dad, next time if you want to get things from the attic, tell me and I'll help you."

"You act like I can't function for myself, boy. I get plenty done around here without you. And I'm still in good enough shape to bust your damn head."

"Why, hello there. I wasn't sure you were coming." My mother stands in the living room waiting when I return from Dad's car.

She reaches out to me, and as I have for the past thirty-three years, I ignore the locks clicking over my chest and throat, and go into her soft, strong arms. The long, fluffy hair for which Roberta Middleton is famous swirls around my face. I both love and abhor her lavender-and-chamomile scent.

"I left you voicemail messages this week. When you didn't call back, I figured you were… tied up in Houston. How did your promotion bid go?"

"Oh, yeah," Dad spins around and throws his arms open. "The promotion! You got it?"

The question cooks my lungs, and the smoke sears my windpipe. "It's complicated."

My mother's excitement fades. "What does that mean?"

"I have more responsibilities, higher pay, but not the title." No matter how much I rub and massage my pecs, I can't reach the insides of my lungs to clear out the smoke from the thirteen years I've given to Houston PetroChem. "They say they'll hold the CEO title open while our family clears up our little 'issue.'"

But again, I know why they're really withholding it from me.

As we stand here, my parents throw accusations between their eyes, over whose fault it is that we're suffering this way.

Instant recognition and pain drifts between my father and me, our mouths closed shut as we accuse my mother.

Her gaze veers between us.

Tired of yelling and slamming things after all these years, our family now argues in pregnant silences.

Of course, firm in her defiance against us, and eager to sweep aside how we feel, Mom hikes her chin up.

"We'll be fine. We'll get through it. Baby, I'm sorry. You do such a good job for them. They'll come to their senses and reward your—"

"It's cool, Mom." Interrupting my mother is how I dismiss her. "Dad, you ready to hit the golf course? Duncan's fundraiser starts in a few minutes. I don't want to be late. Brendan in yet?" I inquire about the middle of my two brothers.

"No," Mom replies for Dad. "But Kevin and Cher are in town. Kevin was saying he wants to talk to you about something." She swallows hard, which tells me her next disclosure is one I'm not interested in.

"People in Hell want ice water. He can forget it." I peer over her head at my father. "The lawyers want a conference call, Dad. And also, Toni, the reputation management consultant, is asking for some face time. We should start gearing up to fight the bad press."

I'm not ready to break it to him yet about the IRS, Boston city attorney, and all the other investigations our family's attorney, Percell, listed.

"Fine." That response is flat as his voice.

"Lion," my mother implores, "don't be this way toward your brother. It's important. He needs you." She plops her hands on her hips. "You and him need each other. There are serious issues happening in Explore with these other Black men, and while you're here for the next few weeks, maybe you could pitch in."

"Explore? That playground thing he's doing? With Solomon *English?"* I nearly spit. "Come on, Mom, how *dare* you." My heart shudders as that name ricochets through my body. "First you, and now Kevin. I would *never* hurt Dad that way."

Fortunately, he has disappeared from the room and absented himself from this ludicrous request of hers.

I slide on my Bulgari watch, and gel my fine curls into a slick wet mold. "And I didn't come here to see Kevin. I came here to see my family, my *father.* The man who is literally the reason we are even here." I say all this while conditioning my beard and giving the whiskers a quick snip.

"Explore is flourishing, Lion! They've got that big Sasha Static concert in just a few weeks."

"Mom." Through the mirror, I shoot her a warning with my stare. "Don't try to sell me on some BS the English brothers are doing."

But she's determined, and leans against me, invading my personal space like I'm still an embryo connected to her body. "This is not about them. Explore is the *Black community* coming together. They are growing faster than they expected to, and they've come up against headwinds. This is a perfect job for you. Kevin is doing an amazing thing and you could be a part of it. He has never asked you for anything."

"The smartest move he's ever made." I disconnect from her and leave the bathroom.

"Stop being resentful." She races to catch me down the hall. Those elegant, ageless fingers wrap around my face, with nary a scar, lovely natural nails, and veins finer than lace. Her jade-green irises plead with me once more. "You and him have never worked together in your lives. Don't be a fool. Push your anger with me aside, and at least *listen* to him. The two of you could help this community."

I finally spin to confront her. "Don't you mean the family of your former lover?"

Her hand is swift. But I anticipated her reaction when I decided to say it, and dodge her attempt to smack me.

The hurt and upset on her face still lands a blow to my gut.

"Dad! You ready?" I call to him in another room, closing off this conversation.

I labor to maintain my respect for her, despite her bringing up the English boys. Their grandfather is the very reason our family name now lies at the bottom of the social ocean, alongside the shipwreck of the *Titanic*.

He comes to stand at the edge of our curving central stairway. "No, son, why don't you go on with… without me. But give your friend, Duncan, my regards and tell him we will consider supporting his Senate run."

"Come on, Dad." I am near begging now. "Now that the reporters have died down, it should be a good time. Seeing Earl and your friends will take your mind off things."

He's been stuck inside for months, where he's been holed up since last October. Since Madison Rouse, Chriselle Rouse, and Adella English McLain leaked his darkest secret—Smeralda Costa.

On his shoulders, he lifts the pain he won't admit to me, and lets them fall. "You enjoy yourself, and tomorrow morning we'll hit Sharon's."

Between him and my mom, another intense exchange flares and dies, and he retreats to his movie room.

I shape my lips to kiss the woman who birthed me and pay her respect I often question if she still deserves.

"Just consider it, all right?" she pleads.

"I will not, so you can drop it now," I respond. There is no way in hell Kevin will ever get anything from me as long as my father hurts this way.

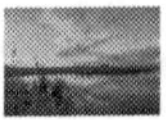

INTRODUCTIONS ARE MADE on the green as the old guard in the Hamptons is joined by the new Black and wealthy families.

The Rouse men of Louisiana—Roland, Sheldon, Jerrell, and their father, Charles—arrive and scope out the scene. I recognize the youngest, Jerrell, the man who snatched up and wifed Maddy before my pigheaded little brother, Kevin, finally made up his mind. I stop myself from congratulating him on besting Kevin.

"Why don't we just move the entire damn ghetto and countryside to the Hamptons?" my childhood yachting buddy, Trane Prescott, mutters.

"You took those words right out of my mouth, man. Pretty soon, this side of New York will be unrecognizable."

Then there's the English brothers—Solomon, Martin, and Lonnie—the family and spawn of Francis Manuel, the Alabama real estate loon who tore apart *my* family. Who now lies exactly where he belongs—his grave.

They gather with a couple of men I've seen around but who are not "one of us."

"Who are they?"

Trane whispers, "More new people—the McLain brothers, Keenan and Desmond, out of Baltimore—construction folks. They're here because Desmond married Adella English."

The gaze of Solomon English locks on mine, in a not-so-subtle "fuck you." On behalf of my father and grandfather, my chest out and fists clenched, I extend a subliminal invite to step off the green and handle this.

"Dude." A hand slaps into my chest from the other side of me. "Chill and stop mugging that dude." My other little brother, Brendan, just got here from Washington, D.C., and can read me like the newspaper. "Sorry I'm late. Had to catch the redeye. Worked late last night. What'd I miss?" He twists from one side of us to the other in search of somebody. "Where's Dad?"

"Not doing too well. He didn't want to show his face here. Claims he's tired and his blood pressure is up, but…"

Brendan's cavalier expression tightens as he processes what I'm saying. "Shit. He loves summertime out here with his buddies."

"Not these days."

After months of being dogged by bad headlines and reporters, he's now in hiding between our houses here and in the city. He mostly emerges for doctor's appointments and the occasional meal at a restaurant where he knows the owners will look out for him.

"Gerald!" Brendan calls out to one of the brothers we took yachting class with. "Eh, man, what's good?"

Gerald throws up a hand in our direction and quickly averts his eyes, as if hoping not to be seen talking to us.

"Well, damn," Brendan murmurs.

"You should have been at that brewery, Slurp, last night. Some of these folks act like they never knew us. Like they've never done the same shit Dad did."

"They just never got caught," Trane mutters.

"Exactly. Fucking Kevin," I grumble.

"Dude, don't start," Brendan replies. "You know this isn't on him."

"But he could have avoided it. Instead, he just pisses on Dad and leaves him to burn after all Dad did for him. And he's building his rep at our expense. Don't tell me it's not on him."

"Lion! Brendan! Good to see you! Sorry we didn't have much time last night." Duncan struts up. "Come on. Some of these new young bloods don't know who you are. Let me introduce you, man. *Properly* this time," he says with a light punch on my arm.

He turns to everybody. "For those of you who don't know, this man is Lion Middleton, one of the coldest brothers in these Hamptons. I don't know what I would do if my brother had not been by my side, having my back when I was just a shrub at Cornell. You'll be seeing a lot of him. I couldn't think of a better man to stand alongside me. Make sure you listen carefully to what he says. Not just because his pockets are deep," he jokes and pauses for the laughs that don't come. "But because he's one of my oldest and most loyal friends. There are not too many people in this world who I trust more. Lion would never lead us wrong."

That has got to be one of the most touching things anybody has ever said about me.

But I'm not dumb.

There are no cameras or reporters allowed at this private, country club affair. The real test of his loyalty will come when I need a photo op.

"I really appreciate you coming out to stump for me," he says with the afternoon June sun shining in his smile. "Here's hoping you can really squeeze your old pals and the blue bloods around here to get on board for me. Also, Lion, I'll need you to make it rain with your oil executive friends. And Brendan, how about your Pentagon pals, huh?"

Although Duncan is from New Jersey, he is not *of* the Hamptons set. His family lineage doesn't go "way back," and he only started coming up during our years at Cornell as an excellent orator, and later as a presidential speechwriter. His gifts with words then nabbed him a spot as special assistant to the United States president, and later, his first elected post of New York's Attorney General, which has positioned him to now be a candidate for Senate.

Though he may be beloved to the general public and the youth, his opposition is Greg Finley, an incumbent senator who hails from the powerful establishment. Finley wields a campaign chest in the tens of millions and has access to more money bags where that came from. This is the reason Duncan is now dusting off every contact list and deep pocket he can, and why he's asking for the Middleton clout. He will certainly need it.

"Of course, man. You know we've got you," I answer and squeeze him back.

Duncan beams, and he presses me to him. "Thanks, dude. I'll really owe you for this." He reaches in his pocket and unfurls a small, nine-by-twelve, legal-sized sheet of paper. On it is a long Christmas list of Black wealthy people who either currently reside in the Hamptons or who have lived here in the past twenty years at least, all of whom I recognize. "Here's just a few people who are waffling between Finley and me. If you could call them up, you know, start working them..."

It's a good thing I came with my chess pieces lined up. Because if our friendship truly is as thick as blood...

"Sure. And in exchange for the Middletons making calls on your behalf, what press conference would you like my *father and me* to appear at, right by your side?" I ask.

Blood drains from his face.

He realizes what I'm demanding, and his hand loosens on

my arm in an attempt to ease out of my grip. But I keep my arm locked in his, my stare gorilla-glued on him, my determination fastened on his ambition.

Brendan's eyes mushroom to near quarter sized as he interprets what I want. As do Trane's.

Droplets of sweat already form on Duncan's pores and multiply along his forehead. "U-um, of course, dude. Let me, uh, talk with my campaign manager."

"You mean Maddy," I clarify. The woman who single-handedly brought destruction to my family's door. "You need to discuss it with Madison Rouse. The way I see it, she shouldn't have an issue because she owes us."

He shoots a fake laugh while he recovers from me catching him off guard. "Yes. I'll discuss it with her, and we'll get back to you, let's say, next week?"

"How about tomorrow?" I relax my grip and release him from my hold.

He damn near trips trying to get away.

"What the hell did you just do?" Brendan whispers.

"What's necessary. Our family needs this, and if he wants us to work for him, our support won't come free."

"Appearing with a politician will not erase what Dad and Granddaddy did, Lion."

"But it will keep us in the public conversation while we regroup and plot our comeback, so we don't look like we've gone into hiding."

Speaking of blood brothers, Half-Blood walks onto the green now.

Of course, he approaches his new father-in-law, Randolph Germany, first, before he greets his own damn kin. Then he shakes hands with Sheldon Rouse and his family.

Tuh.

Then acknowledges his friend, Brett's, folks, the English family, and these McLain boys.

It's the first time I've seen him since October. He normally goes to stay at Brett's house. But now that he's married, and there'll likely be grandkids soon, Mom is probably pressing him to stay at home. Our last exchange didn't go so well. Dad and I refused to attend his little impromptu elopement to Cher Germany, not after she leaked our Dad's business to the press. As far as I'm concerned, since Cher conspired with Maddy, Chrissy and Adella, she can kick rocks. She'll never be accepted into our household as one of us. And Kevin turned right around and married her. How much more blatantly can he disrespect Dad?

At the first hole, Kevin makes his way to me.

"What do you want?" I mutter.

"So I hear you're kissing up to Duncan."

"And?"

"There's a better way to clean up our family name. You can kill multiple birds with one stone."

For the first time, I stare at him. "I don't want to kill multiple birds. Just one."

"I didn't come here to do this with you. We need to talk business. Can we go somewhere alone for a minute?"

I roll my eyes, as I can only stand to look at him for so long. "That might not be your safest bet. Speak your piece and be on your way."

"Come and work with Explore. We could use your muscle with our supply model."

"No, you don't have the gall to ask me for something."

Kevin squeezes the handle of his golf club. "I have the gall to suggest a solution. To get our family out of this mess."

"Ha. Oh, *now* you want to help. Had you settled your beef with Chrissy and Maddy in the first place, there would be no mess to deal with."

"Set your fool-ass vindictiveness aside for a minute and hear me out."

I breathe and concentrate on the peaceful, rolling green.

He keeps going. "We have a liquor and supply chain backup on the seas. I know your specialty is oil and dealing with the Saudis and the Russians, and large MNCs. But Explore is having problems retrieving its inventory from the ocean."

My neck hairs stiffen into thorns, pricking my skin. "You mean Solomon English's inventory? What the hell is up with you and Mom, huh? If you two are so taken with the English men, why don't you—"

"*Lion*," Brendan whispers forcefully, "lower your voice."

I didn't realize I'd stopped whispering. "How in the hell is that my problem?"

Despite him surely knowing I'm about to clock his ass, Kevin presses on. "I heard you didn't get the promotion you wanted."

How did he know that? Mom wouldn't have told him that fast. *Shit.* The answer dawns on me. In my realization, my chest overheats. "You don't know what you're talking about. Just *shut* up."

Kevin's face hardens in that rebellious, taunting way that unnerves me. "Tell me I'm wrong."

My nerves overcook, and not from the sun.

The men around us stare and whisper.

"The two of you need to head to the clubhouse," Brendan whispers.

The runt is smart in how he stares straight at the course, so cavalier, and mutters through his clenched teeth, "Your job will burn you, Lion. We both know it, like I told you all those years ago when you moved to Texas. As long as this whole Smeralda Costa scandal hangs over you, Houston PetroChem won't fuck with you. I notice you're not walking around here with your chest out, bragging that you're the new CEO. Could it be because they don't want you on the masthead?"

My little brother keeps his stance casual, hands relaxed and folded over his club, with no hints he is using the green to plot and scheme.

He continues, "Slurp and Taste need a business structure that will be seamless among its divisions. Assign roles and responsibilities accordingly and help them turn Explore into a well-oiled machine. You didn't really come here to help Duncan start up his campaign. You came to save face. Your job is in trouble, and you need to buy time while you figure out what to do next."

I crack my knuckles. Roll my shoulders. His mouth is moving too much, and it stirs the old urge to put him in his place. Through the locked gates of my teeth, I warn him a final time. "You're the reason Dad is in this to begin with. This is my last time telling you to get out of my business and shut the hell up."

Kevin continues, "Even if that's true, I'm offering you—"

"*Offering* me?" As if I'm one of his minions or some starstruck kid looking for a job?

His snicker is a mix of sinister and amused. I do give my brother credit for one thing: Kevin's not scared of shit. He always took my big brotherly whippings with heart.

"Yes. Offering. An option. If you can't score a big client or a win while you're here, you can say goodbye to your precious corporate world. You'll be finished, Lion. All that boot-licking you did, and here you are." Sucking his teeth, the little Mama's boy rocks back on his heels and gloats.

I've heard enough. I plunge my club into the ground so hard the force bends and damages the metal rod. "It's almost like you're hoping I'll beat your ass."

Stubborn determination flashes in his green eyes. "And I'll take that ass-beating if it means you finally realize I'm *right*. There was no future in what Dad taught you. But there is a future in Black independent wealth."

He struts off.

"I hate he was ever born," I tell our other brother.

"I don't think that's true," Brendan replies. "I think you hate he proved you wrong."

THE NERVE OF HIM

LION & KAMILAH

LION

Kevin's words still bounce off the walls of my mind as I enter the Page residence.

You can say goodbye to your precious corporate world. You'll be finished. All that boot-licking you did, and here you are.

Madison Rouse was right to call him out for his ways. But she should have called the Middletons first, so the families could handle Kevin jointly. Instead, she dragged our historic name over the rocks, and has practically brought down our house. She owes us.

For the first time in years, I enter her family's ancestral living room. Vintage sterling silver frames display black-and-white photos dating back over a century, of her ancestors who toiled alongside mine on the high seas. Men who sacrificed their lives in pursuit of life off the plantations. Men who may now be turning over in their graves that one of their descendants tossed another overboard for her own gain.

Over the rim of her crystal goblet, Maddy's frozen expression confirms that she knows the real reason I'm here.

I didn't come for Duncan this time. I'm sure he's still thinking about how he'll use my family name and at the same time dodge our bad press. While he does so, I'm here for Maddy, the woman who maneuvers on his behalf.

One thing I always respected about Madison is she's no fool.

"Dude," Trane mutters at the back of the room during Duncan's spiel. "I'm all for Duncan, but this political shit twice in one day is killing me. Football on the beach?"

"Somebody say football?" another childhood buddy, Fenton, and his son both fidget as if about to collapse from boredom.

Before I dip out, I take one last look at Maddy, to reiterate what I subliminally said when I entered.

With a tiny nod, she acknowledges that we'll talk.

"It's been a minute. Let's get it." I join the boys.

Our polo shirts ripped from inside our pants, one by one, we sneak into Maddy's family's backyard. As if reading my mind, Trane grabs a set of flags and distributes them.

Just a few yards from the wooden picket fence that's gated her property for years lies the Atlantic Ocean. Rolling currents on the ocean bring warm, humid air that hugs our skin and seeps into us along with old memories.

Not surprisingly, a few of Duncan's young campaign staffers tiptoe outdoors to throw down with us.

"All right," Trane whispers aloud, but not so loud we draw attention. "White 80."

In the first play, Trane passes me the ball. I pull back to throw to Fenton's son, and...

... stumble forward.

Did one of these dudes just push on my ass?

I peer at my waist, and my yellow flag is missing. But I could swear somebody also shoved me from behind.

The hell? What man has the nerve? Who out here is funny, and is using flag football to get some sugar? When I spin around, this person waves my flag in the air, as if showing it off to his buddies. But he's wearing a helmet. Who on earth wears a damn helmet for flag football on the beach?

"Eh, buddy, listen up—"

This scrawny Negro's back is to me, and he moves with swagger that's still feminine.

"Say, dude, do you hear me talking to you? Don't fucking touch me on the--"

Wait. Is this a chick?

Our team positions themselves again for the snap. Five of us line up in the sand, in front of... six?

Gentle summer winds envelop us and whistle through the wild, high grass that borders the backyards and separates the houses from the beach. Polo shirts billowing from the night draft, toes sinking in the warm sand grains, we line up again.

Surrounded by the guys I've known my whole life, immersed in the comfort and release of being home again, I squat behind Trane. The New England heat hasn't ratcheted high enough to turn balmy just yet. Instead, mild warm air blows the pressure from work off my shoulders.

My legs carry me while I race to catch his pass. Hit with a shot of defiance and perseverance, I take off and shoot past Duncan's young bucks.

Somebody chases me.

Pushing these thirty-nine-year-old legs as hard as I can, the salty air escorts me to the end zone. I'm home, in my element and victorious. Here, no one can stop me.

"I might be getting old, but I got a little juice left in me!" I brag to Fenton upon hearing the sound of his legs falter behind me. In high school, I was running back, and he was a defensive back.

"You got it, bruh," Fenton manages to say between wheezes.

"When was the last time you hit the gym, man?"

"When he married Patrice," Trane replies with a laugh. "Now *she's* the gym. All those babies they're having, that's the workout."

"Forget you, dude." Fenton bops him with the ball. "Don't be mad because I get it on the regular and you're lucky if Carmen squeezes you in once a month."

The fellas bust out laughing.

"Lion, what are you laughing for?"

"Because I don't have to negotiate pussy." More belly-shakes. "Hell, what's the point of commitment when you get less now than when you were single?"

"It doesn't matter since I'm too tired most of the time anyway." Fenton covers up his face with apparent humor.

"Amen," Trane replies. "Lion's way was the smartest way."

"See, you were laughing at me ten years ago when Ash and I cut the cord, but shit's not funny now, huh?"

Fenton swipes his hand down his face. "I love the hell out of my wife…"

"But…" Trane adds. The rest of us crack up.

"But nothing. Can't live without her. Wouldn't change a thing." Fenton catches the ball, aims it at me. "You just haven't caught the right one yet. And when you do, you will catch all this hell. You feel me?"

"I doubt that. Just make sure you catch this damn ball, because Imma be on you like white on rice, man."

We lean in for the snap. I've got my eye on the French Fry who grabbed my flag earlier.

Trane passes the ball to me, and just as he does, another person comes from behind, snatches my flag.

Dammit!

The two apparent women celebrate with high-fives.

"LM, bruh, what gives?" Trane asks.

I call my team in for a huddle, give them the play. "Let's do a fake pass and try to shake these females."

Trane holds his stomach and laughs. "*What?* Is this Roarin' Lion I'm listening to? Don't tell me they've got you shook."

"*No,* dude. Just give the ball to Cyrus. Cyrus, you can fake and throw it to me down at the fence."

We go for the play. I take off in a sprint toward the end of the fence, turn to receive the pass throw, open up my hands, squeeze my forearms tight. The ball is coming. I've got it locked in.

From nowhere, a hand intercepts my airspace, and fucks up my line of sight. The ball is slammed from my reach, mere centimeters before I secure it.

The arc of her lower back curving into tight, bulbous muscles that slide into her capri slacks, the caramel cords of her lean arms twisting and glistening under the moonlight, and pedicured feet dusty with sand, all coalesce in a work of art that should hang in a museum.

She's already walking away.

"Nice interception," I say loud enough to make sure French Fry hears me.

Silence.

"Damn, Lion, somebody's spanking that ass, isn't she?" Trane trots over to me.

"I don't know her. Who *is* that?" I ask.

"No idea, man." Fenton wipes some sweat off his forehead. "But she's playing like she knows *you*."

"All right. New play," Trane calls. "I'll pass it to Cyrus who will try to take it home. Lion, man, get your shit together and protect him."

"Fair enough." My beer swishes down my throat, and as I

drink sensations that vacillate between curiosity and lust, I set my can at the perimeter of the tall grass.

At the edge of Maddy's yard, the Rouse brothers gather and observe French Fry, chuckling among one another. She jogs to where they stand and gives them fist daps. *Ha.* So she's connected to them. A co-worker or friend of theirs? Family?

I can't pry my gaze from the shapely little seahorse who runs to huddle with the opposing team that seems to be taking this beach game seriously.

Is it her?

Since her head is tucked in that helmet, I can't make out if it's really who I suspect. I didn't see her walk much last night, and I'm still not clear if I've met her before, so it's hard to determine if I'm getting my ass handed to me by somebody who might also out-drink me.

The wind blows her small shirt across her ribs, allowing me a glimpse of her muscular, toned abs. Confident with her strut, she doesn't miss a step in the sand. It's the cockiness that's familiar for me. Like there's no question in her mind that she'll keep whipping me. For the second time in twenty-four hours, I have an itch to knock her off her little pedestal and make her submit.

She and her teammates communicate with their eyes and their body language. They're onto Cyrus. In the next play, instead of running to protect him, I slow up and let her catch him. Then I sneak up behind her.

Right as she reaches to intercept his ball, I grab her and spin her away from him. He runs on and makes the touchdown.

With her squirming in my one arm, I snatch her flag. Next, I lift off that damn helmet, which in turn, snatches her calm.

Now I set her back on her feet.

Stripped of her disguise, a mix of discomfort and shock swirls on her face and gives away that she's not used to having the tables turned on her.

Sure enough, it's my little octopus.

"Touching me is against the rules," she protests from her heaving chest.

"So is copping a feel on my ass," I protest back. "Apparently your helmet was on too tight when I said that was a nice interception back there."

Since I'm quickly learning her defiant type, I deprive her of the chance to dismiss me. The fellas are watching when I pivot, leave her behind me, and toss her helmet over my shoulder.

Her quick reflexes when she catches resonate in my consciousness more than it should.

But I can't stay and explore that. Maddy appears in her back doorway, and I jog off the sand to meet her.

"Duncan told me about your ask," she starts. "You know how difficult that will be with the media storm you're in right now."

"A storm *you* caused, Maddy. All for a petty vendetta. You were wrong for how you handled Kev. Period. And you are obligated to fix this." I'm all over Maddy once we're cornered by ourselves.

Her calculating political game face eases into an innocence that is familiar to me from her girlhood. She dissolves into the naïve girl who once wanted to marry my brother. Who built sandcastles with the Townsend girls and the sickly Adella English and wore big hair bows to the neighborhood barbecues. "Lion, can you just be patient? And make the calls for Duncan until your situation dies down? If he is connected to you now, he's screwed before he even hits the primaries."

I shake my head. "No. You need to make this right. Not later.

Now. I want to be seen at Duncan's side over the next few weeks. In public. On television. None of this behind-the-scenes shit."

Under all the feminine, pricey makeup, those innocent eyes harden again into masculine weapons. An ingenue, no more. "You and I both know it'll take a whole lot more than television appearances to undo what *your father* did."

"Let's call it what it was. You leaked that information only because Kevin was dogging you in this competition between you and him, and you and Chrissy couldn't handle it. So you screwed *my* family in your desperation. It never would have come out in the first place if—"

"I know!" She shoots up her hands in a mea culpa. "I know." Her worried eyes dart around the kitchen, and she starts to pace. "I will help you, but Lion, you have to put in a lot of work beyond just photo ops. The community needs to see that you're regretful and redeemed. For heaven's sake, your dad bribed an Ivy League—"

"Hey!" My upset aims through my index finger. "No talk of what you *think* happened. This community just needs to know the Middletons have still got juice and we're not going anywhere. So book the appearances. Or you won't like the result."

"Ay, dude, why are you standing that close to my wife?" a voice enters the kitchen. "Get your hand out of her face." Jerrell Rouse marches to stand between us, closer to me.

"J, baby, it's okay," Maddy speaks with a deferential voice I've never heard.

"Man, calm down. I've known Maddy her entire life, and we're just talking," I say to him.

"But your talk with her is getting reckless, so I'm ending it."

"J, is everything good in here?" someone else asks. Another Rouse brother enters, maybe Sheldon, the tech guy.

"I don't know. Is it?" Jerrell inquires, with a message that is not subtle in his tight jaw.

I'm never scared to throw. But at thirty-nine years old, will throwing down in the Pages' home put me or Dad in a better position?

"Lion, come on." Trane steps between them and me. "Let's go for some air, man."

Mrs. Page, Maddy's mother, approaches and slides her arms around me. "It would tear your mother apart to see you this way, son. She and I have talked about how the families can work through this."

The pressure of her hands squeezing my arms offers more than the old neighborly comfort on which we were raised. The understanding in Mrs. Page's soft, searching, pecan-brown eyes is a rarity I no longer see these days, especially in the cutthroat C-suite at Houston PetroChem. Her longtime rapport with my mother expresses itself in her firm embrace that is life-giving.

"Not to worry. Madison will work with you and Roberta. I will make sure of it."

On the laborious trip to my car out on the street, Trane tails me. "Have you and your pops thought of cleaning this up by giving money to an HBCU? Setting up some scholarships for inner-city youth? Maybe even opening up your home to—"

I spin on my heels and stop him. "We give back all the time. But still, we don't owe anybody *shit*. My father hasn't done a damn thing these white men around here didn't do. They all paid and bribed their way into positions that didn't belong to them."

His composure counters my anger when he squares his shoulders, raises his chin. "You speak nothing but facts, my guy. But they weren't exposed. And your daddy was. Regardless of who is to blame for that, the mess is now yours to clean up. Be smart about your next moves, man."

"Mr. Middleton! Could I just ask you a couple of questions about why we haven't seen your father?" A man pushes toward me with his phone outstretched as soon as Trane and I exit the gates of Maddy's yard. "Will he ever come out and make a statement? What do you think of the Harvard president donating the bribe property to charity? Will you do the same?"

Before I can answer, Trane runs interference. "Whoa, hold your horses there. You know the laws for media. Keep your distance."

"Mr. Middleton?" the man insists.

"Lion!" Across the street, Brendan pulls up in his SUV. "Come on and jump in. You shouldn't be driving."

I turn to the reporter. "My family will respond to all these accusations accordingly."

Trane and I exchange a quick half-hug, and I take off. But I walk, not run. Because everything—*everything*—a Black man does will be placed under a microscope and inspected, especially a Black man with money.

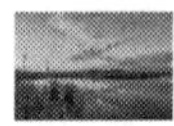

KAMILAH

"Look at his face!" I can't stop laughing at Chase as I give him a tiny piece of baked lobster I've mashed in my fingers. "He doesn't know whether to like it or not."

My friend, Ameera, cracks up at Chase's confused expressions while his gums chew on the soft seafood.

"He's trying to decide whether to smack you for feeding that to him." Ameera's gut shakes.

I nuzzle my nose against his Charmin-soft infant skin. "My baby would never." Of all the nieces and nephews I have —between Roland's kids, Sheldon's kids, and now Jerrell's— I'm most attached to Chase. Though I love all of them to pieces, he gazes at me like he can read all my untold business. The way his tiny hand cups my cheek, or his forehead falls onto mine in his sleepy state, his spirit seems to wrap around mine and poke fun at my rebellion against motherhood.

"Are you using him to hide?" Ameera asks with skepticism in her eye. "You want to go somewhere and talk it out?"

Keeping my tone and emotions even, I answer, "No." The awkward company already takes up every inch of space in this room. I will not give them keys to more rooms in my head. We are all adults. It's been sixteen years. I'm good. "Talk about what? Girl, I'm straight. I've got my leading man right here."

"Whatever, girl. Since you won't tell the truth, I'm going to accidentally spill my drink on one of these men. This Grade A meat strolling around in here shouldn't go to waste, and I need one of these Hamptons vacation houses."

"Ameera, need I remind you that you are married with kids?"

Sister girl sucks her teeth. "I can become unmarried for the right price."

With a chuckle, I shake my head. She married her husband because he's a lawyer and she was thinking of future security, but still, I fear her promiscuous ways will one day catch up to her.

Tonight, Maddy and J run the logistics of the Milsaps' campaign fundraiser—she's hosting and twisting arms for donations, and he's catering and overseeing his Poppin'

Pauletta's staff. With their regular nanny on vacation and J refusing to trust a stranger, we're all taking turns with Chase.

Once I came in from football on the beach, Maddy's mother handed him to me. That lady is a real mover and shaker in these Hamptons, and she's working the room. Who would have thought all these rich Black aristocrats even existed? I'm not talking wealthy Black professionals who went to college in the last couple of generations and now have relatable new money. These folks wield old-world prestige from a hundred years ago that nobody's new purse or degree can relate to. The kind of pedigree that reaches back to when most of our peoples' fingers were bleeding on sugar cane and cotton stalks in the Delta. This New England cachet moves different.

Extended family, they laugh and grab one another in front of diagrams on the wall that lay out Maddy's family tree for several generations, into the late-1800s.

I envy the knowledge of their lineage and bloodline. I loathe the arrogance with which some of these types wield it.

Maddy's family home is as warm and quaint as her parents are lovely. And her sister, Marguerite, and I are definitely cut from the same sassy cloth. But most of these Hamptons women remind me of the tight girls with tampons too far up their butts in college. Like every single exam, every event, every application is a do-or-die situation. I'm trying to place why that bothers me.

Across the room, Tanja hugs Maddy. Two peas in a pod.

I don't think to stop myself fast enough. My gaze already sprints a few feet away, where the object of their efforts, Duncan Milsap, huddles with his campaign operatives. In a moment that blesses and tortures, his eyes connect with mine.

Surprise freezes Duncan's face. Confetti springs out of his smile.

Then he remembers himself. Remembers to step back into the stiff straitjacket in which Tanja has stuffed him.

I hate the way my emotional desert opened for that drop of moisture.

"Duncan," the dry, sandy voice of his wife calls out, "Maddy wants to run something by you. *Sweetheart.*"

My attention drops to Chase again.

Though I no longer observe Duncan, I still know he marches to where Tanja stands. The heavy trot of his wooden, hard-sole loafers is hard to miss.

Glaring at me, Ameera clears her throat and sips her wine in a quick reminder that she knows I'm lying.

Just a few more moments of preoccupying myself with bouncing and walking my nephew, and I'm liberated when donors and campaign staffers filter out the door. As much as I love and adore Chase, tonight was more than I showed up for.

It's time to turn him over to his parents and run. I ache to curl up in my bed, ball up inside the covers and...

"No, I don't understand why you owe him anything. All you did was tell the truth. His daddy is the one who fu—screwed himself." My brother's anger booms through the dining room from where he is in the kitchen.

Not wanting to leave Chase with a worked-up Jerrell, I slow up and wonder who they're talking about.

"J, it's hard to explain, but he's right. I should have let our families work it out instead of taking matters into my own hands." Maddy has wised up over the last year and a half and learned to use her "wife voice." "We were focusing so hard on our fight with Kevin that we didn't think about Lion or Lionel. And I can tell he's hurting."

Lion? Middleton? The mention of his name turns back the hands on the clock, to an hour ago. How his one arm wrapped around me and easily stopped me from besting him again. I was getting in my kicks and embarrassed him for shits and giggles. To see him picking his face up from the sand was the weekend laugh I didn't know I needed. Until he swept me off my literal feet.

And removed the helmet I'd put on so he wouldn't know it was me.

The nerve of him.

Mmph… the *nerve.*

"What's to think about? If his feelings are hurt, so what? He probably deserves it. I've heard he's an ass," J retorts. "Cocky, entitled, talks down to people. That Negro thinks he's white. Maybe this situation is teaching the Middletons they are just as Black as the rest of us. You just need to step aside and let it play out."

"J, I can't. There's the foundation of *us* to think about—the Black Hamptons. That's bigger than Kevin, or Lion, or me." Maddy sighs. "I got so caught up in revenge, I forgot about *all* of us."

"Whatever. Nepotism and unearned privilege," J claps back. "Just get it over with, or I'll have to handle his ass on behalf of every Black person in America who would love to put their foot in him."

Get *what* over with? Damn. What happened between my brother and Lion? I know about J's distaste for Kevin, but the two of them seemed to be moving on these last few months. As well as Sheldon and Kevin collaborating on some business projects now.

Though I'm close with all three of my brothers, I am closest to Jerrell. In J's irritated tone lie his struggles when our family first moved from Louisiana to New York. We were country bumpkins with deep Southern accents. Our father moved us to the Big Apple as teenagers when he won a huge banking promotion that transferred him to Wall Street. My older brothers, Roland and Sheldon, had already left home for college at Brown University, so the move didn't affect them as much. J and I, on the other hand, squabbled with many entitled city folk who snickered at how we talked and dressed. Those fights brought J and me even closer. Which is how I recognize his disgust with the likes of people such as the Middletons.

I walk in with the baby just in time to see Maddy sidling up to J.

"The only thing you're going to handle tonight is—"

"This guy," I interrupt her. "You two are handling this baby duty."

"There's my angel," she says.

It's still strange to watch the metal melt when indomitable Steely Maddy drops her tone and her toughness for her family.

While she takes the baby, J and I hold a silent exchange over her head. My brother loves Maddy dearly, but at times, it seems these Hamptons folks should have come with instruction manuals.

At the moment, my brother's face is loaded with angst, and I'll need a story time. This will require more than a phone call. We'll likely have drinks and barbecue when he manages to get a rare break, but for now, I'm itching to know why J is upset over Lion.

And what is this sharp urge that just sprang through my abdomen, as if Lion's name is transforming from a noun to a verb?

I'll need to find some self-control. Especially since I won't see Lion again, and I only used him with *one* person in mind. What disappoints me is that Lion and his close buddy barely spoke this evening. I might have gone to the trouble of banging Lion for nothing.

Well, it wasn't all pointless. The sex was intoxicating. But I didn't do it for the sex.

BAIT

LION

An elegant strand of saltwater pearls dangles over my eyes and blocks all else as I awaken. My mother rises from kissing my forehead, but her high cheekbones remain over mine and her concerned gaze hugs me. The delicate flesh of her fingers encircles my face and calls up the joys of my boyhood.

"I'm surprised you're here this morning. Your first couple nights home are always spent somewhere else."

Indeed, my phone has been popping off with texts from sneaky links since before I left Houston.

I turn up a brew at nine-fifty a.m. "Wasn't in the mood. There's something about being chased by paparazzi and having people you've known your whole life shun you in public that kills the sex drive. You know?"

"You should come to church and worship. This disturbed spirit of yours could use a visit to the altar."

"Is that where the Lord left the magic wand that'll wave away this circus?"

Along my scalp, she runs her fingers, plays with my curls, and gives them a final tug at the nape of my neck, as she always did. As a man, it is soothing. But as a kid, I cut my curly 'fro that she kept long, so she wouldn't stroke it in front of my friends and embarrass me. And mostly, I did it to punish her.

Her vintage Tiffany necklace I recognize from hanging around my grandmother's neck, and my great-grandmother's, now draws away.

"Margaret called me about last night." She sets down her vintage Valentino clutch on the black marble and gold tier coffee table she just bought from the Black-owned furniture store, Jungalow. "You and I are long overdue for a talk, Lion. I've always felt it was none of your business, what happens between your father and me. But if this family is to stand at all, we need a purging of the truth."

At the thought of my mother airing her raunchy acts in my face, I cling harder to the wicker chair. "No, thank you. Won't it be the same song all you so-called activist women sing?" I stare past how beautiful she is. As much as Diahann Carroll, Cicely Tyson, or Dorothy Dandridge, Mom's high cheekbones are a blend of elegance and rebellion.

Tough, enduring eyes cut into me. "You are your father's son."

I stare at her. "And Kevin is yours."

"*Both* of you—"

"Him more so." My gaze falls to my hand on the chair arm.

"No. You more than any. But back then, you clung to the ways of your father and grandfather, and that's why your ego is so fragile, and you can't see past money and women."

My disdain exits as a scoff. "That's not true."

She ignores me. "But whether you like it or not, you're my son, too. We are a family, no matter the media or politics. Or what happens out in the world. Despite you wallowing in this negative pity party, you could remember all the better times. The vacations, trips and outings on the ocean—lakes and cabins, Disneyland, castles and cruises. Why do you reduce our entire existence to these last few months as if that is the end of everything?"

I stare at her. "When you turned your back on us, that *was* the end. The woman who just loved being my mother vanished."

Her expression admonishes me. "You're wrong. That woman you think changed never existed. She loved being your mother, but she was *so* much more. Her love for you never changed or wavered, Lion. Her love for your father did." She picks up her purse, stands fully erect, and smooths down the hemline of her dress. "I am not going to coddle you, son. But I'm ready to talk when you're ready to meet the *woman* behind your mother."

She strides out of the sitting room, and my attachment to her is a magnet in me, still drawn to the opposing magnetic force, which now swivels my head on my neck to track her. How could she be walking so damn proud when she's the one in the wrong? Yet through the living room my mother marches, past the photos of my great-great-grandfathers earning their freedom and the manumission papers releasing them from slavery. She seems to be releasing herself from a certain form of slavery. Her heels keep clicking by the photos of our Black ancestors from centuries ago, alongside drawings and paintings of our white forebears. Among the portraits hangs that of a seafarer who started it all, August Middleton.

She struts underneath the massive antique whale bones that hang from the ceiling, stretching from the start of the foyer to its end. All of it forms our beginning, and without which the name Middleton would not be.

At the door stand Kevin and Cher, waiting for her in their church attire.

He stares at me underneath our historic bones, as do his words yesterday. *I'll take that ass-beating if it means you finally realize I'm* right. Now he opens the front door for Mom to make her exit.

My phone buzzes with a text from Aiden back in Houston, one of the assistants to the C-suite team, but mostly, he reports directly to the chairman. What part of my being on vacation did he not understand?

Aiden: *Boss wants a phone call with you. Today. A FaceTime.*

That didn't take long at all. They didn't even let the weekend pass. The phone feels like a bomb in my hand, ready to detonate. Over and over in my mind these last forty-eight hours, I've analyzed how I'll play this.

"Dude, get your butt up. Come to church." Brendan now towers over me.

"Uncle Lion, you're not coming?" his son, Braelan, asks.

In tow is my sister-in-law, Kendall.

"What kind of deliverance can I find in those four walls that I can't find here? If God has something for me, He knows how to find me."

"If the Lord has to search for us, bruh, we might not like what He's bringing." My brother squeezes my shoulder again. "It wouldn't kill you to go say a couple words to the man upstairs. You or Dad. Boating later, right? We need to discuss these meetings for the reputation management and press operation."

Just hearing those words, that *our* family needs to repair damage to our unflappable name, clenches my hands into fists all over again. "Yes. We should discuss what direction the lawyers and advisers will take."

"I'll say a prayer for you at altar call, man."

Once he leaves, I get up and do some hygiene. And pull the switch on this bomb.

"Lion, thanks for talking to us on a Sunday morning." Ron, my boss, sits in the sun on a patio next to a pool.

"You're not a work-on-Sunday type, so congratulations on making me nervous." The dryness of my fake chuckle doesn't even fool me.

His laughter is subdued. His chest inflates, and holds, while his eyes dart beyond his phone camera. But he is not in his backyard. I've attended enough cookouts and dinners to recognize that he sits in someone else's backyard, and he apparently holds a silent exchange with this off-camera person now.

As longtime chairman, Ron normally knows what he wants to say and has no problem saying it.

"What is it, Ron?"

"The CEO job you want… we're willing to give it to you, despite your little family fall-out at the moment."

My surprise sucks the wind from me. Now it's my turn to hesitate, the gears of my mind hustling to figure out what's the catch. "You are?"

There is a catch. It's why he's dallying.

"Yes. But I'm sure you know it carries… conditions."

Of course. "Such as?"

"Your brother. Kevin." Ron's gaze sharpens as he assesses me. Whatever he intends to say next is the actual pipe bomb he will drop. "We've learned that quite a few of Houston PetroChem's competitors are meeting up and collaborating on his platform, MoneyCruncher."

The giant whale, almost two-hundred years old, hangs over me. My lungs sink underneath it.

He continues, "Gavin's father is running for the Senate here in Texas, as you well know. He has offered to… show Houston PetroChem very good favor if we can bring MoneyCruncher into our fold."

The sound of his lips sucking his teeth reverberates through my consciousness.

Ron continues, "'Tech can be very good for oil. Your brother's web—the data he controls, analyses, and programs that he has successfully built around the world—is quite promising for our discovery, extraction, and refinement operations."

My boss's words, the prospect of them, the guaranteed fallout, all settle into me.

"Either that, or you will get us other information that... might be useful to us. I know that's your brother, but if you can convince him to sell, you could very well save him... from what may happen to him once the Senate has enough votes." Ron swallows, traces his keyboard in front of him with his finger, as if he clearly sees the line with which he toys. "And you will be rewarded with that CEO position."

I counter, "Anybody can sign into a MoneyCruncher account and join a collaboration. The platform only costs ten K. You can send a ghost spy to do it."

He shakes his head. "Not enough. We want exclusive intelligence on MoneyCruncher that make it ours, or that will bring the whole house down. If you can do that for us, the next time you visit the Hamptons, it will not be as a disgraced heir but as a Fortune 500 CEO. Imagine the leverage that will give you in your bid to rebuild your family's name."

At the base of the stairs stands Dad, his face filled with all the apologies he can't bring himself to make. And I wouldn't ask him to. He taught me as best he could.

After the call, sinking in the chair, I stare at the ceiling.

Kevin asked for this.

He's enjoying the thrill of showing up Dad and me while our backs are against the wall. He finally sees his older brother weakened. Or at least he hopes I'm weak. Dad may have played foul with the president of Harvard years ago, but Kevin *directly* benefited from that move. Harvard University will *always* be on that Negro's résumé.

Kevin still bullies tiny social media competitors, devours them and ousts their owners before their contracts are up. He still plays hi-tech cyber games against his detractors and uses their information to blackmail them for what he wants. Granted, that kid learned shrewd business from my father, but Kevin takes viciousness to a whole other level.

"Just as I thought, they were holding back the position I busted my ass for so I could be bait."

"What are you going to do?" Dad asks.

"Force that little prick to make this right."

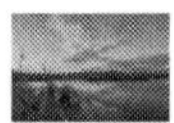

LATER THAT AFTERNOON, out on the ocean, Braelan and I return to the family yacht after riding jet skis.

"Can I help you drive the boat back in, Uncle Lion?"

His innocent voice slices through my agitation.

"I don't know. The last time I let you help, you almost ran us into the dock."

My nephew's small body shakes with humor in my arms. "No, I didn't! You were pretending we would crash. It wasn't real. Daddy said you were just messing with me."

"Your dad only told you that because he didn't want you to feel bad that you almost buried us in the ocean and blew up our yard," I joke with him.

His head swings from side to side with so much energy that I envy. He's so unaware. Unscathed by life. As we all once were.

"Dad said we are natural sailors and captains of the sea. It's in my blood. Just like our ant chasers."

Wait. "Just like our what?" Now I'm listening carefully as this kid repeats what he just said.

"Ant chasers."

After I think a moment, it dawns on me what word he's attempting. The moment of pride that rolls up from my stomach gives me a temporary reprieve from my stress. "You mean our ancestors."

"Yeah! That's it!"

"So now say it to me again, and this time, correctly. Tell me what you think you know about our ancestors." While listening, I maneuver the jet ski to the lift attached to my dad's boat and start scooting it onto the trolley.

"Dad said my great-great-great-granddaddy was a sailor who caught big whales and sold their oil and skin for a lot of money. And that he made good ships. And then his son became a sea captain with his own crew. They sailed to a lot of countries buying really nice things and brought them back. So we know the water really good, and I can't mess up."

"We know the water really *well*," I correct him. "And the next time you tell that story, break down for me what nice things they bought. What will you buy and sell today that will keep money in your pocket?"

"I already know. They bought ivory, silk, gold, and people." Little Braelan's scrawny body pushes alongside me, and he tries to help with the jet ski.

That last one stuns me. "Your dad told you about the people?"

"Yes. He says people are worth more than gold because they can earn us a lot of money," the kid states to me what my father taught us and his father taught him. "So I always need to be in charge of the people. Nobody should ever be in charge of me. I will buy my own ships, and I will be in charge of people bringing me money."

Decades ago, my chest also swelled up the same way his does now, as I once declared those same ambitions.

My father comes down to help us and stands next to the switch that activates the lift.

"Did you hear what this boy just said? About investing in property that brings him wealth?" I ask him.

But Dad is somewhere else, his attention drifting somewhere on the endless ocean. In his face, the world doesn't appear so endless as it did thirty years ago. From his grimace, he may have found the end of the world. "I caught some of it."

"Aren't you proud of how he's talking, Dad?" I coax the old man to find some of his grit. "Of owning a business already, at just six?"

"He knows he's damn smart, just like his daddy and uncle."

I notice that last word is singular and not plural, to indicate *both* of Braelan's uncles.

No need for me to pry Dad's thoughts out of him. From the depths of worry lines around his mouth, Dad's not sure what the world will be when Braelan grows up.

Will humans still be working on boats? Or will they be manned solely by machines? Autonomous marine technology—navigation systems, sensors, and propulsion—is already being used on the high seas. Robots are now taking over an industry where my forefathers found their freedom—both physically and spiritually—and made their name.

Will humans even work for other humans in the future? Or will we all report to work at a machine? With just a handful of companies owned by the few super-wealthy groups on Earth. These seem like stupid questions now. But thirty years wasn't all that long ago. Landline telephones, pay phones on the street, typewriters in the office, calculators, paying in actual cash, sticking a car key inside the door to unlock, taking Polaroids with an actual box camera and waiting days for developed photos.

I understand Dad's uncertainty, how yesterday's promises now close in on him as today's curses.

"Careful, young man," he says to Braelan, who's started horsing around. "If anything happens to you, your mom and grandma will use us for fish food. Why don't you go on upstairs to your mama?"

"Yes, sir."

Once the youngest Middleton runs off and we've got the jet skis secured, I go to face him and lift his spirits.

All my father can't bring himself to confess, he presses into my arm. "I'm sorry about your job, son. You know I'm proud of every step you took. You've brought nothing but—"

"Old Man, don't start. Let's just see what the consultants say in a couple days. We've pulled through a lot before."

Angst swings his head to and fro. "Never anything like this. This damn Manuel scandal is way bigger than us. Francis Manuel..."

He rubs his chest with one hand, and the other stabs the wall to prop himself up.

"Dad!"

He sways to the side, and I rush to catch his stumbling body.

"It's all right. I'm all..." The decades in his age lines defy his words. "All those years ago, I thought..." His words slip out in mumbles of confusion. "I loved her. I was protecting the fam..." Ocean tides clash in his eyes. "I loved her. I *do* love her."

He doesn't want me to hug him, because in his head, that's a sign he's weak. So I hang close, unsure what to do with my hands that idle at my hips, ready to be whatever he needs. "I know, Dad."

Only it's not me he's talking to. "We had everyth... I thought if I made him my own..."

I can't take seeing the mountain of a man I'm proud to call father as he sinks. Nowhere in my sight is the presumed ruthless villain who's been scorched in the *Times*, the *Post* and other newspapers.

"Just chill for right now and breathe. And don't worry. Don't you worry about anything."

Still caught in his own mental typhoon, he shakes his head. "It's over."

"Hell, no. Never." I finally touch him, grabbing his neck and bringing him to me. "After all you've done for that ungrateful runt, if it's over for us, it'll be over for him."

Kevin Middleton was only able to become Kevin Fucking Middleton with *our* name, *our* money, *our* connections and privileges that he never would have had as the son of an Alabama slum lord.

He would have gone to a regular college and had a regular career with a regular life as a regular nobody.

And Francis Manuel *knew* this.

When he had a child with my married *mother*.

A parasite from the swamp bottoms may as well have slipped his dick into the Middletons' inestimable bloodline.

A while later, I've ruminated on my plans for Kevin.

Back up on deck, at the back of our yacht, my mother and sisters-in-law chat and sip mimosas underneath their floppy hats.

Kevin, Brendan, and Dad discuss Department of Defense weapons and technology that Brendan's been working on.

"So, Kev, talk to me about the problem at Explore," I say to him. "It turns out I'll be holed up around here longer than

I planned. Since I'm here, I may as well come and check you all out."

Disbelief paralyzes his face. "You're serious? What changed in the last twenty-four hours that you went from telling me to screw myself to now joining the Soul Train line?"

I shrug. "I want free Sasha Static tickets."

"Is she really landing from outer space?" Braelan crows.

"Not exactly the outer region. Let's call it inner space," Kevin answers. "You should come by and see the guys build the stage and landing preparations." As an afterthought, he looks over at Dad. "The rest of you are welcome to come see also."

I hide my disgust at that paltry invitation for Dad to go, only so Kevin can wave his clout in Dad's face.

I'm not surprised when Dad takes more comfort in his bourbon. "Sasha Static is outside of my age range, but you young folks have a good time."

In the tango of our gazes, we take turns snatching salty air off the ocean surface.

"You were just pissed and going off on Maddy a couple nights ago about"—Kevin continues, pausing to peer at Dad —"the family situation. Now you want to help Explore?"

I stare into the heart of the same kid who would blow a gasket when I would laugh that he couldn't throw the ball far enough, or run fast enough, or get tackled without being all sensitive about it.

"Trane won't stop riding me about it. He says I'm missing out." I toss my arms up and let them drop again. "So I'll come have a gander, and check out this new Hamptons dream you're building. That I'm apparently missing."

"We have family business," Dad reminds me.

"Not to worry, Pop. I can walk and chew gum."

"Fine." The telescopes of Kevin's eyes zoom in on me. "If

you stop at the Explore office, Laney will have your passwords to the computer set up. You can hook up with Miracle at Taste and Desmond at Slurp. They'll show you around."

If I know him as well as I think I do, I'm pretty sure what lies on the other side of his eyes. The calculation, underhanded moves, and element of surprise.

There's only one way he can come for me, because he's expecting I'll attack him.

I'm counting on that. In fact, I'm praying he'll do what he does best—scheme.

STRUGGLING FOR AIR

LION & KAMILAH

LION

The young hostess's eyelids flap a couple of times as her gaze lands on me, breezy in leather flip-flops, Dsquared2 khaki shorts and polo shirt, with waves slicked. Soon as I walk in the door of Taste, this chick's attention jogs over me, from my head, down my torso, and over my…

"Hello, sir." She clears her throat, and reclaims her composure. "Do you have a reservation?"

I suppress my instinctive grin. Good to know if I get bored, she's an option. "No. I wasn't aware I needed one."

At the entrance, she shakes her head, and her nervous fingers flick her pen back and forth. Her chest heaves up and down as she tries to guess if I'm a major celebrity or public figure she's about to piss off. Apparently, she's a new girl not yet accustomed to telling rich people "no." "I'm *so* sorry, but I'm afraid, s-sir, that y-you'll need one. With it being summer now, we'll have a lot of days that we're fully booked, so you should call at least two weeks in advance."

"And I'm afraid you must not know who I am." Since I'm here, I may as well have a little fun.

Already, she cringes but presses on. "W-we receive a lot of important people in here all the time. Mayors, executives, celebrities, and like I said, they all need reservations b-beforehand."

"Even the people who are here to help you find your supplies and inventory?"

Wide-eyed, her face sinks from the weight of recognition. "Oh, my goodness. I am so—"

"No worries." I accept her hand, hold on to it a hair of a second longer than necessary, let her feel my smooth, manicured palm and my fingers wrapping around hers, give her a closeup of the beard and natural waves. "I'm Lion. And you must be Miracle."

Her eyes flutter, her pulse speeds up in her throat, and she enters a state of momentary confusion. Typical reaction. "I should've seen the family resemblance. No, I'm Olga. Miracle is the manager of Taste now. I think she'd prefer to introduce you to the person who's helping you. I've met her already, and she's amazing."

"Helping me?"

"Yes, sir. You and her should get along great. While I run and grab her, why don't you head to the bar and let the bartender take care of you?" On the way out, she trips over the door sill.

I sidle up to the bar area. To where a slender, well-dressed snack stands behind the wood-grain counter, her back turned to me. Petite, shapely, and svelte, she maneuvers the bottles like she might know what she's doing. Solomon English might be related to an asshole, but at least Solly doesn't have bad taste.

"Say, Lady Bartender, what do you know about Old Fashioneds?"

She whips around, whips the air right out of me, and knocks the sense out of my right mind.

We're both sucked into a vacuum of shock.

Her glare now levels me as it did when I removed her helmet the other night.

"Actually, I know a lot, but it doesn't matter since you can come over here and make it yourself." Picking up her drink, Mystery Chick spins the liquor in her glass.

Despite my sudden elevated heart rate, I'll be damned if she catches me off guard. "You're doing it wrong."

I rub my beard and start around the bar, block her path, reach around her. Bergamot aroma flirts with my nose and forces me to restrain myself from grabbing her. Instead, I grab a glass, go for the bourbon, scoop up some bitters and a sugar cube.

While I make my drink, she calls herself swirling her whiskey. Once she has irritated me enough, I grip her wrist.

"Don't you ever—"

In her hand, I push up her glass until it sits on her finger pads. "Swirl from the bottom of the Glencairn, not the top. So the legs can rise higher and without splashing. Keep the rim at your chin to smell. Don't *snort* the damn liquor." I retrieve my own glass. "You're welcome."

Walk away, Lion.

"What are you doing here? Stalking me?" she asks.

"I actually have business with these guys. Since you're not making drinks, why are you standing behind the bar giving attitude?"

"Shit."

Did she just say that?

And what the hell do all those twisting muscles in her neck mean? Is her eye about to twitch out of her socket? "Please tell me you are *not* the operations and supply chain guy."

Astonishment sends me backward to the wooden bar. As my Old Fashioned pacifies me, I can barely hide my amusement behind this glass. "I am. Oh, and please, Lord, tell me Christmas came early and you *are* my trusty secretary. Girl, do I have work for you."

"Quite the opposite." She struts until we face one another. "I'm who you're reporting to."

That fucking Kevin.

I inspect her for any signs this is a joke. "Reporting to? I don't report."

"You do now." She drains her whiskey. "So when you finish your drink, what *you* can get *me* are the costs for expedited deliveries of aluminum cans from Ball Corporation, hops from Idaho, malted barley that has not arrived yet from the Port of Hamburg, or chocolate still stuck on the Conex containers from Belgium and Switzerland."

Her rose-petal lips keep moving.

"I'd also like to know the value of supplies you have on hand, the value of all inventory in transit, your outflows, cash on hand, debts, and at least a six-month outlook for sourcing supplies. We'll need a list of your top investors, Explore's benefits and rewards tier system, the cash value of those rewards, and the dollar amount patrons must spend to acquire them. In addition, there are non-financial returns, such as the cash value of other benefits your patrons expect —premium liquor and top-shelf versus standard product. How is that being tracked and monitored?"

She ends with a flip of her bob and exposes more of her long, thin neck.

My dick flips as I swirl my inner attraction with aggravation.

"Why don't we try this again? I'm Lion Middleton. And you are?"

Mystery Chick pours another glass. "Demanding." She

raises her drink to her lips, and they slowly suck… her liquor. That mouth curls inward, and her tongue licks off the excess. The muscles in her throat swallow.

"Hmph." I lean toward her so that few inches remain between us and I can assess if she really is as tough inside as she acts outside.

No lipstick paints her lips. No eyeliner, eyeshadow, or powders stain her face. Only smooth honey skin cascades into a bordeaux mouth that scowls at me.

"Listen here, Ms. Demanding, when you're asking me for—"

"Who said I was asking?"

"A large amount of—"

"Quite small actually—"

"Information—"

"Compared to what I *will* want."

We talk over one another while I resist the overwhelming urge to stick something through those rose-petal lips.

"Try civility. Let's start with the magic 'p' word," I insist.

"I'd like that small amount of information…" The vanilla extract liquid in her irises rolls backward and disappears under her eyelashes before her gaze returns to me. *"Pronto."*

"Oh, good! You two found each other." Another voice tries but fails to invade our pissing match. "I'm Miracle!"

KAMILAH

Rampant, uncontrollable exhilaration thrashes alongside my blood through the cable lines of my veins.

He was a one-off. No harm, no foul. This changes nothing.

Arms folded over his chest, stewing under his auburn, scruffy beard, he towers over the woodgrain with all the swagger of a Black oarsman who owns the sea. Or a lumberjack about to swing through a forest.

I'm here to do a job, just like my brother wanted. The moment I can hand off this assignment to one of my coworkers, I'm out.

"Are you sure we don't already know each other?" He examines me through squinted eyes.

Ugh. Him recognizing me is the last thing I need. "I'm sure."

Reyna. Hamp. Danny. Mazie. Fletch. All the slackers back in the office who could have taken this assignment but have families, who use their kids' summer activities as an excuse to dodge. All of them owe me.

Until then, I'll get through this week. Easy.

"So, Miracle, enlighten us about Explore's biggest challenges." I shift my focus to the young woman who leads us to the rear of Taste.

"We have a kind of chocolate emergency," the young manager answers. "Chocolate is getting harder to obtain, especially at a reasonable price. We have enough here in storage, hopefully, for the rest of this quarter's regular traffic."

"Regular traffic?" Lion asks.

Once we arrive at Taste's refrigerated storerooms, Miracle's cheeriness melts off her face. "We don't have enough inventory for the Sasha Static concert in August."

"Wait. Don't you have a ton of special events planned around her performance?" I ask.

"Yes. But that inventory is currently stuck on boats from Belgium and Switzerland." She pats a sack of cocoa. "We will need to open up these sacks to substitute. But we still need more."

She unlocks a room. "These are the refrigerated storerooms Solomon had specially built to store all stages and types of chocolate."

Within seconds of us entering, I rub at the chill bumps rising across my arms. Lumberjack peeps me shivering, and he offers a devious grin that intimates the ways he can keep me warm. As easily as he extended it, he slides his attention away again.

"So you risk running out of chocolate before fall and the holidays," Lumberjack thinks aloud. "With no guarantees of when your new supplies will arrive."

"Correct." Miracle's response is more of a panicked breath. "Our lead times have been anywhere from twelve to fourteen weeks, but now we're cutting it close. More like four to six weeks."

Lumberjack's fingers stroke his whiskers, while he inspects the shipping and importation labels. "Talk to me about where you're sourcing these different types of chocolate."

I avert my eyes.

"Dark chocolate ships from Belgium and milk chocolate from Switzerland," Miracle explains. "But we still run into chocolate shortages. So Solomon flew to West Africa to purchase semi-finished cocoa powder and cocoa paste directly from the source instead of relying solely on our third-party distributors based in Europe."

At hearing this information, Lumberjack's eyes flutter. "From Côte d'Ivoire."

Miracle smiles. "Yes, sir. You've been there?"

"Many times." Deep waves rise and fall in his voice.

"Of course, you've roamed in Africa, Lion." Miracle winks.

He laughs.

She chuckles.

Ugh. Eye roll. I clear my throat and twitch every time she mentions a different country. "How much does it cost to import through so many countries for a product as simple as chocolate?" I ask.

Lumberjack aims his stare at me. "So you're an accountant, here to be the budget master."

Miracle answers, "You're right, Ms. Rouse. Transporting the product here to our shores is not cheap."

"Nothing of quality ever is," Lumberjack adds.

I continue, "Yes, quality is our goal. But are all these extra expenses, red tape, and shipment routes necessary? For a plate of food? It sounds like Explore needs more efficiency with its operations, especially shipping, and to acquire our inventory in a way that doesn't eat profit. I've also heard that any Explore boss or manager around here can take whatever ingredients he wants, as he chooses." Despite shivering in this ice box, I press on with my questions so Lumberjack understands I'm playing no games. "We may need to modify some of these expensive dishes."

"No, they don't. Now's not the time to skimp on their plates and offerings," he counters. "Summer is high-traffic season in the Hamptons, a chance to show off for celebrities and politicians. A strong performance over these next two months is the perfect word-of-mouth advertisement for *next* summer."

With my boss face, I inform him this is not a negotiation. "I'm not sure if you and your brother read the memo, Mr. Middleton, but Explore is not a college frat party or a *Girls Gone Wild* episode. It's a business." I scrape my hands up and down my arms to generate friction for heat while I address Miracle. "And all these high-profile cooks Explore has in its kitchen will need to take a seat. How many of Explore's partners have unfettered access to this inventory?"

The young manager's face scrunches up in a silent admission. "All of them."

Pieces of the puzzle form a clearer picture, and I'm taking note. "So, Explore is basically a loosely run boys' club. Not much accountability, anything goes with no real hierarchy or clear roles, and too many exceptions to the rules."

Kevin Middleton has sent his Fortune 500 executive brother to supervise me so I don't do too much damage. Explore doesn't really want to clean up its act, only to pretend that it does. They've only called in our firm's auditing branch to rubber-stamp their *"Wolf of Wall Street"* party scene.

Now Miracle shivers along with me. "Ms. Rouse, why don't we step outside and thaw out? Besides, we should head over to Slurp anyway. I'm sure the two of you will talk about a good solution to all this."

Miracle's legs rush away from me and toward the front door, her hands coiled into fists. I may have offended her with my no-holds-barred interrogation.

"Look, Miracle, I'm not judging your performance. You and Solomon have held this place down phenomenally. I'm just assessing the lay of the land, to help you all so you're still operating next year." I hold out my hand toward her because I will definitely need an ally to navigate my way around this herd of spoiled men.

Her teary eyes blink away her upset, and she shakes it off.

Atta girl.

I'm a lightweight instructor compared to some of the women who trained me.

"Of course. I'm not offended. I know Taste isn't moving like we should, and I'm hoping to learn a lot from you."

"We can learn a lot from each other. You ready to make it happen?"

With an understanding nod from her, we head out.

Once I hop in the Explore Mercedes SUV, the lion already sits and waits.

"Hm," he hums from his chest while settling comfortably into the seat. "You're one of the Rouse clan. Now it all makes sense."

I stare at him. "All *what* makes sense?"

"You're angry like that because you grew up in the swamps of Louisiana. Backwater country. You're probably not accustomed to the large amounts of money we New Yorkers spend on fine foods that we eat with *utensils,* not our fingers."

In the driver's seat, Explore's concierge, Laney, is on the phone arranging for our arrival at Slurp.

Damn hypocrite. "Then how do you New Yorkers eat your oysters, lobster, and other delicacies?" I challenge.

His teeth grab his smooth bottom lip and I hate how his gaze grabs me. "I'm good at sucking."

Reminding myself this is business, I lower my voice. "Talk shit about Louisiana one more time, and I wouldn't think twice about shoving your silver spoon right up your spoiled rotten a—"

"Ms. Rouse, Mr. Middleton," Laney calls to us from the front seat. "What would you like the chef at Slurp to prepare for your lunch?"

This Negro has no off switch. He leans across the seats toward me, his silk summer shirt stretching tight over the contours of his sculpted chest. Just before he starts talking, his phone buzzes. "Saved by the bell," he murmurs.

"Nobody needs to s—"

"Hey, man, what's up?" he asks the person on the other end of his call.

Dressed like he's boarding the Love Boat instead of attending a business meeting, his strong aromas of sandalwood, leather polish, and cigar smoke serenade my nose.

His voice is a glass of bourbon. Smooth and rich as it pours out, I'm not so annoyed that I'm forced to overhear his conversation with lawyers.

"No, I don't want to withdraw the motion to dismiss. Full court press, man. Throw the whole kitchen sink at them and make them sorry they ever tried us. I don't care. They wanted to sue, so now they'll pay. Yep, later."

He retargets me.

"Just so we're clear, I wouldn't be offended if you"—he pauses to circle his finger in the air—"wanted to stick something up my ass. I get women who are into that. It can stay our little secret. Like last time."

So what? He's funny. I *refuse* to fucking giggle and blow up his head even more.

His scent refuses to leave my head, and it transports me back to the silvery beer fermentation tanks where he fermented my liquid lust. Flashbacks cross my mind of Lumberjack tossing me with more energy than I expected.

Now his big body hovers at my side. The curved slopes of his thighs sit idle, ready to spring into action. They lead to hairy trunks that are his calves. He motions a manicured hand between us. "Maybe you can also show me some of your football moves, 'cause me personally, I *like* the swamp. And I wouldn't think twice about jumping in your slimy—"

"Get *off.* Now."

His lips twitch, and he returns to his side, like he's laughing in his head.

My phone buzzes with a text.

Ameera: ***How's it going?***

Me: ***You wouldn't believe it if I showed you a crystal ball.***

Ameera: ***Oh, snap. Spill.***

Me: ***This isn't a text convo. Come out this weekend.***

Ameera: ***Done.***

I use my texting with her as time to tighten up my mental armor. I have zero respect for privileged guys like Lion Middleton, who had everything handed to them. And yet, a part of me is also... *God, no.*

"Ms. Rouse, Mr. Middleton," Laney calls to us from the front seat. "What would you like the chef at Slurp to prepare for your lunch."

With his eyes on me, Lion shifts his hips in the seat. "I know what I'd like."

"Just surprise me," I reply to her. "I want the same experience every other guest receives." That will help me assess where they're lagging.

At the Slurp location, Desmond McLain is waiting to greet me with a giant bear hug.

"Kam! Oh, hell. The Hamptons had better watch out. The sheriff is in town!"

"Not so fast, bruh. What's this I hear about you becoming a dad soon?"

Just a year ago, Jerrell was training this guy on how to be a polished gentleman, helping the Baltimore native adjust to high society.

Now the man's chest sticks out as if he's right at home. Desmond's smile couldn't grow any wider. "Yep. It's pretty wild. Adella is due in a few months. Me, a dad. Crazy, right?" Now he casts his thousand-watt grin at me. "First Jerrell, then Sheldon, and now me. You're up to bat next."

The possibility of a child? Me giving in to a man? Never.

One time was enough.

"I'm good, friend. I'm out of the game, and my life is way too peaceful to mess that up."

"You can't be serious, Kam," Desmond retorts. "You're too

much fun. Got too much energy. There must be a brother on the planet who can handle you."

"Shut it down, bro. I'm just fine handling myself." Right as the words come out of my mouth, I regret them.

"Handling yourself, huh?" Lumberjack butts in. "Sounds like a drag."

"I entertain myself better than most men can," I mutter.

"But not better than me." He comes and towers over me. *Daring* me to rebut that. Not an ounce of humor on him now, he whispers, "I'm not most."

We're standing right above the basement where he thrilled me days before, and I work to push the flashbacks out of my head.

A mystified Desmond stares between the two of us.

"So." I whip out my tablet where I've already downloaded some of Slurp's brewery software and numbers. Swiping through digital charts, I address Desmond again. "Tell us what's going on around here."

The spoiled prince pulls up a barstool and plops down on it, crosses those same thick arms that tossed me up like pizza dough. "Or better yet, show us what you've got going on, brotha, this all looks real good. Tell us about your beers, man. Show us your product," Lumberjack states. He sucks his thin, smooth lips tucked away in that full beard, while staring at me. "I enjoy slurping on good shit."

The act of suppressing my clit requires focus. "We don't have time now. You should be on the phones f-figuring out where..." *Focus, Kam.* "Figuring out where his supplies are, and why. And how we will find substitutes—cheaper substitutes—quickly."

"Can't you see the man wants to show off his product? We have plenty of time." Lumberjack pats the barstool next to him, and eyes me. "Unless you'd like to sit some place... more exciting."

Tuh. This Negro did not just proposition me… with my own damn words… *publicly*. "When I find some place more exciting, I'll go sit there."

Stuck in the middle, Desmond curiously scratches his head. "Uh, so I'll bring you out a flight of samplers. Why don't we start with ales?"

"Sure, that sounds excellent," Lumberjack replies. "A good cold one will help me think clearly. I've been put under a ton of pressure in just this past hour."

"Oh, you think this is pressure?" I remain standing. "We have a lot to do, so you have no idea the pressure you're about to undergo." It flies out of my mouth before I have a chance to think.

Too late.

The mischief already oozes out of him, and amusement skips out of his eyes. "Then by all means, please put your pressure on me."

TOUGH, BUT NOT IMPOSSIBLE

LION & KAMILAH

LION

I forgot why I was here.

Oh, yes—putting my little brother in his place, but all I want is to watch Ms. Rouse pretend she's not laughing. This unflinching stubbornness of hers is… I might want more of it.

My main motivation for walking in here today was Kevin, but the added bonus is watching Ms. Rouse's ass march around in her tight business attire that borders between professional and prurient, while she barks orders and actually expects me to follow them. Shit makes my dick jump.

And dammit, I know I've met her somewhere before. I just can't put my finger on it.

Desmond claps and snatches me from my daze. "Slurp hasn't opened formally. So far, we've only had a handful of private events with just friends and family. We open to the public a few hours a week. But this has mostly been an experimental, part-time situation so far, while Martin's been mashing and fermenting taps."

"What's stopping you from opening full time?" she asks.

Now Desmond's face tightens. "Barley, hops, bottles, and aluminum. We are short on barley and hops. Not only are prices skyrocketing, but goods we paid for several months ago still haven't arrived yet. So we've brewed enough beer to open our doors full-time, and to host tastings in August for a lot of Sasha Static events. But we also want to start selling our product. Sasha Static is our chance to advertise Slurp's opening, not just here in New York, but nationwide. We have enough materials to start—"

"But not to last you through quarter four. The holidays," Kamilah finishes.

"That's not the worst thing, though," I add as I try to throw my head in the game. "Holidays are slow around here. You can roll out strong in August, eke it out during September and Labor Day, and once traffic slows in fall and winter, you can assess where you went wrong and self-correct for spring."

Desmond leads us yet again through the aisles of wooden, polished tables. He calls to the bartender, "Say, Virgil, how about you hit them with some beer-battered catfish, slaw, sweet potato fries, fried pickles, you know. I'll take them down, and we'll be back."

He walks us down to the basement where those shiny fermentation tanks sit. To where Little Red Riding Rouse rode every drop of beer out of my tank. I swap a little eye affection with her, and French Fry shifts focus. Yeah, she remembers.

"How many barrels do you have for all that?" she asks. She's smart to stroll ahead of Desmond instead of me.

Since she wants to play coy, I follow along, my eyes drinking up what they see.

Small beads of sweat on Desmond's face, pride gleaming in his eyes, he shoots his arm around us to show off what he clearly loves. "So far, we've brewed a little over nine hundred barrels of beer this year. With two half-barrel kegs to a barrel, that's about three hundred and thirty bottles of twelve-ounce beer to a barrel, and two hundred and seventy thousand bottles of twelve-ounce beer in that group. We've got six tanks here. That's three fermentation tanks, four Brite tanks, and one mash tun. My Christmas wish is that we'll be so lit during Sasha's performance and August high-traffic season that we can even afford a centrifuge to clarify the extra beer and sell it. But it costs one hundred and thirty thousand dollars."

Of course, the CPA is eating up all these statistics.

"I don't like that high a number," Kamilah warns.

"A beer centrifuge would make the money back in about six months," Desmond retorts. "It'll gain us fifteen percent more beer from the malt and hops per tank, and that's more money in our pocket."

"I had no idea beer was your passion," Kamilah says with a smile at him. Apparently, they know one another through her brother.

Damn. She is actually capable of joy. When she's not parading how tough she is.

"Me neither. Not until I started thinking about how much I love drinking it. Last year, after I married Adella, I wanted a lot more from my life. Being with a badass woman like her will have a man rethinking what he's done with all his time, you know?" He winks at me as if he expects me to relate.

No, I don't know, even though I've been married.

"I'm happy for you, bruh. Tell us about your beers, man. I want to hear about your brews," I remind him. "So this is where the cereal smell comes from?" I ask at the mash tun vessel.

Desmond pours me several more sample glasses and then points out the machines. "Sort of. This is the mash. After this point, we transfer it to the kettle where I add hops."

But I swear, there must be hops spicing up the man's face. His gait picks up a certain swagger as he swings his torso from one side to the other, motioning and explaining.

"This area over here is where I get creative, and add ingredients like apple, watermelon, or strawberry."

While he elaborates, I sample more, rolling the different beers around in my mouth to distinguish the flavors of ales and lagers that take me from sweet to spicy to nutty. "This is the business right here. Congratulations, sir."

This dude, Desmond, beams. And he deserves to after spending the better part of this year in a basement, brewing up drinks some people will guzzle in mere minutes.

"Some of these crafts were made with premium hops from Germany. But those are very hard for us to acquire, even harder in our run-up to the Sasha Static concert."

"Why can't you get the hops from Washington, Oregon, or Idaho? Right here, stateside?" Kamilah asks.

I can't stop my eyeroll at how she's disrespecting the distinctive and finer points of his work.

Desmond opens his mouth and starts to explain.

"It's okay, bruh, don't worry about it." I hold up my glass. "Your quality speaks for itself."

Kamilah's face scrunches as if weighed down with formalities and paperwork. "Desmond, my guy, you're doing an amazing job on all this craft brewing. But I've got to be real with you. If you want to see quarter one next year, we will have to cut back on some of these lofty visions."

Desmond's chest that was swollen with pride now shrivels. "I'd really like to avoid that if I can. The brand of Explore is 'Black is the New Adventure.' How can Slurp do its part in building up brand awareness for a quality experience? How can we truly be adventurous, a notch above our competitors, if we're cutting corners already?"

"The man has a point," I add while sipping his damn good IPA. "What did you brew this with? Chocolate?"

Desmond snaps his fingers and chortles. "Good call, man. Solomon loaned me some of his chocolate." He catches a stern side-eye from French Fry and returns to business. "So we have a crunch time situation. To hit six hundred more barrels of beer by year's end. And to package sixty percent of our current kegs for sale by August."

"August?" Kamilah blurts.

"Mm… yes." He squirms at her shock.

"Tough but not impossible." I offer the poor man some hope, because Lord knows, optimism is not why she gets paid.

"We have our work cut out for us, starting with profit and loss statements, charts of accounts, and inventory lists. We'll need to start right away," she rambles from some mental checklist in her head. Then spins to me. "How soon can you give me reports on where you are with supplies requirements and shipping arrivals and at what cost?"

Her relentless urge to control everything and dictate to everybody would be sensual if she could just loosen up. On that note, an idea comes to mind.

"Desmond, I'll take care of you. If you do me a favor?"

Relief spreads over his face that he might have an ally in me. "Anything, man."

"Can I borrow one of those pails over there? I'm going to fill it halfway. I'll pay you double for the supply. Is that all right?"

Confused, Desmond replies, "Um, yeah, okay."

I sweep my hand around. "Thanks. And could you give her and me a little minute, so I can lay out how this here works?"

Ms. Rouse retorts, "I don't need help understanding—"

"Have a seat." I drag over a stool and set it next to her.

Desmond hesitates, and he and Kamilah swap perplexed glances. While I go for a pail, rinse it out, and fill it with beer from one of the tanks, Desmond rounds up his staff. French Fry's glare follows my every move. She is clearly intrigued but plays it off as irritation. I set the pail of beer alongside the stool.

Desmond points upstairs and motions to her. "I'll just be up there."

She answers him while glaring at me. "I won't need help. He's harmless."

I can only laugh as he and the others leave.

"What are you doing?" she asks.

I grab a napkin and slip out her pen from her bag. Then I pour my heart and full truth into the next five seconds and push the napkin at her.

"What is this?" French Fry holds it.

"My report you wanted me to submit."

On it, I've drawn a sloppy smiley face.

Wadding up the smiley-face napkin and throwing it at me, she snaps, "You are not funny."

"And you were a lot more fun a few days ago," I point out, shoving her down on the stool. Leaning over the pail of beer, I close the space between us.

"That was before I found out I was stuck with you."

"Mm," I think aloud. "No. That's not it."

I examine her, in search of the actual woman behind this stiff, professional facade. I'm close enough to observe her toes all tensed up and pressing into the fabric of her shoe. Nervous? She rolls her head around her neck, grips it and massages.

Once she notices me noticing her stress, she tries to cover it with a flip of her shoulder-length, flat-ironed hair. I move toward her before she can react. Quick to reach her lace-up shoe, I yank out one of the ties.

"What are you doing?" She jabs at my shoulder.

"What you need."

She tries hitting my shoulders and arms, so I clench her slender wrists, and collect them in my one hand. I place my other hand on her calf, and feel its tension.

"Let go of me." Her drink from Taste remains on her breath. Even as she jerks in my grasp, the muscles along the crest of her collarbone ripple with excitement for what she really wants.

"Several days ago, the moment I laid eyes on you, you were carefree, loving life, and breezy."

Down her other calf, I slide my hand. And snatch apart her other lace tie.

I could be mistaken, but her eyes tear up and she starts batting them.

"Lion, I'll say this again. You need to—"

"Why is your voice shaking, sweetheart?"

Her shallow breaths answer. I slip off her first shoe, and lace up her gaze in mine. Then I take her now-bare foot in my hand. The hollow of her throat ripples once my fingers hug her foot and dip it in beer.

"Now as I said..." I slide her other foot from her shoe and dip it in the pail also. "When I saw you at the bar, you seemed like a fun woman." In the beer, I massage her feet. "Thirty minutes later, you caught an attitude. And jumped on me to fuck. Something happened."

"It's none of your business," she murmurs.

"Fair enough." I stroke and lavish affection on her feet that she attempts to pull from me. However, I don't let go, and bring a foot to my mouth. "But you could stand to learn a few finer points on liquor and beer. You clearly know your way around a bar, but you could use some education."

"I'm being pragmatic. This is a business, and he'll need to—"

"Nor should your lack of knowledge on the taste and purity of beer, hops, and malt imported from Germany hold up a promising idea. The sourced ingredients are *not* all the same. The German hops are known as noble hops. Kind of like people."

Shock flies out of her in a gasp, her muscles contracting.

I place her beer-soaked toe in my mouth.

I match her unblinking expression, and suck the beer off her flesh.

"Some hops are only so-so. While other hops…"

I slide my lips and tongue down the row of her other toes. "Are excellent. Unparalleled. The best of their kind. Fruity and sweet."

I set it down. Take her other foot. "The contents of beer are even healthy."

She squirms at the gentle pressure of me massaging the hills and valleys of her foot.

"With vitamin B, healing properties." I feast on her second toe.

"Dermatological benefits." Nibble on the third.

"Anti-inflammatory properties." Lick the fourth.

"Increased metabolism qualities." I kiss the final toe.

"Beer is also," I explain, pausing for my hand to explore her calf, "highly relaxing and therapeutic." I press her flesh. She works out, maybe even plays basketball or runs track. "For those reasons, people have bathed in beer for hundreds of years. For craft beer brewers, it is not simply some mass-produced drink anyone can go pick up from a grocery store."

"That doesn't negate the need for budgeting and financial restraint." Her voice is hoarse now.

"No, but it does require keeping an open mind." I rub my

thumb up her bare, slippery arch. "Maybe one day, I'll get the chance to bathe all of you."

"You will not," she protests, though her throat strains to push that out. "But thanks for the free massage. Now will you please take this seriously?"

"I am. Can't you see I'm busy with product research?" I lean into the pail of beer and slurp some of it very loudly.

She wants to laugh but stops herself. "How will I do this with you?"

"I can think of a few ways." My attention on her feet, now that she's relaxed some, I continue, "I have business to take care of tonight. But tomorrow, accompany me to dinner. I volunteer as tribute to help you work those kinks out of your neck. It'll be a tough job, but I'm willing to sacrifice myself."

The possibility crosses her eye. "No."

"Why not? We already have the introduction behind us."

Her lips part, and she snatches a breath before slamming them shut. "I don't do that with clients."

"But you *do* do it with randoms?" I challenge softly.

Twisting in her seat, she squirms and finally snaps her feet from me. "I don't have fiduciary and ethical duties to randoms."

"I'm not your client either. I'm only here at Explore to help out." Standing up to wet a paper towel, I wipe off her feet. "You have no obligations to me either. Trust me, no strings is *exactly* how I like it."

"But your brother is a client."

"Good thing he's not the one asking you." I begin placing her shoes back on. "Look, Ms. Rouse, I want you to give me all your goddamn attitude… in bed. The balcony. Pool. Hot tub. Hell, kitchen pantry. You choose." That wins me a chuckle, so I push on. "You can be as mean to me as you want. I've even got ropes."

For a breath, her eyes soften. And immediately, she stiffens again.

When French Fry stands, her attention zooms in on my beard. Taking the paper towel from my hand, she dabs at droplets of beer in my whiskers.

I sling my hand around her wrist. "Put your hands in my beard one more time," I whisper.

Ffffuck, I love that shit.

Our faces hover blessedly close.

"Mr. Middleton." Her gorgeous mouth is seducing a brotha. "We have work."

In the back of my mind, this feels a little too familiar. I swear I know her from somewhere.

My phone buzzes again and breaks my chain of thought. Dammit, I hate breaking the moment but I've ignored this call all morning. "Toni, what's up?"

"Lion, you said you would call me as soon you got settled in New York," the reputation consultant fusses. "We really need that sit-down video conference to line up your press operation this summer. It's crucial that every move you and Lionel make tie into positive branding of the Middletons."

A few feet away, an agitated Ms. Rouse swipes through her tablet.

"Toni, let's do a conference in the morning then. I definitely have a few ideas for media stories we can plant."

Explore will be part of the brand messaging for the Middletons. It will not just benefit Kevin. He used my father's money to elevate himself, and we will use him.

I need to bounce and start backing away from the CPA, toward the stairway. "I'll see you later then, gorgeous."

French Fry's jaw slackens with panic. "Where are you going? The chef is cooking us food. Don't be so damn rude."

"Golf. I'll have to take a raincheck on the meal. But lemme know how it is. Will ya?"

"It's five in the evening."

"Night golfing is the best." I suck my bottom lip. "Call me when you're ready for your next beer lesson, princess."

KAMILAH

"You should've been there! You should have seen him! He strolls in like it's some keg party in his flip-flops and oily legs, holding all the girls' hands." I'm hardly able to keep my seat. Bouncing in my chair, I plead my case to my family.

"How do you know his legs were oily, Kam?" my sister-in-law, Chrissy, asks with a suspicious side-eye. "How'd your eyes get down there?"

"Right?" Jerrell chimes in.

I suck my teeth. "We rode in the car to the—"

"Did any of those women… have a problem with him holding their hands?" Roland grins and waits for my answer. He slides another bite of shrimp off his fork.

"That's not the point," I complain.

The table busts up, and he and Jerrell slap the table.

"Dang, Kam, why are you so worked up?" Etta asks.

"She wanted him to hold *her* hand," Roland shoots back.

My family is back to chuckling and eating over lunch.

Of course, I'm not telling them the whole story. Of Lion testing my will while he tasted beer off my toes, massaged it over the pads of my feet, and how I sat there, stupidly petrified.

Now my organs are floating, suspended in my chest as if someone set them loose. That cannot continue.

"Roland, I'm asking you to reassign me someplace else."

"Can't. It's summertime, you know folks with kids have to stay close to home and activities around the city. Or they're going on vacation and can't commute here. So staff is stretched thin. We need you to do this."

I can't shake my head hard enough. "He's pompous." In my mind, his tongue still rolls across my pedicure. "Arrogant." Lips still careen on the tips of my flesh. "He thinks he knows everything." As he breaks down the health benefits of damn beer.

"Shut your mouth!" Roland slaps the table and fakes his surprise, with all the drama worthy of an Academy Award. "Arrogant? Say it isn't so! I can't *imagine* what person could think they know everything!"

My siblings crack up again.

With her eyes, Princess hugs me from her seat of silence across the table. "Ro, couldn't you switch out with Kam and alternate working at Explore on some days?"

I always appreciate Sister-in-law for coming through for me.

Roland's gaze on her deepens in a weird moment I can't decipher. A kiss on her forehead testifies to all they are sharing but not saying.

"You know the answer to that," he says. "My attention is required elsewhere, and that's where it'll stay."

"Some place like where?" I insist.

The eldest of us flashes me a warning glance. "I'm busy with other priorities. So that leaves you."

"I have an idea, Kam," Jerrell starts. "Why don't you take Lion for a drive? Scare the hell out of him on the I-27. I swear to God, he won't act up anymore after that."

My family erupts again.

"No, I know," Roland adds. "Take him bowling with you, so you can practically knock out his kneecap like you did Dad's."

"Just hit him in the mouth with a baseball the way you did that guy in high school," Etta jumps in.

Busting up with jokes, they take turns recalling moments of me in my competitive element, when I focus so hard I forget anybody else exists.

"You guys, this is not funny. He is not there to work. It's a game to him," I plead. "Free beer. Free ass. It's one long summer party. And everybody runs to kiss his butt because he is a corporate executive and a Middleton. He's not going to do any real work, and he's only at Explore because his brother posted him there to schmooze."

"Yes, it is funny, Kam," my sister Etta shoots back. "You finally met somebody whose head is bigger than yours. The only thing wrong is you can't intimidate him or boss him around, because you're on his turf."

"Etta, can you please take a break from judging me for five minutes? I'm not putting up with Lion Middleton for a week."

"A week?" Roland repeats. Now his humor fades. "Who lied to you? You're probably going to be working there the next *several* weeks, Kam, and helping Explore ready up for the Sasha Static concert."

Forget about my heartbeat. I no longer have one. Stuck *here*? In this boring-ass countryside that's so quiet I can hear myself slowly dying. "I was only supposed to go in, assess the situation, give them recommendations on how to operate better, and then jet once my written assessment is on the books and they know what to do."

Roland sops up the remaining sauce with sweet corn-bread, sucks his fingers, and wipes off the excess with a wet cloth. "Explore is your baby for the next several weeks, Kam. I want you to clear your whole schedule for this. Whatever happens at that organization, it's in your hands."

This is not happening.

This cannot be happening.

I press fifteen years of upset through my finger pads and onto the table. "That's not fair. You should've told me that I would be working with *Lion Middleton* as supply chain head."

Roland shrugs. "How was I supposed to know who they would assign to that job? You are a professional and you've been doing this a long time now. No excuses. I'll come by in a couple of days, we'll have a sit-down with all these guys so everyone can come to the same understanding. Will that work?"

No.

"Kam, just show him who's boss. You're good at that," Etta says while wiping her son, Colman's, mouth.

On its face, her remark sounds supportive. But I know my sister. She is throwing shade at my refusal to marry or submit to a man.

"I tried."

"Say what?" Roland mocks me again. "And he didn't give a rat's you-know-what? Imagine that!"

I shoot Jerrell a look of SOS. He offers me a sympathetic expression, but we both know Roland's not going to listen to whatever Jerrell suggests if he won't even listen to Princess. The others leave the table to head inside for drinking. Chrissy springs off to play with their children while her husband and my brother, Sheldon, takes their new baby, Krishna.

Sheldon leans over and kisses the top of my head. "But if he's disrespectful and gives you an actual problem, you know we're just a phone call away, right?"

The fluttering in my womb, the memories of banging in the back of my mind, are not the "actual problems" my brothers can fix. "Yeah," I reply anyway.

This leaves Princess and me. She reads the real story in

my uneaten food, twisted hands, and bottle of Bellini at my right flank.

"It'll be over before you know it," she murmurs. "You'll be working most of the time and won't even see him. Last Friday was just a random fluke."

But I douse these flames in the pit of my stomach with more Bellini. "I hope so, but even if it's not, I'm fine. I'm good."

Princess's head tilts to the side, and she spins her wedding ring around her finger. It's no longer clear if she's still here with me or lost in her own thoughts. "I know you don't want to hear this, but Lion doesn't sound all that bad."

Rolling my eyes, scratching the back of my neck, shifting my shoulders, I'm restless.

My eyes meet those of my sister-in-law, who sees through me, to the twenty-one-year old girl now peeping from the cracks of my emotional fortress.

Though we sit here, Princess finds me in my senior year of college. Fifteen years ago.

P keeps her voice low. "Are you scared of running into you-know-who? Or are you avoiding something else?"

That direct question forces my focus downward, to my drink, to swim in search of my real answer. I sweep my gaze around, checking for bystanders, and release it. "I had sex with him."

I hold my breath for her disapproval. But the sun brings out another reaction on her face. Wonderment? "Do you know what you just did?"

I'm dumbfounded. "What?"

"You didn't call it a fuck."

P's whole face lights up, and now we're both laughing.

With her microscopic lenses inspecting me, Sister-in-law continues, "Oooh, it was good, too. You kept that one locked up in your secret compartment."

Now I realize I'm contorting my legs under the table, spurred by flashbacks of Lion sucking my toes. At my silence, P giggles again.

"When we did it, I didn't think I would actually be stuck with him." Another sip of Bellini fails to numb the past *six*teen years... when I first met Lion, and his little fucked up friend.

Though he clearly doesn't remember, I could never forget. A warm, New York City night at a rooftop party. Beautiful and handsome at once, his chest peeking from his button-down, teeth arresting every girl on the rooftop who clamored for his attention, he had eyes that zoomed in on any person with whom he was talking. Just as they do now.

"It makes sense, Kam." P breaks into my thoughts. "It's been a long time, and seeing them again probably had you in your feelings. You needed to punish ole boy by using somebody connected to him."

Now, P's assessment sends me back to the day she picked me up from the train station, my womanhood in shreds.

It was ten months after the dream of that summer night. Mere weeks before my graduation, what should have been the beginning of the rest of my life was instead a life-changing end.

"I shouldn't have come to the Hamptons. I might leave Roland's branch of the bank and go out on my own. Find a new job. There are plenty of places where I would be welcomed that need CPAs." My voice shakes now, in a way that I hate, with vulnerability I never let anybody hear but Princess. Not even Etta. Especially not the cool, put-together Etta.

Yet, Lion heard me shaking yesterday.

Shit. How could I be so weak?

"Karate Kam, you are the strongest, sassiest person I know. Beatrix Kiddo's got nothing on you. Prove them wrong. Run those numbers and give them facts, girl. Show those men they have no choice but to listen to you. Even Lion Middleton. Even though this is his playground. Unless…"

I massage my neck. And remember Lion's offer.

Princess stops spinning the ring around her finger. She slips her hand inside the hand of that twenty-one-year-old girl and squeezes.

"Unless it's not the work you're afraid of."

YOU'RE SCHEMING

LION & KAMILAH

LION

"Tell me you're not doing what I suspect," my brother panics.

I greet the Bogards, who just entered my fraternity's sky box. "Fine, I won't tell you," I respond to Brendan.

My secret operation has begun.

"Lion! Man, damn, my heart goes out to you," our childhood friend, Ryan Bogard, calls to me.

I wave him and his cousins into my luxury suite at Yankee Stadium for the game against the Cubs and then issue a final warning to Brendan. "Just stay quiet and don't go on and on about it."

Ryan continues, "Bruh, my mom was definitely where you are a few years ago, with the whole insider trading thing. I've got great press reps if you need a referral or a phone number. I've also got a couple of reporters over at TNN. You probably know the same people. Just hang in there, my guy. You'll push past this, and the media will move on to which Instagram model had a baby by a governor or some shit."

"Good looking out, chief."

"Mr. Middleton, your guest is here. Should I have him come up?" a kid calls from the concierge service that organized my gentleman's day party.

"Yes, please, Quincy. I appreciate that. And when you're finished, come and indulge yourself in some of these beer-battered ribs. All right?"

I'm truly home among the guys with whom I summered, yachted, and played beach sports. Here with me are the brothers of our childhood fraternity, Blade and Key.

A nervous Brendan occasionally peers toward the window where Braelan plays with a couple of other boys. "You'll never convince him to sell. He doesn't trust you. And Ma's not going to let you pressure him. I don't care what information you dig up on him. We have more important issues to worry about anyway."

"And I'm handling it all. He asked for my help. I'm doing reconnaissance. What's the harm in that?" I mutter back.

He lowers his voice. "It's not just recon. You're scheming."

Other blue-blood Hamptons men extend handshakes and offer sympathy. At my request, they've come to hang out, using their presence to subtly "show support" for my family without making any formal statement to the press.

Since my overthinking brother is a drag, I'm relieved that my boy, Trane, arrives. He turns toward another guy who enters not far behind him. "I'd like you to meet Kelly, one of the higher-ups over at the Port Authority."

I've organized this all under the pretense of a seemingly innocent men's summer day party.

"Kelly, I appreciate you meeting me," I say. "Pull up a seat and kick back. We've laid out a full spread here. If there's something extra you want, say the word. It's on me."

As if on cue, Quincy from the concierge service escorts more guys in the door.

The brothers of Blade and Key know not to take attendance. Not having an official rollcall allows for plausible deniability. If the press ever questions these men about why they're here, they can simply say they came to watch a ballgame with friends. Not that Blade and Key is formally supporting Lion Middleton.

We're not doing anything illegal, but men in my position always consider the power of perception and how the court of public opinion loves guilt by association. If we're ever interrogated by a reporter, or if an ambitious prosecutor wanted to kick up dust, this is a mere afternoon kickback. Totally innocent.

"So Trane tells me you're wondering about the import situation for some of Explore's goods," Kelly starts.

His eyes grow once a platter is brought to him with well-seasoned scallops, oysters, and caviar.

"Yes. I hear your containers are jammed up," I comment with a gentle laugh. "Particularly the freight from Europe. What's your lead time looking like?"

As he dives into the seafood, his face forms a question. "Don't you work for Houston PetroChem? You all's port is in a completely different state, isn't it?"

"Yeah, but you know how it is. Fortune 500 business never stops at the state line, does it?"

I pause so Kelly can enjoy that delectable, rare bay scallop with its tender, sweeter meat, that's not found in more common sea scallops. And since it's dry, it's fresher. For a moment, Kelly journeys to seafood heaven, where he savors this fine dining before he returns to his nine-to-five tomorrow.

"We've still got competitors, contractors, and partners, and whatnot so we're securing our supply interests here in

New York. My buddies in autos tell me you're still working out your logjam."

I lie and use my job as cover so he doesn't sniff out the real reason I invited him.

A few paces away, Brendan pretends to watch the baseball game.

Kelly shrugs. "Actually, it's not all that bad here in New York the way it is in L.A."

I slurp down some bourbon, and then reach for the bottle and a glass to pour him up some. "Try some of this. Ever had Four Roses?"

"Oh, hell yeah, that's some good stuff." He's already smacking his lips.

"Well, this here is that limited edition. My friends in Kentucky make it." I give him a moment to gulp it down. "So, my guys who tell me there's still a container backup in New York, they're lying?"

Kelly kicks back. He's good and relaxed now. "Haha. Either they're lying or they don't know squat. I mean, we're behind by a few ships, got the occasional backup here and there. But for the most part, our goods are mostly flowing."

Hm. I think about that.

"So do you know anything about shipments headed down the NY-27? Trucks going in that direction? How are they moving?"

Kelly strokes his chin. "Same. No real problems. A hiccup here and there for a week or two, based on occasional issues. But we're moving things pretty well around here." He takes a quick beat to towel the garlic butter cream off his fingers. "Except for that Sasha Static deal. Now that's the real headache, right there."

"Oh, I bet it is. Sounds like a nightmare. I'd hate to be in your shoes, dude." I shove gourmet stuffed lobster at him that I had flown in from Maine.

"Oof, you don't want to know the half," he replies. "Tourists have already booked up most of the hotels for that entire week. We're having to close harbors and ports, block traffic for boats. Shutting down a lot of parking lots and all that to make room for her stage the size of an entire block. It's pissing off a few locals out in the Hamptons."

"Shit, man, my old ass barely even knows who these young kids are these days." Downing a swig of bourbon, I pass it around.

My guys follow my lead.

Now that he's loosened up and feeling the liquor, his conversation flows a little more easily. "You know, they say those guys in charge of this Sasha Static business will have hell to pay."

I toss my liquor glass back, even though there's nothing in it.

"You know what? I don't blame locals one bit. That's what stadiums are for, right? I mean, who has the audacity to come from space and do a concert? What the hell makes her so special?"

Kelly grunts and reaches for more top-quality bourbon I've strategically placed just within his grasp. "Yeah, exactly! These boys who came up with it—call themselves Discover, or Adventure, or I can't remember, but they're pissing everybody off. You heard of 'em?"

I chuckle. "Mm! I can't be too sure. Sailboats or something like that?"

"Nah, nah, man. These boys are bringing a bunch of the ghetto out. Chocolate and beer and yachts. I've been to a couple of their kickbacks, too. I won't lie. It's dope."

With all the fake-laughter I can muster, I lean in. "For real? Dope, huh?"

"Oh, yehhh. And the honeys." He whistles and shakes his head. "But these young cats are fighting, and those Hamptons businessmen aren't playing around. They don't want too much dark skin in those marshes, you know? So they're holding up the goods, and they swear that concert will never see the light of day."

Brendan, Trane, and I share a quick, silent team huddle with our eyes.

The crease between my brother's eyebrows warns the conversation has gone on too long. Media outside shooting with long-range telephoto lenses will no doubt speculate in the tabloid rags on what this gathering is about.

I throw my head back and laugh. "Oh, damn! I ought to hire these Hamptons business boys to come help me out in Houston. I could use guys who'll keep order. I take excellent care of good supply workers. You know?"

After I say this, I stare at the program booklet that lies between Kelly and me. It contains five thousand dollars cash.

It was prepared before I came in here, out of view of cameras. And in case he's wearing a wire, no offer has been made.

Kelly cogitates a minute and processes what I'm saying. "What do you want to know?"

Looking straight ahead now, I park my eyes on the baseball field and casually munch on a piece of shrimp. "Where are they hiding the inventory?"

I'm not asking him to change his official actions, so it's not bribery. I didn't make a threat, so it's not extortion or blackmail. I simply want information.

"Chocolate trucks usually head to a warehouse in Teaneck, New Jersey."

"Isn't that Aragon Distribution?" One of the largest food corporations in America.

"Yes, it is. And they are not playing about a single link in their supply chain." Even in his tipsy state, Kelly's matter-of-factness pulls no punches. He continues, "I might have also heard the guy who runs that chocolate restaurant, went to Africa and bought his own chocolate directly from Black farmers there. When he did that, he pissed off Aragon. They want restaurants to buy direct from them. Now they're raising prices on Taste."

"So, Aragon is pressuring Taste to stop importing from Africa and to only contract with Aragon?" Distributors in every industry always run this game.

"Exactly."

"I see. You know anything about beer inventory like barley, hops, grain? I've got some friends on the beer side, too, who've been wondering."

"Many of those goods are already stateside. Either it's been redistributed to other breweries or it's held at warehouses."

I understand now. There is no shipping delay on the ocean, as Solomon's chocolate distributor lied and told him.

"Are these Hamptons businessowners willing to negotiate?" I ask Kelly.

"Possibly. But they will most certainly want to know what's in it for them if they release the shipments," Kelly reports. His jaw works around before it locks into position.

"It's been good kicking it with you today. Real glad you came to join us. Enjoy the game, Kelly. And anything else you want around here is on me. All right?"

I just happened to leave behind my magazine that's filled with money. How unfortunate.

For the photographers with long-range cameras, I circle the room for more schmoozing, so it doesn't appear that I only came here to do what I just did.

As far as Explore's opponents, and the customs agents who help those businessmen hide Explore's shipments, I know better than to report their activity that's illegal as hell. The schemers will only find a worse form of screwing over

Explore, and they'll "lose" Explore's other containers in the future.

No, this must be dealt with in some other way that's under the radar.

As casually as if the meeting never happened, we hoot and clap for the American pastime.

On the ride back to Long Island, I think this through. Then I call up my boss, Ron.

"So you've made a decision there, Lion."

"Yes, I have. I'll do it."

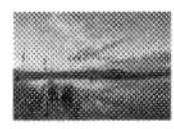

KAMILAH

"Thank you, Laney." I take more printouts of shipment orders from the arms of the young woman who is concierge for all of Explore. While we hold interviews for an assistant to help with the brewery's business administration, she's been gracious enough to help me organize scattered, poorly maintained packing slips, customer lists, balance sheets, and other reports.

Her side-eye declares that I might be about to catch her hands.

That's when it dawns on me. "Oh, Laney." Palm to face. "Girl, I'm sorry. Did I snatch it from you?"

Hands on her hips, she joins me in chuckling. "Yes, ma'am, you did."

"I apologize. For real, Laney. My bad."

"I get it." She motions to the boxes and papers surrounding me. "This is a lot, and if all this madness was my problem, I'd be doing a whole lot more than snatching a box."

"Treat you to lunch?" I offer.

She grins. "The rest of us have eaten. I already asked the kitchen to whip you up food."

Now I cover my face. "What time is it?"

"Past two." In comfortable capri slacks and a button-down cotton blouse, my laptop open, I've been entering numbers into spreadsheets and hunting for missing reports all day. Once again, I glance through the office windows to Slurp's taproom. "The King of New York still hasn't blessed us with his presence?"

Laney shakes her head. "Afraid not."

He didn't bother showing up for work yesterday. In front of Explore's staff, particularly these young women, I attempt to hide how the nerve in my eye jumps. A courtesy phone call was clearly beneath him. I was right the other day when I warned Roland about Lion Middleton.

My fingers can't speed dial my brother fast enough, but I'm left talking to his voicemail on the third call. The several hours it takes for him to call me back have fired me up more.

"What took you so long?"

"Kam, you don't remember I have three kids and it's summertime? On a workday?" Ro claps back. Apparently, my normally silly older brother is wrestling some issues of his own.

Hands over my eyes again, I check myself and wrestle to put a lid on the angst pouring out of me. "Sorry. Look, I'm sorry."

"It's fine. But I don't have long. P's headed to an appointment. What's up? And, Kam, I swear you'd better not be calling me because he didn't fill in a form correctly."

I huff at his reference to a similar call I made a few years before about a colleague. So I might have earned some of that disdain. "Ro, the Middletons are not serious about this. They only have us here to keep up pretense and front to their investors like they're on top of outflows. He hasn't bothered to report at all. He's not even here. What's worse is none of them will consider cutting back on these high-end materials they keep importing from Europe. I've been told that Solomon won't either. They pay out all this money for ingredients that are now stuck on boats. They are too used to doing whatever they want."

"Where is Desmond?"

"Ro, he's not the real one calling the shots. He sticks mostly with the brewing, but he is not a majority owner yet. He reports to Keenan, Kevin, Solomon, and Martin, and the reason we're here is to help Des get all these owners under control."

"All right. I'll shift my meetings tomorrow afternoon, give Jalen my conference calls, and I'll drive out there. Can you have Laney round up the guys?" he asks.

I barely manage to ramble the answer out before Ro says his goodbye and cuts off the call.

The bite in my brother's tone leaves me with guilt over whether I should have tried harder to resolve this myself. But no. Ro is the one who accepted this project and forced me to take it. I need cooperation if we're executing a plan to have Explore fully optimized for Sasha Static.

Still, Roland rarely gets upset. The life of the party, having all the jokes, he is the king of shaking off drama. Sometimes so much so that his goofiness comes off as juvenile and insensitive. For him to sound tight is another concern in and of itself.

I start to text him and tell him not to worry about it.

Instead, I pull up P in my favorites.

Me to Princess: ***Hey, honey, what's up w/ bro?***

An hour later, no response from P. The kids must really have them running.

My gaze strays out to the marshes, swaying in the

distance, that lead to endless, boring ocean. All those sailboats floating on the water look so fucking peaceful. Lion Middleton is probably out relaxing on one of those boats and tossing back a beer without a care beyond what kind of suntan lotion he'll rub on those legs.

Staring at all these sheets and lists, I pick up a phone and call for the tap room.

"Yes, Laney, could you have the bartender hook up a surprise drink? Make it strong. I'll be here for a while."

I swear I'm about to light him up, and all his spoiled rotten privilege.

FEELING THE BURN

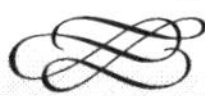

KAMILAH & LION

KAMILAH

The next morning, I enter the doors of Slurp, and if my heart doesn't fail, some body part in my chest damn sure does.

A figure from the most humiliating period of my life awaits me.

After smoothing over her short, sleek haircut, her hand returns protectively to the Dolce & Gabbana dangling from her forearm. "You know why I'm here, Kamilah."

I set my Givenchy on a nearby table and use that quick moment to reset my emotional clock, from age twenty-one to now. "No, but I do know why you should slither the hell out, Tanja."

My exterior is tough, impenetrable.

But my interior…

… flails in the air, the rug having been yanked from under me sends years of dust flying.

Sends my heart grappling for a soft, sane place to land.

"I understand your family runs in the Hamptons now, so we'll inevitably cross paths. And you're probably using that as cover to revisit old shit." In her attitude, she seems nervous.

Despite my emotions tossed somewhere near the ceiling fan, my brain just landed. "Why did you come here after fifteen years? Marriage on the rocks? Tired of only being a prop?" I fish out my lip gloss and roll it on to emphasize how she's unworthy of my full attention. "Worried about where he is when he's not with you?"

The princess-cut diamond she so happily waved in my face all those years ago now clashes with the red dreariness in her eyes. She must realize coming here, showing me her hand, was a mistake.

"Just make sure all this stays kosher, and we won't have problems."

Rummaging through my purse for nothing at all, I don't bother giving her eye contact. "Leave now and I won't share this audio of you I just recorded."

As if struck by lightning, her body jolts, and she backs up.

Of course, I don't care enough to record a thing. But that has nothing to do with her. Despite how he devastated me, I could never humiliate Duncan. He's not mean, more a prisoner of his ambition.

Her heels go clicking out the door, but not without one last parting shot. "Just remember your lane. Stay away from *my* husband."

LION

The scent of roasting cereals and grains enters my nostrils at 12:45. Though I'm awake, my brain is still waking up, and Slurp is the last place I want to be.

I've got far more important things to worry about than missing beer and chocolate.

Our family name sits in mud, and it's slowly killing Dad. All the pressure could cause him to have a stroke or heart attack when he's still relatively young, but one goal pushes Slurp to the front of my priorities.

"Well, there you are. Good afternoon, Mr. Middleton, glad you could make it!"

I spin around. "Hey, Laney, so Ms. Rouse called a special meeting. Let me guess. There's an emergency over missing toilet tissue or too much beef in the burgers?"

Laney's obligatory smile is just that. Stiff and all business. I head toward the bar to order up some food and drink.

Before my butt can hit the barstool, she speaks louder. "Actually, they'll be starting the meeting soon, sir."

"They?" Chuckling, I motion for Virgil. "And that would be who? Kevin and Kamilah?"

"All the owners of Explore, sir. Wanting to make sure everybody is on the same page."

"Same page?" I ask. Once I put the order in for a lamb burger and home fries, I scan the premises for a big, black, pointy hat and crooked broom.

"Yes, sir. The meeting should start in just a few. In case you wanted to prepare for it or something."

Down one of those dusty hallways, through a window, a small, determined figure jerks up and down, tossing papers across a table. Nose to the grindstone, she organizes stacks and scans her computer, as if her life depends on it.

The owners of Explore enter the brewery. I shake hands with all of them but two.

"So you're Lion? Your brother says your skills and supply chain know-how are not to be played with." One of them offers me his hand.

I shake it and immediately find Kamilah's features in his face. "I am. And you must be Roland Rouse."

"The one and only."

The family resemblance is striking. Slender, strong, prominent nose, medium lips, high cheekbones and square chin, although his face is fuller than hers. Poor man's energy says he's tired and has a million other places he needs to be also. I notice the wedding ring. The sprinkles of salt and pepper in his goatee and on his head places him around my age—late thirties, early forties. So not only does he have the headache of a wife, he's probably got two or three kids.

"Ah, the Rouse clan. I've heard you guys practically run New York City now."

Pride in his chin juts outward. "Not all of it. Just the parts with money."

"A man after my own heart." I see why Kevin hired him. My brother is a lot of things, but dumb's not one of them. "Looks like you've got places to be, bruh."

"But never too busy for our clients," he retorts with the obligatory grin we all give clients. He then texts all the way to his seat.

Next up, I come face to face with the spawn of my father's enemy—Solomon English, the grandson of Francis Manuel. I've known him since we were kids. Back then, he and I were actually friends and played together, until I learned the truth.

The energy he's giving tells me, after all these years, he's figured it out, too. That the premium land my father took from his grandfather had nothing to do with real estate and everything to do with Francis Manuel receiving the punishment he deserved. Now his family is suing ours.

Solomon has every right to be pissed, but so do I.

His grandfather took my mother's heart. My grandfather and father took their Italian property. I'd say it's a pretty even exchange, but it's one of the reasons we're now getting slaughtered in the press.

"Lion." He acknowledges me anyway, setting down his leather carrier on the table.

"Solomon."

My little brother and I exchange silent "fuck you's" from across the room.

French Fry enters the area, not with an angry march, but more of a commanding strut. Intentional, her movements are crisp, from the ease with which she cracks open her laptop to the smooth laying out of her leather document carrier. She spreads her arms, extends them across the table, and nails down her finger pads at each corner. Doing this stretches her opal silk blouse until the open spaces between buttons reveal her lace bra underneath. Her confidence and intense focus so move me that I'm compelled to stare around the table for what requires all that attitude.

The sight is not one I see very often. In fact, other than a fraternity meeting at college, I'm not sure I ever have: six expectant, Black business owners stare back at me, their faces all locked and loaded. This vision of black power and prominence hits different than an exec meeting at Houston PetroChem.

"I called this meeting so we can reach an understanding of what Explore's priorities are for the next six to eight weeks, leading up to Ms. Static's performance." Kamilah's gaze sweeps each of us.

"I am not in favor of chasing expensive goods across the ocean, Mr. English, Messieurs Middleton. And it's my position that, as long as I'm here, we should not wait unreasonable timeframes for inventory to arrive in the States that we need now. In their absence, I'm asking you gentlemen to start purchasing more of your goods domestically. I've prepared—"

Solomon sucks his teeth in apparent disapproval.

"Solomon," she continues, "I know your brand is premium quality and I'm not suggesting you cut out all foreign chocolate. Just some for the time being while you wait on the food situation to—"

I reach in my shirt pocket. And pull something out.

She freezes.

I hold the fabric to my nose. Sniff.

Curiosity floats around the table as the others wonder why she's fallen silent.

"I know where Explore's chocolate is," I say. "And Slurp's barley and hops. We'll have to work out minor logistics for the aluminum and glass bottles, but that shouldn't be a problem."

Desmond sits up straighter in his seat. "You do?"

"Yes. And I can have it all delivered next week."

Mouths drop, one by one.

In his swiveling chair, Roland now swings toward Kamilah and delivers a scorching stare.

After clearing her throat to collect herself, she gets back on her mental horse. "While it's commendable you managed to obtain this information in the three days you've been absent, Mr. Middleton, you have not produced an accounting of the quantity and value of this inventory. When you can acquire more, how long it will last, and where you will source the next orders."

She peers down at her laptop and plants her hands at her sides, giving me another peek at the lace displayed between gaps of her silk button-down blouse.

"Say, man, that's a cool little red handkerchief you're wearing with your day suit. Where'd you get that? I might want one," Keenan says.

I smile at the appalled Ms. Rouse. Sniff it again. "Sorry, man, this is a gift from someone special, custom-made. Can't be bought in stores." I take a moment and wipe my nose, dab my mouth, with the seat of her panties.

Wide-eyed, Kamilah rises real strong, like she's one of the Dora Milaje.

"Like I was saying," I continue and tuck her panties in my jacket pocket so the red fabric peeps out at her, a reminder for her to be a good girl. "I can retrieve your supplies."

While she complains, making her case, I text the young man, Quincy, from the concierge service. He enters with a tray, and now the men's faces grow confused.

My younger brother is intrigued.

Kamilah tries to rebut me. "Chocolate here can be purchased far cheaper once it has arrived stateside. No need to order from other countries."

"I disagree," Solomon retorts. "Taste's brand depends on luxurious offerings. The details set us apart, and we've already spent the money upfront for our first two years of cultivating that painstaking nuance."

"But you can't obtain chocolate reliably and consistently right now," Kamilah replies. "You're facing a dry spell. So I'll need to reduce the amount of imported chocolate per month until deliveries are more reliable and consistent."

"Kamilah makes excellent points," I say. "And I won't argue with their validity. We could spend less where it won't hurt the brand and integrate more readily accessible stock. But here's why that would be a mistake right now."

As I speak, Quincy walks around the room setting sample cups next to each man. As well as flights of the beer that swell up Desmond's chest.

An astonished Kamilah grinds me to a pulp with her eyes. But she needs to understand that not all trust-fund babies are idiots.

"I've had them all numbered. Sample the first." I watch them partake of the chocolate from Switzerland. Then they taste the chocolate from Belgium, plus the chocolate from standard American imports after it has been mixed.

"The chocolate from Belgium is dark, strong," Desmond points out.

"And the chocolate from Switzerland is milky and rich," Roland notes.

"American chocolate tastes like a regular candy bar. Not that special, but these others have more of a gourmet flair to them, from Europe," Kevin points out. "You taste more of the cocoa. American is definitely sweeter. Not everybody wants so much sweet with their savory."

"Very good. Now for the beers."

I take them through the process that I went through the other day with Desmond, and his chest puffs up with pride.

Continuing, I note, "The flavors and variety provide a different experience. Not everyone wants the same experience."

I study a silenced Kamilah as I explain to the room, and to her, why cheap is not always the best way to go.

"The long-term effect is detrimental, especially here in the Hamptons where people come for the best of the best, and these gentlemen only have one time to impress them. It's my suggestion and recommendation that you use all your best quality ingredients you have on hand in July and August instead of spreading it all out for six months until year's end. July and August are critical in the Hamptons. I'll get you what you need for the rest of this quarter including Sasha Static events."

Kamilah listens intently, facing me down from the opposite end of the battlefield, or rather, the other end of the table.

"Lay it on heavy with the quality right now," I continue. "And then, in the winter months when traffic slows during off-season, over Thanksgiving and Christmas, you reserve premium and foreign goods, and serve it only to top investors and select guests. But in July and August, pull no punches. Spectators who come here to watch Sasha land from space will go back to their homes and make plans with Explore next summer. And at that point," I pivot to Desmond and Solomon, "hopefully, you will be more prepared." I shift to Kamilah. "But for now, just accept that this summer, you're not the most prepared. These events will be a sloppy rollout for Slurp. Slurp can open its doors—Desmond's got enough beer. If he runs out, that's not a bad thing. People will hate they missed out, and that increases demand."

Desmond turns to the owners. "Where did you all find this man? We need about two or three more of him all throughout this organization." He laughs nervously.

"I agree. We also need the money to pay for more of him," Keenan says, finally speaking. Notably, though he is the CEO of the entire Explore conglomerate, he has been quiet and mostly engaged in his phone throughout this meeting. Texting and chuckling, he smiles occasionally into the screen of his phone.

Kamilah fumes. "I think you'll regret this, and while I understand the points you've made, you shouldn't take that big a risk when you don't have your quarter four stock."

"And you make equally valid points about the need for efficiency. I will make sure Explore's operation is efficient."

Despite the harsh conditions on those chocolate farms in Africa, and what I know is required for cocoa paste to be sourced faster. The slave labor and child workers who suffer to deliver those cheap goods Kamilah is demanding, I'm too aware of it.

"So this is resolved then," Roland says with an exasperated breath. He's been emailing and texting throughout most of the meeting and seems distracted, very clearly annoyed with his sister.

Now I'm worried he might come down on her too hard, so I speak up. "I tried to obtain this information earlier, but I've worked it up over the past couple of days and waited to share it with Ms. Rouse until I was certain. She wasn't aware of my moves before today."

In the meantime, as we wrap up the meeting, my own younger sibling approaches me.

"Good to see that money isn't completely going to waste," Kevin mutters.

"Don't think my services won't come at a price."

Kevin snickers and glimpses from Kamilah's end of the table back to me. "I would take this moment to light your ass up."

"You can't light my ass up, Negro."

"But somebody in here thinks she can. I'm about to go outside, where the view is good, and watch."

Once the table clears out, and it's just Kamilah and me remaining, I saunter over to her. Now that I've shown her who's the real boss, we can make nice and proceed.

I did my job that she clearly thought I couldn't do.

"Kamilah—"

Her hand zips up fast, shocking me.

Wham!

"Ohhhhh!" The taproom full of spectating men crow at the same time, and jump back like they're at an exhibition match.

I'm reeling at the blunt force behind her hand, and my jaw stings.

Kam's finger in my face, she straightens me out. "Don't ever make me look like a fool again."

"I didn't make you—"

"You think this is a game. And you don't have to take it seriously? But the rest of the world does. Your paycheck may not depend on this, but ours do." Her tone remains low and lethal, a weapon. Anger ratchets up in her chest. "You can blow all this off and just walk away, back to your Texas corporate job and your mansions. But for some of us, this defines our careers, our résumés. It's not playtime at the beach!"

The harder smack on me is the humiliation reddening Kam's eyes.

I'm not sure I'm the one who put that hurt there, but now I wish like hell I could lift it out.

"You were not prepared to listen to me," I explain. "So I had to get your attention."

"You thought you could lure me by showing off, because that's what you're used to," she snaps. A quick flick of her gaze to the red panties sticking out of my shirt pocket makes her point. "Impressing women with your money and connections and boats."

"Is that why you're so emotional?" I lower my voice and sit back on the table. "You hate people with money, and the only way for you to react to it is jealousy and rage."

Kamilah's lips curl over her teeth. "Don't diminish my legitimate concerns about you. Try caring about something other than what newspapers say about you, or your stocks, or which high-profile friend you're taking out next."

"Stop expecting me to apologize for it. I won't. So I wasn't born poor. There is no shame in that. My family and I have a lot on our plate right now, so ease up some, all right?"

Any other time that argument would nab me some sympathy. Maybe even some pussy.

Kamilah's face flares. "Read the room, Little Boy Lion. Nobody cares about your rich-boy problems. And if you really want to help your family, *do something useful!* Instead of setting up a bunch of photo ops where you *pretend* you bring substance to the table."

Just as tough as she strutted in, an upset Kamilah barrels out.

On the other side of the taproom, betting money changes hands. I don't give a damn that they saw, only that this meeting, in front of her older brother and all these men, was clearly important to her.

Kevin stakes out a good position where he can stand and gloat.

"Don't fucking start," I warn him.

He folds up his money he just collected. "Dude. That wasn't some casual, workplace slap. That was more like a you-must've-fucked-during-a-trip-and-fall-and-now-you're-catching-feelings slap."

"Kevin, stop aggravating him." My mother's voice only barely manages to tear my attention from Kamilah's path. "Give us a minute."

"Ma, what are you doing here?" I ask her.

The last thing I need is her trying to "talk some sense into me."

She reaches for my face where Kamilah hit me, and instinctively, my head escapes her mothering.

"I heard there was a big meeting and I came to make sure you and… nobody tore each other apart. Although I see somebody is keeping you boys in line," she says. Her eyes veer in Kamilah's direction before returning to me. "What did you do?"

Poised and collected in her ivory linen blouse and airy capri pants, my mother is the outward image of a midsummer oceanside day. But her eyes scream at me. Every argument, disappointment, and revelation we've ever flung at one another pours out of her graceful and stalwart frame now.

"What have I told you?" she mutters. "Despite what your daddy did, women are not *play*things, Lion." She unleashes forty years of her hard-earned marital wisdom. "Apologize."

She's repeating what she has said many times before, especially during my marriage to Ashlyn, but for the first time in my life, apparently, the soil is fertile in my heart. The seeds of my mother's words may be landing, seeds that are finally finding a home in me.

THE HILLS & VALLEYS OF ME

KAMILAH

KAMILAH

The next night, I slam down my beer glass. Lick the foam off my lips.

"All right, Karate Kam! Don't hurt 'em!" Ameera cries.

She and Katessa left their husbands and kids behind for the weekend and drove from the city.

The young man in front of me can't be a day older than thirty.

"Sorry, Finn, I give you an 'A' for effort." I stick out my hand. "Time to pay up."

And now for the only good part of being in the Hamptons. This boy in his Birkenstocks, cargo pants, backwards Abercrombie and Fitch tattered baseball cap, and Gap faded T-shirt takes out his wallet and unfurls it, slips out $5000 easily, and places the bills in my hand.

"Kamilah," he slurs while trying to keep his focus straight, "you have got to be the greatest fucking woman I've ever met, and that includes my mother."

His friends hoot and holler around him as he practically teeters off the barstool but manages to find his chest and hold his hand against it.

"It would be my honor and my privilege if you would allow me to make you my wife."

The bar erupts with laughter.

"Finn," I reply, "you look really rich, like you've got a lot of money I'd love to spend, but hon, I gotta tell ya. You don't look like you can fuck."

His friends let out roars that send the place practically off its hinges.

"Will you please give me the chance to prove it to you?"

"All right now, bud, that's it!" His friends start hauling him away.

"Girl," Katessa starts, "why don't you marry you a rich white boy and live in luxury the rest of your life? That might be the perfect answer for you. Let him spoil your little spoiled ass."

Ameera pipes up. "Because she knows Charles Rouse, Roland Rouse, Sheldon Rouse, and Jerrell Rouse will drag his blond-haired, blue-eyed behind down every last one of these here streets."

We all bust up from Ameera's crazy ass.

Katessa laughs over her martini. "Chile, please, they gon' do that anyway. Po' man could be black as dirt, and them Rouse men still gon' get his ass together."

I met these ladies in my twenties, once my career had started, and I had long left behind memories of my senior college year and…

Katessa, Ameera, and I started out together as CPAs, ambling about in New York City while growing up. Arguing with our parents and breaking away from what they taught us as kids, we ran the streets while all our friends got married. But once we hit our thirties, the others found love and I'm the last woman standing.

Hip-hop music fills the bar, and all these Hamptons twenty-somethings turn up.

The bartender is Black, older, likely older than me, probably in his forties—those are the best. Older men know *exactly* what they're doing in bed.

Now he leans over the bar, and his muscles gleam under the track lights. His sly, half-cocked grin offers me a good night. And my kitty could certainly use one, after Roland read me the riot act yesterday and I've been dealing with rich Middletons all week.

"So," Ameera interrupts my flirting. "Back to this Lion guy. You mean he just stood there and let you smack him?"

"Not exactly. I caught him off guard. He wasn't ready." I recall the astonishment that jarred his eyes, the way he leaped in the air, maybe entertained, maybe wondering if he should return fire. "Hell, I wasn't even ready. So much was happening in my head the entire time he talked. He kept spouting off all this information he hadn't told me. Like he had been hiding it and saved it for the meeting, just to make himself look good at my expense."

To be honest, my conduct even shocked me. I've never hit any man in my adulthood.

"I'm still at the part where he let you," Ameera comments. "He didn't file a complaint with Roland or you all's bank, or anything?"

Katessa shrugs. "Even if he wanted to, no real Black man would do that. Other guys will perceive him as a punk. Did you apologize? Talk?"

"I went off on him and left. Though he deserved it, hitting somebody didn't feel good. It was a spur-of-the-moment thing and I'm not proud."

"Shiddd, he was sniffing your panties in a meeting, and

you slapped him. Sounds like foreplay to me." Ameera cracks up.

"Kam, girl, all I'm saying is your life wasn't this damn fire when we were twenty-seven!" Katessa focuses on me.

"Okay?" Ameera adds. "I mean, let's you and me trade places. You take my husband and two kids, and I'll come pick one of these white boys and travel the world, lounge around in the Hamptons, and complain about how I have to work at a brewery all day with spoiled men who get on yachts and plan big concerts with major stars and celebrities."

Katessa chuckles while Ameera goes on.

"Girl. I would gladly swap my life for yours. Because nobody told me parenthood would be this damn hard. Everybody paints having kids as some happy wonderland or some shit. And mind you, I love my little girls to pieces, would give my right arm for them, but oh Lord, what I would not do to have my freedom back. Especially if I was juggling your options!"

"Preach!" Katessa sips loud from her martini glass.

I chuckle at all this talk, because truth be told, my life isn't all that interesting. It's basically working, fucking, and event-hopping to keep myself occupied.

But when I'm done, I always have to go home. To the silence. Yes, I run the occasional marathon, go hiking, or to the nightclub, and volunteer with youth. My life is full. I've got a lot of associates. They come hang for drinks, lunches, brunches, shopping sprees, but then leave for their families. New York has been good to me, and it's been a damn good time. Life owes me nothing.

It's just hard not to wonder… what would have happened if Duncan and I…?

I brush that question from my mind.

Let's just say my very full life took a sharp turn I hadn't

expected when I first saw Lion on the other side of Taste's bar.

"All right, ladies, I hate to be the one who breaks first, but I'll have to call it a night. Your girl can't roll like she used to," Katessa says and addresses the bartender. "What do we owe you?"

He shakes his head. "Her future husband over there already paid."

I smirk. "Thanks."

"Thank them." He slides his hand across the wood-grain bar. Gives me a final stare. "I get off in thirty if… you need a man whose ears are bone dry."

"Bitch, I hate you," Ameera mumbles as her gaze roams from his fingertips to his Afro.

"No, thank you," I say to the bartender. One-night stands can be useful to scratch an itch. But at almost thirty-seven, I already know how that ends. One-offs are only a temporary Band-Aid for a deeper emotional longing. Been there, done that, too many times.

Stress-fucking is just that. A momentary stopgap.

The bartender extends a hand and rubs mine, his rough thumb scraping down the back of my hand. "The offer remains if you change your mind, Karate Kam."

He was paying attention earlier when Ameera called me that.

"Oh, wow, look. It's that guy who's running for the Senate. I've seen him and his wife on TV. Such a good speaker. And damn, even more fine in person," Katessa murmurs, her gaze stuck on some point over my shoulder.

No. I spin on the barstool to see Duncan, the Lion King, and two other guys coming through.

My eyes meet Duncan's.

And then Lion's.

Duncan's characteristic hesitation holds him back. He's

ever the overly cautious politician, carefully examining his next move.

But not King Lion.

He strolls over in jeans and a silken, long-sleeved button-down, a tall glass of ice-cold beverage all by himself. I could swear his eyes just changed, but I'm not sure if it's upset or eagerness they display.

"Lady Rouse."

"Little Lion. Isn't there a water vehicle somewhere you should be showboating on?"

He shrugs. "You're not there to watch me do it, so why bother?" He takes a gander at all the quarters lying around. "Beer games. It's been a minute."

"Don't lie. You probably just played 'em last week."

Somebody in our midst reminds me of her presence when she clears her throat.

"These are my friends, Katessa and Ameera. Ladies, this is Lion Middleton—my co-worker."

I don't go into any more detail than that since I won't be working with Lion long.

While they shake hands, Duncan and I hold a quick, fifteen-years-long catch-up over Lion's shoulder. My gaze snaps back into place when Lion returns his attention to me.

"We didn't talk anymore yesterday," he says.

"Why would we after you played me?"

"Let me make up for it," he offers in his low, husky voice I'm just now noticing for some reason.

"Sure. Start by submitting your reports to me as soon as possible, and not doing anything behind my back again."

He licks smooth lips, though I can honestly say he may not be flirting, but truly being thoughtful. He wedges his big body between me and Katessa, who's now picking the brain of a vexed Duncan.

"Kam, how did we get off on the wrong foot? Huh?" The

Lion asks. "What is it about me that's got you all... hating me?"

All right, so his voice could probably coax a bear into hibernation.

I don't fall asleep, but my subconscious does backtrack to the first time we were all together. How loud and rowdy he and Duncan were at a private rooftop party sixteen years ago. Three years younger than them, I was still in college, an intern in a summer program at the mayor's office auditing division, and Duncan was a law student while Lion was a young businessman just starting out.

I wish I had never gone to that party. All the beer and alcohol I've drunk tonight won't wash away the hole at the pit of me, into which I'm still falling.

"Kamilah? Girl. You good?" Katessa asks.

In front of all these guys, especially Duncan, I'll be damned if they see a speck of weakness in me.

"Of course, woman. Are you crazy?" I flick my hair in Lion's face. "What time is it? I'm bored."

"Why don't you all come to the game room and we can shoot some pool? Did you ladies eat?" Lion asks.

Duncan's discomfort matches my rising indigestion, and I don't want Little Lion to think he can buy and schmooze his way out of being held accountable. He needs to understand that when we arrive at the brewery on Monday, we won't be friends, not enemies, nothing. And he won't be a distraction that knocks me off course.

"I'm not hungry."

To emphasize this, I stand to leave.

Swift with my subliminal messaging, I catch the bartender's eyes and give him a nod. Though I told him no earlier, his wink acknowledges that I've changed my mind.

"Ladies, see you back at the rental."

Ameera's mouth flattens. "Yyyeah, I guess."

"Before I jet, I need to hit the girls' room."

As he observes what's unfolding between the bartender and me, Lion's jaw tightens. For some reason, his annoyance isn't as gratifying as I'd hoped.

"What are you doing?" Katessa rushes into the bathroom behind me. "I thought you turned down that bartender? Now you're going home with him?"

"Who says anything about going to his home?"

"Are you trying to make this dude, Lion, jealous?" Katessa asks.

The bathroom door busts open a second time. "Girl! You didn't tell us Lion looked like *that*!" Ameera busts in now and takes the next stall. "And got some pretty, curly hair, too? He can play as many games with me as he wanna!"

"Ameera, you are married," I reply.

"Days like today, when they come in swinging it like that, I'll make an exception."

Katessa yawns. "It's eleven-fifteen, and we had a good run. My old ass is sleepy anyway. Are you sure you're doing this with some guy you don't even know?"

"He needs to be sure if he's doing this with me." Swiping a few hairs back in place, reapplying my gloss, I check my outfit, and swing my hair.

"Kam, are you trying to make Lion jealous by leaving with somebody else?" Katessa presses her question again.

"One thing about being single is I don't have the luxury of live-in dick. I've got to leave with somebody at some point."

Ameera replies, "I see you're not answering her question, but let's sync phones so I can at least know where you're going."

After we do that, I follow them out the bathroom door. Whatever happens in the next hour, I deserve that momentary emotional Band-Aid.

"Kam."

That mix of confidence and hesitation. Like he knows what he wants but is terrified of what happens if he pursues it. His presence, after all this time, stops me but doesn't turn me around.

"When I heard you were at this bar, I had to come and speak to you while—"

"You heard I was here?" I ask him.

"Yeah, some of us were over at Maddy's for a strategy session, and your brother, Jerrell, mentioned you might be here." Now he stands behind me, only inches. The warmth of his hand slips inside mine. "I'm glad you're here in the Hamptons, Kamilah. I'm happy to see you. I've been thinking about what I would say to you if I ever had the chance."

"You mean all the things you should have said fifteen years ago, if you had only been a man?"

Behind me, he pauses for a breath. "I deserve that. Not a day goes by I don't think about you flipping your hair, setting somebody straight, or arguing your point of view. I want you to know if I had it to do all over—"

"Duncan, did you use an outing with Lion as cover to sneak away from Tanja? You can't even look at me when she's in the same room. So you come here and speak to me behind her back, like some child."

"She's my wife."

Hearing that no longer quite stings, just tastes like vinegar. *Now* I turn around. Facing him is weird. We're older. Even in this dark bar, I can make out the few grays sprinkled around his head now. The regret in all his eye-batting tells me he wishes he could take back those last words.

Same intense eyes. Same studious expression. Same silly dreamer. Same fucking coward.

"And what was I?" My voice echoes through the mental hallways of my disgust. I start off.

He tries to stop me. "My love. My heart. Whom I failed. And I'm sorry."

I no longer think of what we could have been. Unlike meeting him at age twenty, I know too much now. All I see is the counterfeit standing in front of me, and what a welcome surprise. I'm no longer impressed.

I shake off his grip. "I'm not sorry. Your big moment to tell me that, after all these years, is in the back of a bar. I only lost one thing in this deal."

"What's that?"

"Our child."

Duncan's face explodes. I am complete. That felt better than fucking his close friend, Lion.

"Hold up, Kam. You can't just walk off after saying something like that. What do you mean... you never—"

"Hell no, and why would I? I wasn't going to put myself through having a baby to compete for you."

A deer shot in the woods couldn't seem more dismayed. "You left, and I never heard from you again."

"And you didn't come find me. Your family's lawyer came to see me with legal papers. So I signed them."

A last look at him reveals he just might carry some regret.

Hell, I'd carry some, too, if I had to wake up to Tanja every day.

With him all crestfallen, I leave him and head to the front, where the bartender is now off work and awaits. "I thought you had changed your mind *again* and dipped on me," he says.

"Nah. Ready when you are." After hugging my friends and promising I'll see them off in the morning, I palm my crossbody purse to confirm I have my Mace and stiletto knife.

Over my shoulder stand a dejected Duncan and a bothered Lion.

"I'm Parker, in case you wanted to know," the bartender interrupts my thoughts. "And you're Karate Kam."

Is it that obvious he doesn't really have my attention? For his part, Parker is handsome, a gentleman who opens my passenger door to his Jeep.

"What brings you to the Hamptons, Parker? Is this where you're from?" I'm trying to play it cool and pretend I'm one hundred percent invested in this, and that my head isn't still back in the bar.

"No, but it's where good money is. I have a little boat where I sleep in the summertime. In the winter, when things slow down here, I'm in the city."

He starts up his truck, and we head out. But he keeps peering in his rearview mirror while we talk. Why does he keep staring behind him? Two miles down the road, he pulls to the shoulder.

"What's up, Parker?" As I ask, I reach for my purse and loudly unzip it. Maybe I was wrong about him and I will need this Mace after all.

"Where would you like me to drop you off?"

Wait.

In the driver's seat, he's perturbed. "You only left with me to make those guys jealous."

"Those *guys*?"

"Yeah. The one you talked to in the back for a full five minutes, and his friend who practically wanted to jump me to keep you from leaving."

Jump him? Embarrassment creeps up my neck. I've never punked out on a hookup.

"It's all good," he continues. "I've been doing this a long time. I get all kinds of offers from women mad at their boyfriends, or showing off to catch the attention of a crush or whatever." His smile is friendly, even if tight. "But I prefer not to be caught up in..." He motions behind him, toward the back window. "Whatever you've got going on here."

"Whatever I've got going on?"

He shakes his head, points at the rearview mirror. "You have company. One of them followed you. Having some other dude on my ass kills the whole one-night-stand vibe, you know? I wish you all the best... Karate Kam."

He's putting me out? Swinging around to see who's behind us, I almost have a mind to tell Parker to hold up one moment so I can go put whoever it is in his place. But one more look at Parker, and it's clear he's already over it.

Once I jump out, a Ferrari sits a few yards back. The sports car is not really Duncan's style, and that car doesn't belong to one of my siblings or girlfriends. I scope a better peek at the figure inside staring at me.

Flabbergasted, I do a hundred-and-eighty-degree turn. Parker is already pulling off, so I start walking in the direction of my parents' home. According to the GPS on my phone, it's one-point-six miles. Why would he follow the vehicle I'm in, like he's tracking his property? With him behind me, I proceed on the thirty-minute walk, his bright headlights illuminating my path.

The loud-ass engine of his car roars up beside me, the perfect approach for his personality. "You can stay mad at me all you want. Just get in. I'll drive you straight home. You know I'm not going to do anything to you, Kamilah."

"You did not just piss on my hookup. I'd rather walk alone since you want me to be by myself." I also need to process what happened with Duncan, the encounter that finally went down after all these years.

"You shouldn't have been leaving with him anyway, but fine, I'll just hang out over here and mind my business."

"I'm not your business."

"Until you get home, you are." His one hand on the

steering wheel, his eyes veer between the street and me, with him driving and talking. "I'd like you to be my business even after you get home, though."

I ignore his flirting and try to sweep aside thoughts in my mind of those hands on me. "So you knew what you were doing and you're a stalker."

"You were leaving with somebody you didn't know."

I keep my eyes ahead. "How did you know I didn't know him?"

A couple of other cars pass him and blow their horns.

"While you were in the bathroom, your friends were describing you to him. How you could put hands on a dude and jack him up. They wouldn't need to describe you to somebody who already knows you."

"So you didn't have anything better to do than stalk me."

"I choose to ignore whatever else I could be doing."

"Lion, shouldn't you be somewhere throwing money out of a window?"

"Only if I can throw it at you. Otherwise, I'm not interested."

Another car approaches and slows down. An elderly couple rolls down a window and peers out at me.

"Everything all right here, young lady?"

From the driver's seat, the woman's husband quietly flashes a police badge where I can see it.

"Just say the word, and he'll help you."

I stare back at Lion, who tails them now. He could easily drive off. But he doesn't.

"No, ma'am." Now I'm concerned with avoiding trouble, especially for a Black man with money. "He's a friend of my family, and he's making sure I arrive home safely. I'm perfectly capable of taking care of myself." I whip out my flip knife and display it so the blade flashes.

"You need us to stay close?" the man asks. "In case he steps out of line."

Why is it that on the night I've been reminded of my early life screw-ups, and just want to be left with my thoughts, everybody in New York shows up? I don't want anybody following me. They can all leave me alone. "Absolutely not." I give them the most assured, confident expression that Karate Kam can muster up. Finally, they're convinced and wave before driving off.

Lion pulls over and shuts off the car. Behind me is the steady, undeterred crunch of his feet on dirt and grass along the path.

"You were not concerned about my safety. You know the bartender didn't look like a perp."

"You're right. But he doesn't know shit about what your hands can do to a man, and since I have personally caught your hands, I'm the one who should be taking you home. Not him."

A tiny part of me—very tiny—wants to laugh at that. "You're such an entitled ass."

Now he picks up a light jog until he's at my side. "Yes, I am an entitled ass. But I can be other things as well."

"All I need you to be is competent. Work *with* me to organize Explore, Lion, and not for your own interests. I don't want to be here in Southampton. I would really like to leave this place sooner than later. The faster we get Explore squared away, the less we'll have to deal with each other."

My family's house is just another six or seven minutes. In silence, for the next few minutes, he accompanies me down the two-lane country highway, past thick, lush greenery, swaying high grass, and vast spreads of unhurried Hamptons quietude. I'll admit this hideout from the rest of the world soothes my muscle tension some.

Through the small crevices of my mental wall, his cigar-

and-leather scent sneaks in, and joins the night air to further disarm me.

"What if I like us dealing with each other?" he finally asks.

"I don't." Somehow, that is just as much the truth as it is a lie. His scent and presence are opening more than my lust, snatching me too far back in time, and it's an inconvenience I'd rather not deal with.

Hands in his cargo pants, his arm occasionally brushes mine. His scent keeps swirling around me.

Heat rolls off him as easily as smoke from the smokehouse. With Lion so near—swathed in all his sickening wealth, a constant reminder of the night I met him and Duncan, and my foolish decisions I made after—I can't think straight. Or properly wallow in my misery.

Lion's presence is…

… titillating. Uncomfortable.

Unwanted and yet…

… wanted.

Maybe all of them.

The tranquil highway finally leads us to my family's driveway, where all the Rouse cars are lined up along the pavement. It's surrounded by tall, wrought-iron gates they had installed now that we have mini-celebrities in the family —Maddy and Chrissy.

I pause before entering the code that opens our gate and glare at him to look away.

Amused, Lion rolls his eyes and pivots. Playfully, he peeks out of the corner of his eye.

"I see that!" I snap with humor I can't help.

Under the sheet of night, we are alone.

In the time that the gate creeps open, maybe in a suspension of time, his footsteps crunch along the dirt.

Along my heart.

They travel the hills of my hesitation. Through the valley

of Duncan, across the desert of shithole men I've been rejecting before they can reject me, and they navigate my forest of terror at being humiliated again.

Until Lion's steps close the distance between us.

The arrival of his pelvis at the entrance of my womanly domain is an arrival at more than me. The tips of his fingers take a risk at my hips. On my scalp is his warm breath that joins the gentle night draft.

"I'm sorry."

So low it almost drifted into the high grass unnoticed.

"I was presumptuous."

His finger strokes me deeper than my pelvic bone. The seismic response rushing my head, ears, and neural network drowns out the swell of ocean tides crashing ahead of us. I step from his grasp and cannot find the wherewithal to face him again. Because I know the next time I face Lion, it won't be as casual co-workers. All my good sense would evaporate.

Once I escape into the house, my mother sits in the sunroom with a book at 12:30 a.m.

"There she is. I thought you and your buddies were wilding out this weekend."

I kick off my slides. "Not so wild when your knees give out on the third song while you're trying to get low. And if you drink too hard, the liquor won't come out of your deepest brain folds for a week."

Verona Rouse's little giggle always sounds like tinkling china wares. I surprise her when I plop next to her, hike my feet under me, and fall onto her lap. The silk fibers of Mama's pajamas absorb all of my stupid shame and crumbling strength I cry into them.

My hair is swept from my neck.

"My strong, rebel girl," she whispers into the same night quietude as Lion did. "You finally ready to tell me what happened?"

Tears march across the bridge of my nose and down my temple as I recall Duncan's dumb-ass expression. I should have been smarter. My brothers taught me not to be stupid, how to recognize game. I came from a close-knit family that sharpened me. As a girl, I had zero problems with my self-esteem. There was no excuse for letting a man make a fool of me.

Which is why it's never happened again, and never will.

FEAR

LION

"Old Man, what are you doing here by yourself? Why aren't you out on the golf course? Or on the boat? I hear Mr. Page is in Sag Harbor. And Mr. Townsend."

"Yeah, since their daughters iced out our family, we haven't been on the best terms," Dad replies. Pain shakes his eyes that swivel to me.

"I'm discussing that with Madison. And her mother is working it out with Mom. We'll handle it."

As I say this, I peer down at today's Sunday newspaper. Duncan graces the front page in a tuxedo and delivers a speech at a snazzy event, one that I knew nothing about.

My family has often received invites to nearly every function in New York, even if it's Upstate. During the high-traffic season of summer in the Hamptons, we've often required a social secretary to arrange our appearances and social calls. However, this year, since the Harvard leak, our social calendar isn't completely dry but has dropped to about a third its normal size.

This vexes me. When Duncan first landed in college with me at Cornell, and he didn't know anybody, he sometimes came home with me to New York. His family was doing all right over in Jersey, his father being a school principal and his mother an insurance agent, but they lacked connections or extensive financial play money. So during his internships around the city, my family allowed him to stay at our homes. I looked out for him when he needed connections and wanted to join our fraternity. I have given him the clothes off my back. But after college, he married Tanja because her father was doing well in Albany politics.

It speaks volumes that, these days, he can only find me when he is in need.

"You've been spending a lot of time with those adventure fellas. So Kevin's reeling you into that business. And away from the more serious affairs you should be attending."

I no longer wither under the wrecking ball of Dad's stare, as I did when I was a teenager, because now I realize it's no longer about discipline but fear. All the old ways—family dynasties, hidden wealth and power with little accountability, and men being masters of our destiny as long as we had our own coin—are dying. Most of all, he fears he was wrong.

"Dad, I'm not distracted at all. We are on the right path with media messaging. We've donated literally thousands this year to charities, inner-city programs, and troubled youth around New York. It's in the press, on websites, and letterheads of organizations. The good part is the Black community doesn't really care about a Black man with money buying his son's way into Harvard."

I sit to face him and stare directly into what I've never seen before—shame dismantles his tough, proud spirit that raised us. Over the last nine months each time I've come home, he seems to retreat more and more into himself. It makes me want to go outside and break every camera, tackle every single press reporter. To avoid the press treating him like O.J. Simpson, a man who got away with murder in the eyes of the public and is flaunting his freedom on the golf course, Dad's mostly remained in the house. But I refuse to allow him to punish himself forever.

"A lot of Black guys actually admire you for having that kind of influence and financial weight, Dad. You've popped up in at least three rap songs since all this blew up. You've become a pop culture figure."

"I don't find that admirable, Lion August. Fads and trends and damn popularity contests are not what made this family what it is."

My father's got fan accounts on Twitter and TikTok. He ignited a wave of group discussions about the secret Black upper class and fired up talk show debates everywhere.

This week alone I've turned down no fewer than twenty requests for my father to appear at various conferences or gatherings around the country. I don't want those appearances to give the nation—particularly government authorities—the impression he's gloating. Or for gossips and press to interpret his public appearances as arrogance, that our family escaped accountability.

"I'm not saying it's admirable, Lionel Augustus. Only to point out to you that all is not lost, and we do have a way around this. There are some bright spots, mostly that you have a path to a new generation of young Blacks who are curious about men like you. They want to know more about quiet Black wealth. But we must navigate it carefully. And strategically."

"Unfortunately, Boston city prosecutors are not influenced by a damn rap song. They won't close their investigation."

I rub the aged seams along his neck. "But they're beyond the statute of limitations, and they know they can't do shit at this point. It's over. The lawyers say prosecutors are still fishing so other rich people won't think you got off easy. The city of Boston doesn't want the public thinking that the failure to indict you means they're condoning what you did. So they're dragging out the process."

"What about your oil promotion? Your bosses. What do they want from you as far as convincing Kevin to sell?"

"I have a plan for that also." Among other things I'm planning. "Dad, you should take Mom out. Maybe the two of you can go to the city, see a show, fly out to L.A., Jackson Hole, or Miami for a few days." I stop short of suggesting they visit our family's ancestral home in England, where we still have relatives. I'm hesitant to give the public any impression he's attempting to flee or that he won't stay here in the States and face the pressure like the solid man he is.

"Here the two of you are," my mother says, coming in from the back. She slides her arms over my shoulders and kisses my head. "I'm finally seeing your face. Since you've been home, you've been living on that laptop. No yard parties, boats, sports? What did you do with my son?"

"Your other son's put him to work. My vacation is no longer a vacation."

After kissing Dad, she takes a seat next to him.

"So I've heard." Gladness crinkles up in her eyes. "I'm happy the two of you are working together. But I hear work's not all that's happening over at Explore. I've had the chance to meet Professor Verona Rouse. She is an outstanding lady. And I hear her children are, too." She can't beam hard enough.

Me finding a woman to "tame me" as she puts it, is her dream.

But I have a dream of my own. "Have you two given any thought to renewing your vows?"

That knocks the spark right out of her and stuns my dad such that his eyelid twitches.

Awkward hesitation might be the only thing they share as the two of them squirm and avoid one another.

"What about therapy first?" Mom suggests. Now she takes a gander at Dad.

Panic rips through his eyes and across his face. "No."

I share his immediate horror. Therapy requires truth. All of it, and neither of us is interested in hearing the sordid details.

The door to the house opens.

"Hey, everybody." My new sister-in-law, Chenera, enters the house, followed by Kevin.

Kevin and I have mostly been avoiding one another during our stay this time, other than the meetings for Explore.

"Why's everybody so dead ass?" he asks us. "You all expecting a hurricane I didn't know about or something?"

Since Dad nor I wish to repeat it, my mother does so. "I suggested that your father and brother join us in therapy."

Jealousy leaps ahead of my curiosity. "Join? You and him are having therapy together?"

She nods, "Yes," and holds out her hand to halt my coming protest. "Only because we knew you and Lionel wouldn't do it."

Now it's my mother's emotion quivering on her chin. I'm not sure if it's shame, hurt, remorse or what.

To silence the already-silent accusations, she keeps going. "Kevin started therapy a few months ago to… process our issues. He's invited me to attend with him. Now I've started going on my own. It works wonders, Lion."

"I'm glad to hear that for the both of you," I respond for myself and, I'm sure, for Dad, too. "But you should have discussed with us first how much family business you're disclosing to complete strangers. Especially right now, when the nation watches us, and the press is on the hunt for any little detail on us they can find."

"Therapists are professionals who have an ethical duty to keep it confidential," she responds.

"What about your duty to *us*!" I bellow back, stronger than I should have, with a lot of resentment packed into those few words.

Kevin moves to stand at her side, as if he needs to protect her from me, as if she's his to protect.

"My duty to you is healing us, Lion."

I lean toward her, not giving a shit about him standing there. "We wouldn't have anything to heal if you hadn't done it in the first place. And I don't want to hear about Dad cheating. Two wrongs don't make a right. You didn't just ch…"

I choke. On the memory of my father's sobs that still echo through my mind thirty-two years later. I was only seven. He and my grandfather thought I was still down the street at Trane's house. I saw the way my father's strong body collapsed at the fireplace, forcing my granddad to catch him.

"You didn't just cheat on him. You cheated on *me*." I stare into her. Then I shift my anger to Cher, the person directly responsible for the "Harvard leak." "And you…"

"Don't come for my wife," Kevin warns.

I shoot up from my seat. "Your *wife* came for us!"

Mom throws herself between us with desperate energy and slides her soft hand under my chin. "Now let's all move on."

"Say you're sorry." I need to hear it.

And I'm not talking about the simple, trite apology that people spout off to sidestep responsibility. I need to hear that my mother regrets her ongoing love affair with another man that produced an entire child, pitted two houses against one another, and started a quasi-civil war in the Black Hamptons.

For these last few years, now that her sons have all become grown adults, we had reached an uncomfortable peace. We had learned to talk around it, tried to fool ourselves into thinking our stiff, carefully guarded dinner conversations amounted to forgiveness and family unity.

Until the Harvard leak.

Nine months ago, Kevin's enemies blew the roof off our lives and security, off our house of glass.

Mom closes her green eyes that she shares with Kevin, and opens them again, brimming with tears. "Will you demand the same accountability from your father?"

"Son," Dad murmurs. An ask for me to stand down. He can't bear to hear any more.

Mom hurls her entire body to grip my shoulders, shaking me and unleashing tectonic plates that rock me, too. "The fact that you hold *me* accountable, and me alone, is why I'll only say it to you in *therapy*. Come with me, so we can heal and finally live life."

I throw her hands off me. "You've always had all these rules and stipulations when it came to me. Your love for Middleton men comes with conditions. But you gave your love so freely to that Manuel hustler. I'll never go to therapy where you can make excuses for it. So I guess from now on, this *is* life."

KAMILAH

LION

My watch tells me it's 10:15 a.m.

I'll be late for my first breakfast with Kamilah.

Seagulls take off from the rickety wooden pier and fly over my head near the business and warehouse district. The ocean tides are high enough today to bounce off the rocks and spray me. Energetic and vibrant, that's a surfing invitation.

But I have more important matters, like putting the smile back on Kamilah's face. The thought douses me with extra vigor.

A youngish gentleman walks around the harbor, emerging from the warehouse. "Mr. Middleton! Quite honored somebody of your stature would stop by here and bless us with your presence."

"You Allen Stafford?"

"Oh, no, I'm his son."

This is the location where beer distributors and bottlers are apparently hiding Explore's barley malt and German hops, without their identifying labels. It's not uncommon for businesses to conspire and form blocks against newer competition to shut them out of a market, and this especially happens with beer distributors.

"Son, you should go and get your father so he and I can talk specifics," I say to him.

The boy budges and then remains steady. "No, you can talk to me."

"Do you know what a bill of lading is?" I ask, arms folded.

His mouth twitches and he blinks. "My father said—"

"Not that I don't believe you, but go get him and let him say it himself."

A couple of minutes later, out comes an older, half-put-together man in a polo shirt, who shifts all his body weight when he walks, as if he's asserting authority he wishes he had. "The famous Mr. Middleton."

"I'm not the famous one. Wrong Middleton."

"Ah, I see. So your brother then? He's starting a big-time adventure operation and stepping on a lot of toes in the process. Some folks aren't too pleased about this whole Sasha Static getup."

"And you're punishing him?" I inquire.

"Naaah! Nah. What kind of men do you think we are?" He, his son, and a couple of other guys laugh. "Other businesses around here—restaurants, beer-sellers, tourist companies, would just... like to be compensated for our inconvenience. This Explore outfit, and those girls—what are they called? Dream Stage? You all have been making a lot of noise around here and—"

"You mean the Black people," I interrupt him. "*Black* people have been making a lot of noise around here."

He swings his head. "Nope. Don't go there and start with all of that 'woke' mess. I'm only talking about the businesses who bust in here and shake up our quiet little community."

Yeah, right. When white people start talking about "their

quiet" area, without a doubt, this is code for "Negro-less" space. But I motion my hand toward the pallets his workers are bringing out. "Is this all of Explore's shipments?"

"That's what they ordered four months ago, in February," responds the clean-shaven man with a deeply peach-colored face.

I start calculating in my head. "Sea freight shipping from a German port should only take a month and a half. No more than sixty days. So you've had these shipments sitting here for how long?"

His peach fury burns to an apricot color. "That's not important. If you don't like it, Explore can go to Germany and pick up its own damn hops instead of spending all that money on yachts, parties, and pricey entertainers."

That means the goods have been here for a while. "How soon will we receive the next shipment of barley malt and hops from Frankfurt?"

"Depends on how much you are willing to pay for that express mail." His head tilts up while he waits. These types are all too rampant in oil.

Translation: Anti-competition. Diverting the goods of competitors, or buying them up altogether, to suppress sales and gain the upper hand in a market.

Before I open my mouth and tell him where to go for trying to screw me, I think of Kamilah. The tough CPA's eyes fired at me the other day with bullets of hurt. That meeting clearly meant more to her than me.

Stafford's demand for money to give us what we've already paid for is illegal, but I came here with a plan so, "Fine. How much?"

"Twenty-five thousand for every shipment."

"Ten thousand."

"Thirty thousand."

I stare at him. "Don't be ridiculous."

He sniffs and chomps on his gum. He reminds me of Jon Voight's seedy characters he portrays in films. "I don't think you understand how this works. I've got you all's shit sitting right over there. And my boys aren't going to haul it out of here without my say-so. Now, do you want to seriously participate in this conversation, or do you want to jump back on your yacht and sail your oily ass back down to Houston?" Allen asks.

Kamilah.

But this bitch *will* feel me before it's all said and done.

"Twelve thousand," I counter.

"Seventeen thousand, and I won't go any lower."

"I'll have to clear it with the guys who will pay for this."

"By close of business then, and I'll know we have a deal." He sticks out his hand.

Disgusted, I ignore it. "You'll have an answer by COB."

He snickers, and his face burns deeply red. "I don't give a damn if you pay a *million* dollars. There's no deal if your high and mighty Black ass can't bring yourself to shake my hand."

"Fuck y—"

My goal for Kevin crosses my mind.

And another priority is indeed overtaking that of me putting my brother in his place: Kamilah. At the thought of her, I check my wrist. 10:39 now. Disgusted, I take the man's hand.

"Your next shipment should be here in two weeks. We'll have it all lined up."

"Are you sure the extra hops and cans are not here already?"

"Young man," he mutters, "I don't give a damn what family you come from. If I say two weeks, that's the date."

Which means he may have Explore's other inventory held up as well. Competing beer retailers and distributors have likely paid him to sit on it. The result is Slurp's slow production that might cripple them for Sasha Static.

I walk away to call my boss. Aiden gets Ron on the line.

"Lion, we were wondering when we would hear from you."

"It will take seventeen thousand a month to move this product off the docks. But I have an idea."

Indeed, I do.

"And what's that?"

"That we control Explore's inventory and product. Now that Explore sees I can deliver, they trust me. Once we have access to all of it, I'll go to Kevin and use it as leverage to make him sell—MoneyCruncher in exchange for the materials for his precious Sasha Static concert."

"Won't he be pissed you're doing that? Why would that compel him to play ball?" Ron asks.

Inhaling the ocean air, I consider my answer in light of my scheme that's even bigger than Ron. "He's too vain, wants to be great. His devotion to MoneyCruncher only serves his vanity. This is one of the biggest concerts in history. Kevin will sell his business in order for the concert to move forward, and his name to be on it. Then, he'll go start another company, same as he always does."

"I like how you think. Pretty soon, Houston PetroChem will be calling you CEO."

As I'm leaving, another couple arrives in their truck.

"Can we find a Mr. Stafford?" one of them asks a warehouse worker. "We've been calling with no response, and we've driven from Bridgehampton to get answers."

Of course, they are Black.

And they are frustrated. So it's not just Explore, or the Sasha Static concert, that the restaurant and beer community are conspiring to destroy. These anti-competition and unfair business practices target all rising Black businesses, particularly those that sell liquor and spirits.

"I'm sorry, ma'am," Stafford the younger says, "but Mr. Stafford is not here. He only works here once or twice a week, and he's not here today. I'm afraid we'll have to connect you to our headquarters."

I open the internet on my phone to research Allen Stafford. Indeed, the guy I just met with is him. My skin crawls at this pirate operation these guys run against Black Hamptons businesses, but I need to stay focused on the biggest goal—putting Kevin where I want him.

ON THE DECK of Explore's sixty-footer, I'm a little breathless, and not just because I rushed from the car onto the boat. Kamilah stuns in a body-hugging teal dress. Hopefully, the serving staff laid out the specific order I called in on Friday.

Clouds darken the sun as well as her greeting, and she glances at her watch.

"It's only thirteen minutes," I start. "Good morning, by the way."

"Late is late." After a sip of coffee, she removes her sunshades, slips her computer out of her bag, and sets it on the table. Her eyes aren't red, but they are somewhat dark and dry. Ultra-focused, maybe even stressed, she flits from her tablet to the computer keys and her phone, apparently wanting the job done fast so she can move onto wherever she belongs next.

"I was at the distributors, finding out what I can. I think we'll receive our next orders shortly, in about two to three weeks. And as we speak, the truck should be delivering Explore's wish list to Taste and Slurp."

"I'm happy to hear it. How many pallets?" she asks without looking up.

"Check the Eros app. It's already loaded in there."

Finally. The glimmer strikes her eye. She blinks several times with upbeat surprise. "That can't be right. I just checked it yesterday evening. There was nothing about new inventory yet."

Her face blooms amid the steely backdrop of today's platinum sky as she opens up the app and the figures and numbers populate. "This is awesome. When did you do this?"

Are parts of me shifting with her mood?

"Don't worry about all that. It's in there."

Quincy approaches. "Good morning, Miss Rouse. Mr. Middleton."

Kamilah stares at him, confused. "This is the young man from the meeting the other day. Good morning. But why are you here?"

"So he receives a 'good morning' and I don't?" I insist on knowing. "I've hired him as my assistant, to help me take care of things."

Kamilah's momentary happiness falls, and her face turns to silent accusation. "So you've found somebody else to do your work for you?"

"What difference does it make as long as it gets done? You're happy with the result. Explore's supply chain progress is in the works. I don't see the problem, other than you searching for reasons to be upset."

Poor Quincy stands vexed between the two of us. "So am I staying or going, sir?"

Kamilah starts in. "Always need someone at your beck and call, huh? Do you ever do anything for yourself? While everyone around you hauls ass?"

"Assistance makes me more efficient, so I can focus on the more important responsibilities, like meeting with critical players in the line of production who can speed it up. So beautiful, demanding auditors who want things done now can show me they're capable of smiling."

She sucks her teeth. The penetrating knife point of her stare matches that of only one other person in my life.

My lungs fill with a breath of capitulation. "Quincy." I'm still staring at Kamilah. "Please visit each one of the Explore sites, check in with Desmond, Miracle, Rocky, and Keenan, and ensure that *everyone* has the proper assistance they need for this week. Even if you have to go through a staffing agency. Ensure that all of Explore's managers receive administrative support and inform me on how much that costs so we can maintain our budget."

Kamilah replies, "You can't keep paying for more workers as a way to speed this up and complete the tasks."

"Check the operations systems charts. And you'll see my plan for bringing in special summer staff to meet traffic expectations. They would only be temporary through Labor Day. Staff should be hired, especially for the canning process and packing, and to work the events that Kevin, Keenan, and Solomon are all planning. Explore will need extra hands and you can't avoid that."

"But we can keep them to a minimum." Her finger taps the laptop keys. Then taps again. "I can't see your operation setup. None of it. It's not in here." Flustered, she swings her hair. As she has a tendency to do, she slides her hand over the back of her neck, flips her hair, and twists it in frustration. "You didn't do it, Lion."

"Log out completely. You must have closed your laptop without logging out of the program, and the software hasn't completely updated yet. It does that. I was experiencing the same problem yesterday. That should solve it."

She stares at me, apparently stunned. Her eyes ask the question her mouth won't.

"Yes, I worked yesterday."

"You or Quincy?"

"Does it matter? Right now, I'm telling you how to solve that, so I must know how to do some work on my own, right?" I sip my coffee.

A few moments later, she reviews the figures and projections I've provided for Explore to achieve efficiency over the next several weeks and then the next three to six months once high-traffic period is over. A tiny smile creeps up at the corner of her lips when she sees the money this could make for Explore and how they could stand to grow over the next few months.

Her joy creeps into other spaces, inside me.

"This will take some discipline," she says, her focus fully immersed in the screen. "A lot of discipline. They will not want to hear this, especially Solomon, who's very choosy."

"But it will allow him to keep sourcing his chocolate directly from African warehouses and farms, and he can cut out the middleman distributor, Aragon, on some of his shipments. But when he uses Aragon, I'll have to call up guys there and see if they will renegotiate so they're not penalizing him."

"Do you really think you can do that?"

"I really think I can try." As I sit here and observe the color return under Kam's eyes, I suddenly think I can try to drink the ocean so this joy on her never goes away again.

I've met some of Aragon's execs in the past years, at supply chain conferences and corporate executive conferences. They are among the biggest food distributors in the world. But I know personally how under-the-table activities go down on the other side of the globe, the forced labor and slavery they employ. For them to cooperate with me, I may need to leverage what I know.

Where she seemed overwhelmed when I got here, Kamilah now scans her digital charts with new vigor. While she attends to that, I scan her.

The yacht staff lining the wall have started texting and playing around, and I wave for them to begin. They snap into place and bring over the first course of entrées. Warm sauces and dips with croissants as a starter. They set down escargot flown in from France that I had delivered by a friend.

Kamilah's eyes flutter at all the dishes placed around her on the table. "What is all this?"

"What does it look like?" I fold my napkin in my lap. "Breakfast."

Ready to dive in, I wait to hear all the girly gasping and excitement, and look up from my lap to receive my reward.

Her expression is a full red traffic light.

It stops me in my tracks, so I protest, "We can't eat?"

"We're *working*. You should've eaten already."

I deliver my hardest "give me a break" face. She doesn't flinch and adds the eyebrow for emphasis.

"There's nothing wrong with food."

At least now her eyes shine. Somewhat. "And there's nothing wrong with waiting until the appropriate time for that. Other hard-working employees are watching."

In rebuttal, I spread my hands. "Then they can come and join us."

Suppressing a little smile, Kamilah crosses her arms on the table. "If everybody stops working to accommodate The Lion," she says, her hair swinging over her shoulder with the tilted head thing again, "how efficient is that… Operations Manager?"

Her lips… *God*, the lips on that face. Not small, not thick, they remind me of the curl of a petal or a seashell.

Shit. Seashell.

The opening. Her other opening. I remember it. Slick, long, her muscles…

"Lion."

I raise my hand. The servers stop, confused.

"Take it away. Thank you."

A humored snort escapes her throat before she pushes her fingers over her mouth to hide it. Well damn, if all this effort at least got me a small laugh, I'll take it. The hoops I have to jump through…

"So where were we?" She returns to business.

"Blue balls. That's where we were. At least that's where I am."

The open-mouthed smile breaks free. White, glorious, it reminds me of Whitney Houston. Yes, that's who Kam is with her coppery skin, wiry curves, and inner shine when she lets herself open up. A Whitney.

I press on. "So, can we have breakfast after work then?"

"No, because we work together."

"We don't work together. We're on a temporary assignment. That's all. You work for your company, and I work for my regular company, and I'm just trying to have some breakfast."

French Fry's shoulders shake as she chuckles and glances at the schedule on her tablet. "The Black Business Council is having a meeting later this week. Since the guys are busy, maybe we should go on their behalf."

"What for?"

"Other Black businesses could benefit from our presence there. Not everyone can afford auditors and Fortune 500 corporate executives. Maybe we can go, listen to their concerns, and help out," she explains, with her mouth as well as her eyes.

This might be the first time I've seen her open up.

Despite how sensual she is, I have Dad and my family's situation to contend with. "I can't. I have other commitments. Maybe next time. Don't forget I'm doing this while I juggle my family's affairs also."

"Fine. Fair enough." She swipes up on her digital calendar. "Also, the BBC is sponsoring inner-city children here in the Hamptons this summer. I was thinking maybe it would be a good idea for you to teach them some history. Being that your family is the oldest Black family in the Hamptons, who better to tell it than one of you?"

"You mean when I'm not mastering software apps, arm wrestling to negotiate commodities from foreign countries, and thinking of ways that I can persuade you not to hate me?"

Over her coffee, Kam is now relaxed. Maybe it's just coincidence how the sun emerges from its fortress at the same time and showers me with vitamin D and new energy and new… attraction.

"Yes, Mr. Middleton. When you're not performing your job duties, could you consider doing something good for someone else? Outside your own interests?"

"My family is sponsoring two of those inner-city youth and their accommodations. And we've already written a check to the Black Business Council this year."

She flicks her pen between her fingers, perhaps a representation of how fast her thoughts are traveling. "Then let me guess. You made sure a magazine or newspaper reported all about this, and your family probably received some plaque on a wall at a country club, or the city inscribed your names on a sidewalk, right?" she asks. Her bone-straight bob swings around her shoulders to emphasize her point.

I silence a call from my lawyer, because now that Kamilah smiles, whatever he has to say, I don't give a shit. "What's so wrong with that? Does it matter that the press saw? We still gave. Why can't we be recognized for it?"

"Those public displays only remind the world that you're vain. And you're not really trying to change or improve the circumstances."

"Kamilah, why can't I do both—receive good press *and* improve circumstances? You and I accomplish goals and get results in different ways, but business is handled just the same."

"But is there anything you do that you don't need the world to see?" No sooner than she speaks does she catch what she just asked, and she notices that *I've* caught it. "Don't answer that."

"You can find out for yourself."

Her ice is thawing, lips twitching, and breasts rising and falling, like she may want to find out.

She stands.

So I stand. "Where are you going?" I'm already rubbing my heartburn at the sight of her packing her things. I'm realizing I've longed for her nearness since Saturday night.

"I have to head to Taste and work with Miracle. It's my understanding you're staying here to direct the yacht staff today. That shouldn't be too hard for you." She smiles, drinks up the last of her coffee, and sets the cup back down.

I don't miss this chance. Hell, I miss her. And she hasn't left. I brush her hand with the back of mine. Inches separating us, I inhale her, learn her.

"Thank you for the figures and diagrams," she murmurs.

Her eyes say more, but I don't know her well enough yet to interpret what.

"May I have a thank-you kiss then?" I murmur back.

Her amusement lifts her face and the inside of me. "Do you really need to be rewarded for everything?"

"Yes." I peer down at her. "When it comes to you."

More joy overtakes her, and she chuckles. We've come a long way since I sat down. I walk around the table and pull out her chair. It's really a setup to do what I've wanted all weekend.

When Kamilah moves to leave, I go for her arm, step to her. And lower my head so no one sees or hears me but her. I'm taking a huge chance. "I know I shouldn't say this at work, and you can slap me again, but I'll do backflips the day you let me put my mouth on you. Everywhere."

Her wall of composure cracks.

For a slight moment, the shuddering of her one eyelid…

I brace myself.

Her finger twitches next to mine. She pulls her hand away. "Employees are here."

"Does that mean… I'm getting a thank-you kiss when employees *aren't* here?"

A hint of humor flashes. It disappears. "You have a good day, Mr. Middleton."

She leaves behind more than her scent.

A PROMISE

KAMILAH

"This is so lit," Desmond gushes. "I can't believe it. Kamilah, I won't lie. I had my doubts. You were talking like you were trying to shut down all the hot moves we want to make."

"And I won't lie. I intended to."

We both burst out laughing.

"These numbers, though," he says, thumping his tablet, "they look really good. You mean, I'll have this inventory to last through September plus key promo events for Sasha Static?"

"Yes, you will." I nod as we talk.

The workers at Slurp are unloading the pallets and lining up the bottling machines that have sat dormant while Desmond grappled with the shortages.

"So your brother was right. You're amazing."

I think about Lion and the last time I saw him yesterday afternoon, how he smelled so incredibly male, like ocean and smooth linens and rich bourbon. All-American. How strong I had to be so I could stay focused, the way the spotlights of his eyes centered on me. It was a complete turnaround from the jackass in the backseat of the Mercedes last week.

"Actually, I can't take credit for this. These are Lion's numbers. You have those pallets of aluminum and your latest shipment of hops and barley over there, thanks to his negotiations and contacts. I would be lost on where to start making calls if I had to bring your shipments in myself."

Desmond smirks. "So you smacked some 'act right' into him, huh?"

I don't join him in the joke. The other men mocking Lion was the last thing I wanted. It wasn't some performance for their enjoyment. In fact, I didn't even think when I did it, and was operating on my humiliation that's been in my baggage for years.

"I should not have done that, especially not in front of an audience."

Desmond lowers his head as if about to share secret information. "Oh, a few folks around here think you should've. And that it's about time somebody did it."

I suck my teeth, keenly aware that Desmond's wife, Adella, is currently suing Lion's family over property in Italy. Though I have no idea what that's about, I've learned for myself that there are always two sides to every story.

"Just remember to give Lion his due credit for hooking you up. All right?"

The man might fall on the overly confident side, but as he pointed out to me yesterday, he is clearly capable of handling business. I might have prejudged him.

Desmond nods slowly as he processes how I won't stand for Lion being disrespected after the work he put in. "I will give the man his respect then."

Our conversation has me reevaluating Lion's motives for coming to Explore. Maybe he didn't ride in here on Easy

Street the way I originally thought. He had to know he'd have naysayers, starting with Desmond.

Desmond is friends with my brother, Jerrell, and married to Adella, neither of whom are fond of the Middletons. Desmond may be respecting Lion now since Lion appreciates his beers. But I'd imagine that, before we all met, Desmond probably objected to Lion being on this project. Since Lion is smarter than he acts, he likely anticipated he would have detractors and he agreed to do this anyway. I'm guessing Kevin believed in his brother's skills enough to ask him for help.

These men may have some friction among one another and are having to work together despite it. They seem to be coming together for Explore, despite some personal issues. That is not the party scenario I had prejudged them for.

Maddy breaks into my thoughts when she comes in with the baby.

"Hey, Aunt Kam, thank you so much for taking Chase while Daddy and I are out of town." As always, harried, scattered and rushing, she's toting three bags. "I'll go put these out in the car."

"No worries. Just sit them on the table, and I'll take them out. Mama and I will be glad to have him."

While Maddy coordinates Duncan's campaign, Jerrell is opening a new store in the city, and from there, he flies to Atlanta, where he and Solomon are partnering up. There, Jerrell's business with my grandmother, Poppin' Pauletta's, will partner their pastries with Solomon's chocolate menu at a potential Atlanta-based Taste. So Maddy's family and our family will take turns juggling Chase between our houses over the next two days. That's as long as she's willing to stay away from him.

"Say, Maddy?"

She keeps checking and rechecking Chase's things. "Yeah, girl?"

"Got a moment? I wanted to ask about Lion."

Now she stops in her place and stares up at me. "Don't tell me he's doing something to Duncan."

I shake my head. "No! No, that's not it. I..."

"Yes?"

I force it out. "Do you have intel on him? All of you grew up with his brother, Kevin, and Lion was a few years older, but do you know much about him?"

"Oh, that's right. You and him are working together around here for the concert."

I nod and pretend that's the real reason I'm asking. "Yes."

"I heard things got tight between you two the other day."

I scoff. "God, who is not talking about that? No big deal. I flew off the handle. It was really inappropriate."

Maddy's expression dismisses what I just said. "But so is he. Lion can be a handful. He's been married before. Cheated on his wife. Sometimes he doesn't recognize boundaries, just like Kevin has a tendency not to recognize them either."

"He's been married?" So, Lumberjack actually tried to commit to somebody?

"Yes. I believe she's still down in Texas. Nobody we know. She was nice, though. Lion and Kevin are..." She looks around in search of words. "Incredible men. But arrogant. They are both so very different, and in so many ways, much the same. Lion is the jock. Kevin is cerebral. Think of Roland on steroids—smart-ass, clever, condescending. Lion is all that Roland would be if he'd grown up wealthy with no limits. So there are times when the Middletons don't realize they need to come down to planet Earth with everybody else." Sister-in-law eyes me now. "Wait, don't tell me you like him."

I shrug. "I don't know. I'm just asking. He's..." The spread of breakfast he ordered for our meeting yesterday, the way everyone jumped to do everything he said. That must be how he was raised. "It sounds like his parents overcompensated for him being Black. By lavishing them with too much privilege and not enough balance."

Maddy nods. "Bingo. But to be fair, Lion is not a bad person. When he was around, he made sure Kevin didn't pick on us. Although, he was harsh on Kevin."

My face must have follow-up questions, because she continues.

"Kevin could be such an asshole, and Lion would come out and make him apologize. Or Lion would embarrass him in front of us to humble him some. There is definitely some rift between those two. We've just never known what it is. You'll have to guard your heart where he's concerned. He's a playboy. He thinks he's entitled to everything, whatever woman he wants, however many, just like his father." Her phone vibrates. "Look, I have to go. But be careful. If there's anything else you want to know, you can also ask Chrissy or shoot me a text."

We exchange hugs.

"Be safe in your travels, girl. And good luck with…" I stop myself from wishing her luck getting Duncan elected to one of the most powerful political seats in the nation. "Good luck with your new consultant role."

"I'll call in a few hours and check in on my baby." After kissing and hugging him until he squirms, she turns him over to me.

Chase doesn't cry since he's used to being shuffled between family members.

His eyes are already surveying the hanging overhead lights, shiny knobs behind the counter, array of tables and chairs, and foreign objects he'll try to attack if I'm not watching.

"Oh, how precious is this little guy?" Laney asks as she enters the brewery to help out.

"Can you say hi to Miss Laney? Can you wave?"

He waves backward as if motioning her to come to him.

"We've got to get that wave together."

"He is so cute. Is he yours?" she asks.

"Oh, no. I don't plan on having any," I respond. My chest squeezes tight at that thought. "All my nieces and nephews are my kids."

She waits for me to explain myself, and when I don't, she continues with a smile that's sympathetic and forced. "I respect that. An independent woman who enjoys her own company and doesn't want a family slowing your stride. You must travel a lot and have so much fun, huh? I saw your first night here when you were crushing those guys left and right in a drinking contest. You were a real badass."

Of course, she guesses wrong on my reasoning for skipping kids. I appreciate her compliments, but I don't have the time or patience *or* headspace to justify myself to yet another person who stares at me as if I have three heads for not expressing a maternal instinct. "We're heading to the corner to do some work. You can find me there if you need anything."

Desmond returns. "You know what? I have an idea. What if we throw open our doors full-time on Juneteenth in a few days?"

I shift Chase from one hip to the other while he wrestles his way out of my arms to go crawl about. "I don't know, Desmond. We really should stick to the schedule and numbers that Lion crunched to a "T". Those figures are all based on our current estimations of foot traffic per day, and working with a highly organized crew, plus preset forecasts of beer served per person. Since we are having inventory problems as it is, I just think we should—"

"I can adjust those charts. It won't take much," a voice speaks behind me, low and husky.

Somewhere inside me, my brainwaves might be reversing course, akin to tides turning.

"I can call up other warehouses and use my connections in the beer distribution industry in other states, see if we can purchase substitutes and recalculate what ingredients Slurp will use and in what priority. But I agree with Des. Slurp should aim to become full-time operational sooner, figure out its flaws and weaknesses and correct them. But of course," he pauses and comes to stand beside me. "I don't mean to undercut your judgment."

Desmond's hopeful glint in his eye is enough to light up the place all on his own.

With a deep breath, I assume the risk of… trusting his judgment? "What do you have in mind?"

Chase wiggles to leave my arms so he can explore. I remove some of his toys from the bag, make sure the brewery floor is clean, and spread out his blanket for him to play. Unsurprisingly, he wants to play with everything but his toys.

"I'll show him around while you two talk and come back to me with recommendations. I could use the practice," Desmond offers. "And besides, Chase and I already know each other."

I turn to Lion. "How long have you been here? Listening?"

Tasty and fine in khakis and a silk polo shirt with leather sneakers, right now, he is the cold brew. Like I have no self-control, my eyes spontaneously drop down to his bulge and I force myself to look away.

Bitch, stop it.

But our gazes already connect, and he smiles. He caught me. "He likes staring at you, too."

In the brief moment I need to come back to myself, we

swap bashfulness that lightens my mood, lightens the taproom, lifts the day.

"And I've been here long enough to hear you crushing my dreams."

"Your dreams?" I ask, confused.

"You don't want kids."

His drama's got me smirking. "And you do?" Why are we discussing this, as if it *matters?*

He shrugs. "Maybe. If the right woman came along who I could see myself doing that with."

"And at the age of forty, no woman has come along, huh? Imagine that."

His gaze dances all over my face. "Who says no woman has come along?"

Before my vital organs can soften like Chase's baby food, I switch subjects. "So, you believe Explore should have Juneteenth celebrations."

"Keep it small. Don't promote too much. Maybe just within the Black community if they want to stop by. Nothing big, since this is last minute. But, yes. You were just saying the other day that incorporating our history is important. I agree."

I think about that. "Laney and Miracle would have to work quickly on word-of-mouth and advertising."

"I'll call some marketing folks to help them out, and I'm sure my mom will be all over this with her social clubs."

My breathing can't be speeding up at the relaxed richness of his voice. "That all sounds perfect."

His lips curl in. "So, about dinner."

"So, about that BBC meeting on Thursday."

Lion flings his head back as it becomes clear I'm twisting his arm. Then the realization dawns on me—I have the ability to twist The Lion's arm. My insides cannot be lighting up the way Chase's eyes did. What the hell?

"Kam, I told you I already have some commitments around that time," he protests, which isn't really a protest. He swipes his hands over his face and returns his attention to me again.

The softness of his eyes pours over me and seeps through my emotional fortress.

"I'll see if I can move my meeting with some reputation people." He bites his apparent sensual thoughts. "Does that get me dinner?"

"It gets you my appreciation."

"Will there be a time whennn… your appreciation will get me some—"

"I think Desmond is waiting for you to come and explain how this Juneteenth mini-celebration will work, Mr. Middleton." And I need a minute to calm my throbbing clit.

"That's too bad. I thought the celebration was already going down right here. But I'll go if I must." He touches my arm.

I fail to think first. Instinctively, as naturally as I draw breath, I'm moved to touch his hand, too.

We meet in my womb, and his eyes promise me. Before I can blow out this flame by dismissing him, he walks away, as if he's learning me and preempting how I tend to run.

WAKE UP. WE'RE HUMAN.

LION

By Thursday, I'm carrying a full plate of priorities.

My time and attention are split between helping with Explore and achieving my own ends—using Explore's business needs for my leverage.

I now have a "special relationship" with Kelly at the Port Authority, who informs me when containers for Explore's goods arrive at the ports, unbeknownst to the racist liquor distributors who've teamed up against Explore. In this way, they cannot hide product from me, even if the greedy assholes want to charge more for delivering it. I've been thinking of how I will handle that also.

I also haven't forgotten about Duncan and the fundraising phone calls he wants me to make to my friends. But he and I have hardly spoken since that night at the bar with Kam. He talked big when I arrived back in New York and buttered me up with all the compliments and speeches in private groups. But I've seen in the papers where he's held several lavish galas and charity events and has invited our family to none of them.

We're in some hot water right now, but the Middletons

are not criminals. To the contrary, we are bastions of the Black Hamptons, and his ignoring us while we're down illuminates his true motives behind our longtime friendship.

One glimmer of light shoots across all the conflicts and stress plaguing my day.

Kamilah and I sit in the Black Business Council meeting, as she discusses the idea of Juneteenth collaborations. The Hamptons typically don't do much beyond a few museum showcases and a couple of barbecues. But this year, the Black businesses are deciding to come together.

Our family attorney, Percell, shoots me a text, and I am discreet to peek at my phone while Kamilah is talking.

Percell: ***Great news on the Smeralda lawsuit against Francis Manuel's family.***

Me: ***Fantastic. What's up?***

Percell: ***The judge denied their motion for discovery to compel evidence concerning other international properties your father had purchased the previous years.***

Me: ***This is awesome news. Dad will be glad to hear it.***

I happen to see another text from one of the new co-chairmen at my job.

Gavin: ***Lion! Dude. Heard you're making big things happen for us in the Hamptons. Got time for a call today? Ron wants to flesh out your little plan.***

My "little" plan? Gavin is younger than me. He arrived at the company seven years ago, six years after me. He only got that job because his father is a political heavyweight in Texas, now running for the US Senate. Houston PetroChem needs favorable federal laws, to win federal contracts that allow them to keep pumping oil, and to sell it at a price of their choosing.

I think about what my job is asking me to do—hand my brother to them on a silver platter. My fingers cannot reach the headache rising under my skull. This is how the game is played, only, my dad is the one who got caught. I'm a fool if I don't play it, and Kevin deserves to have his ungrateful, pompous ass handed to him.

Me to Gavin: ***Yes to the call. In a meeting now. In a couple of hours—***

"Mr. Middleton?" A voice breaks me from my plans.

Kamilah and the Business Council are staring at me.

I have no clue what their conversation was about.

An embarrassed grin all over my face, I answer, "My bad."

"Miss Sharon here was just telling us she's having a hard time securing her shipments of ingredients from Aragon," Kamilah explains. "They've been slow, and she's had to cancel some of her restaurant's top dishes. You've done such an amazing job negotiating the delivery of shipments for Explore, and she was—*we* were—wondering if you could work your magic for Sharon's."

Playful and teasing, Kam waves her magic wand across the table at me.

"Sure. Miss Sharon, I'd love to. Just tell me who your shipping people are, give me your order slips, and I'll look into it."

The elderly woman who's been serving brunches and breakfasts during Hamptons summers for decades practically jumps up and down in her seat. "Oh, Mr. Middleton, we really appreciate that. You've become such a sparkling man. It was a real joy watching you grow up." She wags her finger. "Your *mother* raised you well."

The mockery and shade in that statement toward my dad… Fury bumps over my cup of water that splashes my tablet.

"If I'm not mistaken, Miss Sharon, hasn't my *father* sponsored your annual charity baking contest every year for the past thirty years? As well as given large sums to your Sharon Feeds the Homeless project, no?"

The woman squirms where she sits, mouth twitching to cough up that apology.

It's funny how short people's memories are when they think you're dead in the water. Dad has supported most of the businesses at this table, in some form or another. He's broken bread with these people, held their kids at birth, taken them sailing and taught them golf. Yet all it takes is one fuck-up. One wrong move, and that becomes the sum of a man's entire existence.

"Of course, Mr. Middleton. Your father was… certainly a fine man in his day."

"It's *still* his day."

"Let me grab you some paper towels," Kam murmurs.

I stand. "I'll get them." It gives me a chance to walk out before I clap back with my actual thoughts.

At the condiments table, my hands shake as I jerk up napkins. All the little dishes and packets in front of me blur. Snapping my eyes shut a moment, with my back facing the room, I pull myself together. Over the years, I've faced down the worst of the worst. Gossip, snark, rumors, and subtle digs at my family from the press and my rivals. It's not like I can't take some heat. But this is different.

These people would love to dance on the grave of my family name, a name that has come to their aid and sustained many of them during their own tough times. It won't happen.

Soon, they'll be calling me Houston PetroChem's CEO, and like they've come to our family for numerous other favors over the years, many of them will come begging for help again.

We'll see if my plans are so "little" or if my dad's day has passed, or if they'll continue this disrespect.

The light pressure of Kam's hand on my arm coaxes me from my anger.

"You good?" she asks. A tiny crease appears between her brows. Is that concern?

My throat is closing up, and my frustrated brain cells can't come up with a wisecrack fast enough to dismiss what just happened. So I lie. "Yes, beautiful, I'm good. Thanks."

Her arm crosses mine in her wiping up the mess, and I check my electronics for whether they still work.

"But I'm going to take off for the rest of the day."

Kamilah's eyelids clap several times, and she's apparently stunned. "Let me treat you to lunch," she offers. "Since I don't grace the Hamptons with my presence too often, I'm ignorant about the good food spots. Why don't you show me?"

Just as I shake the hell out of my tablet, her hand over mine stops me, her concern piercing right through the center of my anger. I'm caught off guard with her fingers gripping my bicep. Damn. But I'm too fucked up and need to deal with this storm that's brewing in me.

"Let's take a rain check, baby girl. If Miracle or anyone needs anything, just tell them to hit me on my cell."

As natural as the sun came up this morning, we shift toward one another, like we're a standard couple accustomed to working together all the time, as if it's nothing for us to kiss one another goodbye.

We realize what we're about to do—and freeze.

The others filter out, and she and I stare, wide-eyed.

I tilt up and press my lips on her forehead, let my affection linger while I decipher what exactly is happening. "I'll see you later, gorgeous."

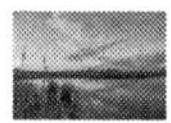

"We should have all of this ready in the next month, and that's when we can move." I peek over my shoulder to ensure no one is home. Dad's supposed to be at a fraternity meeting, and Mom is out with Braelan, but just in case, I stroll through the living room, onto the terrace. "If I'm in control of his product he needs for the Sasha Static concert, he'll be backed into a corner," I explain to Gavin over the speaker.

"Dude, that sounds awesome. And what will be the justification for HP having the checks sent to the distributors, rather than you?"

I rub my hand over the back of my head. My ribcage barely manages to hold my heart that races off the rails. Deep whiffs of ocean air fill up my nostrils. What is this weird reaction in me? I'm hoping it will stop. No such luck.

Her concerned face pops up in my mind, how she wanted to have lunch. I wonder how that would have gone for us, how her smart-ass mouth feels when it kisses. I'm confident she's a damn good kisser.

"Lion?"

Got to get my head back in the… "My bad, man. Yes, so…" I finish clearing my head. "By paying for those products, Houston PetroChem becomes an official sponsor of the concert. Which is the truth. HP's name will be on the billboards, marquee, and all the promo materials, of course."

"Excellent. Wow, man, you are a beast. To come up with this. Ron will be pleased. Consider it all done. We'll take care of it then. So, are you sure?" he asks.

"Sure about what?" As I ask this, I use one of the columns on our back terrace to hoist me up.

"Putting your brother in the sling like this? Man! I hope I don't ever piss you off."

Honestly, I'm torn.

First, I think of Dad and how badly he wanted that property in Florida for a chain of Black-owned resorts. Kevin didn't give it the time of day. But on the other hand, no one can ignore all Kevin has accomplished—to build an investing platform that large companies are fighting to buy is no small feat. I give the little runt credit for proving himself, though his actions are laced with vindictiveness.

Because I know my brother as well as I do, I select my words carefully. "I'm not pissed, just doing what's necessary. Kevin's a big boy. When Ron makes him the offer, he'll know what he needs to do." I'll make sure of it.

Once we're off the phone, I take a moment.

It's not Kevin's money Dad wants. My father wants to be acknowledged as the man who paved the way for him. Kevin has never publicly thanked Dad for shit. And Kevin's stingy ass can't bring himself to do it.

"What are you doing?"

The demand spins me where I stand.

"What are you doing here?" I ask Brendan. "I didn't think anybody was around. I thought you were out with Mom and Braelan."

My brother's sweaty face clenches into a tight weapon on his way from the end of the house, on the other side of the bushes. "Mom asked me to clear out the pool house for her relatives she's got coming for Fourth of July. Now, your turn. What are *you* out here doing, Lion?"

Dumbfounded, I try to play off that conversation as if it's nothing. "Just making some plans for Explore and the inventory I'm arranging for Slurp and Taste."

"With your *job*?" B's face opens a can of whoop-ass as he sets down the mop and pail he was carrying out from the shed. "*Lion.* Answer me, man."

"Don't worry about it, B. Just go on about your business the way you always do, and sit in the middle watching, instead of doing something to help."

"What can I do with you?" The normally mellow Brendan

grows tighter. "All you think about is being ornery, and making Kevin bow down to you. It's clouding your fucking judgment."

Pouring myself a drink at our outside bar, I shake my head. "Lay off. He'll be fine. Dad is in trouble, and he is my priority. Kevin needs to make himself more useful in our family's situation, and I'm doing what it takes so that'll happen."

"Stop lying to me, dude. He asked you for help with Explore because he genuinely needed it. This is a chance for you and him to finally combine your talents and not be at each other's throats. You two can help the Black Hamptons, but here you are, working against him? What kind of shit is that?"

Whisky burns my throat. It's either that or the sting of his anger, because even-keeled Brendan rarely ever gets worked up.

"Kevin helps Kevin. And I'm helping our family and Dad. That's all. If you don't like it, stop listening in on conversations that aren't meant for you." I start for the door.

B blocks my path and pushes his chin up in a challenge. "Miss me with that bullshit about how this is all for the family and has *nothing* to do with you wanting to be CEO."

"There's something in this for everybody, Brendan, so stop tripping."

"Lion, you and Kev fighting like this would be a new low. It'll devastate the hell out of Mom."

I bristle at this idea that I should be so considerate of her. "Don't talk to me about how Mom feels. She never gave a damn about my feelings."

"That's not true."

I push up on him until we're chest to chest. "B, move."

He presses his body onto me, and we stand nose to nose.

"No." His face is firm. "I heard what happened the other

day. That Mom asked you for therapy, and you got upset. But you need it, Lion, you *and* Dad. This backstabbing and trickery aren't the moves. Neither of you would do this if you just dealt with your anger at her."

"Therapy is for weak people. Middletons are not weak."

He examines me. "Wake up, Lion. We're human." My brother starts to back off. "We're not the invincible masters of the universe Dad taught us we are. Look at what's happened to him. At what's happening to you on your job. We *are* weak right now, and sabotaging Kevin will make our house weaker."

I sip more whisky and let it numb me while I mentally check out. Give him time to unload all this from his chest.

"You can ignore me all you want. But you know the real reason you're going after Kevin? You're scared. Having money doesn't make you invincible anymore. You moved to Texas thinking you could trade on the Middleton name and the Middleton money in some place new, and you would build up your own street cred. But those racist ass people down there used you up. Dad did not prepare you for that, and it's scaring you. So you're on some desperate shit so they'll finally give you the power you think you deserve. Because you don't know what it's like to be without it. You don't know what a world looks like where you can't manipulate the name 'Middleton' or the money that comes with it."

I point at him with my drink. "Don't go there. You've got an attitude with me, but this is about Mom. If she hadn't done what she did, Dad would never have needed to go after Francis Manuel. If Kevin had settled up with Maddy, we wouldn't be—"

"If, if, if... Lion, enough."

I'm stunned at this coarse tone he's never copped.

"You know what I notice? For you, it's always everybody's fault but Dad's."

Now it's me rolling my eyes in disbelief. "Okay, here we go."

"Yeah, let's go there," Brendan insists. "Dad went after Francis Manuel because he didn't want to deal with the real problem—himself! And you're just like him. You'll hurt whoever you need to, instead of checking your own baggage."

I press my fingers into my eyes and try to squeeze the emotion back inside me. "While some of that might be true, all of this is Mom's fault for being with that man. Dad made him pay, as he should have. As for Kevin, I will humble him some, and make out nicely for myself in the deal."

"Do you think that will change him? No. Even if you force him to sell MoneyCruncher, he'll work *another* five years and build *another* company. You ought to be proud that he can, but instead, you'll be mad about that. He's never going to lay down for you or Dad as long as all of you destroy each other like this."

Brendan abandons his post from blocking the door and goes to fix his own drink.

I don't move, because this kind of upset from him blows me away. And because… My fingers dig at the quiet storm in the center of me.

"I know you don't want to hear this, and I'm not saying Mom is justified. But I get why Mom slept with that dude."

His words may as well be dynamite in my heart. "B, if you want us to keep talking, cut that shit."

He aims his drink at me. "No, and you're going to listen, Lion."

"The hell I am."

"You always put Dad on this pedestal. You love being a Middleton. It's who you are. You got to be the hero and have everybody worship you, walking into a room already crowned the king. I kind of just followed and caught your shadow."

The scoff from my chest is audible. "So that's what this is really about. You're jealous."

"*No.* I love the hell out of you. Worshipped you. Still do. I will check somebody quick for speaking wrong on your name. No, this is about me understanding how *Mom* might've felt."

He sways with emotion where he stands. "She gave up who she was to be the wife of Lionel Middleton. Didn't have her own identity. No voice of her own. Stuck with a husband who cheats and then apologizes with material possessions. I get how she may have felt walking in Dad's shadow since I always walked in yours."

As the shock of his words fall on me, I stare at him. "Why didn't you speak up? You know I'm proud of you and have no problem supporting your shine."

B shakes his head. "It taught me how to be something more than a Middleton. I created a light of my own, became an engineer. Learned to thrive beyond Dad's name. I never had to bear the pressure you did, of wearing it."

Now I'm skeptical as hell and refuse to believe what he's selling. "How did you snag your job at the Pentagon, B?"

"I used Mom's maiden name."

"You're lying."

"I'm not. My bosses didn't find out about my family until later in the interview process, once they ran my full background. But at the beginning stages of me just submitting for it, I did not use Middleton."

His gaze sharpens into a knife that twists in me.

He continues, "Kevin created his own light. Despite yours and Dad's abuse, Lion. You took your anger about all this out on him. And you're *still* doing it. You always said you were making him stronger so kids wouldn't pick on him. But it was abuse. He built his own success."

"He did it with Dad's money!" I bark.

"Kevin could have turned out a rich crack addict, but he didn't! He's out here building empires! Give him some credit and stop being so goddamn pissed and jealous about it!"

I no longer have the energy to lift my glass and sip.

Brendan continues. "Mom created her own light. With the only power a woman has—her heart. Men are powerless to control that." He sinks his drink, and his face flinches with the burn. Then he faces me head-on.

"But *you,* Lion, the name Middleton is all you have, it's all Dad raised you to rely on. And you might have leaned on it too much, because now it's under attack. So *you're* under attack. And what will you have if it loses its juice completely?"

With his angry voice narrating my thoughts, I stare ahead of us, beyond lush trees and hills, into my future, as I've been asking myself the same question.

Brendan must have been carrying all this on his chest for a long time and is now feeling himself. "Dad always acted like a necklace or ring, bracelet, or a car would make up for his infidelity. He always tried to fix his relationships with his money. As if that's all his marriage amounted to. As if that's all we were worth. You tuned out the fights between him and Mom, but *I* remember. I was only four when she cheated the first time, but I remember when she started cheating again later. Kevin was twelve. I was fifteen. You were eighteen, about to graduate and head off to Cornell, and you were rarely ever home."

Now it's Brendan who stares out at the greenery. "Dad had fallen into his old routine, coming home with lipstick on him. One time he even started to call her somebody else's name, right there in front of us. He was flagrant. He thought he was untouchable. And Mom showed him he wasn't. I don't know shit about Francis Manuel, but what I can tell you is that man probably made her *feel*. In a way that Dad knew nothing about and didn't care to learn. I can tell you *for a fact* she was happier when she started up with Mr. Manuel. For Mom to experience that joy for a little while in her life, I'm okay with it."

I'm processing what he's saying, though he drops bombs I wish he wouldn't. His memories assault me. "She brought another child home to her husband, B."

"And she taught Dad a lesson he never forgot." The liquor spinning in his glass might not be nearly as hard as his side-eye. "I'm okay with that, too. Mom didn't take Dad's shit lying down, the way so many women do. Accept it."

"Why didn't she just leave him if she wasn't happy?"

"That's a question you should ask her. But if you do, humble yourself and listen."

I love my mother, but I'm not feeling that option. "She was our mother, B. *Ours.* And we were not enough for her. She needed to step outside of her house and find happiness with a man who wasn't one of us."

Brendan's glare calls me out. "Do you think that same way about Dad?"

Pissed, I jerk away. His question instantly transforms me back thirty-three years, to the sorrow I heard in Dad, which will never leave me.

He's nn... he's not mine.

The image pops into my head of the astonishment on my grandfather's face when Dad said it.

My father's big, strong back on which he'd given me piggyback rides, hoisted the sails on boats, carried firewood for our cabin fires, and chopped our Christmas trees, was now curled over the mantle of the fireplace. Weak.

A seven-year-old standing on the terrace, I was young and powerless to hold him up as he'd always held me.

Not wanting to watch him that way, summoning some imaginary power to do something and realizing I had none, I could only slide to the floor and hold Dad's hand from across the room. Behind the couch. I kept my tears silent and silently joined Granddad in his promise that we would all make this man pay.

"It's different!" My seven-year-old self now snaps at B through my thirty-nine-year-old body. "Women are built different. They are nurturing and..." I search my mind for strong logic to defend why I'm justified in expecting my mother to be my *mother* and not some man's whore. "Loving and comforting. They are for us. She was for us. Not somebody else!"

"You're on some bullshit!"

I set my glass on the table because, in more ways than one, I'm finished. "And you've been hitting up too many of Kendall's women's activist meetings."

Brendan hypes up again. "*No*, Lion! The reason Kendall married me in the first place, and we're still going strong ten years later, is I paid attention to Mom. The reason your marriage to Ash fell apart is that you did not." He now beats the air between us with his finger. "More than that will fall if you don't start placing accountability squarely where it belongs!"

He pauses only for a few breaths. "I only haven't said all this to you because I've always tried to play peacekeeper, and I never wanted you to blow up at me the way you did Kevin. You weren't ready to hear it. But it's time you heard truth from somebody who doesn't have a dog in this fight."

Over thirty years of heartbreak tosses in my unsettled mind. "You and Kevin have always been Mama's boys, so you *do* have a dog in this."

B now pursues me off the terrace and into the house, his voice at my back.

"And you were *Daddy's* boy!" the normally chill B bellows. "Stop punishing Kevin! Stop blaming him and Mom when we all know who's really to blame! And stop acting like you're invincible and can't be touched! Those days are over, Lion! Money will not keep protecting you and Dad when the two of you do foul shit!"

Ignoring him—or escaping him—I rush up the stairs to get dressed for barbecuing at Trane's.

He yells up the stairs at me, "And you have to tell him it's time to step up, Lion! No schemes and tricks! Dad's not going to listen to anybody else but you." My brother drills it in. "You won't get him out of this with press releases, soundbites, throwing your money at charity, or photo ops, but by actually humbling yourself and showing the world you're just as human as the rest of us!"

Tired of hearing it, I slam my bedroom door.

BUT YOU WANT TO...

KAMILAH

"You are wearing him all over you." Princess observes me over her coffee.

Staring into my own cup, I can't hide the smile. "He wasn't there yesterday. I hope everything is all right." I really do.

Miss Sharon's words the other day were an apparent insult to Lion's father. And Lion's hurt spilled everywhere, the first time I discerned that the man has feelings. That despite his money and influence, he hurts, sweats, and bleeds. Like every other hotblooded man. Though I rushed to comfort him, he had already disappeared somewhere else in his head.

"Have you and him...?" P finishes the rest of the inquiry in her facial expression.

I shake my head.

"But you want to," Sister-in-law concludes.

At the mention of that, my carnality returns. Hard. It hasn't shown up in a long time. These past few years, sex for me has been mostly transactional. The way it was with Lion the first night I saw him again, the way it would have been with the bartender last weekend.

For years, when it comes to men, I've been leaving my emotions at the door, but the last few days, I've been fighting fantasies. Nothing about our exchanges has been simple. Him walking me home in silence on a summer night was no simple transaction.

Unlike the first time, I want more than his dick. I want to make love to the thoughts in his head when he's staring at me and he thinks I don't notice. Whatever compels him to stand down and give in to my demands, I crave it inside me.

At family breakfast, P and I whisper among ourselves while the others catch up on gossip back home in Louisiana. Our extended relatives are still there. And while I go home to Louisiana once every year or two, and still chat with my cousins there occasionally, right now my mind is only consumed with one subject.

"We haven't even kissed."

P's looking slightly weaker than last weekend. But still, the love on her face comes through for me. "That sweetens the feelings."

Where is he? Why wasn't he at the brewery yesterday with all his come-ons and jokes, pretending like he's dumb before he provides all the answers, noting the differences between Desmond's craft beers, regaling the staff with his appreciation for culture and fine food and drink?

"His dad has gotten all that negative press for buying Kevin's way into Harvard years ago. I can only imagine how upsetting it must be for people to disrespect his parent. Right or wrong, that's still his father," Princess says.

Fortunately, Maddy's still not here. And neither is Chrissy, who is over at Dream Stage this morning. "I hear that Maddy and Chrissy are the ones responsible for that."

"But we don't know what's going on with all of these Sag Harbor people. Not our circus, not our monkeys. I'm praying they will all work that out. So it's understandable why he might've reacted the way he did. Maybe he could use a pick-me-up." Mischievous, she stares at me with a hint in her expression.

"Come to think of it, I don't have Lion's number. This entire time, we've communicated through Laney."

Only now does it dawn on me that he never asked for my number.

"Your brother is working with his brother. I'm sure there's a way you can get it." She nods toward Sheldon at the other end of the table talking with Roland.

"I don't know, P."

Lion is Duncan's close friend, and though I screwed Lion the first time hoping Duncan would find out, I wouldn't dare play with Lion that way now.

She seems to read my mind. "Yes, you do. But whatever happens, you should tell him about… your mutual connection. If Lion hasn't figured it out already, tell him. Let him choose whether he wants to date his close friend's ex." Even while slightly tired, she fans herself with her hand. "I'm so happy for you. You deserve all that going on right there." Those fingers now wiggle at me.

But I can't help wondering if this is idiocy, allowing myself down this path again. "There is nothing to be—"

"Girl, please, and when you and him do it, it'll be so…"

"We are not—"

"Don't even finish that lie."

"Kam, you ready?" Sheldon asks.

He's on duty to pick up his and Roland's kids from sailing class, and then he'll come over to the Explore properties to run tests on their financial payments network. Plus, he'll check on the security of their integration with Money-

Cruncher. So I'm riding with my big brother today, and Miracle will drop me off at home.

"As I'll ever be." I get up and kiss Princess on the cheek. "Work calls."

As I do so, she stifles a cough.

"Have you been to the doctor yet, P?"

"I'm getting it looked at. They prescribed me with some pills. Hay fever."

But I swear, she's a little frailer than she was two weeks ago.

My dad comes out as I clear my plate from the table. "Hey, baby, heard you had some problems with one of the Middletons the other day. One of us doesn't need to stop through, do we?"

Sheldon intervenes. "Oh, don't worry, Dad, I'm already on it."

"No, Dad, Sheldon! Please don't." I kiss Charles Rouse on the cheek and grab Chase before we head out.

Sheldon has a baby seat in his truck already that I stuff Chase into. There are plenty of babies around the Rouse household these days, it seems.

"So, what *did* go down between you and Lion Middleton the other day?" he asks in his SUV.

"I was tripping and went off. It was a misunderstanding. I'm tired of people talking about it and asking me. He and I have resolved it."

"But you'll let us know if it hasn't resolved, right?" Shel reaches over from behind the steering wheel and playfully shoves my head to the side.

"No, I will not, because I am just as capable of handling it."

"Okay then, Superwoman, I see you. What else is going on with you? We don't see each other anymore."

"You mean, ever since you and Jerrell went on lockdown, the family doesn't see you two anymore," I correct him.

"And now it's time for the family not to see much of *you* anymore, my dear." My older brother glances at me and returns his attention to the road. "Out here in the streets, running circles around these poor, unsuspecting dudes grows exhausting after a while. Trust me, I know. There's only so much dick and so many bars and parties and restaurants you can move through before it gets old. You're too smart for that, Kam."

Now that word choice is confusing. "Too smart?"

"Yes, too smart. You deserve so much more emotionally. When Chrissy and I first met and we competed against each other, it pushed me. She reawakened my synapses and reminded me of my hunger to achieve. Until then, I'd just been"—he shrugs and steers the wheel—"going to work every day and distracting myself from sadness with one chick and then the next. But when I met her, she was so determined to fix her situation and rebuild. That inspired me, and we inspire each other. Then I found out about her dreams she had been sitting on for years. I wanted to be everything for her so I could help her reach them all. And she wanted to be everything for me after Eugenia. We lift one another up. So yes, smarter than the shallowness of bars and one-night stands that only leaves you empty."

While he steps out to go pick up the kids, his words remain with me.

Sheldon is considered the brain of my siblings and me, and it's only fitting that he would describe bed-hopping as not smart. And he actually made it make sense.

I go for Chase in the backseat who has grown impatient with waiting. For a moment, I walk around with him outside the truck. "You see Uncle Shel over there with your cousins?"

When I'm pointing, a familiar figure captures my attention. Taut muscles twist along muscular arms under the morning sunlight. Underneath a silk polo shirt and khaki shorts are those massive calves. The clear bulkiness of his lower legs indicates his past as a football player and all-around athlete. He bends over on one of the boats as if he is instructing and pointing.

And to think, I never gave a damn about sailing. Until now.

After the class ends, he interacts with the other parents, shaking hands. Black boys surround him and pepper him with questions. I venture closer to where he holds a captive audience.

"Bend from the knees and not the waist. You don't want to strain yourself and hurt your back," he explains. "Make sure you've got a good grip. And don't forget to tie that knot real tight. Practice it at home. Next weekend I'm giving a quiz. If you get any wrong, you'll be sweeping the docks."

The boys laugh.

Sheldon gathers his son, Chrissy's son, and Roland's children, all of them jumping up and down excitedly. "All right, young men, let's roll out. There's another stop before we head to the beach." He extends his hand. "Mr. Middleton, you've got the boys all worked up. I didn't know you taught yachting. Good to know. I might want personal lessons myself at some point."

Lion has not turned around yet, so he has no idea I'm here.

"Not a problem. I'd be glad to. My family loves the water. We'd be happy to bring you guys along."

"It's a deal then." Sheldon stares at me standing not too far off. "That's assuming you and my sister are on good terms, though. Right?"

Lion spins around now. All the giddiness in his face

washes ashore in me, too. I approach until we're only a couple of yards apart.

"We are on good terms." My voice sounds different than I intended. "You weren't at the brewery yesterday."

A slight wince crosses his face. Something else is bothering him behind the brave face. "I had family stuff."

I peer around at all the boats and change the subject to one he obviously enjoys. "You went out and picked up a new gig and didn't tell us about it?"

"I'm doing the same thing I was doing last Saturday, Miss Rouse." His gaze takes a tour over me from top to bottom. And I don't mind. "You're looking rather weekendish today."

"Weekendish?" I haven't stopped grinning.

My brother is dumbfounded. Puzzled, hands on his hips, Sheldon stares from Lion to me.

"Yeah," Lion replies softly. "Breezy, chill, not flipping out over a quota or a spreadsheet. Relaxation looks good on you."

"Well, I have certain people to thank for pulling our organization together. I can afford to breathe a little easier."

"Hey, Chase." He touches Chase's foot.

"The boys are getting restless. Kam, don't forget we're meeting Desmond at the brewery. Mr. Middleton," Sheldon says with a wave. "I'll be taking you up on that private yachting lesson." He motions to the children. "Come on, fellas."

Shel's suppressed amusement promises me that our ride to the brewery will be lit.

"So are you also coming to the brewery for the stress test?" I ask. And hope.

Lumberjack's lips spread over his teeth, and I swear his eyes are sparkling.

"You clearly haven't checked the team schedule for today, Miss Rouse. I'm due over at Taste to make sure Miracle and her staff have inventory and are prepared for Monday's Juneteenth."

Damn.

"That's too bad." Now it's my turn to offer the admiring once-over. "I had no idea you taught yachting on Saturdays."

"Yeah, sometimes these guys on the docks tolerate me while I'm in town. I give the regular instructors a break. The gossip rags don't tell you that when they're reporting how much money I throw out the window." Lumberjack's admiration dips to a new level when he sucks his lip. "I teach other subjects as well."

"That sounds… interesting. Well, you will be missed at the brewery."

If we stand here like two kids in a schoolyard much longer, we just might start acting on our juvenile machinations.

He leans toward me. "The brewery will miss me, or *you* will miss me?"

I roll my eyes. "The brewery, Mr. Middleton."

Skepticism wrinkles up his features. "Mm, I don't think somebody here is telling the truth."

His playful flirting doesn't mask how his smile only reaches half of him today. There is still a melancholy mood about him I wish I could fix.

Chase pouts and points to the boats, dock, ropes, and all the activities surrounding him so now he wants to roam.

"I have to get him out of here." But I don't want to leave. "So the next time I see you will be—"

"Monday for Juneteenth," he answers. "Unless…"

Should I do this?

"Kam!" Sheldon calls from his Escalade.

"Why don't you come and eat Sunday brunch with my family and me in the morning? That's if, you're not doing anything with your own family."

Lion's mouth drops in protest. "Whoa. Time out." He puts his hands perpendicular to one another in a "timeout" symbol. "You mean to tell me that my first date with you will be all your people breathing down my—"

He observes the matter-of-factness on my face.

"Of course," Lumberjack answers. "I'd love to join you and your *entire* family, so your brothers can threaten my life."

I wasn't intending on it being our "first date," but now that I think about it, this would be our first meetup that's not work-related. Are these boats rocking in my chest? Are they rocking on his face? Cheesing and eye-fucking, we finally give in to whatever force keeps bringing us closer. And carry on with what we almost started the other day.

It's been a long time since I anticipated a kiss, for a man to touch me.

"Nnno." Chase's tiny arm shoots out and pushes Lion off me.

"Chase!" I marvel. "I think that was his first word!"

Lion busts up. "It was the wrong word. Look here, Little Man, I've been working hard on getting this sugar."

We close in toward one another again, and Chason Rouse is more insistent this time. "No!"

We both crack up.

Lion notes, "I guess he said what he said. He is indeed his mother's son."

"*And* his dad's. My brother definitely had something to do with this attitude he's got. Speaking of his parents, I should probably call them so they can hear this. They'll be so mad the word isn't mama or dada." But I'm hesitant to leave the ocean's electromagnetic fields that conduct some form of electric flow through me the closer I stand to it. Or is that force coming from the ocean? "So I'll see you tomorrow morning at ten?"

The water must conduct an energy field through Lumberjack, too. "You will."

Once I'm back in the truck with Sheldon and the kids, he's perplexed.

"What the hell was that?"

"Just two co-workers—"

"Co-workers, my ass. And here I thought I needed to regulate. How did you go from slapping him to…." My older brother shakes with humor and a pleased grin. "Never mind. That was Chris and me. Forget everything I said earlier. I'm happy for you."

"There's nothing to be happy over."

"Yeah, okay. So, that slap you gave him the other day was really a love lick, huh?"

A few minutes later, we enter a Slurp that sings.

My nephews run inside, faces excited at the shiny tanks, barrels, cans, bottles, and systems. Desmond's got the different stations set up and operating smoothly, with staff circling in systematized fashion from one task to the next.

Lion and Quincy hired extra hands to speed up the canning and packaging process. At Lion's recommendation, Explore secured more money for Desmond to purchase the extra Brite tank he wanted to hold more beer. Teams have now begun to can as much beer as possible before the Sasha Static concert. It's part of a special promotion for Slurp's new brand of beer that they'll sell across the country.

Though he's not here physically, Lion's fingerprint is everywhere. I rub my chest. *Every*where.

Sheldon sets up his laptop so he can test the financial payment system and its vulnerability to hackers. Although Kevin is one of the key investors of Explore and is a techie as well, some of the owners have handed off their duties so they can be ambassadors for Explore. Not to mention I had a concern about the ethics of Kevin approving his own monetary system and signing off on the security of Money-Cruncher's online integration with Explore. So Sheldon serves an extra pair of eyes.

Staring around the place, I'm realizing that in just this past week and a half, we're already moving fast and far. Where Desmond had an organized mess on his hands a few days ago, we're now achieving optimization rapidly. He's loving it, as his feet dance across the floor from one area to the next.

"Say, Kam! Is your man—I mean—Mr. Middleton coming in today?" Desmond smirks.

I give him my side-eye and Sheldon also peers up, before they swap smart-ass silent commentary.

"Mr. Middleton will be here tomorrow for Juneteenth."

"Juneteenth is about slaves?" Sheldon's nine-year-old son, Hadar, asks.

"Not quite. It's about liberation of slaves. Freeing them. And don't forget, not all Black people were in chains on June nineteenth. The Emancipation Proclamation freed some people but not all of them. Some Black people were already free."

"For real?" Roland's son, Rome, asks. "How do you know, Uncle Sheldon? I didn't read about that in my history book."

"Of course you didn't," Desmond adds.

"I don't mean to call you a lie, Uncle Shel," Rome continues, "but where is proof of this? My dad tells me to always ask for the proof."

Shel nods. "As he should. So, we'll research it for ourselves later. We'll learn that not all Black people were enslaved during the Civil War. The Civil War was not needed to free everybody. Some Black people had already taken risks with their lives and achieved freedom with their skills, their intelligence, or by birth."

Laney happens to be here helping out, and she strolls

over. She and I exchange glances, the same idea seeming to form in our heads at the same time.

"Isn't it true the Middletons were never enslaved?" she asks.

Come to think of it, I've heard the same thing. "I think so."

"Why don't we have Lion or Kevin come and share with the boys the proof of Black people who were not enslaved in 1865?" Sheldon suggests. "People who were already living for themselves and building their own communities."

Laney adds, "Explore still has some kids from the youth camp staying in town. Why don't we bring them over, too? I would love for them to hear this lesson."

"Lion will be at the house tomorrow for brunch," I say. "I'll ask him then."

Sheldon's face turns quizzical. "Really now?"

"Don't catch any ideas, Shel," I reply. "Play nice."

"I'll think about it." He squeezes me to him. "I haven't ever seen you so excited about brunch, though."

With Lion's handiwork surrounding me here in the brewery now, the brunch isn't all that excites me. It's the man who I clearly misjudged, who never ceases to rise to the occasion.

CALM DOWN

KAMILAH & LION

KAMILAH

"Girl, will you sit still? How will I finish when you're doing all this fidgeting?" Etta asks. "You weren't this bad twenty years ago for prom."

"Mama, he's here!" my niece calls to Etta through the door.

"Kamilah!" my mother calls from downstairs.

"Kam!" Shel yells. He's only doing this to tease me.

"Let me get my pistol," Daddy says aloud from downstairs.

"Why is everybody making a big deal out of this?" I ask. But my lungs have stopped functioning. "Where is he?"

Princess peeks out the window. "Getting out of his car." Her jaws surely must hurt from all the smiling she's doing. "Ohhh, Kammm. Good job, girl. And, oh my Lord."

"What!" I panic, while Etta finishes hot curling my top layer of hair so it's wavy.

"He brought flowers. And *gifts*. He was raised old school for real."

My inner chambers shake.

Scratch that.

Everything trembles.

"Girl, raise up," Etta complains. "Just go on. Since you won't be still, this is the best I can do. I'm through with you."

Princess comes and cups my face, and we exchange nervous energy. "Oh my God, girl. I knew this was promised for you. You could never tell me any different."

"Don't say that. It's just brunch. Stop hyping it up." But I don't believe the words coming out of my mouth.

Princess's hands intertwine with mine. "You're about to be so blessed. Let's pray."

I draw back at this suggestion. There's not much P says that I disagree with. "Chile, I have every intention of doing nasty shit with him later. I don't feel right asking God to bless what I plan on doing with him."

P's eyes water up, and she holds my hands tight, rubs them with a sudden feverishness that unnerves me. Her examination of me penetrates deep, as if she's communicating things she can't say. "Kamilah Dawn."

"I'm thirty-six. I shouldn't be acting like I've never done this before."

Etta and the others have all gone downstairs to meet Lion, and it's just Princess and me now.

"You haven't done *this* before," she whispers. "You may be thirty-six, but your heart is still stuck on twenty-one. Back at that clinic. And my spirit is telling me we need to pray this time. So close your eyes and bow your head."

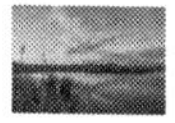

LION

"I'm praying to God this is finally your hour," my mother had said while sniffing the flowers the florist delivered.

I didn't want them sent to Kamilah's house and preferred to give them to her myself.

"I don't know what you're talking about, Mom. This is not some major move."

"Yes, you do. You've done well for yourself, Lion, but you haven't moved with purpose. This feels different." Her hand taps my chest. "It already seems you being here this summer, meeting this girl, working with your brother, God is ordering your path in a way that won't involve your Daddy's money or status this time."

As always, I kiss her flawless forehead and make out the door. I can't have Mom talking that way when I'm already a ball of nerves. This is unlike me, to get worked up over a date. It's been a long time since I've shown up at a woman's house—actually, intentionally stepped inside and met her family.

Maybe not since I was in my twenties. Even when I met Ash's folks, it was more of a quick "hey" at a bonfire in South Padre Island. But with Kamilah having such high standards, demanding so much respect for herself, I cannot half-step. She has clearly been taught by parents with little tolerance for laziness. So it's not lost on me that I must represent my own proper and vigilant upbringing, and for class to represent class.

I spent a full hour this morning deciding on the right 'fit. Trane's wife helped pick the saltwater Tiffany pearls I'm giving to her mother.

Now Kam's brother, Sheldon, opens the door.

"Lion, dude, what's all this?" he asks with a peek at the gifts. "You do realize she's already spoiled, right?"

I laugh along with him. "So you would agree she could be spoiled a little more."

"All right, player, I see you scoring points."

As if he is still figuring out what to make of this, he sizes me up, the way I size up people who want to be around my folks. I might be working hard on this first impression because I'm acutely aware of the numerous misjudgments about my family. And keenly aware of my reputation as a playboy in the Hamptons.

Sheldon offers a smile that's polite, even if undecided. "Calm down."

"It's that obvious?" Why am I so nervous?

"Understandable, bruh. She's a lot even for me, and I'm the one who schooled her."

A not-so-subtle-hint right there. But hell, I'd be the same way about my sister hanging out with the likes of me.

"So you're the young man everybody's so worked up about?" Charles Rouse starts toward me. He squints and examines me harder. "Hmph. You ain' all that young, though."

This is hilarious, and I can't hold in my guffaw. "You know, my knees told me the same thing when I got up this morning."

"Oh, honey, he's just pulling your chain," Verona Rouse says, strolling up and inspecting me. "You are quite the stallion all the ladies say you are. But I also hear you're a sailing instructor and athlete. My grandsons can't stop talking about driving the boat and being masters of the sea."

"And trust me when I say your grandsons are the liveliest and most excited to get out on the water. I'm glad they enjoyed it. These are for you." I hand her one of the bouquets.

Mrs. Rouse beams. "Well, now, I see why you're the first

man my daughter has brought home in almost twenty long years."

"Twenty?" I repeat. *Damn.* A nagging suspicion rises in the back of my mind, one I've had since the night Kam and I met. *Again.* For now, I dismiss my hunch.

"Yes. Twenty." Mrs. Rouse's gaze hits the ceiling and falls. "That girl runs harder from commitment than she ran from those water moccasins back home. It's awfully brave of you to come in here and be such a gentleman to her anyway. I heard you walked her home the other night. Thank you for seeing she got here safely."

"I wouldn't have had it any other way, despite how much she fought it."

"I've met your mother, and your manners are definitely a tribute to her class."

She doesn't say it with the same tone Miss Sharon used the other day, so I don't take that personal. "My dad is actually the one who drilled that into me, about a woman in my presence always being safe."

His lessons ring in my head now.

Don't let a woman be disrespected in front of you. You keep your wits and head, no matter how she acts. No matter what she puts you through. A real man doesn't go to a woman empty-handed.

"Excuse me. Of course he did," Mrs. Rouse's smooth face turns serious. "How is your father, by the way? We've met him a few times over the years, out on the golf course and various dinners. Funny man. Very business-minded and knowledgeable."

I sense she's asking about Maddy's Harvard leak. "He's a strong guy. Can't really knock him down. Thank you for asking. I'll tell him you inquired about him."

"Please do," Mrs. Rouse replies. "And that lovely mother

of yours. Tell her I want to come shop in her closet real soon."

"She's got more than enough in there for you to take away."

Kamilah comes down, and I do mean exactly that—in a ripped jean skirt and an off-shoulder, frilly peach blouse. It's very casual, nothing particularly dressy, and yet it's everything, showing off slender, shapely thighs on her tiny frame. With just the right amount of meat, perfect and blemish-free. Smooth shoulders and arms pour out of the slightly see-through blouse. Her normally straight-as-a-rod hair is wavy, like her stiff exterior is taking the day off. My eyesight and involuntary reactions are... involuntary.

Yeah, I could have just said she's gorgeous, but that wouldn't do her justice.

She walks up to me with this gigantic-ass smile from ear to ear. "Hey." She eyes the flowers. "Those for me?"

"Maybe."

I hold them out of her reach, and she grins harder before I bring my hand down and give them to her. I also pass her the medium-sized gift box and hand the other to her mother.

"Why is everybody standing around?" Kam asks.

"Because you don't ever bring 'em home," another version of Kamilah replies. The lady extends her hand to me. "Hi, I'm Etta, her sister."

"You might be the first in twenty years, but it's no pressure, Lion," Sheldon cracks.

Kam and her mother smile at one another as they open their boxes.

The entire family observes, like we're sixteen years old. Her face is blossoming, as if this moment is doing more for her than I might understand.

Kamilah unwraps the Hermès purse I picked out myself, and her eyes pore over it. "It's gorgeous. But you didn't have to do this. You know if I'd had my say, I would have asked you not to."

"I took advantage of you not having a say. Finally." I eat up her smile while we exchange chuckles.

"Lion, these pearls are exquisite. I'll repeat what my daughter just said that you didn't have to." Mrs. Rouse reaches for me. It's something about the arms of Black mothers that feel safer than a bomb shelter.

Kam ushers me to the family's dining room.

"So, Lion, I hear you're in the oil business," her father starts. "You wouldn't have had anything to do with that oil spill off the Gulf Coast last year, would ya?" he jokes.

I joke back, "Actually, sir, since I'm Vice President of Supply Chain and Operations, I oversee the shipments on the seas. That falls under my authority. So, yes, I suppose that oil spill was me."

Mr. Rouse and Sheldon swap awkward expressions.

"Just kidding. That wasn't our company. But I enjoyed watching your face, though."

The table cracks up.

Three hours of shit-talk spans all the subjects from stocks, to football, basketball, politics, and music over the last forty years. It's a whole other vibe than my family table. Kids play and laugh. Older siblings rib on each other without the bite of resentment. Her parents gaze at one another with loving longevity, as if they've walked through hot coals together and at this point, like Daenerys Targaryen, they stand unburnt.

I've sat at a few other family tables, but now I pay attention.

Afterward, Kamilah walks me through her family's colorful backyard garden to the gazebo.

"I can hold the rest of them off for about thirty minutes.

Don't be too long out there," Sheldon warns his sister with what looks like a knowing wink.

"I love the purse, but I wish you would take it back," she says.

"I love it, too, which is why I want to see you wear it. And why I'm not accepting it back. And I will be highly offended if you donate or regift."

Her instant amusement pushes her smile into her cheeks before she curls her lips in and hides it.

"You're not used to that, are you?" I ask. "A man who wants to just see you light up when he does things for you?"

"Can you make a woman light up without your money, Lion?"

"I can... and I *do.*"

We both break into hysterical laughing fits.

"I light women up all the time. It's my favorite."

Still chuckling, we pass by honeysuckle vines that tease their saccharine fragrance and compel me to pick a couple of off.

"So, Ms. Kamilah, why'd you come to the Hamptons if you didn't want to be here?" I ask. "Seducing men in breweries, teasing them in football, and slapping them around?"

Her lips tuck in with another suppressed smile. "My brother assigned me here for the job since no one else was available. And I don't mind breweries and bars, liquor and that sort of thing."

"What do you have against the Hamptons, though?"

"Too quiet, boring. All this green can put somebody to sleep. I love New York, but the city is exciting. There's always something to do. Where Louisiana is slow and stagnant, here I'm always moving and shaking."

I can't help wondering if that answer is the full truth.

The more I think on my suspicion, the more I believe I'm right. Now the tension between Kam and Tanja that first night in the basement of the brewery makes more sense to me.

"Moving where?"

She peers up at me. "All right, Quiz Master. What's with all these questions?"

"Because the only time you talk, it's about what you don't like. What you don't want. What *do* you like?"

That question must've thrown her off.

My hand mingles with hers, not holding it, just loosely hanging… toying with the possibility of holding. "And why can't you accept generosity from men?"

"Lion," she starts with a laugh. "I'm not good at that kind of thing."

"What kind of thing?" I press.

Her expression becomes a question, as if she expects me to know. And to some degree, I do. But I want to hear it from her.

"At being a girly girl, and letting a man get to me, Lion. You can't tell? Do you see me running around talking about a boyfriend or chopping it up on the phone? No. Haven't you been married before? Don't you feel the same way after your divorce?"

I study her. She examines me right back.

"Ha, yes, I guess I did feel that way until you slapped me."

Half laughing, half scoffing, French Fry turns stiff. She glares at me now, as if questioning if I'm being a smart-ass. "What?"

But I'm serious. "You heard me. No, I didn't see me ever being married again. I had already disappointed one woman. Ash was a good lady and I didn't want to hurt another."

"How did you hurt her?"

"Now it's you with the questions," I point out.

"Much easier to ask than to answer, huh?"

I think as we walk. Twirl the honeysuckle in my fingers. I still haven't pulled the nectar out yet.

"I cheated." May as well be honest. "It was too soon. I loved her. She was a lot of fun, and we had a damn good time, but..."

"But?" French Fry's gaze sharpens.

I thought I could have it all—Ash and any other woman I wanted. Just like Dad with Mom. But unlike Mom, Ash didn't hang around and play marital games or try to get even. She just left.

"I wasn't ready for us to be something more than a damn good time." Was not ready to carry the more serious load of honesty and vulnerability. Those virtues simply were not how we lived in our house.

"What's your ex-wife like?"

Ash's face pops into my head. "You."

We both chuckle.

"I have a thing for feisty women."

"And none of them have held you down?"

I shrug. "None of them have slapped me."

Perplexed, French Fry gives me her side-eye. "Tuh. I don't believe that."

"Believe it." I reflect on what I'm trying to say that I still haven't really clarified in my own mind yet. "You are the first who's knocked some sense into me, literally. And that day, you commanded my attention."

Flashbacks of that brewery meeting, and Kamilah's vulnerability she didn't intend for me to see that day, must weigh heavily enough on me now that it sits me down. I land on the seat under the gazebo, nestled behind high rose bushes, a far enough distance from the house that we can have semi-privacy. A kaleidoscope of leaves dance in the afternoon sunlight, casting shadows and sunbeams across our faces, and in this array of light and dark between us, I pull her between my legs and sit her on my knee.

"Maybe it's because life is forcing me to grow in ways I didn't know I needed to, according to my brother who just chewed me out the other day."

Kam's head dips with intrigue, and she's a smidge too gleeful. "Kevin cursed you out? I wish I could have been there for that."

I suck my teeth. "Yeah, I bet you do. But no. That little..." I stop myself. "No. We have another brother, Brendan. He has a family of his own and a plum government job, so his time around here is limited."

"If you don't mind sharing, what did he say to you?"

"He told me to be on the lookout for... women nicknamed Karate Kam who beat men at beer games, walk the streets by themselves, and have a fast right hook."

This time she laughs and shoves my head aside, and I press her closer to me, because she just feels good. She draws my face to hers.

With my mouth, I knock on the doorway to Kamilah. She knocks back, our lips barely dusting one another. Tentative, hesitant, we flirt with temptation. Parting her mouth, she cracks the door and invites me in, and I play at her threshold. Slow, gentle, I tease her lips with my tongue. Nibble. Down her chin, over her jawbone, I suck until I coax the gasp out of her.

Her breasts rise with expectation. Elevated breathing pulsates along the thumping artery I lick. Along her neck, I trail my tongue and appreciate her supple skin.

Even over her blouse, her breast is jelly, sweet and plush, in my palm. "You put this on to tease me."

"Guilty as charged," she huffs.

I bite her naked shoulder. "Edible lotion."

"Right again."

I suck some off.

The dick jumps off.

Once French Fry grabs and squeezes my shaft, the pressure weakens me, sending my forehead against her arm.

On the honeysuckle I picked off the vines, I slide the piston through the stem, so the nectar oozes out of it, to the base. My fingers trail honey up the crest of her cleavage and follow it with my tongue. Our mouths play. The suction muscles of Kam's cheeks tugging on my tongue, her taste buds massaging me, are a dirty promise to my dick.

I place my mouth in the valley of her neck. "Are you on birth control?"

She nods.

"When I make love to you, I want to be inside you raw."

Her mouth hangs open. The fantasies dangle from her tongue.

"Do I have your permission?"

Her nipples clap under her bra. I felt one rise against my chest. Eyes wild, pupils dilated, her open mouth is moist.

"What makes you think we'll make love?" she asks, her throat gulping.

I nudge the honeysuckle along her inner thighs and stroke her skin inside her skirt. Along her feminine lips, I twirl the flower and rub it in her juices. Kam's pussy ripples with anticipation before I pull the flower back out. Hold it up for her to see. "This flower is soaking wet. Like I knew it would be."

She inhales and exhales. Skin in the center of her chest, over her heart, is break dancing. The pleased smile at the corners of her mouth can't hide from me now.

"I'll arrange quick testing," I suggest.

"Because everybody jumps at Lion's command," she whispers, flashing me her smart-ass face.

I drag my mouth over the hill of her shoulder, stare up at her, bite. "Not everybody. Not yet."

All those perfect teeth, lips as smooth as fresh rose petals, fuck me up in Kam's laugh, while her hair shifts on my face.

"I'm never jumping for you, Mr. Middleton."

Her thighs tremble. She can't hide the spontaneous tap of her neck artery jumping so fast it telegraphs to me in Morse code.

I lay my head on her breast and listen to her heartbeat. In her skirt, between her moist inner thighs, I move aside the satiny panties blocking me from heaven.

Moist and oozing in my fingers, her folds are fat. Swollen. Smooth. I push my finger past her creamy opening, into Kamilah. Her back arches, thrusting her titties onto my face. In the kaleidoscope of our lust--jelly titties, nipples, dick, and her juices--swirl the shadows of us. I'm even weaker with my fingers buried in her slick, plush home.

"Your pussy begs to differ."

In the middle of exploring as much of one another as is permissible in broad daylight, she squeezes my dick harder over my pants. Thumbs the head, and my wood is at full swell. My manhood answers her with a squirt of precum she must feel, and we gasp at the same time.

Consumed with heat on a mild day, we stroke each other and let our mouths hang against one another in a long, open kiss. Her pussy walls clamp around my fingers, and the plush sensation is so exquisite my dick thumps in her hands. Our breathing swirls in an erotic whirlwind, heads pressed together from the strain of our attraction. We keep our movements small, as she strokes my dick in my pants.

Around my fingers, Kam's pussy contracts and overheats, her legs tighten, her foot curling around my calf.

Urrrrgh....

She buries her guttural moan in my hair. In her ecstasy,

her sandal slides off, her balled up toes scraping my leg muscles.

I nudge my finger upward, into her wet pool, intoxicated on how she burns hotter as she loses herself.

Faster. Deeper. Harder.

Tongues slipping and dancing.

I can't breathe enough to fill my lungs.

"I'm coming."

Under her grip, I squirt in my pants.

"Mmm," Kamilah hums.

Her pussy oozes cream on my hands.

Eyes closed, heads glued together, we squirm through the tremors, catch one another's breaths.

Reeling, pulling myself from a daze, I withdraw my fingers from her, stick them in my mouth, and suck off her essence. "Let me wipe you before we go back."

As subtly as I can, I lift her so I can inch down her panties. Kam's hands on my shoulders, her titties shove onto my face. I bite one.

In my palm, her knees wobble.

"That was just the appetizer, girl. You'd better be stronger than that."

French Fry's laughter is genuine, and her sunlight breaks through her barricade. "Don't get too cocky, Mr. Middleton. You still have a lot to prove."

I use her panties to wipe the streams from her thighs. "Finally, a task you want from me that I actually look forward to."

I fold the panties and shove them in my pocket.

She gasps.

"I'm starting a collection and I'll never wash 'em. We should go."

Hesitant, she replies, "Yeah, we're probably past Sheldon's thirty minutes."

Before we leave the gazebo, she pulls my shirt down over the wet stain on my pants.

"Hopefully, your dad won't jump down there and check," I joke.

She smiles. "I wouldn't put it past him, though."

I'm still figuring out what inside me needs to grab her hips, taste more of her—experience her rose-petal mouth, her tongue. My manhood wants more of this joy that now dances all over hard-ass Kamilah, to see more of her humanity, more of her eyes luminescent, hopeful, expectant.

"Oh!" She leaps a little. "We want to hear about the history of Black people who were not enslaved on Juneteenth. Tomorrow at Slurp. We were wondering if you'd come and talk about it."

I smooth down some of the flyaway hairs on her head and take in this tiny moment in which she is not self-aware. My insides smile to see her excited vulnerability.

"No, I won't do it. But I know somebody who can tell it far better. Either way, you'll get your story."

"Good." She tugs me back toward the house.

Since I like what's in front of me, I follow.

Suddenly, she whips around. "Say!"

I chuckle. "Say."

"Why haven't you ever asked me for my phone number?"

I roll my eyes and pull her under my arm. "I knew you wouldn't give it to me."

THE ROYAL FAMILY

LION & KAMILAH

LION

"Dad? Dad!" Excited, I rush into the house a few minutes after leaving the Rouses.

I'm on a mission now.

This opportunity presents a perfect opening for Dad to start rebuilding his name and the family's image.

Silence.

He's normally in the television room.

Now my pace picks up. He didn't mention going somewhere today. I rush through the house. When I don't find him, terror grips my trachea. The worst scenarios filter through my mind. He can't leave Earth under these circumstances—suffering and in silence.

Going to his favorite rooms first, not seeing him in the theater room, or the game room, or the living room, I stumble, as I would without him. Once I'm back down the stairs, I even search the floor for drops of blood or some sign of the worst.

"Dad!" I'm desperate now.

With a burst onto the terrace, I snatch up a huge breath and fill my lungs that had been deflating.

He's in the pool. With Braelan. Splashing around.

"I looked all through the house and..."

"Braelan asked me to help him with his backstroke so he can impress the little girls at the country club," Dad replies.

Inhaling a few more breaths, I wait for my vitals to return to normal. "We've worked on his backstroke. He's just trying to sneak some money out of you for the water rides and games next week."

I make a face at Braelan, and he frowns at me for putting his business in the street.

"You've been real busy lately. I thought you forgot I was here," Dad says and backstrokes away from me. "Your mother told me you were out with a woman—somebody related to Maddy, who tarnished our family name."

My eyes fall, simulating how my mind is laden with thoughts. I don't know how to explain Kamilah or how she has nothing to do with any of that. He wouldn't understand, so I won't touch that right now. "Old Man, I've been putting things in motion so we'll have options. Now we have some."

"Is that right?" he asks with skepticism.

"Yes, the Juneteenth celebration is tomorrow."

"Yes. And how does that concern us?" He sips sweet tea on the opposite side of the pool.

"Do you already have plans to go out?"

"No. Couple of the boys and your uncle were coming over so we can play cards."

I plug my hands into my waist and ready up mentally. Forcing him out of the comfort zone of this house will be harder than moving a mountain, especially as it involves any part of the English family. "There'll be a Juneteenth presentation. This woman who I was with, she suggested we share our family history with a few young people over in Montauk."

"Isn't Juneteenth about liberating slaves? Our ancestors didn't need liberating. That wasn't us."

I squat on my haunches. "But we have a different perspective to share about freedom, a story and beginning that is unfamiliar to most people. These days, kids need to hear as many sides of Black history as they can, especially about successful Black communities who thrived and did not have somebody's foot on their neck."

Already, his scowl says no before his mouth opens. "I don't think so, son."

"Aaah, come on, Dad, what's really going on here? You've been in the house for months now. You can't hide forever."

"I'm not hiding. There's just too much risk in going out there."

He's afraid and on the defensive where all this legal stuff is concerned.

"Not if we do it right." I stare at him. "And I believe the perfect reason for you to venture into those streets, and reintroduce yourself to the world, is for Juneteenth. I can't think of a better occasion." I address my nephew. "B, why don't you head inside and get a snack or something and give us a minute?"

"Lion, I know you mean well." Dad rises from the pool. "But stop trying to force me to go around people who I thought were my friends. I can no longer stand to *look* at them. You don't know how it feels."

"You're right, I don't. But I have tasted a little bit of it. People turn their heads when I walk by. My job withheld the promotion I earned and are playing Russian roulette with my career after I took a lot of risk for HP. Press reporters jump in my face and catch me off guard. After what I've been through, I can only imagine being you, Dad. But I'm telling you right now, I will not allow you to sit here and die. I won't."

"I'm not dying. I'm all right."

"That's a lie!"

I didn't mean to do that, but it snuck from somewhere in the furnace of my chest. From the heart of that seven-year-old kid who's seen this weakened man before. He still doesn't know I saw. Or that, in my own mind, I was holding his hand.

I'm still holding it. Especially now that I'm scared for both of us.

He lifts his head from the towel he's using to dry himself and glares at me. "Watch it."

"I will not." I rarely backtalk to my father. But we've never stood on the precipice of life and death. I continue, "Dad, that is not meant as disrespect. But the man I know is full of life, loves people, to laugh and party. He has so much more to live for." I go out on a limb now. "You have people around you who adore you and are here for you, no matter what." I move closer to him. "And we will not leave your side. *No matter what.*"

He faces me head-on, and breathes in and out real deep, as if each breath to stay alive requires too much effort now.

"You are not alone, Dad."

"If I go in that prison," he barks in a dry, wretched voice, that comes so devastatingly close to the one I heard the night I learned Kevin shared only half my blood, "nobody else is going in with me. Just me. I *am*. Alone."

"I've fought like hell to make sure that doesn't happen. And you're still here with us."

"For now." He sways, clearly overwhelmed. "This Juneteenth event, where will it be?"

"At the brewery over in Montauk."

"Is it that place owned by Francis Manuel's grandsons?"

Though my throat is somewhat clogged with emotion, I try swallowing it. "The man who oversees it is Mr. Manuel's grandson-in-law, by marriage."

"Then how could you ask me to—"

"Because tomorrow is not about Francis Manuel or his family. It's about you rehabilitating your image, no matter where you do it, Dad."

All his hurt pumps his hand up and down. "Let me make sure I understand this right. The man who slept with my wife didn't have to jump through all these hoops. He escaped accountability. But I need some publicity tour to rebuild myself and ask society for some kind of forgiveness that I don't owe them."

One time he even started to call her somebody else's name. Right there in front of us. He was flagrant. He thought he was untouchable.

Brendan's words beat a drum in my mind.

My father's strong back shudders under the weight of all this.

"The world doesn't see it that way. They don't know your private struggle. You took his land, Dad. His family went into financial decline. I'm sure he did suffer. You made him pay." My voice is low, and I'm certain I shouldn't say this. "And what did that do for your marriage to Mom?"

Leaning back on his heels, Lionel Middleton gives me that stare that has always chastened me. "Boy, watch your mouth," he warns.

Some instinct or force inside me pushes forward. "I'm sorry, Dad. I can't. I've done everything you've ever asked but I can't do that. Maybe you're still here and Francis Manuel is not, because you still need to learn a lesson."

His eyes squint the way they would before I had an ass-whipping coming.

"What did you just say to me?"

"I said... maybe there's a lesson in all this you haven't learned yet. There may be some purpose or calling in all of this for you, Dad. And we can never be too old. Or too proud. Or too rich to come to terms with it. Our family has always been masters of our own destiny. So we *can* conquer this now. And that might take doing *whatever*. Even if it means taking off your big man armor. And just being a bigger man."

Slowly, my eyes never leaving his, I square my shoulders. "I remember watching you hurt when you told Granddaddy about Kevin."

"I don't want to talk about it."

I press on. "Your pain was my pain. I hurt with you."

"I don't want to talk about it!" He throws his finger forward as a weapon at me.

"So I rode with you, because nothing or no one was going to hurt my dad, who could never be anything but strong."

He yanks up a chair and shakes it at me.

I jump back.

His aging arms hurl it off the terrace and into the pool. "I said I don't want to talk about it!"

My damn hand quakes hard on its path down my face.

Explosive, he glares at everything but me.

"She still loves you and she never left."

"It was the money that kept h-her here!" he bellows so hard the phlegm in his throat chokes him. "Bert could never give Kevin the same life on her own that he could have with *my* name! *That's* why she stayed!"

"I can't speak for Mom, but plenty of women have left their husbands and been fine. Just ask Ashlyn. Maybe Mom just wanted to get your attention. I did things all the time as a boy so I could have your attention. But you didn't leave her, and she didn't leave you, so where does that leave us all, Dad?

You've got to walk out of this house and go face consequences."

I inhale a sobering breath, because I suppose I really do need to believe what's coming out of my mouth. "You can't keep hiding. Like you always taught us, it's time to be a man and get on out there. Chin up. Shoulders back. And turn this thing around. It's time for you to practice what you preach. It's what you damn sure taught me."

Dad's anguish is also mine, but we have to start repairing his reputation, and our legacy.

Still simmering, he considers it. "And you think this history lesson will do that?"

The question shocks the shit out of me.

He's staring straight at me, waiting for an answer.

I wasn't ready.

"Image is everything now. Making good use of our history is a start. I believe it'll open doors and minds."

"And Kevin?"

"Why do you think I took the job at Explore? I have a plan for him, too."

His face plummets to one side, and his focus drifts somewhere else. As if he's conflicted. He runs his wrinkled hands over an area of his heart. "Stubborn-ass boy built his own damn company, just like he said he would. That boy succeeds to spite me." Walking by me, Dad heads toward the house. "But there's enough hurt in this family to go around. Don't hurt him. He's still mine, even if his blood might not be."

"I won't. I'll only humble him a little."

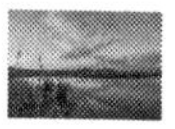

KAMILAH

"Don't wear that," Princess fusses.

"Why not?" I ask.

"Girl, it's too stiff. It's too 'businesswoman.' This is summertime. You're in the Hamptons. Here. Wear mine."

She holds up a maxi dress that screams "rip me off as soon as possible." Though she's a couple of sizes bigger than me, the looser areas actually complement me nicely, with the dangling shoulder straps giving me a sexy, helpless damsel look.

I'm cracking up laughing. "Princess, you do remember this is a professional event, right?"

"For everybody else, yes. For you, no. Today is a holiday. This dress is appropriate and respectable. Enough." She winks.

"Bae, are you sure you should be going to this?" Roland cuts in. "Why don't you stay here and spend the afternoon enjoying some peace and quiet? You've been watching the kids since school let out. Somebody's always in the house with you. You could use some time to yourself."

Concern creases his forehead in a way I don't normally see. My brother's been more and more stressed every time we cross paths now. He even seems extra protective of P, like he's scared to let her out of his sight.

"Whatever, boy. I want to hear this illustrious history of the Middleton family. I'm going to meet these Black descendants of folks who were not in chains on Juneteenth. We hear about the Creole families back home in Louisiana and families from the Boulé. But not that often. It's rare to actually meet some, and who can recall several generations of history. I want to be there for this."

"Wait a minute," Jerrell breaks in. "What did I miss while I was in ATL?"

Before I can answer, Sheldon speaks up. "Lion Middleton was here yesterday. He and your sister were out under the gazebo for over an hour."

Jerrell directs his vexation at me. "Hold on. What happened between last week, when you slapped him, and now?"

"It wasn't a real slap. It was a love lick," Sheldon reports the latest news while we hang out in the backyard. "He tried to kiss your sister the other day, and Chase wouldn't let him."

Jerrell presses Chase to him. "Give me some, my guy. That's what Daddy's talking about. Protect your aunt when she's not thinking straight."

Chase talks back in his baby babble.

"Excuse you?" I ask.

Jerrell turns to me. "When did you start entertaining cocky Negroes who look down on the Black people around them? I thought we had an understanding the Middletons are not cool. This whole Harvard thing, and the Italian property, and them railroading Adella's family. And here you go, selling out like Sheldon."

Two weeks ago, I was on the same page.

But Lion has not ceased to amaze me. He is working on being more perceptive and more sensitive. "It's possible for people to change. Didn't Kevin Middleton fly you to your wife when the Capitol was under attack? And Maddy changed you, Jam 'Em Jerrell."

"Yes, Kevin and I have a truce, but he's still a general prick. And me enjoying my share of women is not the same as mistreating other people," he complains. "I'm not having it, Kam. You're too good for them, and you deserve better. If he keeps coming around you, I will have to let him know it."

I love my brother—all my brothers, to pieces—but their faces don't do what Lion's did when he saw me coming down the stairs. And their fingers can't do for me what his did yesterday.

"Stay out of it. If you talk to him, I will go mess with one of your friends. And I have several to choose from," I reply, allowing that threat to drip. Of course, I'm not serious since my head is on something else these days. But it still shuts Mr. Jerrell right on up.

Once we reach the brewery, I marvel at what we all did with the place. A tall, gorgeous and thick woman who resembles Desmond stands in the center of the place. Solomon flirts with her by grabbing her butt or pulling her to him.

She approaches when I enter. "Hey, I'm Chaitra, Desmond's sister."

"Chaitra McLain?" I ask as we shake hands. "From Baltimore? I'm Kamilah Rouse, Jerrell's sister."

Her mouth opens wide. "Oh! I heard you've been keeping these two in line."

I shrug. "Girl, I try, but they won't let me. Haven't I heard your name, a long time ago in basketball? Didn't you play some women's summer pick-up games? I might've played you years ago, in Newark and D.C."

From her happy surprise, she remembers. "Get out! What a small world. This summer I'm teaching basketball to some of the kids, helping out for the Black Business Council connection to New York City youth. If you have time, we'd love for you to come through. We need all the help we can get."

"I'd be glad to. But I'm honestly shocked you didn't go pro. Your skills were dope." I'm genuinely curious to know how somebody as talented as Chaitra is not in the WNBA.

Chaitra might be averting her eyes now to hide some emotion. "You know how it goes. The real world calls, and you have to stop bouncing the ball. I work with my mom over at McLain Construction in Baltimore. I'm co-chair for the company, CFO."

I love meeting another Black woman who's into numbers. "Look out now! CPA here. I see you with that math."

Aside from her tightness when I asked about basketball, her smile is easy and broad, and she has a chill vibe, comfortable in her skin. Just my type. "Girl, what do they have you around here doing? "

I laugh. "Auditing. Making sure all these glitzy events add up to a profit."

"Get them right. We will have to go to lunch and swap tea pretty soon."

"I'm game."

"Kamilah," Solomon calls and throws his arm around Chaitra, "I hear you've been giving Lion and Desmond the business. Your elbow grease is helping us pull all this together. If you want an exec position in Explore, just say the word."

I shake my head. "No, no, no. Don't be giving me more work to do, Mr. English."

"Because we've got aplenty, Ms. Rouse."

As we banter, more people enter Slurp.

"So is it true?" My sister-in-law, Chrissy, asks me. "You had Lion over to the house for brunch?" She stares at me with skeptical eyes. "Right after you hit him last week?"

I inhale for round two. Or is it round three or four by now? "Chrissy, didn't you go off on Sheldon and *try* to slap him at a Village Council meeting?"

Her lips curl in. "Listen, I'm not judging. Just, I've known the Middletons my entire life. I know people he's burned. He can be very smooth and sweet when he wants. So be careful, that's all."

I know my family means well and I'm not surprised at their concern. What does surprise me is how they tend to forget their own relationship struggles—hell, human struggles.

Which is why I could never tell my parents, with their sky-high standards, about Duncan. Or how I rushed to the abortion clinic, devastated when Tanja showed up at his apartment. It's why I am eternally grateful for Princess picking me up the next night after I rode back to New York from college on the train, with my body *and* my spirit in literal shreds.

"Kam, this is so lit. A Black-owned brewery? A Black-own…" Princess stifles a cough. Several coughs. Her body quakes, and her shoulders curl over like they convulse due to an internal war.

"P, you good?" With my arm around her waist, it's my turn to hold *her* up now. "What is going on with you? Forget concern. You've got me shook."

"I'm fine, g… girl. Don't worry. I just… need to blow my nose." With the speed that she nails her hand over it, there must be something underneath I shouldn't see. "Be right back."

Now I pursue P to the bathroom so I can lay into her for lying to me. But an instant hush falls over the room that stops my feet.

At the front of Slurp, Lion enters. Behind him are his parents, and his brothers.

Astonishment widens my eyelids. I've never seen his father in person. Spitting reflections of one another, the only break in their resemblance is the salt and pepper sprinkled in the older man's head and goatee. Otherwise, they are equally comely, of equal height, and matching stature.

"Well, praise the good Lord," Etta murmurs outside earshot of her husband. "They are God's personal footmen."

Only now do I realize that, peering over all the other

folks standing on their tippy-toes, I've made my way back to our little group.

"I want one," Ameera comments. She's driven down from the city so she can be nosy. "I'll take any one of 'em. Doesn't matter which. Old. Young. Married. Single."

Kevin and Lion introduce Mr. Middleton to the men of Explore and their significant others.

"That's strange," Etta comments.

"What?"

"Lion's dad didn't acknowledge the owner of that chocolate restaurant, Solomon. They didn't even speak. Just passed right by one another."

Today isn't the first time I've made the same observation. Lion talks to just about all the other Explore owners except Solomon—and Kevin. Even now, between them, there's little of the natural camaraderie I share with my siblings. The inside jokes and ribbing among us, I don't find between them.

Their mother works the room and says hello to the community, hugging Hamptons residents and holding on to them while she whispers something in their ear. Like she's a Black Jackie Kennedy and should have been the wife of a senator or president herself. Her daughters-in-law, Kendall and Chenera, network along with her.

"God, she's so beautiful," Etta whispers.

"She looks just like Dorothy Dandridge," Princess adds, having returned from the restroom.

I consider confronting her now, but she actually appears to be all right. Later, we will address those doctor visits for whatever that cough is about.

In this moment though, we Hamptons outsiders stand in a line and wait for the Middletons to come by. Like they're the royal family.

"I feel like we should curtsy or something," Etta says.

Lion approaches us, zooms in on me. Teeth biting down on his lip, he zooms his admiration up and down me.

I recall his fingers playing with my pussy in the garden yesterday, and now she's in full bloom. To keep our exchange professional, and to mask the carnal thoughts in my head, I offer him a handshake.

But his excited eyes suck me up, followed by his gigantic football arms.

The sinfully slow kiss Lion lays on my cheek flirts with the boundaries of civility. He whispers, "What are you trying to do to me in this dress? You must want me to say fuck it all and we do this shit right here." Straightening up again, returning to his normal voice, he shifts to his mother. "Mom, this is Kamilah and her family."

It really is stunning how fast these rich folks switch up.

"Kamilah." She says my name as if it's being announced in the heavenly roll call.

Butterflies flutter in my chest and throat while I reach for my words. "It's such a pleasure to meet you, Mrs. Middleton. How could you still have your right mind after raising this one?"

"Just call me Bert. He does make it a challenge." She cuts her eyes at her oldest before focusing on me. "But I wouldn't trade him for anything. Thank you for having him over yesterday."

While she talks, she rubs my hands, and I swear hers feel like satiny wedding cushions. Whiffs of her refreshing lavender-and-chamomile aroma enter my nose. I looked her up on the internet, and I had no idea there was a such thing as "aristocratic" Black women. But this one attended finishing school and is actually related to Marie Antoinette, the beheaded queen of France.

"We had a lot of fun. He's a riot."

"Sometimes too much so." Though Roberta is all class, she

stares at Lion with half-chastisement, half-love, like she is indeed the woman who pushed him out and knows every nook and cranny on him. "But you apparently have no problem handling him. I hope we can repay the social call and have you eat with us soon."

I squeeze her velvety hands just because. "I'd love that."

"And if you need anything at all, don't hesitate to come and see me. Your mother has my number."

She moves onward, down the line, as if she's got this socializing thing down to a science, knowing exactly what to say, perhaps not a pretentious bone in her body. And yet she can still be elegant and on point with her realness.

"Oh, my God, the way Sis talks…her voice is liquid satin," Princess murmurs.

"Girl, but did you see how Lion kissed her on her damn *cheek*?" Ameera asks.

Princess half chuckles, half coughs. "I sure did."

"Heffa…" Ameera declares, rolling her neck, "for him to act like that in public, when he gets you by yourself, he is going to fuck… you… up."

"Shh!" I swear I can't have her out anywhere.

People standing nearby wonder why the three of us are breaking out in fits.

"Ya'll are doing too much. It's not even like that! We just w—"

"Aht, aht. Don't you dare speak against this blessing, Kam," P chastises. "We've got eyes. It's about to go down. Did you tell him?"

"Did I—" I stop mid-sentence, realizing what she's asking me, if I told him about Duncan.

"Come on now, Kam. If the shoe was on the other foot, you would want to know. Don't forget to tell him before this goes any further."

I nod in silence.

Just a little more time.

What if Lion is one of those guys who refuses to date the ex of his friend? They've been boys since college.

Contrary to what I expected during my stay here in the Hamptons, Duncan doesn't dominate my every thought. I haven't seen as much of him as I feared. My biggest surprise is I'm not screwing other men to erase him and Tanja from my head or to prove to myself I'm over what happened and perfectly happy as a single woman. I may have even overreacted in the beginning and pushed Lion away, precisely because he's Duncan's friend.

But affectionate with some of his neighbors and former classmates, lined up with his family, I'm seeing Lion through different lenses, as a man instead of a rich asshole, or as Duncan's friend, or as a revenge fuck. Instead of ire, admiration rises in me at the sight of Lion draping his arm around his father, almost protectively.

An afternoon of Juneteenth commemorations and presentations wind down, and the three brothers take the center of the floor to thank everyone for inviting them. Desmond has turned on a sort of spotlight. Mr. Middleton, the eldest, stands alone and his family disappears. Hesitation drags his feet, and he forces himself to the center, almost like he abhors the light.

"Isn't he the one who's in all the papers? Bribed the Harvard president?" Ameera asks.

"That's him." Jerrell is present now, and the warning in his eyes couldn't be clearer.

For a moment, I'm not sure the poor man can remain standing. Lion's father covers his mouth with his hand, and it becomes clear to me and everyone else in the room that he's having a moment.

From the sidelines, Lion emerges. Carrying two barstools, he sets them down and circles an arm around his dad, mutters in his ear. They lean into one another as if the man needs Lion to survive.

Lion may as well have thrown his arm around the taproom, drawing us into a collective hug, the way their raw emotion has us clinging together for what comes next.

One at a time, the audience picks up a clap, urging them on.

Someone gives Lion a microphone, and he turns to the audience. "Residents of Sag Harbor, family and friends, I'd appreciate you all giving another round of support and encouragement to my father, Lionel Middleton. He is here today, despite the intense public scrutiny, prepared to face whatever consequences that come for his decisions."

"It's all right!" people call out around the room.

Notably, Solomon and Adella and their family members quietly exit.

THE LONG HAND OF HISTORY

LION

More people showed up than we expected. People pack the walls everywhere, some of them pointing their cell phones and cameras straight at him, and neither Dad nor I were anticipating that.

Since this event was thrown together last minute, we had little time to go over how we would present the history. Though he's recited much of our family lineage many times, the audience is different now. Surrounded everywhere, it's unclear who's a friend or foe. Who's recording for the significance of this moment and who's recording for darker purposes?

The spotlight shining into the center of the floor, waiting for him, might also wait to illuminate his dark secrets.

I pull up two chairs and sit him down so he can gather his thoughts.

Making sure he rises from the ashes is my only concern. He has a stunning heritage. Many families do also, and just as others do, the Middleton journey should be heard. We need to work through some things but we also have a lot to be proud of. I refuse to let him lower his head with shame, not when we are blessed with a heritage that does indeed set us apart. It does not make us better, but it sets us apart.

"Dad," I whisper.

His eyes have turned fearful. I press my reassurances into his shoulder.

"Our history goes back as far as Chatham Dockyard in Kent, southeast England, in the late fifteen hundreds," he begins. "My forefathers served under Queen Elizabeth I. Our family worked on the royal dockyard making ships for the Royal Navy."

Audible gasps fill the brewery. Shocked teenagers remove their earbuds, hold up their phones, and start recording. Kids set aside the games on iPads.

"Our family were free people who arrived in England from West Africa, during Elizabeth I's reign. During her era, many cultures and races grew on English soil, as people ventured from places such as Bangladesh, Spain, and Guinea. British merchants and traders began making quite a lot of money off the trade of Africans in the fifteen hundreds."

He pauses a moment because listeners always need a minute to react to the sale of slaves.

"It was only natural that diverse populations grew in that era. During her time, Shakespeare wrote the famous play, *Othello*, where the main character was a Black man. Black people intermarried with citizens of other races, and many of them roamed the country as freely as whites. Black people were a peculiarity to many whites who had never seen Blacks, and some of them inevitably came across deplorable mistreatment in their lives as well."

My father swallows, struggles with his throat as it gets dry. Desmond brings over some water, which I appreciate, especially since his wife and her side of the family have left. I express my gratitude with a quick nod.

Desmond's affable jock persona makes it easy to forget

he's related to Francis Manuel by marriage. The man's granddaughter manages Manuel's estate and is now suing Dad. Despite the history and bad blood, Desmond has been nothing short of gracious. He does it for the sake of his brewery, I'm sure, but I've never gotten bad energy from him.

Dad takes a sip. And I help him with the blown-up photos our family has collected throughout history. We've used them at schools and presentations over the years during Black History Month.

"In the fifteen and sixteen hundreds, quite a number of Blacks served in the courts of King James IV, King Henry VIII and then Elizabeth. Some were performers, others domestic servants. My family ancestors were fortunate to have mastered ship-building. They resided far outside of London, in the rural countryside. Meanwhile, British merchants had begun taking European goods to Africa—such as sugar, hides, and spices—and trading those goods for African people who had been captured from that mainland."

Every person in the room hangs on to Dad's every word.

"Those Africans would then be transported by boat to the Americas. This horrible practice exploded during the sixteen hundreds. Our family was already living and thriving in England. But many families were not so fortunate." The gates of his chest seem to open, and he remembers to breathe, but the room is so quiet it may have lost its collective breath.

"To make ships and refit them for one of the greatest monarchs in history, on the premier naval base of the time, was an honor. Having this unique knowledge kept our family out of the bonds of domestic servitude. Most Blacks in England worked as cooks, maids, dressmakers, many women as sex workers, and in arts and entertainment. My family avoided this type of labor with our understanding of the seas, tides, and how ships navigated them. As a result, every member of the family—men and women—had to learn about ships, the ocean, and nearby waterfront terrains. War was prevalent for England, Netherlands, Spain, and Portugal, and later the Americas. It was the source of British power. Blacks who could help Elizabeth I build up the British Navy ships made ourselves indispensable, which made it harder for the aristocracy to force us into involuntary servitude."

I pass him another poster.

"Great Britain at its height was the largest maritime power on Earth. Chatham was an important strategic dockyard during the Dutch Wars. Two hundred years later, in 1760, one of the men in my family, Domingo Middleton, in addition to being a builder, was also an excellent musician and could play the flute very well. He captured the attention at court of Queen Charlotte."

Though he sips water, what nourishes him more is the sea of mesmerized souls.

"The tension with the colonies in America was growing. Many British Blacks were curious about opportunities to build wealth in America, just as British lords and merchants were doing. But they were very afraid of being captured and placed in slavery. Families like ours feared losing two hundred years of freedom with all the stories we were hearing about Blacks being brutalized. By the seventeen hundreds, some of my ancestors had spread across England, and some had entered the Queen's service in her court as instrumentalists, poets, and writers. A few of my forebears did go to America, wound up fighting in the American Revolution on the side of the British as Loyalists, and had to return to England poor after they lost.

"Others remained as shipbuilders on the dockyards. For the several members of our family who wanted to leave for the Americas, she granted permission and gave them special status as friends of the Queen.

"After the war between the colonies and Britain, the racism was much deeper and more entrenched. Many shipyards in New York refused to hire Black men to build their boats, and white ship repairmen did not appreciate the competition. So my forefathers went into ferrying people on boats and whaling. Whaling was very lucrative, the fifth largest sector of the economy in 1880, a way for Blacks to establish wealth, real freedom, and status in that time."

Dad has picked up his flow now and is on a roll.

"Although racism still existed in the Navy and on boats, a great deal of freedom came with work on the seas. Discrimination and oppression occurred for all Blacks, but Blacks who worked on the water were treated better than those who worked the land. We used this to our advantage. It has always served us well."

Mesmerized kids observe as Dad flips from one blown-up poster to another, displaying paintings of our ancestors who pose next to boats, in our family parlor rooms, at weddings, and in businesses.

"Some of our ancestors sailed from America to various countries and brought back trinkets from Africa and the Indies for sale. On the ships for months at a time, white men had to depend on Black men for their safety, which required trusting your co-worker. If a Black man could do his job as a good seafarer, it earned him great respect. So on boats, there was not much opportunity to treat Black and white separately when they needed each other to stay alive. This provided a path to respect and liberty for Black men on the high seas that did not exist on plantations."

People only move to make themselves more comfortable. Even I listen to this story like I've never heard it before, every time he tells it.

"Over the eighteen hundreds, for our relatives who were stolen and sold into slavery, my relatives purchased their freedom when they could. We also purchased the freedom of other Blacks. My great-great-grandfather purchased the freedom of my great-great-grandmother. But the problems grew for our family in the lead-up to the Civil War. The whaling industry began to decline in the late eighteen hundreds. After nearly a hundred years on American soil, some of the Middleton men had used the family's wealth to venture into other professions, such as doctors, lawyers, dentists, shopkeepers."

He holds up another poster of more relatives in later New York.

"But due to extensive racism, whites sometimes destroyed our businesses. Set them on fire or raided their homes or shops. So our family maintained much of our history and artifacts in secrecy. For years, we buried some of our memorabilia and placed them in boxes in the ground. Whale bones from sailing exploits, jewels, fine fabrics, photos, and letters, we hid under houses and churches."

People marvel at the drawings and later photos of underground caverns my family had dug.

Dad pauses and takes in the quiet awe throughout the room, the young audience drawn to the history. It seems their energy keeps him going.

"Although Middletons endured rough times, we do not regret coming to the Americas and making our wealth. We were able to increase our fortunes greatly on these shores. Some Middletons suffered, but we also gained and achieved esteem, privilege, and wealth that made the sacrifices worth it. Though we came here freely, many other Blacks did not have that choice. It is the liberation of our brothers and sisters, tortured for generations, that we recognize today. The liberation of all Blacks, so they could also pursue their destinies and their dreams, as we did. We still have distant relatives in England."

As a few people clap and pass the poster boards, I can't help surveying a scene I hadn't prepared for—kids and parents pointing and wondering, with more questions they want to ask.

"Just as the whaling industry declined in the late eighteen hundreds, and before that the Chatham Dockyard began to decline after the Dutch Wars, New York's shipyards declined in the early nineteen hundreds. The Middleton family always had to adjust to the times, and the ever-changing priorities of society. Now, we Middletons find ourselves at a crossroads once again."

Emotion fills up Dad's face as he concludes.

"In the technological era and digital era of the two thousands, we Middletons must carve out our path and find our way to a new destiny. As m-many of you, we are having to look forward to the future."

He chokes up some, and I hope I'm conveying to him how I've never been prouder.

He continues, "My family has always survived with our skills and intellect. Just as many of you, we are figuring out how we'll use those now to have a meaningful place in the future. Often, the future can be scary."

A heckler calls out from the audience. "Are you building your future by taking opportunities from the poor and using them for yourself? Is that helping the community?"

I prepare to deal with this person. Desmond seems tense, unsure of what to do.

Dad holds up his hand and stops me. He addresses his heckler head-on.

"I'm not here to argue with you, son. What I will say is that times have certainly changed—over the past centuries, the past decade, and just these few years. Practices that were totally acceptable half a century ago, when my father was ensuring my future, are no longer acceptable today. Our family is willing to change to meet the times. We will evolve as we always have and serve our people. Now is no different. We hope you will show us grace as we get there. The Middletons have risen to meet the challenges of changing social and economic times before. I have no doubt we'll do it now."

He turns to me.

"My sons have taught me this. I'm proud of them for showing me they can thrive on their own, just as their forefathers did. I could not ask for better teachers."

In the pressure of his hand squeezing mine, he conveys his sentiments. Tears in his eyes, he rubs my face.

"I have not always been the best example, like many fathers. But I can learn how to do this leadership thing better."

My father stands. I stand with him. He walks over to little Braelan and kisses his head, then kisses an emotional Brendan. He searches around the room, to where Kevin stands with Cher.

"I am part of an old generation who must learn new ways. I'm willing to learn if they are willing to teach an old dog new tricks."

Kevin comes forward and stretches out his hand.

Dad pulls him into his arms. "I'm proud to call you my son. Whatever you decide to do."

The rest of the room does not know and cannot fully process what this is about. But it's obvious to them that another event just occurred alongside the history lesson.

Dad looks to my mom. "The women in my family, who marry a Middleton man, put our feet to the fire, and hold us accountable. There would be no Middleton without the strength and grace of our daughters, sisters, and wives who are great in their own right, including my wife. Whom I love dearly and I could never live without."

I can't really describe what it means for me to see my

parents embrace each other in a way they haven't done in years. There are no metaphors I can employ to put an outsider in this moment. Between my parents, layers of hardship, struggle, and longing crystallize in a way I'd hoped for but wasn't sure was still possible. They stare at each other and can say things with their expressions, in a room full of people, that none of us can decipher or understand.

I love my mother. I do. She might even be one of my closest friends who knows me better than anybody. That's why the wound she sliced through me never healed.

Still, when she comes to encircle my face with her lovely fingers, and pours her emotion into me, I do my job as her son and express love and caring back to her.

But the full emotional circle does not close for her and me.

"I'm proud of you for this. For getting him here."

I nod. "I know."

"Lion." Though she stands next to me, too many years and a hell of a lot of betrayals still stand between us.

Next up, Kevin and I exchange uncomfortable, terse glances. We both know the bystanders are eying us, the two most visible Middletons. Forcing ourselves forward, we share a half-hug.

"Lion," another voice intervenes.

To which we both redirect our attention.

"A moment?" Madison Rouse asks.

Mom squeezes my arm. "Hey, Maddy, glad to see you again. Lion, we'll talk later."

I place my frustration on my hips. "I haven't heard from you lately, as you said I would, Madison."

"A lot is going on. But I'm here now."

"Yeah, when there's an event you can leverage for your press operation."

"Go easy, okay?"

While she says this, her husband, Jerrell, Kamilah's brother, makes his way over.

I couldn't care less. "Madison, I'm holding you to your word. You said we would talk, that Duncan would be in touch—"

"I actually have a better idea than you and Duncan. This here"—she points at all the people surrounding Dad—"this is a book, Lion, a bestselling book."

She has my attention as she shows me her phone. "Your dad is already going viral on the socials. I've been watching the numbers. He's picking up thousands of views by the hour. That's good for a book tour, which gives your father and your family a platform for connecting with a Black America that's hungry to see itself beyond oppression. You would have to be careful in how you present it, to avoid the appearance of bragging or indifference. But as long as you are concerned about the well-being of our race and actively engaged in the community, they will stand with you."

She slips her hair behind her ear and seems to mentally prepare for her next words.

"What is it?" I prod.

Steely Maddy's expression sharpens into a blade. "Lion, if your father wants to redeem himself, he can't half-ass it."

"What do you mean?" I'm confused. "This was a big move for him, coming here today with all the pressure he's under, at the risk of accidentally incriminating himself."

Her disdain cuts across her face. "Smeralda Costa. You need to resolve it."

"It *is* resolved," I mutter.

"You know that's not true," the shrewd politician and organizer insists. "I will help you all get a damn good deal and book tour. But Adella is my friend. Now I don't know what personal issues exist here between your families, and that is none of my business. But what I do know is I can't help you in good conscience if your father does nothing to rectify the injustice to the English family."

Now I absorb what she's saying. I stare at Dad, how relieved he seems after getting through that history retelling. I believe with everything in me that Smeralda Costa helped him keep his sanity in the face of another man tending to the woman he loved.

"I don't know about that, Maddy."

Francis Manuel is mine and Dad's shared enemy. We can forgive Mom. And hell, I can even tolerate Kevin. But no, not Smeralda Costa, the one piece of security that buffered the betrayal and humiliation. That was the unspoken deal for Dad taking and raising Kevin—pristine beaches and turquoise waters on the Italian Coast.

"Think about it," Maddy presses me. "Duncan can come around, and I can start leaning on my publishing contacts, once you and your Dad make amends."

Brendan, his wife Kendall, and my little nephew, Braelan, step up.

"I know that took a lot. For both of you. Hopefully, other mature moves will follow. And no dumb ones," he says with a side-eye that puts the fate of our family directly on me.

In a sense, he was right the other day. I suppose the glory of House Middleton was bestowed on me, and now I'm charged with protecting the name.

"Thanks, B."

In a bear hug, we grip one another.

"Proud of you, man." His fingers dig deep. "Always have been."

"Just make sure you let Dad know that, too, all right?"

The loaded moment where he stays silent speaks volumes. I understand it. He and Kevin don't connect with Dad as easily as I do.

Nevertheless, "Don't call me on my shit if you won't address your own, man."

"I hear you, and I will." Once we let go, he nods toward Kamilah on the other side of the taproom. "So who is that over there?"

Now flagrant, spoiled me can't find my tongue all of a sudden. I'm not ready to put a definition to Kamilah's magnetic pull on me since day one.

"Oh, shit." B turns to his wife. "Ken, babe, you see this?"

"I do. I also saw that hug and kiss before the presentation. So will she be joining us for sailing out on the water pretty soon?"

I hug Kendall. "I actually like her, so why would I put that poor woman through a full afternoon with this family?"

"She's probably a breath of fresh air compared to you," B shoots back with a big grin and squeezes me.

Trane, Fenton, and our friends rake me over the coals since I haven't seen them much. But the entire time, from across the room, Kamilah and I have our own vibe.

Suddenly from nowhere, Kevin is at my side. "You know Desmond had reservations about you coming here. He really tried to talk me out of bringing you in, considering there's beef between you and his wife."

I shrug. "We're having a good moment right now, dude. Don't ruin it."

"Lion, I'm just saying. I'm also aware that Madison came to you with options. I hope you're giving weight to what she said… for you *and* Dad. Don't let all this goodwill go to waste. Plus, Desmond trusted you with his dream."

"And Explore is seeing results."

"We are. Imagine the bigger impact you could have if you were all in, rather than half here and half in Texas."

But I've already checked out of what Half-Blood is saying,

because a beachy Kamilah strolls up in her sunset-orange floral dress.

The loose fabric, sweeping perfectly around her frame, allows her slender, curvy hips to roam. “That was mind-blowing. When we came up with this idea, I didn’t know you were coming with five hundred years of history.” She displays her approval in all those perfect, gleaming teeth. “The fifteen hundreds, Lion? Elizabeth I? You all should be doing a whole lot more with that history than telling it in breweries.”

Spontaneously, my hand reaches for her. I need to touch her to confirm this relaxed, engaged version of her is real. “When it’s your history, it’s easier to take for granted. Thank you for inviting him to share it.”

Is it me, or did her thumb stroke the back of my hand?

It was an accident.

Maybe not?

Is she wearing makeup?

“I didn’t invite your dad. I invited you.” Her lips are shiny. Gloss? “But I’m glad you brought him instead. No offense, but I’m not sure someone else telling it would’ve been so powerful. He seems really dialed in to his heritage and he tells it from his gut.”

Definitely gloss. Flavored?

This is our second time standing in Slurp, not as businesspeople discussing its operations but as two people. Happy the event went well, chattering and bubbling, she’s almost a different woman than the one I met two weeks ago. With her skin sun-kissed and hair breezy, she smells like fruity candy.

“How’s your day been?” I ask. Because she’s standing here. And now that Dad is okay for the moment, I don’t give a damn about anything else.

"Really well. But it's been weird not seeing you around here these past few days."

Every other gorgeous woman I've dated, sexed, lusted after, has not made me bashful, unsure of what to say next, hopeful I don't screw up. I'm striving for my every word to be on point and for my shit to be together.

"Weird as in… you miss me."

Kam's gaze dips, as if she's making a decision, and when it hikes back to mine, the skittishness in her eyes matches what's in my chest. But she tries to cover. "Weird like the *brewery* misses you, sir. When the new hops arrived for autumn—"

Cupping her chin, I connect to this open version of Kamilah, who is no longer agitated, whose presence here exceeds numbers and math calculations, who is no longer referring to my presence as a job or assignment, but as "weird."

In the middle of all these people I've known my whole life, I lay claim to her rose-petal lips and kiss her.

FRENCH FRY

KAMILAH

Lion's mouth, tongue, touch…

He must be sampling a delicacy, inspecting a rare gem. His thumb graces my chin, fingers crest my jawbone and neck. The heat of just his finger pads… care and tenderness of his head action…worships and adores what his mind is sucking.

The way he nudges his taste buds along the opening of my mouth is at once respectful and wanton—a complete contrast to our chaotic, hasty, rough initial fuck.

"The first time we ever met, I asked if I could suggest some place more exciting. What are your plans for the rest of the evening?" he asks me.

Only now do I realize I'm in a stupor. "Uh." Smart-ass Karate Kam has taken a hike.

Once I locate my senses and scan the taproom, Ameera, Princess, Etta, and my mother all gawk on the other side. Alongside an irritated Jerrell, with Desmond clearly laughing and giving him shit.

"Ms. City Girl, I want to show you something," Lion says.

I don't hear what else he says after that. Inches away, his

toned, athletic chest hovers over me and emanates a deep scent of saltwater and fine leather, as if he was working on his boat before he came here. The top two buttons are undone on his light, short-sleeved shirt, and where tiny, curly hairs are interspersed along his oiled, wheat-colored skin…

I stop myself from…

My clit registers an objection.

Involuntarily, my body answers him. A tickling sensation forces me to shift my legs where I've squirted in my panties.

What is happening?

My brain goes on a mission to hunt for tough-as-nails "Karate Kam" Rouse, for her smart-ass comebacks and unshakable fortress, who has no fucks in her pocket for anybody outside her family, but while I'm doing that, Lion's muscles ripple beneath his shirt and reach for me.

I'm kind of watching from the outside of my body when that twenty-one-year old girl I put in a box and locked up, reaches back to him. He guides her out of these walls where she first entered in her military armor, and now leaves unguarded into the gentle breeze on this liberating Juneteenth evening.

We both grab the passenger door handle of his Ferrari at the same time.

A giant smile spreads over him.

My gaze drops to the ground, and since I don't know what to do with myself—rare—I scratch my head and laugh.

"Look here, French Fry, I've been waiting two weeks. May I please be the man in this situation?" he jokes.

Shaking from humor and nerves, I extend my arm and invite him to open my door. He might be opening me in a few ways, maybe.

"French Fry?" I ask when we're in transit to wherever.

"My nickname for you in my head," The Lion answers

with a devious grin as he and his muscles maneuver the steering wheel.

My mouth drops, and I scoff. "French Fry! What else in your head do you..." Thinking better of where that might lead, I back off. "Never mind."

We both crack up.

"Smart woman."

My window is down while we ride past the large green spreads of land, the sky changing colors from azure to tangerine. Mild wind blows my hair around, and I don't bother to remove it from my face.

"How often do you come here from Houston?" I ask him.

"About once or twice a month, depending on my work and travel schedule. Sometimes, if I'm making deals or checking on ships and drilling locations overseas, I'll stop through New York for a few days, check in on Mom and the Old Man, before heading back down south." Though he's chill as he focuses on the rural highway, he seems to shift in his seat and his eyes twitch.

"You miss this place?"

"I do."

"So why did you move all the way to Texas, of all places? Why not take a job here?"

"Right out of college, I did, but building my career was rough. With people knowing my family, they often have their own agenda. They tried to hijack my career or my job so they could get something out of us." He lifts his hand from the gear shift and uses it to talk. "For example, they offer me X assignment or promotion if I can hook them up with tickets to Y or dinner with Z. And that's certainly not a bad thing. Sometimes, swapping favors worked out well for me. Other times not so much, especially when someone gets greedy or pissed. If they're higher up the ladder than you, you're at their mercy. And you're being denied opportunities you deserved or worked hard for, out of spite. I've had jealous bosses sabotage my work file, just to feel power over me.

When he says this, his eye twitches again. Behind it, he seems to wrestle his thoughts.

He continues, "So being from a New York family with connections is a strength, but people can also make it a weakness. In my late twenties, I received an offer out of state. I thought it was good to spread my wings some, earn my way to CEO on my own, in a region where not many people knew me. Dad didn't like it too much, but he understood. I needed a way to neutralize all the haters who misjudge me as a spoiled Black dude who doesn't know shit."

In exaggerated fashion, his head tilts toward me.

I can't help erupting with unladylike laughter for him calling me out.

He takes a deep breath. "My brother, Brendan, likes to say I lean on my name too much." Taking a pause and staring out at the road, he definitely grapples with some burden now. "To some extent, maybe that's true. But I *have* tried to carve out my own reputation. It's almost a no-win situation. So here I am again."

I'm not even sure if Lion's still talking to me or himself.

He steers from the rural highway onto a tiny road that shoots past more emerald, swaying grass to one of the restaurants sitting the distance of a football field off the main road. The smell of cooking seafood greets us along an embankment that empties into the Atlantic. The clapboard house has been transformed to an eatery.

This time, when he exits the driver's side of the car, he stares at me through the windshield and moves slowly around the car to test me. Laughingly, I watch him watching me to see if I'll go for the door handle.

How long has it been since my shoulders shook from

laughing and I was comfortable enough with a man to just be... *goofy?*

"Good girl." He swings his weird ass sports car door up, and stuns me when he scoops me out.

Literally being swept off my feet is a big leap from one-night stands in bars, and will take some getting used to. Entering a restaurant, our fingers flirt cavalierly, and the summer humidity preps my body for the hotter festivities to come.

Inside, we walk underneath beer bottles that hang from ceilings, past distressed wooden tables, chairs, and a bar area, and admire chipped, faded paint that gives it a humble, distinctive fisherman's character. Families laugh and kick back with seemingly no worries, and it really is summertime in their tousled, unbothered hair, attire, and tempo. Yet again, it reminds me of the slow pace of country Louisiana, but with wealthy white people.

After he introduces me to his friend who owns the place, we grab lobster rolls, and I turn back for the car. But the grip of Lion's hand stops me. He guides me in the opposite direction, to an exit out of a narrow backdoor of the restaurant where people dine on a wooden patio. Beyond that is a small wharf you would miss if you blinked. It's kind of like a parking lot for boats. Lion heads to the end, where a work of art awaits him.

My eyes meet a masterpiece. Graceful from the bow to the stern, even the low-hanging sun that gleams along the hull and flares off the cleats, seems to worship it.

"What are we... this is yours?"

"Don't tell anybody," he cracks.

I don't realize he's giving me the food to hold, so he can undock. Then, he boards and extends his hand to me. Hoisted into the air, it feels like I'm being transferred to different dimension.

I've been on boats with my brothers and family, not that often. With just him and me on the open water, all this peace surrounding us instead of my raucous family, this excursion is altogether different. Inside is beautiful wood grain and tan leather outfitting a surprisingly spacious cabin.

"What kind of boat is this?"

"An express cruiser. One of the smaller sport boats that goes fast and lets me sleep overnight when I want to. We can eat up here in the cockpit." He's already leading the way.

Beyond the beautiful wood-grain steering wheel, the sun fades ahead of us on land, preparing to disappear in about an hour minutes. He moves to the control panel.

"You ever driven a boat before?"

"No, never been interested."

He nods toward the key in the ignition, so I start it up, and follow his directions.

"It's easy. Just like riding a bike." Lion stands behind me, his chest at my back, as it was the night he walked me home. He hits the gear and his voice murmurs the instructions in my ear.

Of course, I hit the wrong gear, and the boat jerks forward. He immediately jumps to shift it properly.

"Oh, shit!" I cry.

"Next time, take us *away* from the land. Not out to the streets of Montauk," he jokes.

My horror at what almost happened tickles me, and him, but he slides a hand around my waist and pins me to the steering wheel. We sail away from civilization, with me between his arms.

"Take over," he murmurs, his mouth in my hair.

"What if I crash us?"

"I'll make sure you don't crash." His chest rises at my back. "Ever."

Again, just as the night he walked me home, and we might

have bonded for the first time, he whispers that last word so low I almost lost it to the wind. But the hopefulness inside me catches it.

He pops open one of Desmond's brews and passes it to me, lets me have the first sip.

"Desmond's got a knack for these brews." The beer taste is rich, not bitter, and has a fruit-tinged aftertaste.

I pass it behind me to Lion who sips it loudly, drinking and sucking the excess from his lips.

"Pretty damn good actually. He found his calling after football. He's onto something with this stuff. We just have to help him get it out the door and on shelves in a few weeks."

"Tough, but not impossible."

His hands next to mine, I steer the boat, trying to stay as careful as I can.

"I'm letting Karate Kam Rouse steer my favorite boat, so no, nothing is impossible."

I can't describe these next few minutes that we depart the world, with Lion at my back and the horizon in front of us. Evening colors spread across the sky and stretch down to the ocean's surface. There is nothing blocking us from that amazing slice of heaven. The moment he leaves my side to grab the food, the air turns cooler.

Unwrapping our lobster rolls, he hands mine to me. "I know you're from Louisiana and that's the mecca of seafood and all, but you are going to lose your mind when you taste this. This boy's skills are nothing to sleep on. You want a plate, or are you good?"

"I'm good. And *this* had better be good, too." I'm hungry and ready to dive in.

My hand brushing his, I take the box he hands over with so much giddiness. This man watches me bite into the soft white bread, tear into seasoned lobster meat, and chuck it into my mouth.

Butter, garlic, peppers, parsley, and other spices I can't immediately recognize, all come together for a concert on my tongue. In my fervor, I snort it and choke. Amused, he holds out water for me to wash it down.

"You might have a little taste in food." It's damn excellent and disappears faster than I'd like. "You're taking me there again."

"Maybe," he replies, already finished with his. "That's the side of the Hamptons people don't know about."

Kicking back, he reclines in his seat, props his leather loafer on the cockpit, sips beer, and relaxes. "What about you, Ms. Kamilah?"

"What about me?" I tuck my feet under me.

"What made you follow me down to the fermentation part of Slurp that first night?" The way he eyes me, that question doesn't feel casual.

Shit.

Duncan.

Does he know?

We're out here in the middle of nowhere, and I'm trapped. He knows.

I should come clean, just explain what I felt when Duncan and Tanja crossed my path for the first time in fifteen years. All the betrayal and humiliation that swelled me up until I almost couldn't see straight, the way Tanja hovered at his side possessively, victoriously. That pathetic apology on Duncan's face before he turned to address his adoring supporters.

The entire episode burdens me until my gaze falls in shame for what I expressly went down to the brewery basement to do.

Lion reaches over and strokes my neck. "It's okay, French Fry. Whatever man put that sadness in your eyes, I'm sure that punk didn't deserve you anyway. So you had a broken heart and you needed to work that shit out. I've been there. Not with a romantic interest per se, but I've had my heart busted."

I shudder and find the strength to meet his eyes. Care and concern are all that gaze back at me. Coming toward my trifling ass, he lays claim to my mouth again.

The tides of our tongues join these waves, rolling and splashing and twisting. For the first time in quite a few trips around the sun, this grown woman who had to push forward in life, forget a hurt heart and shove her feelings aside, now feels.

This man who seems to be wrestling his own shit triggers more than a superficial attraction in me, opens up my locked doors. I suck his tongue, curl mine around his. Nibbling and tasting and inhaling each other, already alone physically, we lose ourselves mentally.

Lion's hand massages my titty and cajoles an urge in my womanhood that whines in my throat. My eyes closed, my whole body savors how he expertly kneads the stress from my flesh. Up and around, against his soaking taste buds slipping and sliding on my nipple, as naturally as if he were born to sup there.

I had forgotten. In all my quick ten-minute trysts I've been having, just to avoid men getting too close… I forgot.

My breaths come in desperate gulps but still don't relieve my lungs.

Wetness drizzles over my skin, shocking me.

My eyelids snap open. Jaw drops.

Beer runs off me from an open can as Lion pours it. The bodice of my dress is down. I was so mesmerized I didn't realize my titties hang exposed to him.

With a hunger on his face, he leans to my nipple, opens his mouth, and drinks beer that slides off my titty. He's still pouring, and his tongue stretches out and laps up the stream of beer running off my tip. Wet and weak from watching him, I can hardly move. But when I touch his dick, the size is a whole other boat to cruise on.

Soaking me, drinking beer off my titties, he laps and drinks on me until I can hardly see him through my hooded eyes and blurred vision. I've never just let a man do what he wants with me.

"Lion..." I murmur.

Leaving my bodice down, he stands me up, but he remains seated and spins me around. Faces me toward the endless horizon.

"Yes?"

Before I can speak again, he massages my ass through my dress. *Oh God.*

"Mmph."

I just squirted again.

The pressure of those large, muscular hands cups the meat on my cheeks the way he palmed that football the second time we saw each other. While he's squeezing, pressing, pulling, and rolling, my breasts lunge forward every time his thumbs rub devilishly close to my pussy. Once I'm good and tender, he eases up my dress.

Through the corner of my eyes, I watch a new can of beer disappear.

His hand rubs my ass. The lips of my womanhood clap, and the juices of my lust trickle out of me.

My entire adult existence anticipates his tongue. He pushes me forward. Directs my hips until my pelvis faces down, puts the arch in my back. My ass poking out toward him, The Lion slides down my thong.

I jump at the touch of a wet cloth. He's wiping my lips and opening, and finally, my ass. With each touch, his hands journey over me like he's rubbing his treasure.

Behind me, the lid pops off a fresh can of beer.

My titties jump, as does my breath, at liquid that streams along the small valley in my back. Beer fizzes up on the way down my ass crack, sliding until it circles my opening and streams to my clit. Hell, I'm practically intoxicated from the expectation, so much so that I can hear the spit in Lion's mouth when he opens it.

He must know I'm on edge because he's dragging this out.

"I like how your pussy wiggles while it waits for me."

"Nigga…" In my angst, my class loses out to my ratchet for one moment, and he thinks it's funny.

Finally, he relieves me. Easing my leg open, he drinks beer off my pussy, and starts pouring into the glass of my need. His tongue gently laps at my clit, the hairs of his beard scraping my inner thighs.

His hands around my stomach, Lion draws my ass to his face. Lays his entire tongue on my folds and drags it up, pressing repeatedly, slurping the foam.

"Ah!" I buck at the pleasure rippling deep into my core.

He doesn't stop at my womanhood but continues to my trunk, pushes in with his tongue.

I'm not used to this. The times I've gotten buck with a dude, I'm normally strong. This is different. I'm feeling. And crumbling.

"Kam," Lion warns.

He stands. So fucking focused. He takes my hands that I'm swatting at him with and plants them on the dash.

"I've been fantasizing about making you a meal since I first laid eyes on you. Now, you always play like you're real tough, French Fry." He leans against my ear. "Do you think I'm going to hurt you?"

The scent of my essence emanates from his mouth.

His beard brushes my face, and I stare at him staring at me. "No, Negro, I just… nobody ever…"

"Good. So put your big-girl panties on." He tightens my

fingers on the dash. "And keep these here."

His one hand on my ass, his other cupping my breast, those palms scrape over me, to their original position. He returns the arch to my back and resumes pouring beer down my crack, and into my soul. The thrust of his soft tongue follows the stream.

I shiver at the feel of his moist organ cleaning my asshole, whiskers of his beard scratching my skin. So I'm enduring pleasure juxtaposed with light torture. His face in my ass, he teases my clit, and my naked titties bounce up and down, kissing the glorious sunset.

His fingers massage my womanly lips, slather my juices mixed with beer on my nub. Lion sloppily feasts on the stern of *my* cruiser. Up and down, he wipes his face with me.

Squirming and curling my toes to escape, I can't. Animal in how his mouth pursues me, Lion does not let up. My legs out and ass cheeks up while he tongue-fucks the daylights back into my dark womanhood, I can only grip the woodgrain dashboard for dear life.

"Lion!"

These ocean waves rock in my womb, splashing and tossing, to and fro. My inner walls contract as I touch the colors of the sky, literally and figuratively.

Face plastered to the dashboard now, I buck through the hurricane of his tongue and appetite. The torment strikes through me, down to my toes. Behind me, his mouth sucks, and he drinks and swallows my juices while I squirm through a savage orgasm that cracks toward my brain.

The sun sets on me like it signals my transformation, the sky metamorphosing from orange to lavender and then purple in what might be a toast.

Seconds later, I still tremble from the aftershocks, both mentally and emotionally. It's been a long time since I've allowed a man into my head.

He slowly wipes me off. Kissing my thighs and butt, he rubs and worships me as he does so. Then Lion brings me onto his lap, where he tugs my bra and dress bodice back up, slipping the straps over my arms again. I can't even recall how they came down.

I'm swept into his arms and carried down to the small cabin, laid in his bed. How in the hell am I so weak I can barely move? Why is he placing a blanket over me?

"Night-night, French Fry," he whispers.

When I open my eyes again, it's dark. In a strange place, I practically jump from my skin.

The silhouettes don't resemble my condo, and a big body lies at my side. The smell of saltwater and the motions of floatation remind me of where I am. My movement awakens him.

His hand on my hip, Lion massages me. "You straight?"

If I'm honest? I should have told him. I still should.

"No."

I feel my way to his beard, and his silhouette faces me in the dark. Quickening breaths from his nostrils tell me my touch in his scruffy whiskers stimulates him.

He grabs me and squeezes me to him, and I discover he's not wearing a shirt now. My fingertips are tickled by the forest of intermittent hairs on his chest, until he lifts my wrist and tastes the inside of it. The man is so fucking sensual.

I can't recall the last time I lay in bed with somebody else, his arm around me, warming me, cherishing me. Like he senses how I'm lacking, Lion grips my head, draws me to him.

Our sloppy tongues and spit and heavy breaths are all the needful energy I've avoided. The moments are long in which he clings to my ass, and I claw his pecs, and he bites my jaw. His feverish way he grips me is energy I return to his ass cheeks, holding on to his taut muscles like I've wanted this for sixteen years.

He's changed into sweat shorts. And his full-sized dick insists that I open up and let him in. Lion's precum smears my stomach.

His fingers slip between my legs that I open wider for him. A little gasp floats out of him at the feel of my slickness, and he twirls his fingers in my folds. "You're ready."

Since the night I first met him.

Since I first laid eyes on him and I knew if we hit, I'd never be the same. Time is up for how I keep resisting it.

"I've wanted to do this to you again since the first time."

"What?" I whisper.

Sliding down in the bed, he caresses my feet. In the dark, my toes turn wet. One by one, he sticks them in his mouth and sucks. "You got a lot of nerve walking around with an attitude and these damn pretty-ass toes."

I bust out laughing, my fingers in his hair. It's no longer gelled into place, and his long, carefree strands atop his crown fall into my fingers. He nibbles and kisses his way up my calves, the backs of my knees. Along my inner thighs, he sucks and nips, until his beard is back at my womanhood again.

His appetite feeds me, too, and nourishes me so I'm alive again.

I can't tell him.

I know my silence is wrong. But I don't want Lion seeing me as I've seen myself—as a woman Duncan already pissed on to mark his territory.

When I came down the stairs yesterday and Lion was waiting with flowers, when he greeted me today at the brewery, when his eyes consume me, he's only seeing me. For the first time since I can remember, Duncan is finally *not* here.

THE WHISPER OF HER TRUTHS

LION & KAMILAH

LION

In her hesitation, the occasional aversion of her eyes, there's something she's holding onto, but at the same time, she needs this release.

I don't press for why she followed me, a man she supposedly didn't know, into the basement the first time we met. I don't ask why she pursued the bartender, whom she didn't know, as we all stood at the bar. I'm too selfish, too wrapped up in what she can't hide:

The way her loose, floral dress whipped around her thighs, her hair blew in my face, and she nearly wrecked the boat but tried to sail it anyway. The way she starts to laugh before remembering to play it off, how she fights to be tough, but at times, displays slivers of her vulnerability.

In the dark now, I barely see her silhouette, but her body whispers her truths to me. The involuntary wheezing in her throat tells me she especially enjoys when my tongue goes easy, not hard.

With every tremor through her pussy lips, Kam's brick fortress crumbles.

All that fierce facade yields under the pressure of my tongue sliding in her pink meat, slurping every drop of her cream.

She can't stop the spontaneous contractions of her ass against my mouth that not even she's aware of, but I am.

Her toes tense up and pussy twitches, only provoking me to nibble more, to lift her leg in the air, spread it out until her clit pushes out of its hiding place and glides right to me. And my tongue sings to the center of her soul.

Kamilah forgets herself, and she bucks on my face like I'm her new rocking horse. She squirms with me attached to her inner thighs licking the depths of her, until whatever troubles she carries convulse on me.

Out pours her spirit. She leaps from the bed, squirts, gasps, and sucks in damn near all the air in the cabin. Karate Kam falls like a rag doll. Rising onto my knees, I move over her. Even in the dark, the whites in Kamilah's eyes stare back at me. Her silhouette reaches for me, and I kiss her hands.

Then I enter all of her fierce womanhood.

Our sexual ocean sucks us under as we connect and meld together. Deep, intertwined breaths. Her muscles melt around my shaft, allowing me in. Finally, she relaxes and trusts me. Her moist layers hug my erection and stoke deeper parts of me than lust. Kamilah's legs strap around me, her exhilaration hanging from her open mouth while I penetrate her womanhood.

I thrust, and she throws it back. Raising her legs over my shoulders, I pull one of her feet to my mouth and suck her toes again because there's no part of Kamilah I don't want to taste and discover. The tension in her thighs eases and she lets go. In another peek of her personality, her nails pull me into her by my ass, and I push past the apex of her.

Leaning my head into the pillow, I leverage my weight and maneuver my hands under her butt cheeks to open her up more. In the deepest parts of her ocean floor, Kam's pussy squeezes and compresses around me. Soft, throaty moans of pleasure fill my ear, rock up my dick, fertilize my heart.

I plunge harder, deeper. Pull out. Savor her tiny, stubborn gasp. Twirl my wood just at her opening. Feed her a little of this dick.

"I know you're not mine. But when you walk around in tight skirts, I don't like other dudes looking at you. I have to leave and go to Taste so I don't beat the hell out of 'em."

Jerking my meat up and down, I tease her opening.

Kam's womanhood gushes on my shaft. The sound of her throat swallowing with anticipation for me to put it back in, tempts me to keep teasing her. I slip in only the tip, circle my dick barely inside her opening.

"Lion..."

Just a bit deeper.

The thrill sends her breasts upward, against my chest. Her canal welcomes me back in. Cream all over my shaft is my gift, and I taste her jaw again. Legs falling open wider, she's indeed releasing, and her walls grab for more of me. Her breaths, deep, exaggerated, her moist pussy trembles around my dick.

"When you left with that bartender, I wasn't having it. You weren't going in his house with him."

She tries to protest, and it comes out as a whine. "Lion, I'm a grown-ass—"

"You weren't laying with him."

Her pussy answers me when it contracts. Kamilah likes it —me being possessive over her. I whirl my hips against hers. Hold up one of her feet.

While I lick inside her ear, my wood pushes past her

stomach. Her back arches, and she clings to mine. I thrust up, and her moans come out.

"You wanted me in you as much as I wanted to be in you. You deny it?"

Kam's soaking wet walls contract and grip me.

Since she's silent, I pull out.

She shudders from her empty canal. "Asshole."

My erection hovers at her entrance.

She will not treat me as just another dick for her whims. Her haughty, bossy ass *will* yield.

"Princess…" I dip in, thrust the tip of my dick against her G-spot. "With your feisty ass."

She whimpers.

I drag it out. Linger at the edge of her. My mouth against her mouth, my dick strokes her entrance, my fingers rub her essence over her female lips. She turns to my ear in the dark, claws me to her.

"Yes."

"Yes, what?" I clarify.

"Yes… I slapped you because I wanted to fuck the cocky right out of you," Kam finally admits between jagged breaths.

I reenter her sweetness, and the glorious sensations intoxicate us both. So deep my manhood practically twists and knocks her bones, I burrow past every resistant barrier she tries to throw at me. I sweep her hair from her face so I can see the silhouette of her giving in.

"Fuck it out of me now, precious."

The folds of her womb overheat the nerves along my dick. Above her head, I pin her arms and our hands intertwine. With my dick sailing in Kam, any other thought I have sinks away, until nothing remains but her.

Mentally, sexually, we glide over the same ocean, the loving so immense her back arcs up and her ass muscles clench me. Kam abandons herself.

The tides roll through her and crack across me.

The scream she lets out…

Kamilah's slender body is an explosive, and she clings to me with her whole being. I pick her up and give her as much of me as her frame can handle. Like I fantasized since the first time, I unleash all I have into her.

Grunting and moaning and rocking, we're a thunderstorm. Kam is satiated and her pussy drenches me. Shit, with her firm, wiry legs strapped onto my shoulders, the ferocity of her womanhood sucks the cum from me until I'm not sure I have anything left.

KAMILAH

"I have a meeting this morning. We overslept. Shit." I wake up panicking. "Where are my p—" I rise to stare at him.

Mischief all over his face, Lion looks like he swallowed a canary. "You know the rules. You're not getting them back. Why are you so worked up?"

Pantyless, still feeling the soreness between my thighs of the best sex I've ever had, I limp to search for my other lace-up espadrille. "Why are you so calm? We're *late*." Picking up his shirt and shorts, I continue my hunt. "I don't normally…"

Stay the night.

My hands shake. My insides shake, in a way that has nothing to do with some meeting. To preoccupy myself from fright, I keep digging for clothes while I try to make sense of what I've done. Thoughts race in my head of how this might get out of my control. How do I regain the upper hand? I'm vulnerable now. And weak.

Again.

No.

I'm bent over when he comes up behind me and bumps my butt. To either side of me are those bare, muscular calves. I rise and turn. He's dangling my other shoe.

In front of his very naked chest that cascades down to his naked torso.

At the sight of his dick, I avert my eyes. As if I wasn't just bobbing on it like I was hanging from the monkey bars at the playground. A giggle comes from... *where* does that keep coming from? Since when am I some shriveling pansy?

"What's the matter, French Fry?" he murmurs on my forehead after one of his sensual kisses.

"Nothing." I move around him, because...

Rushing up the steps, I head back to the deck. The morning sun hits my face, and it takes a moment to see that the boat is docked at the restaurant where we took off yesterday. Only the dock is mostly empty now, and his yellow Ferrari sits alone in the otherwise empty car lot on the other side of the property.

I whip around to him. "Why aren't you getting dressed? I have to go and I don't have a way to town."

Lion holds up his keys. "I have some things to take care of first. So take my car."

"Which... which one?"

He grins. Points to his car sitting in the parking lot. "That one. The only one that's out there."

Of course, you knew that. Why are you asking fool-ass questions?

"Then how will you get home?"

"I'll take the boat over to my house and pick up another car. Or bum a ride. And I'll just pick up mine from you later." He says this like it's literally nothing, jerking on a shirt and shorts as he talks.

Before I can think of another stupid question to fill the time and divert attention from the real reason I'm so rattled, he reaches for me.

"I need to change clothes, and I don't have time to stop at the house and... change clothes." My mind keeps racing... with reasons and thoughts and excuses.

Lion folds me into him. "Use my credit card. There are boutiques not far from Slurp. Just pop in and grab whatever you want."

His magnetizing presence, the pressure of his hands on my hips, his leather and cigar scent, the ocean waves tossing against the boat that makes it bob under my feet, all put me on unsteady territory.

"When our co-workers see me drive your car into town, they're going to talk, and know our business, and then..."

"So?" He speaks calmly, his voice unbothered. "You're a professional woman who's damn good at her job, and that's all they need to worry about. Besides, after I claimed you yesterday—in front of everybody, your family, and mine—I think we're a little too late for that." He talks against my forehead. "Why are you so nervous?" His fingers scrape up my neck and along my scalp.

Because fifteen years ago, I was humiliated. The girl who had three brothers and was too smart to be played, got played. After three years of college bullshit, I fell for a young law school student with a smooth tongue during a summer internship. And was stupid enough to think I was the only one. The worst part wasn't the actual betrayal but constantly questioning my intelligence.

Last night, I took off the armor. I opened my legs too wide, let him in too far, slept in his arms, let go and got lost. For Christ's sake, I even admitted I wanted to fuck him at first slap.

Tell him.

Taking my hand in his, Lion lifts our intertwined fingers until they're tilting up my chin so I face him. He kisses my hand.

"It's okay for you to just say you like me."

We both crack up.

"I don't know what I'm doing either. But it feels good. So, step one. Can we agree to just savor this and enjoy our day?" he asks.

I nod. "Yeah." A small part of me relaxes. Small.

Tell him.

The tenderness in Lion's eyes…

He guides me to the exit, hands me his keys, and takes out a credit card.

I accept the keys for the ride but wave off his wallet. "Oh, I don't need that. I've got my purse and I'm fine."

He gently holds my hip the way he tends to do. "I didn't ask if you were fine." Jerks me closer, shoves the card inside my bra. "Based on where you kept your cash when we first met, I'm guessing this is where your valuables belong. I don't know why you carry a purse."

Yet again, our stomachs shake with kee-keeing. He steps off and reaches to swing me from the boat onto the dock, as if I weigh nothing.

Grasshoppers, crickets, and frogs serenade us from the marsh on our walk to his car. What do I say now? I can't stomp away from him with an attitude or dismiss him when I've already let him in.

He lifts the car door, talks me through a few basics, helps me drop into the deep bucket seat. Leaning against the door-frame, he stares down at me with humor. "The road is that way. It works like every other street."

With a smirk, I throw him my side-eye. "Right."

Lion takes my lips for one more trip on his that expertly bid me goodbye. "See you later."

With my heart and head and lungs and toes and abdomen doing all the nervous-girl things, I nod. "Yes, later."

"Please don't wreck my shit."

"Your insurance papers are over here, right?" I joke.

He laughs with me, and after one last look, he brings down the door. In this cushioned, tight space so low to the ground, he may as well be snapping me into a vault.

In town, I stop by Taste before heading to the brewery in Montauk. For a moment, I grapple with his GPS system. Then, there's the embarrassment of actually having to exit his spaceship of a car. Soon as I let up these ridiculous rising doors, clapping heels come toward me on the pavement.

"Oh! Hey, Lion, good *morning*, it's been a while since I've seen you. I—" a female voice starts before she peers down to discover me. "Oh."

"Good morning, Olga," I respond.

She clears her throat, apparently stunned that I'm not him. "Ms. Rouse. Morning. I… how… nice. I wasn't expecting you."

"I'm sure you weren't. As it turns out, Mr. Middleton is indisposed. Something I can help you with?" I ask while climbing out of his time machine.

"Just…" She swallows and thinks but can't conjure up a lie fast enough. What could the hostess possibly need to discuss with the supply chain guy? Dejected, she seems about to cry at the sight of me in his car. "No."

"Enjoy your day then," I tell her.

"Certainly." With a sharp pivot, she damn near flees.

A part of me heats up in a way I wasn't ready for. When did *that* go down? Saturday night? On Sunday? Right after he ate with my family? Did he give it to her raw, the way he did me?

Then there's the awkwardness of swiping somebody's card besides mine or my family members'. Finally, I enter

Taste to check in with Miracle, go over their schedules and today's projections, and I then head to the brewery.

I'm preparing to meet with Laney and potential concert sponsors who've flown in to tour Slurp, when a harried Desmond intercepts me.

"Hey, you're already on top of it?" he asks, his normal affable greeting now flat.

"On top of what?"

"The new shipment of barley we're supposed to get—it's not coming." Sweat pooling at his armpits and beading across his forehead, he's breathless. "We've tried reaching our distributors, and they say we haven't paid. I thought we had worked this out and we had paid them." In a panic, he huffs in a nervous frenzy. "With Lion's direction, we thought we had enough to commit to shipments of beer across the country, to Atlanta, D.C., and Chicago. They're our commemorative cans for the Sasha concert. If we can't have those ready and these shipments don't go out..."

"Okay." I walk with him. "We'll handle it."

Now Laney comes and joins us. "I'm about to head to Taste and help Miracle. Apparently, Aragon is giving us an issue there also. The supply of chocolate for quarter four needs to be resolved."

"How is all this happening at the same time?" Desmond asks. "It's Lion. He negotiated the inventory for Explore a couple weeks ago. So what gives?"

"Let's just be a little patient and handle our meetings, continue production as planned. I think Lion will be around later. I'm sure he has a credible answer." I squeeze the arm of an upset Desmond.

It's not lost on me that he's an expectant father who's taking a real risk on Slurp with his money and future, and he's got everything to lose. The same exhaustion and panic I saw on my brother, Jerrell, when he first started out, is now apparent on this man.

"I mean," Des continues, "we trusted Lion not to screw this up. Kevin suggested his brother. Solomon had questions about it. Kee had some doubts. My *wife* told me not to bring him in, and I even went around her. She said the Middletons railroad people in business and that sounded shady as hell..." He rambles on our way to meet a set of potential sponsors.

As much as I want to give Lion his time, I pull out my phone to text him.

Me to Lion: ***We have an inventory situation.***

I await a response, but nothing.

Now I don't just fret for one reason but two. I still have a job to do here that requires me keeping a clear head. And not only have I opened myself up with Lion Middleton, a reputed playboy, but I slept with a colleague. Workplace sex complicates things, which is why I've only ever done it once.

The potential sponsors meet with Desmond and me, but while he leads, I'm hardly paying attention. I scroll through my tablet for the distributors Lion used and their contacts. I'll start calling them myself if I have to. But this is not my field of expertise.

I pick up my phone again, still no response.

Even while I'm sitting on the edge of several seats, it's hard to shake off flashbacks of him sucking my toes in the dark. Pouring beer and drinking it off parts of me I can't see. I've done some weird things, but never that.

Does he think my submission in bed means he can slack off at work?

And to think, I drove here *in his car*... for all the other employees to witness. For Olga to see.

My palm smacks my forehead.

Now she'll probably attempt some silly competition between her and me. Every exchange going forward will be awkward. Especially if she throws herself at him or flirts in front of me.

Goodness, I was stupid.

This is why I don't date. Anxiety over literally every little incident is not a headache I've missed.

THE WRONG WIFE

LION

"We need more details from you. We haven't heard anything on MoneyCruncher yet, Lion," Ron says to me through a video conference.

When I left Kamilah, I had several messages waiting for me, including from a Duncan who sounded worked up and irritated in his voicemail.

Before I started this call, I made sure my mom was somewhere planning a charity event, Dad was watching baseball, and that my brothers were gone.

Yet still, I maintain a low tone. "It's taking some time. Selling his flagship company is not a move I can sweep in and convince him to do overnight. But in case you haven't checked the media lately, the tides are turning. I'm making a little headway."

Ron nods. "Have you even talked to him about it and raised the prospect?"

"That's not how we operate."

"You've been there for two weeks."

"I'm telling you I've needed those two weeks. We haven't been around each other much the past few years since he's built MoneyCruncher. So it wouldn't make sense to just bust in and tell him to hand over his baby on a silver platter. Come on, Ron. You really can't give me time?"

I'm staring at him on the computer screen, but I'm thinking beyond this conversation, down the pipe, over the last few years. At the lengthy history of Houston PetroChem sending me to some of the worst drilling locations at offshore sites in places as far away as Angola, Denmark, and the Arabian Gulf.

In locales with the worst reputations for safety precautions and numerous injuries, oil workers who were poor, sick, or who had some other weakness complained about injuries. I paid them off.

I was the Black man who the company viewed as "relating more" to the working people. It's where I sharpened my skills for wheeling and dealing. Young and ambitious, with a keen understanding of people's wants and needs, I used my humor and affability to cultivate relationships with pipe layers, pipe fitters, and pipeline walkers—the deadliest jobs. Then, I shelled out under-the-table cash in exchange for their silence when they became hurt or sick. Houston PetroChem always sent me to do its dirty work, and I went.

All for prestige, influence, and my name to be atop the masthead.

Now my mother walks through the patio door.

"So, keep me updated on how things are going. I have family here that I need to check in on. I'm glad you all reached out to me this morning, and I hope I was able to help," I say to Ron and Gavin, subtly informing them I can no longer talk.

Ron figures it out. "Sure, Lion, we're glad you could help us, uh, sort some of this out. Most likely, we'll be in touch with you again, so you can give us more guidance."

"Are you talking to your job while on vacation?" Mom asks with a loaded side-eye.

"They're just keeping me in the loop about some of my projects while I'm out, running some issues by me that came up."

Burning her skeptical stare into me, she nods. "We haven't spent much time together since you've been home. You're so involved with Explore. And you didn't come home last night."

"Yeah, and I need to head over there now." I collect my laptop and start to get up.

But her hand shoots out to stop me from running. "Lion." She pauses for a beat, an indication of what's coming.

"Mom, I don't—"

"I got closer to Kevin, not because I love you less, but because Lionel had more of an influence on you. And I knew Kevin would need protection because of the circumstances."

My throat closes up. The chambers surrounding my heart instantly slam and lock. "I don't want to hear this." I can't stand to be reminded.

"But you need to." She places her other hand on my shoulder, and those beautiful chartreuse eyes jab straight into me. "If it stops you from going after him."

Like I noted before, she knows me so damn well that she's my best friend of sorts, because who else knows me better.

Through her fingers on my arms, she applies the pressure of her concern.

"I know you and Lionel want Kevin to sell, so his cash becomes liquid for Lionel's beachfront resort he's always dreamed about in Florida. He wants to own it with all of you, for future generations, the passing of property, just as the Middletons have done in the past. Lionel doesn't want it with anybody else, only his sons."

My mother's clarity reflects what I've slowly come to realize over the years.

"Son, that's Lionel's dream. And I know you're pursuing it for your father. Stop letting your daddy chase his dreams through you. He was wrong. Just admit it."

Her face is an earthquake as it trembles.

"All right, Mom, fine. You really want to have this conversation?" I ask, feeling her upset and hurt now well up in me. "Dad's not perfect, but he *tries.* Meanwhile, you found your comfort somewhere else. Your children were not enough. When did you go out with Francis? Hm? Where did you find the time? When I was at a ball game? At school? When I was six and seven, playing football and checking the stands for you, because you hadn't arrived yet? And I thought you were at some real estate showing? When you were at one of your real estate conferences? And you couldn't come be with the Boy Scouts?"

A red cloud spreads across those riveting eyes. "That's not fair! I was there for you all the time. Always did pick-up and traded with other parents to ensure you had transportation. Or it was your sitter. *I'm* the one who chaperoned your school trips or organized them, cooked or arranged meals, kept the house going, and all your activities. *Not* Lionel! So why does he get all your affection and admiration?"

I think about how I simply expected her to be there every time I looked over my shoulder, that Dad was supposed to be out conquering the world and Mom was supposed to be home...being my mom.

The demand rips from me. "Who were you thinking about when your eyes zoned out over dinner? Or when you were whispering and giggling on the phone? Or during my conversations with you and you weren't fully paying attention? Were you juggling us and work? Or were you juggling us and *him*? You and Dad were busy with work. That's what I thought."

Her face is stunned and wide-eyed. "And most of the time I was, Lion! But I needed a piece of *me*. I needed to remember the woman who enjoyed music, dancing, nightlife, plays, skinny-dipping! Foods I actually like—Indian, Peruvian, Mediterranean."

I'm not about to listen to some shit I don't need to know, and try to move around her.

But she's insistent and keeps jumping in my face. "I found out your daddy was cheating when I was pregnant with Brendan, and I felt very alone, with nobody to talk to because most of the people around us are secretly happy if we fall. They secretly want our misery. And I got tired of crying to my mother and sister. I wanted some freedom for myself, to not feel like I was trapped."

She swipes away at tears. Spreads her flawless hands and shakes out her frustration through them. "I was *stuck*. I had given up my life. I thought I was getting a fairy tale. Lionel thought he was getting a housekeeper."

The memories stream from her eyes and down her face. Snot creeps from her nose. The chartreuse jewels staring back at me are strong, unapologetic, unyielding, but they reach out to me while she still stands her ground.

I suppose I've never wanted to talk about it because I wasn't ready for this. I longed for her to be remorseful and sorry that she was not all I expect her to be: a dutiful mother who is one hundred percent perfection, and who only exists for her family. Because *that's* what the hell mothers are.

"Why can't you understand I'm just as human as anybody else on the planet? I still tried my damnedest to be there for you, but you punish me for it, Lion."

Our family was hobbling along fine. All these years, we've

had an uneasy peace we weren't aware of, but it was peace. Then came the death of Francis Manuel, Adella being appointed his administrator, the lawsuit she filed against us. A few months later, the Harvard leak. The press, the hard spotlight on Dad. All of it picked the scabs off old-ass wounds.

We could no longer keep up the pretense. With the constant reminders, everywhere I went came fresh resentments. Maddy, Chrissy, and Adella threw the closet door open, and out came our skeletons, at least in our house.

"When Francis Manuel died a couple years ago, I was happy," I murmur to her. "I thought it was over. And you were finally ours."

"I was always yours, carrying my ball and chain. Even if I took a little space to escape for myself, I was still yours. I'm still here."

"You may as well have left."

My words throw salt in her eyes.

"Trust me, I certainly wanted to in those early years. I only stayed for you and Brendan. I knew you loved Lionel and you would never come with me if I left. And I would never leave you. But now that you boys are gone..." Mom wrings her hands. "I don't know. I guess a part of me still hopes..."

"Did you love Dad?"

"Yes. With everything in me. Still do. It's why I was so hu—" The rest of that word chokes her.

"So what was it about, Mom? You fulfilling yourself or getting revenge on Dad?"

My eyes don't veer anywhere else, so I'll know I'm hearing the truth.

"Both. I started up with Francis because I wanted my power back. I thought I could hurt Lionel the way he was hurting me, and I'd hoped maybe I would even get him to stop. That he might change. I was devastated when he did not. So I *wanted* Lionel to know I was cheating. I told him."

I think back to Ash, her despair when she came to find me on my lunch break on my job. The memory flashes behind my eyes, of her finding me at a hotel when I'd lied and said I would be at a basketball game. The wreckage on Ashlyn's face is apparent in my mother's eyes now. I'm a fool if I don't learn from seeing the same dynamic on more than one person.

In my mind, I expected the same from Ash that Dad expected from Mom—that I would go do whatever I wanted, and she would be waiting for me until I grew out of my selfish phase. The plains of Texas weren't big enough for me to run when Ash demanded more. She served me with divorce papers, because I believed she wouldn't go anywhere.

"Since he didn't stop, you brought Kevin home."

Those words quake across me, though she's the one who lived it.

"I thought Lionel would kill me. I expected him to hit me. But I've never seen him so weak. He couldn't even raise his body, let alone his hand. I feared he was having a heart attack. But your daddy managed to get up and walked right out the door. I didn't see him again for weeks."

Shuddering, she scrubs her legs over and over.

"I had no idea what we would become. I was shocked when he came back. We made an agreement that lasted a few years, and that's between us. Instead of being happier, we were empty. Even when he was faithful, I still didn't have the man I loved and wanted. I was young and foolish."

She has disappeared someplace else and strums her mouth with her fingers.

"I couldn't change Lionel any more than he could force me into the submissive wife he wanted."

A disturbing laugh rises from her throat as she seems to recall it all to herself now.

"But he wanted another son, another heir to carry the Middleton name. That man loves Middleton so much he would tolerate my unfaithfulness if it meant building his dynasty. That's how I… I finally understood he truly loved Middleton more than me."

No longer able to stomach her this way, I walk away.

Behind me, she breaks down.

That breaks me down.

I grab a tissue and come back to her, surprising her. Squatting before her on my haunches, I take the tissue to her face and wipe away the strain of years.

I can't bear to see either of my parents in pain. But I am simply clueless on what to do with hers.

"I love you, son." Her hands shake around my hand that wipes her face. "So much."

The trembling in her voice is a lot to bear. A lot of reality I can't possibly understand but which digs into my stubbornness.

Her and Ashlyn.

And now, Kamilah.

"You're still the prettiest girl in the world." It's what I used to say to her all the time as a kid, before I overheard Dad. "And I love you, too, Mama."

Shit, I'm forty but I'm learning.

Mom's arms are far stronger than they look, squeezing me tight. "Thank you, baby."

It always takes a while for what she's saying to sink in. I'll definitely need time to wrap my head around this other version of her, where she is an actual person, beyond just the woman who bore me.

I mean, my mother likes to skinny-dip.

"You have a chance at love again, son. With a phenomenal

girl who comes from a beautiful family. But don't go into it the way you did your last one, thinking she's a possession you can own. You Middleton men have that bad."

"Give me a minute. I'm trying, Ma."

"Mr. Middleton?" The housekeeper comes in. "It's Mr. Milsap here to see you."

"Go on. You need these partnerships. Just remember what I told you about your brother. This family is not strong with you two going at each other. It's the only way you'll save House Middleton."

Before I go to meet Duncan, for a moment, I sit with this, rub my eyes. My classy, graceful, perfectly put-together *Town and Country* cover model of a mother… is nasty.

I bring myself to ask what I know I'll be thinking about for weeks. "You haven't ever skinny-dipped with anybody I know, have you?"

"You should go see about Duncan, son."

I NEED to get out of here and over to the brewery. I made some different arrangements with the liquor distributors, which include contracting with new barley sellers. So I intend to make this talk with Duncan as quick as I can.

"Sir." He greets me with open arms.

"Took you long enough to get here, brother." In dramatic fashion, I feel his hip with my hand.

He cracks up laughing, already knowing where I'm going with this.

"Whoa! You mean Tanja's not attached to you? How'd you manage to escape? They must have pried her off you at the door!"

"Get out of here with that, dude. You know Maddy Rouse has me hopping around the state, going from house to house, making all kinds of calls, dialing for dollars. Which is what I was hoping you would do for me."

And that's why he's here. Not to see if Dad and I are okay, but because I haven't done anything for Duncan.

Originally, I gave my bosses at work the excuse that I needed extra vacation time to come here and help Duncan get his campaign off the ground. Since oil companies love having senators in their pockets, I knew my story about Duncan's senate campaign would be perfectly acceptable. Not to mention I suspected they would want to use me for access to Kevin.

I roll out the game plan that I flew into town with. "Say less, my guy. But there's also a couple of things I need you to do for me."

"Now, Lion." He's queuing up his small violin.

"Come on, bruh, don't you start." I can already hear what's coming.

"Just listen. Let me win the senate seat first, okay? And then I promise, I've got you. I will take care of you."

I can't believe what I'm hearing. After years of me swimming through bullshit, nobody can wrap it up and sell it to me.

"Duncan, who helped you pass your damn macroeconomics exams, business concepts, anything concerning math which was never your forte? And now you ask me to wait?"

He holds up his hands in a mea culpa. "I'm just asking you for eighteen months. So I can get sworn in, and then I will endorse you once I'm in the seat. You already have an open door to a ton of politicians, so you don't even need me."

"But I will need *Senate* approval." I reference my prospects for either being appointed as a US ambassador or awarded government contracts for my other business endeavors.

"And I will secure that for you," he replies with conviction. "But you had better spend this next eighteen months hauling ass. Nothing else can come up. Not anything that you did over in Åfrica or the Persian Gulf to move your oil off those rigs. Or that's my ass for supporting you. I'm already putting myself in jeopardy by having you at my events."

At the intimation that *my* presence hurts *his* image, I fucking snap. "I don't want to hear about *us* jeopardizing *you* when your ass wouldn't have made it out of college without me!"

"I said I've got you. And I mean that, man," he mutters.

Through the lens of my skepticism, I stare out at the ocean. "If you say so… my guy."

"Well, I do." He looks at me. "I can't stay long. But I wanted to come and tell you I will do whatever I can behind the scenes to help you and your father. Even if I can't say it in the press just yet."

Behind the scenes? "Right. I should bounce out of here myself. I'm headed to Montauk."

And Kamilah.

She's been texting me all morning, with her exacting demands and rigorous standards and vivacious attitude and gorgeous smile when she decides to let me see it.

But Duncan's slow to rise. Instead, he hangs back, his gaze wandering aimlessly around our backyard.

"What's wrong with you?" I ask as he seems to gaze into the distance at nothing.

"I think I might have fucked up. Big time."

I shrug. "Happens. Fix it. Just like you're telling me to do, Negro."

His laugh carries some burden. "Can't. I'm in it now."

"What are you talking about? It can't be that bad. You're running for the US Senate."

Now his entire manhood dives through his eyes into our coffee table. "I picked the wrong goddamn wife."

"When you say 'wrong,' you mean you had another alternative?" Now my suspicions resurface from the other day at Kamilah's house.

He lifts his head, drops it. "Yeah. You might not remember her. I met her when I was in law school. This one chick who was just bad. I mean, *bad*."

I don't have to try and recall. "Before you married Tanja? You haven't talked about anybody like that in a long time."

"Yeah, because I thought I was over it." He wipes his face. "For years, I didn't see her. Sometimes, I tried calling her. Followed her on social media. Sent an occasional email just to check in and say hey. She never responded. Nothing. And then, boom, we crossed paths recently. Shit, it felt like my heart started beating again."

Every word he speaks must be an albatross hanging around his neck. Duncan's pathetic eyes find mine.

"Fifteen years ago, I kept going out to see this one chick who was just..." He rocks where he sits and shakes his head. "*Incomparable.* She was still in college, but she called it like she saw it and was going to use math and business to change the world. You know?"

I don't say shit.

Calm and still, I turn back the clock in my own mind. And let him get it off his chest.

"She was edgy and on point and visionary and raw. I keep wondering what my life might have been. Especially these days while I'm living a front." Big inhale. "Everything I do is orchestrated. Tanja is the symphony conductor. For the labor sector to endorse us, 'we need to do this.' For the NAACP to like us, 'we need to live here.' Every decision is about what the voters will say. And Tanja's damn good at that. But that one time in my life with this girl, the love was real."

Once more, I'm silent as I scratch my head.

"I don't recall you mentioning a girl who put it on you."

Getting up to stand just inside the patio doors, he leans against the doorframe, shoulders rolled back, and seems to struggle with internal angst. On an overcast day, we're surrounded by a bleak sky. "I didn't. But I thought I was over her. Seeing her now reminds me of what I could have had."

Without warning, he reaches in his phone, swipes up a picture.

Duncan shoves it toward me.

We immediately bust out laughing, though inside me, nothing is funny.

I'm reminded of that wild summer night, sixteen years ago. Standing on a rooftop at a New York City loft, we may as well have been standing on top of the world. At the beginning of our careers—me a couple of years out of business school, him on a clerkship with the city before graduating law school and using his time in New York to flee from Tanja.

We had our entire lives ahead of us, and we partied like it.

Adults now, our worlds have changed drastically since those days. We're more driven by our ambitions and money than by friendship or loyalty.

I've already seen that photo, numerous times. I came home and pulled it up the night I walked Kamilah to her house. So there's no need for me to scan all the drunken, excited faces and inspect who's hugged up on whom.

I still know Duncan somewhat. Memories aren't why he's showing me the picture.

And I'm realizing campaign phone calls, or discussions about our futures, aren't the real reason he's here.

This is a veiled threat.

Duncan glares at me, his laughter having faded.

He knows.

But I hold tight the shutters over my emotions so as not to expose a single one.

"If I leave Tanja now, I'll be painted in the press as the cheater who did her wrong. Even though she knew fully well I loved somebody else. But her family had the keys to the kingdom."

With a hand over my chest, I remind him, "You're running to be US Senator, so not all is lost."

"Sometimes, I wonder if the sacrifice was worth it." His accusing eyes linger on me a while longer before he finally checks his vibrating phone. "I should dip out of here. Tanja wants me to meet some of her sorority sisters before they go to dinner at The Countryman."

My own phone vibrates with messages from Kamilah, Desmond, Miracle, and others at Explore. It's already been jumping from Percell and Toni.

I venture to ask this next question. "Why didn't you ever introduce me to this chick you liked so much?"

Duncan snickers. "Hell, no. Not after the first night we met her at the party." He attempts humor to mask how he's irate, but he can't hide the nerve jumping over his eye or how his jaws grind over one another. "I didn't want her anywhere near you again. You were so much bigger than me and larger then life. Girls always went for you. Who could compete with that, man? I liked being the king in her eyes. I wanted it to stay that way."

His sentiments reverberate through me. It sounds like he keeps me away out of low-boiling jealousy—all the events he's been attending, of which he's invited me and my father to none, the fake closeness and the real distance now between us, all that's happened the past few weeks.

What occurred my first night back in the Hamptons, in the basement of Slurp, Tanja must have told him.

Now I think back to the standoff between her and Kam

that night. Tanja's foul energy toward Kamilah on the stairs makes complete sense, and all this shit seems to come full circle. Particularly Kamilah's reason for following me, and fucking me on sight. She probably even hoped Duncan would catch us.

"So you say Tanja will be at The Countryman tonight?" I ask.

Distracted with his texts now, he replies, "Yeah. Whenever we're here, I can't keep her out of there. May as well be her second home. Anyway, I've got to jet."

"Yeah, me, too."

We exchange a half-hug that kind of reflects what's become of our friendship.

LIGHTNING IN A BOTTLE

LION & KAMILAH

LION

It's one o'clock in the afternoon when I finally make it into the brewery. Duncan's earlier distress confirms my prior suspicions, and I now understand exactly why he's worked up.

What am I to do?

On top of that, an irritated Kamilah struts toward me.

Too bad she doesn't realize when she looks ready to fight like that, she's only pouring kerosene on my dick.

Come to Daddy.

"Lion, please tell me you've got it handled. Desmond is stressed out. The latest shipment that was due this morning at nine did not arrive. And the three-hour grace period has passed. The distributors won't even talk to us because we're not you. We're in the middle of Fourth of July preparations, so delays are the last thing we need. You know better than anybody that the success of this depends on all of us moving together. I don't have to tell you that." She lets it all out in one breath.

She worries under pressure.

Eyes popping wider, she presses me. "Are you going to say something?"

"Yes." I chuck my hands in my pockets, inspect her gorgeousness, how she's got it all wrapped up in fabric. "I give you my credit card, and that's what you buy?"

"Lion." French Fry folds her frustration into her arms across the breasts I enjoyed last night.

"Kamilah." Before she can protest again, I stop her. "I'll tell you what. If the inventory is not sitting there by five o'clock this evening, you can do whatever you want to me, in front of all the staff, punish me as you see fit. You can even hit me again. But!" I hoist up my index finger in a challenge. "If that inventory comes *one* minute before five o'clock—and I do mean one—I take you shopping myself."

Giggles break out from behind the bar, especially from the women servers who try to pretend they're not watching.

Kamilah throws a hand on her hip, fighting to maintain her authority, and she squints at me.

I squint back.

"This isn't funny, Lion," her mouth warns, but she's started to relax.

"Do you see me laughing?" I step closer to her and lower my voice. "I asked you to buy some*thing*. Not that." I point at this matronly dress she's wearing.

Kam's head drops to review herself. Then, she whispers, "You told me to grab whatever I wanted, and I did."

I whisper back, "What I meant was 'grab what you think *I* want.' *I* want. Which is what most women would've done. They would have chosen attire that's slightly sleazy to look more sexually appealing for a man. Not something… *professional*."

She takes inventory of what she's wearing. "I like my dress. Don't try to distract me."

"I'm not *trying* to distract you. I just... distract you."

The pearly whites of her teeth bust out as her stomach shakes.

"Lion, I can't have you playing around. We have a big task ahead of us for Fourth of July. I need you to take this seriously," she complains. Then she murmurs. "And *you* need to take *me* seriously."

I address the other staffers. "Do you all take her seriously?"

The others glance up from their duties, confused, and nod. "Yeah."

"Yes."

I turn back to an appalled Kam, who can't believe I asked that. My eyes devour her body. "Girl, I take every part of you *very* seriously."

"Is that right?" Her eyebrow goes up, and she's no longer laughing. In a low tone, she mutters, "Have you been taking Olga *very seriously*, too?"

Her bare-knuckled annoyance strikes a chord in my chest. I've seen it before, too many times. Ashlyn.

"It was just one time."

Her eyes disengage, and she pivots to walk away from me.

"Kamilah, you weren't giving a brother any play after our first little encounter. So I got some ass to take the edge off." I follow her to the back office.

Yet again, Kam's vulnerability peeks through her tough facade. "Were you 'taking the edge off' with her when you were coming on to me? And when you ate with my family?"

I stop her and keep my voice down. This *is* serious now, and Kam cannot think I'm treating it as anything less. "No, sweetheart." I close the door with just the two of us inside. "She was literally a one-time fuck in the Taste stockroom the same day we started at Explore, Kam. No dinner, no drinks, nothing. She's been trying to throw me the pussy ever since, and I've only paid attention to you."

I can't fuck this up.

Behind Kam's eyes, she's still assessing whether to believe me.

"Did she drive up here today in my car? A car I happen to like a lot. And which better not have any scratches. Does she have my credit card in her bra? Where it had better *still* be." Linking my hands in hers, I nudge her to me. "Did I kiss her less than twenty-four hours ago, standing out there in front of the world? Did I follow her from a bar to intercept her fucking somebody else?"

"Shh!" Kam's face turns animated and her apprehension melts.

"And, might I remind you, that you *did* attempt to fuck somebody else? Before I put a stop to it. Do I give a damn who Olga fucks?" I keep whispering, "And I can promise you I did *not* drink beer from the crack of her ass."

"Shh!" Kam's playful side returns to the corners of her mouth. She's struggling to find her smart-ass voice, and I've broken through some of her worry.

"So, back to our bet. If the inventory is here, I take you shopping where I'll pick whatever *I* want. No objections from you. And then—get this—we'll go to dinner at a place of my choosing. *And*—you're going to love this one—I pick what you wear."

Her laughter fills the office while she shakes her head. "I don't let men pick my clothes."

"Yes, and that's your problem. But you're going to do it tonight."

"I didn't actually say yes to this bet."

"You did. I heard you say it in your head."

Her tongue slides over her lip. "This smells like a setup. You did this on purpose."

"Oh, no, no, noooo." I slide my hands in my pockets and start off to find Desmond. "This smells like a hard worker who takes this project"—I pause to pop my hands out in front of me—"very seriously."

KAMILAH

"No, the bodice on that is too high." Lion wags his finger. "Can you bring something that's cut a little lower?"

"How low are we talking?" the sales associate asks.

Lion exaggerates his reaction. "I'm talking here." He's dragged his finger down to his navel.

Of *course,* the inventory arrived at 4:47 p.m.

So now I stand in the middle of some high-couture spot called Cover of Night while boutique associates swarm me at Lion's direction.

"No, the heel can't be any lower than five inches."

The woman's eyebrows shoot up. "Five?"

Pretending to be in deep reflective thought, he sits back in the chair and nods. "Five."

I glare at him. "Five?"

He mouths, *Five.*

She brings me Dolce and Gabbana see-through lace worn by J-Lo, and Bronx and Banco classy cut-outs that prominently display my stomach, chest, and thighs. For the next hour, Lion swivels his finger in the air for me to spin, twist, and pose, to which he shakes his head, grins with mischief, or outright frowns.

I find myself not knowing exactly what to do about this, how much to trust it, how much to give in to his goofy ass.

I leave wearing a sexy summer maxi dress with cutouts revealing my waist and chest, the cloth barely covering my breasts. He arranges to have the rest delivered to my house.

Instinctively, once we approach his car, I go for my door handle.

I'm tugged backward.

"Aht, aht. I see we're still learning," he murmurs.

I try to suppress my giggle fits. His tree of an arm envelopes me while the other opens the door. His hands glide over my waist, lingering, promising, and their warmth contrasts with the cool evening.

Just about every restaurant in the Hamptons takes the form of a clapboard house. Even the really fancy ones are just upscale elaborate country spreads that have been converted. At our destination, he walks me into some place called The Countryman.

Making our way across its polished wooden floorboards, I'm self-conscious suddenly. He strolls behind me, his hand at the small of my back, through decorated, candle-lit tables, past all these eyeballs.

"People are staring at us," I whisper.

"Good," he whispers back.

Normally, I'm not squeamish at all. This is just a different scenario than what I'm used to. But I don't want to be the subject of rumors or gossip or people's attention. For the past fifteen years, I've just partied in my corners of New York and lived my life away from old friends and classmates from Brown who knew about my tryst with Duncan.

As Lion and I move forward now, the walls of my windpipe slam closed and shut off my breathing.

Tanja. Peering up from a table where she entertains other women in their sorority colors, she gives me a searing once-over. I'm inclined to cut my eyes and keep walking, but Lion stops and greets her, kissing her cheek. Then he turns to me. "Tanja, I suspect you two already know each other, but this is Kamilah Rouse, Supervising Audit Consultant at Explore."

She forces her eyes at me. "Kamilah."

I force the back of my hand not to strike. "Tanja."

The women seated with her visually take notes of my attire, their collective gaze scrutinizing me from behind their fake smiles—from a couple of them, no smiles at all.

I already know how this works. Once I leave, they'll ask her who I am, and she'll happily conjure up the worst to tell them about me.

And I feel it all over again—judgment. A group of women assessing me for whether I fit their standards.

For a long time, I've worked hard not to care, to do my own thing. Because I've been through this too many times since college, I've got my fuck-you attitude down pat. But tonight, I'm on foreign territory in foreign clothes. It feels like I'm wearing somebody else's skin.

And that might be the most terrifying.

I'm finally wearing the skin I secretly dreamed of all those years ago, skin I was too devastated to imagine for myself after Duncan dropped me, the skin of a valued, cherished woman. Not just talented and smart-as-a-whip but loved and worshipped in addition. It's the adulation most of us claim we don't need when, in our deepest consciousness, we do. From the level of men around whom I was raised, men like my brothers.

When it eluded me, I resigned myself to bars and one-night stands just so I wouldn't risk a man stripping me of my skin again. And people talking about me as a result.

Now, in my progression toward a table in the Hamptons with one of its most eligible bachelors, I'm worried I'm setting myself up for another embarrassment.

I'm stunned to see someone else I know sitting across the room.

Sheldon. After my big brother does a double take at his tomboy of a sister in a dress I would not be caught dead in around the family, a massive smile crosses his face. His eyes crinkle as he laughs approvingly and chokes on his liquor at the same time. Then Chrissy swings around in her seat and serves up an open-mouthed grin with a thumbs-up. They both wave.

Lion gives them a small salute and returns to pulling out my chair.

"I feel naked in this."

"You're lightning in a bottle, baby. Nobody can resist staring at lightning." He hands both of the menus to the waiter after he orders. "And let me tell you why they're really gawking. In an hour, they'll go back to their husbands who won't do shit with them tonight."

Lion reaches across the table and takes my hand. Not a glint of humor flashes in his gaze over the candlelight. He eye-fucks his way past my inhibitions, down to my most sensitive erogenous zones.

"And they know you're dressed like Miss Universe because I'm worshipping the hell out of your pussy, your mind, and when you and I step out of here, I'm giving you the works."

Suppressing my laughter, I gaze around us and pray nobody heard him talking like that. "The works?"

"And then some."

My head probably spins faster than the ceiling fan over our heads as I brace myself.

But I also wait for his mouth to ask the inevitable question I know will come, about Tanja and me, how we know one another.

Eying me, peeling me, Lion raises his wine glass for a toast. "To 'then some.'"

I still can't bring myself to tell him. This is too heavenly.

"To 'then some.'"

A couple of hours later, he drives me to an incredibly lovely home that sits on a lake. "Lion, I really do have to get home, and change, shower, work, and plan for the grind over the next few days, for Fourth of July—"

"So do it all here," he suggests, circling his arms around me.

We walk to the back porch that has a storybook view of vast greenery around picturesque water. "What is this?"

"My friend's spot that I borrowed since he's not around. Cleaning staff have come in and tidied up. This is closer to Montauk than where you are, so it's a shorter drive to work. You can sleep in a little longer, hang out more in town, leave work as late as you want, without worrying about driving over to Southampton." He takes my hand. "Come on."

I'm led up circular stairs to an expansive master bedroom with a balcony having a built-in stone jacuzzi. Even in the night, we face a breathtaking view of the lake.

"If you want me to drive you home, I'll do it, French Fry." Handsome and elegant in his silk linen summer set, he leans against the open French doors. "Or you can stay a while. And let me spoil you. And we can see where this leads."

I struggle to release that deep breath I've been holding the last fifteen years.

"Lion, why?"

"I'm feeling you, Kamilah. This is what you deserve. But it seems you're distrusting of men… such as myself. Maybe you've been hurt in your past by a man who failed you, so I'm sure you're totally justified." Lion's smooth, deep voice offers reassurance that matches his easy face.

He has an x-ray of my insides.

Hell, I switch away because I need to escape.

But he catches me. With a firm hand, he guides me to the bed, where he sits me on his lap. His eyes steady and scrutinizing, it becomes even clearer there's more depth to him than he lets on.

"You've spent enough time alone, though, Kamilah, knowing you're a badass in your heart but running away from the queen treatment. It's time you had a man who can show you that. And despite me previously fucking around with commitment before, I'd like to be the one to try."

Lion kisses my skin as he offers the skin I lost.

He stares at me through rich, coffee-colored eyes, his smooth skin the shade of light wheat. For the first time, I notice the few freckles sprinkled across his nose, and thin, wide lips hidden in his auburn beard. He draws my mouth down to his. We barely dust one another's lips.

He's laying down a lot right now, and it's pressuring the hell out of my guilty conscience. "Lion, I have something I need to..."

"Kamilah, the next time we make love, I don't want you thinking about whatever foolishness you endured in the past. When my dick is in you, I want that to be your only reality."

His eyes drink me up. And he pours back into me all the lust and affection and intimacy between a man and a woman that terrifies me. I examine the tenderness on his face for any hints of fraud and find none.

But still, I shouldn't be stupid again. Especially not at age thirty-six. "I can't be bought, Lion. Or boxed in or showcased like one of your cars or—"

"Nor would I ever try. I figured you might say that, so I'm willing to show you this isn't all carnal. I'll stay away. You use this place by yourself. I'll only come when you want me to. So there's no pressure."

I didn't think it would ever be possible for a man to render me speechless.

"What do you want in return, Lion?"

"Don't get me wrong. I'd love to fuck you here and now, but for the first time in my life, I'm willing to wait. Because I want something else, too."

With bated breath, I manage to swallow. "What's that?"

He shakes his handsome head, and now I realize I'm playing in the fine hair on it.

"Not now. No pressure. But I'd love to see you this weekend for my birthday. My family won't be around since they've made plans with friends. And I can't go anywhere since I have this demanding co-worker who won't let me leave Explore. She's always on my ass. If I can't get her good loving, it sure would be nice if I could have my favorite strawberry lemon cake."

Scared and exhilarated, I question if I can let down my guard. And be a woman again.

I imagine Princess's voice fussing at me in my head if I don't do this. I'll never hear the end of it. "We can't have you alone for your birthday, can we?"

HIS BIRTHDAY

KAMILAH & LION

KAMILAH

"Get out. Just get out of here right now." Ameera surveys the pool in the backyard, and beyond it, the massive lake. "You're not even giving him any, and you're staying here?"

She and Katessa drove out to help me with cooking a small surprise meal for Lion's birthday. We are packing up the strawberry lemon cake we made, which I thought was more personal and intimate than simply ordering one up from a bakery. That's just not how we do things in my family or where I come from.

And Princess helped me cook up a really good seafood gumbo from my family's Louisiana recipes. Yet, she breaks my heart every time she doubles over and fights to suppress coughs that seem to erupt from her soul.

"Sis, I'm concerned about that so-called 'hay fever' not improving. Your new race might be gray instead of Black," I finally say to her.

"Okay, so I had a little issue come up a few weeks ago that I've been getting tested."

My mouth drops, my heart stops. *"What?"*

She shakes her hands to calm me down. "No, don't you dare make this a big deal. I haven't wanted you to react the way you are right now. No panicking."

"You've been going through something, and I haven't been there for you! The way you've…"

Been there for me.

"Girl, your happiness has been on one hundred since you came into these Hamptons fighting for your life. Do you hear me? Kam, the beautif—" She needs a moment to hack. "The beautiful scenery isn't just out there. It's on *you*. And that is all the support I need from you. I don't want you worrying about my hospital visits for some very small thyroid thing. Doctors are very positive. Your brother and I are working out."

That's why Ro's been so stressed these past few weeks and couldn't work with Explore himself. I approach her and wrap my arms around the woman whose spirit, smile, and overall humanity have been my saving grace.

"Princess, woman, let me be the support you've always been for me."

What I feel underneath her giant, loose sweater shocks me. I'm wrapping myself around bones and flesh, where shreds of her muscles remain.

"You *are* here for me." Her voice is hoarse and raspy. "Seeing this—you in here and the way this man is glorifying you, makes my heart so glad. Yes, the kids miss their Auntie Kam at the house, but watching your life shift is so worth it."

"Tell the babies Aunt Kam will be coming to see them."

"Girl, no, she won't," Ameera replies from the kitchen. "Auntie Kam is about to get her back blown out. I promise you, this no-sex thing won't last long."

Katessa snickers. "Girl, that back is getting torpedoed."

My friends chuckle and pour drinks.

"Okay, so," Ameera says. "Is he a good fuck or not?"

"Meera!" Katessa fusses.

Ameera maintains her unbothered position.

Letting go of my sister-in-law and de facto big sister, I don't let go of my worry for her that builds up in me.

As for my friends' interrogation, I grin and shut my mouth. Scratch the back of my neck and sip my drink.

"Oh, shit! Look at how she's smiling. Where her eyes just went," Katessa notes.

"If Kam was catching bad dick, we would've heard about it by now," Ameera observes.

"Right!" Katessa agrees.

"You would be blowing up our text thread. Whining and crying for Roland to bring you back to the city, begging us to come out here," Ameera replies. "A few days ago, I had to call and make sure she was still alive, because I had not heard a peep since last weekend." She turns to Katessa. "On Juneteenth, you should've seen how he took her away for himself, led her from everybody at the brewery."

Princess nods. "There is nobody else in the room when he's staring at Kam."

"See how she's not saying a word," Katessa notes. "She's keeping all that tucked away in her bra with her cash."

I finally respond to all this speculating they're doing. "I'll keep it real. A part of me is scared if I say it out loud, that I might jinx it. The cards might fall down, because this is too good to be true."

Princess shakes her head. "Don't think like that. Enjoy the moment."

I glance at my watch. "We should head over to the brewery. He'll arrive around noon."

When the others start carrying out the food, Princess

approaches. "So what did he say when you and him talked?"

A guilty sigh is my first reaction. "Don't be mad at me, P. Just, right now, all he sees is Kamilah. His French Fry. And nothing else. No tomfoolery or drama."

Her face forms an admonishment. "I feel you, sis, but you're also underestimating his feelings for you. If that man is into you the way we think he is, nothing will take him from your side."

In my head is the imprint of Lion's tongue the other night, licking my asshole with beer. "I'm being selfish and enjoying a moment that's not blocked by my past."

P pushes back. "You're still blocked if it's keeping you from trusting him with it, so you two can move on."

At the brewery, our work over the past three weeks comes together. American flags hang from the ceiling amid stacks of oak barrels that decorate the taproom. Keeping with the Black history theme that will continue, several stations are set up where each owner of Explore will teach on notable Blacks who fought for American freedom—Crispus Attucks, Prince Whipple, Primus Hall, and George Middleton, among so many countless others who never received the recognition they deserved, and some who never even received their freedom.

I set the cake down, surprised to see my brother, Jerrell, here.

"Hey! What's going on?" I ask as he drops a kiss on my head.

"Desmond's having an issue at the bar with plumbing. Hopefully, some of us can fix it and he won't have to call in a plumber." He eyes the cake and gumbo and sees Princess setting up food on one of the tables. "What's all this? It's been a long time since you've cooked. What's the special occasion?"

Big inhale, because I can already feel his objections.

"Today is Lion's—"

"Lion?" J shakes his head.

I open up the cake container and distract myself, moving around him. "J, don't start."

"I just took you as smarter than him. He's–"

"Dad said the same to Maddy when she started up with you. I know what Lion is, and I also know how he's treating me. So can you please just back off and be happy for me? No matter how it turns out." Wow. Never thought I'd see the day those words came from my mouth.

Concern still grips Jerrell's face, as if he wants to go beat Lion to a pulp. "If you shed one tear, his ass is mine, Kam."

It's a wonder I was able to keep him from learning about Duncan. Though J was two years behind me at Brown, our styles of socializing couldn't have been more different. When he wasn't with his girlfriend Raychelle, he was holed up with some other chick or partying with his frat brothers. College life was good to Jerrell, but not me. He and I had survived high school together, but university drama hit different for me. Sorority girls, cliques, bullshit boyfriends…by the time I reached my senior year, I was ready to go. Jerrell, on the other hand, was only just turning up.

Maybe that's how Duncan seemed so impressive back then. Exhausted from the silliness, I enjoyed hearing about his big ambitions and goals, and he seemed to be above the fray. Jerrell still doesn't know.

Now we trade hugs.

"Where is my nephew?"

"With the Pages today."

"Sometimes, it's hard to remember my baby's got other relatives besides me. Bring him to see me when you get a chance. Have some of the cake and tell me what you think," I say to my little brother.

Kevin walks in, surprising me since Lion said he'd be in

California.

"Hey, what are you doing here?" I ask him.

"Ms. Rouse, what's popping?" He turns to J, and they trade a respectful handshake, despite their history. "Mr. Rouse, I had the pleasure of meeting your son at an event a few weeks back. Charming young stunner. Had a strong grip."

It's good to see the two of them being civil, so I know there must be hope for all our families.

"Thanks. I'm trying to teach him to keep them to himself. I'm going to head over here and help Des get this machine working again."

"I thought you were out of town?" I ask Kevin again.

Confusion crosses his face. "I spend a lot of the summer here in my own backyard. It's my stomping ground." He chomps on a catfish Po' Boy sandwich from Slurp's kitchen. Taking large, bites he motions at the food and cake. "What's going on there?"

A little confused myself that he's asking, I reply, "Lion's birthday. He didn't have anybody to cook his favorite cake, because you all's mom is out of town and..." As the words pour out of my mouth and I watch his expression, the more I feel stupid.

Kevin's face breaks up with pity. "Lion's birthday is in March." He bites another chunk of sandwich, eyes me. "Our parents are at home."

My friends, once they overcome their initial surprise, crack up.

"Yeah girl, he's got you," Ameera says.

I'm laughing even in my irritation.

"What's this?" one of the other employees asks.

"Gumbo," Princess answers and winks at me. "We're waiting for the, ahem, birthday boy to arrive so we can eat it."

Other members of Explore and some of the other Black

business owners—the owner of Cal's, the brother of Miss Sharon, Tom who owns Tom's Candies, Pierre the Black dressmaker, and others—all enter the brewery to help Desmond, who lies on the floor, tinkering with the pipes.

Cal strolls up. "I brought this here. You young boys have probably never seen one of these before. It's called a toolbox."

The older men laugh. Pastor Arnold enters as well, dressed down in his work clothes.

In comes my brother, Roland. "Hey, K.K., I've been hearing a lot of good about your reports and oversight. Nice job, baby."

"Thanks. How are things in the city?"

"You know how it is. Clients mad because we don't do magic math." He flings an arm over my shoulder. "Speaking of the city, I found you a new assignment and I can relieve you from here. You can go back to your nightclubs and book clubs where you pretend to read but really go for a hookup. You'll be rid of this Lion dude."

The city… back to my condo with an amazing view of Central Park and the New York City skyline. I'll hustle into work on Monday morning. Traffic, noises, crowds, standing at a packed intersection waiting for the light to change. My cell phone will blow up with demanding clients all day. After work, I'll entertain myself with single colleagues still in their twenties and early thirties at bars. My life in the city… it's what I wanted.

Lion saunters in, chill and breezy in his leather slides.

Instinctively, my hand flies to the back of my neck and I try to summon up anger with him that doesn't come.

He surveys the spread of food, and the joke is already crinkling up his laugh lines. "Roland, pleasure to see you, bruh."

It's obvious from Roland's expression he has no clue what's unfolded while he's been commuting between the

East End and the city. P likely hasn't told him my business—she never has—and my other family members have likely been too busy with their own summer social calendars.

But now Ro stares between the two of us. "Lion, you also. I've been hearing dope feedback about your supply chain flexes and how you're helping my sister navigate all this. We appreciate you."

Lumberjack eyes me. "You can believe she runs a tight ship."

"Does she now?" My brother shifts positions, and it's clearly dawning on him in this awkwardness that he's missing information. "Where is my wife?" He pivots toward P so she can fill him in.

"Is all this for me?" Lion feigns innocence.

"Hey, Lion, happy birthday," Ameera calls out with sarcasm. Giving him a fist bump, she nods. "My boy. You got her butt good. And I didn't mind driving down here and sleeping on a lake either."

I glare at both of them. "Don't encourage his behavior."

Lion surprises me when he takes my finger, dips it in cake, sucks off the frosting. What's more earth-shattering is how I don't move a limb to stop him.

Loudly, he smacks his lips. "Mmm, strawberry lemon. So you care about me."

"I felt sorry for you and I was being nice."

"You put the time into a custom cake and real Cajun gumbo." He scans the elaborate setup across the table. "*And* you're carrying the purse I bought you. *And* wearing one of my dresses. You're feeling me."

I want to swat him even as I adore him. "You're so arrogant. You lied and ran game on me?"

"No. Okay, technically, yes. But it wasn't to run game, it was so I could spend more time with you. Grow closer. Hear you tell me all the things you find incredible about me."

There's no way I can avoid laughing at him. "I'm not going to say that."

He points across the brewery at Katessa and Ameera. "But you called up your friends, and I bet they told you I'm wonderful. You want me to ask them?" he threatens with that gleam in his eye.

"No! You'd better—"

"Hey, ladies, so how do you like the house?"

"Oh, Lion, it's off the chain. Your taste is 'chef's kiss!'" Ameera and Katessa gush.

He's so cocky and proud of himself. Sexy as fuck in his button-down navy shirt and khaki shorts that display those beautiful defined calves that leave me with thoughts.

"And why is your shirt buttoned down like that?" I try not to stare, but my attention keeps veering to his oiled, golden smoothness. Like one of those shiny Werther's caramel candies.

He leans in closer. "For you to do what you just did."

Despite his juvenile antics, and because of them, I'm glued to where I stand.

My attraction and affection grow by the millisecond, and that scares me. "How many of these women around here have you been wonderful to, Lion? Putting them up in houses, buying their clothes, tricking them so they fall for your personality?"

"None. For a few, I've been sufficient. But I'm trying to be everything for you." The mischief and humor dissolves from his face, leaving only his concentration on me. "They haven't met my mother, they don't drive my car, I don't take them to restaurants where I know there will be important people, and I don't want them thinking for a minute that they'll feed me on my birthday. So, where were we? Back to me being wonderful."

Back to him turning my insides as sweet as strawberry lemon cake.

"Excuse me. I don't mean to break up this...co-worker situation," a vexed Roland interrupts, eying the two of us. "So, Kam, Vivian at the job is waiting for your answer. She wants to know if she should come out here to replace you, so she can make arrangements for her and her kids. What will it be? You coming back to the city?"

Lion and I stare at each other. Only weeks ago, that woman who walked home from the bar after talking to Duncan again would not be caught dead baking, gushing, gazing, and learning the finer points of Hamptons culture.

Now I'm dreading the day I leave peace, tranquility, community, and...

"So are you feeding me some of my cake?" Lion murmurs.

I smirk and throw him this side-eye. "No."

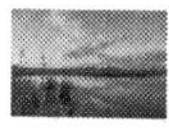

LION

I open wide as she feeds it to me.

When I overheard her brother offering her a transfer, it was the first time since Ash left that I looked down the next few years of my life and feared what I saw. Emptiness, loneliness, and meaningless relationships with people who wouldn't give a damn about me absent of money or title, who wouldn't lift a finger for me if I was in need.

The moment it took Kam to answer Roland paralyzed me, one I hope to never feel again.

Now Kam flips her hair completely different than she did three weeks ago. Rather than scratching the back of her neck with irritation, she now scratches it as a way of hiding her secret affections.

And I have to restrain myself from touching her or grabbing her too much here in front of everybody.

The other business owners enjoy the gumbo she made. She's not really unnerved about my birthday prank, though she tries to pretend she is. Instead of being upset, Kam notices everyone chomping and chatting around food prepared by her hands, while she slowly chomps away at me.

Adella English McLain, one of the co-owners of rival company, Dream Stage, enters with a casserole dish. The moment feels odd, considering our families are suing one another over ownership of Smeralda Costa.

Desmond is busy working on pipe fittings and doesn't notice her. Kevin is engaged in a conversation with Keenan. I suppose this community feel-good moment compels me to go over and greet her.

She eyes the spread on the table. "I came to bring food for everybody who's helping Desmond, but I didn't realize there was already food here," she says.

"I'm sure whatever you have there will be much appreciated," I tell her while clearing out space for her dish on the food table.

"It's just a little basil lobster pasta with yellow tomatoes. Desmond tells me you've been a huge help lining up his supplies for his brews and really juicing up his productivity." Hardness mixes with acknowledgement in her unsmiling face, and she seems to choke up her next words. "Thank you, for being so kind to him, despite your disagreements with me."

"To be honest, Dr. McLain," I start, pouring her some lemonade, "if his brews didn't taste so good, I might not have bothered. But your man's got a couple skills in him."

Her laugh is reserved, proud.

Across the taproom, Kevin watches us interact and quickly diverts his attention elsewhere. This is definitely awkward, if not uncomfortable. She's his niece, and I'm guessing he observes to imagine how both sides of his genealogy might reach conciliation.

"I'll go find Desmond now, see what I can do to help with all this."

We depart from one another, but not from the questions hanging over us. Not from the longtime resentments I detected in her that likely match my own.

My phone buzzes in my pocket from the thread text I've been having with Gavin all morning, insisting that we set up the particulars for their siege against Kevin.

Then there's the separate text thread about my family's press operation and how we will proceed with Dad and me writing a book on the family history.

After I've been at the brewery a couple of hours, across town, Trane and the guys await me to hang out.

I go to give my goodbyes to Kam and her friends. "I'm glad you're enjoying the house. I'll see you soon."

"You're leaving?" Is that disappointment furrowing between her brows?

"I have another engagement, French Fry. I spend so much time around here it's been hard to schedule with my own friends. I do have a life of my own."

Kamilah's eyes flicker in a way I'm not used to. They flicker inside *me* in a way I'm still not used to.

The hand scratches the back of her neck, and she flips her hair to avert her gaze. "Okay then. I'm glad you enjoyed the cake."

"I'm glad you made it." Bending over, I kiss her cheek. "I guess I'll see you Monday then."

Her slow, disappointed nod snatches my heart.

"Monday then." Hesitant, a bit of her brightness fading,

she finally pivots to join the others.

I head for the exit, leaving all the activity. Black business owners burst out laughing as they help one another, rivals and all, unified with the goal of getting Desmond's brewery running full-time, in the lead-up to a Fourth of July stress test.

They're all gathered, some holding up pipes, passing tools and beers, some lying out on the floor, others down on their haunches shining flashlights and gripping cables.

A text comes through from Trane: ***Are you picking me up, or am I coming to get you?***

This Black Hamptons is different than the one I left behind over a decade ago. Different than the high society for which my father prepared me. Different than the cutthroat manipulation and maneuvering for which I was groomed.

I text Trane back. ***Why don't you come hang out at Slurp for a while? They could use a hand with things.***

Swiping up a text message from Gavin down in Houston, I check his last text.

Gavin: ***We're getting pressure from these natural gas startups that connect on MoneyCruncher. Do something. The board wants face time with K immediately. 48 hours.***

Across the brewery stands the young computer hacker and maverick who sought to prove me wrong all those years ago. I recall all our biggest arguments and fights. Including the most critical—who was right and who was wrong about the future of the Middleton family legacy.

He's still the same brat he's always been, who as a teenager, hacked my computers and phones and tested his listening devices on my girlfriends. He did it to Chriselle Rouse last year when she met Sheldon. I've heard he does it to his enemies. I'm not dumb to think he wouldn't do it again.

I'm certain he'll try it with me. Let him. I'm ready.

SWEPT OFF MY FEET

KAMILAH & LION

KAMILAH

On the eve of Fourth of July, it's been a busy two weeks.

I haven't seen much of Lion, not even when we're at Explore. The entire conglomerate has been gearing up for this Fourth of July week of celebrations that are really meant to be a stress test for next month's Sasha Static concert.

I am especially nervous, as that is also a test of my auditing skills. We've gone over the budget numerous times, adjusting it for unexpected expenses, the need for new vendors, the last-minute holiday ideas such as Juneteenth and other commemorations that Desmond, Keenan, or Kevin suggest with only a moment's notice.

I'm not just auditing any beer brewery any more but supporting a community. Every time Desmond comes to me with a gleam in his eye and a new idea, it's back to the calculators and spreadsheets for how we'll make it happen.

Needless to say, it's late when I arrive home, or rather, to the house I'm staying in.

When Lion is not at Slurp or Taste, he's with the yacht team of Explore Adventures, going over those operations with the crew, making sure proper insurance clearances are in place, that we have all the certifications and the necessary supplies and equipment aboard each boat. Because that's the worst catastrophe that could hit us financially—that, or one of the tourists injuring themselves in one of our sporting activities.

Though Explore has captains, experienced tour guides, and lifeguards, Lion's also been running repeated trials to ensure they are prepared. When he's not there, understandably, he's with his parents and helping them hash out this whole legal and press situation with his father.

It's never crossed my mind to ask him about the media or publicity he gets, or his job down in Houston.

What happens when he goes back? What happens when I do finally return to the city? When we have managed to snag quick lunches together, I'm so busy laughing at him, or ignoring the butterflies in my belly, I tend to forget the real-world questions. And honestly, it's been such a long time since a man has melted Karate Kam that, in those moments with Lion, I don't think about anything else.

True to his word, he's stayed away from the house and given me time to learn him for myself, beyond the soul-sucking sex.

And beyond his connection to Duncan.

I will free myself from that burden and tell him. Today.

A series of Fourth of July events are popping off for the next couple of days, where the Hamptons families fellowship at one another's homes.

Last year, Sheldon and Jerrell attended these outings

because of their wives growing up here, but my other siblings and I have never.

Now, as I enter Maddy's family home for my first stop, I wear one of the dresses Lion bought me. He and I agreed to spend some time during this holiday, but since we're making different stops on the social circuit, we don't house-hop together. Plus, we're not exactly "official." I've waited for that next level, until we have the Duncan talk.

Saying "hi" to my nephew and in-laws, I remember my doomed state of mind the last time I was here almost a month ago. The big momentum shift that's taken over me now has me chuckling, in my breezy, relaxed summer dress with my back out, a flowing skirt swishing around my legs and roped around my waist.

My phone buzzes.

Lion: ***Goddamn. Who are you all dressed up for? I don't want to beat his ass.***

Cheesing hard, I whip around, but I don't see him, only my in-laws, Maddy's relatives, and political colleagues and friends.

While I'm pouring myself something to drink, the arms slide around me, muscles lift me from the floor, and his chest holds up my body. A squeal rips out of me as I try not to spill my drink from the cup and hope our silliness doesn't spill too hard everywhere.

"L-Lion," I giggle. "Quiiit!"

"I have a better idea," he whispers in my ear. "We both quit this BS and head for our own private party."

I've avoided us making love again until we've had the talk. It's necessary, now that we've grown to be far more than the revenge fuck I initially intended.

But I want Lion, and to keep growing in my new skin, to shed fear and open myself to the possibility that, even if this doesn't work out, I deserve to let love in again.

I surprise him when I cross my arms over his at my waist and I murmur back, "Say the word and we can go."

He freezes and stares at me in disbelief. My lungs must rise at the touch of his lips laying one of those slow, tortured kisses on my cheek that connects me closer to him every time he does it. Through our clothes, his erection beckons me.

"Say, Lion! Come over here for a minute. We've got a bet going!" one of his friends calls out.

"Let me shake these guys, and then we'll dip," he says in my ear.

"Hurry up."

He bounces out of the kitchen. I'm terrified of how he'll take the news, but P is right. The truth is long overdue, and it's blocking me from completely letting go with him.

To work off my nerves, I spend some time straightening up. Maddy and her mother have their hands full with all these summer events and grandkids. Maddy's younger sister, Marguerite, just had another baby, so they've got a house of little ones they're chasing. And these cleaning staff are only going to half-ass do their job. I already see small pieces of broken glass under the stove that one of the kids could get hold of.

While I'm sweeping up, footsteps reenter the kitchen. They seem to stop at the doorway. Devious Lion must be standing there watching me while I'm bent over.

"That was quick. Are you ready to g—" I accidentally dump the glass.

Instead of Lion, it's Duncan.

His face strained, not apologetic like last time, he's carrying some serious angry energy. "I know you were upset about Tanja, but how could you?"

"Duncan, look—"

"How *could* you?" he demands through clenched teeth,

eyes tearing up as he walks toward me. "You're fucking my friend? And you're only doing it because of me, admit it. You're playing two friends against each other, Kamilah. Whatever you think about my decision, I would never fuck one of your *friends*. There were a million dudes on the planet you could've gotten with. But you waited and came to the Hamptons to go after *him?*"

I'm miffed at his nerve to stand here and play hurt. "Not that it's any of your goddamn business, Duncan, but I have a job to do here for Explore, and I'm handling it, in case you hadn't heard. And Lion is so much more fucking man than your sniveling—"

He shoves his finger in my face, shocking me. "It's a bitch move, Kamilah. I *loved* you. All these years, I emailed you, called your office, tried to explain, and you're the one who didn't respond."

"But you didn't talk to me when I needed you most. I came to New York to see you, and Tanja was at your apartment. After that, I never saw or heard from you. Where were you then?"

I don't give a damn who's around us anymore. It's been fifteen long years this beef has smoked in my chest. "Duncan, I was about to graduate, alone, and pregnant by a fool who talks good for a living. I had to go back to my school and be a laughingstock when my classmates found out. Tanja made sure of it. I don't give two shits about how *you* feel!"

His eyes flare. "And that is *exactly* why you did this, so you could look at me and say that. So you could burn me. Well, you have. I hope you're happy. Let's see how happy you are when he *plays* your ass the way Lion always does. And you'll still be nothing but a shit old maid at thirty-six, Kam."

"What the hell is going on in here?" Lion yells. He snatches Duncan away from me and tosses him into the table.

Duncan jumps up and gets in Lion's face. "You're fucking my ex-*wife*! That's what!"

Lion's astonishment…

I shake my head. "I'm sor—"

"Yeah, that's right," Duncan brags, rubbing it in Lion's face. Like a giant drain, his revelations suck the energy from the room. "We were married. I got her pregnant. I had her *first*. And you're getting *my* leftovers, Lion. For a change. Not you passing me your hand-me-downs or your charity or your women who you passed over. She married *me*."

The others crowd around the door—Jerrell, Sheldon, Maddy, Chrissy… my parents. My brothers stand paralyzed, fists ready, confusion wrenching their faces about what to do, who to hit.

"Duncan, *stop* it," I mutter.

Aiming at Lion, Duncan continues firing. "And the only reason she's fucking you is to hurt me. To get back at me for Tanja. I'm sure you knew. You're supposed to be my friend."

Lion recovers just enough to respond. "Don't talk to me about friendship, man. Not from you, who only calls when you need something, not when all you do is use people to climb up."

Duncan sputters, "We didn't all grow up rich with conniving daddies to buy our way up."

"Common sense doesn't cost a dime, and yet, you still married Tanja," Lion replies.

"But I found enough sense to fuck Kam before you could."

Jerrell lunges toward Duncan.

But Lion reacts faster than all three of my brothers, intercepting J and pushes him back.

Pop!

Right in Duncan's jaw.

Whatever personal animosity existed between Lion and his old buddy had him pre-fueled and already at "go."

"And I got into Cornell on my fucking own," Lion responds. "Daddy or no daddy."

I force my eyes to a red-faced, wild-eyed Lion.

Breathless, embarrassed on so many levels, not wanting to explain my private stupidity to him *and* my entire family, I just let it out. "It's true. We eloped, on Valentine's Day, after that summer I met you two. Tanja found out and told his parents, and he folded. I wasn't important enough for him to stay married to me. His parents had process servers bring me ann… annulment papers… while I was… taking m-my finals," I explain through the sobs I can no longer contain.

My mother and father listen in appall, along with my brothers and their wives and families.

"My folks did it, not me," Duncan retorts, checking his jaw. "They told me you're the one who wanted the annulment."

"And somehow, you never called," I shoot back. "Just admit it, Duncan, Tanja's family could help your political career. And back then, your folks didn't think my family would become the *force* that we have. Go fuck yourself." I continue to Lion, "I am so sor… so sorry. I had every intention of telling you. I never thought you and I would take it this f…"

I run my hands across my wet face, over my head, and grip my neck tight. My legs take me out of here because I'm too damned ashamed that my foolishness is the exact opposite of how we were raised.

My car is blocked in by others that arrived after me, so I can't leave. My family calls out to me, and I hear running and voices back at the house, but I can't do all the questions right now. What do I say? I wasn't prepared for it to come out this way, in front of them all. I'm not sure I would have ever told them.

Hardly able to see through the tears, I rush out of

Maddy's yard. To where, I don't know. Frazzled, I take out my phone and start to call for an Uber.

My feet are swept from under me.

Cigar, leather, and salty ocean encircle me, along with bulky arms, a meaty chest, and a boatful of swagger. He carries me to a wooden swing hanging from a nearby tree in Maddy's yard.

"Let's pray this thing holds up." Once he sits with me on his lap, he gives the ropes a good tug.

My eyes are blurry from tears of shame. With his thumb, he sweeps my hair out of my face and wipes.

"French Fry, what's all this?"

"I wasn't trying to use you, I sw—"

"I know," he whispers. "I knew who you were."

"Wh—" Choking, I clear my throat, clean my nose.

He offers the tail of his t-shirt. "Here."

We both chuckle as he helps me out.

"You did?"

He nods. "Yeah. The night Duncan and I saw you at the bar. Before we got there, we were here at Maddy's, when Jerrell mentioned you would be there. Tanja wasn't around, so Duncan really wanted to go all of a sudden. When we got to the bar, you and him both disappeared at the same time, for about five minutes. You came back all worked up. I'd already suspected I knew you from somewhere. That night, I started putting two and two together. After I escorted you to your house, I went home and pulled out the picture of the rooftop party where we met you. You were in the photo, hugged up with Duncan. I remember that night, wanting to talk to you. Duncan picked up my vibe and got to you while I was preoccupied."

Wiping my face, he examines me and continues.

"That might not be a bad thing, since back then, I wasn't ready for you." He takes my hand and kisses it. "You always react whenever you see Tanja or Duncan. It's why I took you to The Countryman that night, all dolled up. I saw the beef between you and her, and once I figured out they were shading you, I wanted to help you show out."

I'm perplexed. "You mean you knew she would be there?"

"I did. Duncan came to see me. He mentioned it, dropped big hints that he still had feelings for you. I already suspected it, but that day, he confirmed it. So I handled both him and Tanja for playing with you." With a slow kiss on my shoulder and his fingers massaging me, he continues. "I took you shopping out in public to get people talking. Flirted with you in front of the Explore staff. Showed you off at The Countryman, put you up in Cyrus's house, so they could understand, in no uncertain terms, that if they were fucking with you, they were fucking with me."

This is blowing my mind, the way Lion tends to play the dumb jock who doesn't know much, but in fact is slick with his perception.

Our fingers lace with one another.

"The times I've been around, and you see Duncan, your first move is to sleep with somebody you don't know," he murmurs. "Like you've got something to prove."

Called out, hating I'm so transparent, I look away.

Lion nudges my face back to him. "It's why I gave you time. I sensed you needed it, baby." He lays his lips on my bare arm and kisses it. "I didn't want you laying with me and using what you and I have as a diversion from your beef with him." Now he stares at me like he's up to no good. "Plus, I couldn't tell you straight up that you were going to be my lady."

At hearing this, I draw back. "*Excuse* me?"

"You heard me. I wasn't about to come out and say it was a wrap for you being single. You're stubborn, and weren't ready to hear it, so I just started clearing the field." Deviousness in his eyes, his voice drips with sin. "In your head, you were taking your time, but in reality, all up and down these streets, you were my lady. I told you after we left the bar, I wanted you to be my business."

Stumped is not the word to describe me. Damn spoiled ass man. I don't know whether to hit him again or slip him my tongue.

Before that though, we need to clear up how he views my time with him.

"Lion, no. A diversion is not why I laid with you." I brace myself for this next part. To trust him with truth. "I slept with you *despite* me detesting Duncan. Not because of it. I was… I *am*… catching feelings for… a certain… cocky, self-centered, sexy at times…"

His face breaks out into summertime flower gardens. "You *are* catching, or you already caught?"

His lips tug and love on mine, tug and love on my womb, opening me up. The lazy tenderness of our mingling mouths is akin to this soft grass cushioning my bare feet.

"Both." I stop kissing to grab his face. "And I wasn't playing you to get back at him." I think for a moment. "Okay, that first time, yes. I followed you downstairs with an agenda."

His laugh is as sexy as it is gentle.

"M-hmm, that's what I figured. But later on, the more time we spent, I saw you struggling with it. That's not somebody who's straight ruthless."

His teeth are every bit as iridescent and mesmerizing as the night I met him and Duncan sixteen years ago, on top of the world.

I was more attracted to the magnetic Lion, but so was every girl.

After that party, Duncan and I kept crossing paths on the way to our offices in the mornings the rest of the summer.

He held his own. His conversation and ambition sealed the deal. Focused and determined to be president one day, already out of school, he wasn't about the college-boy games. He couldn't get enough of my no-nonsense intellect and intensity in the bedroom, even though I had a year left of school. We were going to take over everything.

I flaunted him on campus to my so-called friends when he came to visit, but I hid it from my family so they couldn't talk me out of being with him. On a visit to see him in New York, I found Tanja there, two months after we'd eloped. I learned why he hid our marriage from his folks. They had already chosen who they approved for him.

The rejection burned hotter than hellfire. Now I'm grateful that went nowhere. "I should have told you sooner."

"It went down as it should have." Tilting up his head, Lion brings me closer to him. The mocha richness of his eyes pours into me, and he glides his tongue along my bottom lip. "Besides, once I figured all this out, I knew you hadn't really loved him."

Puzzled, I stare at a man who sits firm in what he just said.

"What?"

"You only felt puppy love for him. Nothing serious."

"How are you going to tell me about my own emotions?"

Lion shakes his head. "That day we ate with your family, your mother said you hadn't brought a man home in *twenty* years. That means, not since you were sixteen." My cocky Lumberjack grins smugly. "That also means you never took Duncan home to meet your folks. I never bring a woman home who Roberta Middleton will turn her nose up at, so in your heart, you knew it wasn't right." He sucks my lips and hugs me. "But guess who you *did* ask to break bread with your mama and daddy."

Now I roll my eyes. "Oh, my God." I'll never hear the end of this.

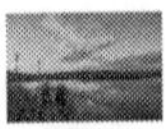

LION

I've never wanted to be inside a woman so bad.

Not my dick inside her, but *me*. This man who struggles to be one of power and influence, when what he may need most are the right influences. People to slap the hell out of him and make him see beyond his own interests.

I imagined the next time Kam and I made love…

… make love.

Not fuck.

Your boy has come a long way.

I imagined she and I would reach roller-coaster heights in the brewery. Some one-off where she would deny me again, and I would tempt her again, and we would lose ourselves in each other again until we climaxed our way to kingdom come.

But watching her strut inside a house—so personal and intimate—and kick off her shoes, hits different. She stops at the base of the stairs.

With that mettle of hers, she tips her head forward and casts lustful eyes at me. "You coming or not, Lumberjack?"

"Who is Lumberjack?" I throw my keys on the little hall stand.

"My nickname for you in my head."

Tickled, I scoop her up. We ascend the stairs while her eyes climb into mine. On our way up, she slides her fingers in my beard.

"Shit." Immediately, my dick hits maximum capacity and I can no longer walk. "Them is fightin' words right there, girl."

Kam giggles as I lower to one knee on the stairs.

I had every intention of doing this properly, in a bed and everything.

By my beard, French Fry tugs my face to hers, tugs my heart to hers, my life to hers, my protection and affection...

Her fingers keep frolicking in the whiskers on my chin.

"You're not allowed to touch another woman. Just so we're clear, no more Olga," she whispers and emphasizes her point with a hard glare.

"And I don't want any more, baby."

To Ash or anybody else, that would have been a complete lie. My mouth would have recited what she wanted to hear, while my heart, hunger, and sense of purpose still longed for more. Although I have no idea what my life will entail tomorrow, no part of me feels incomplete or unsatiated with Kamilah.

Kam fumbles at the straps of her dress. Since I picked this gown, I memorized *exactly* how to undo it. Once I unzip her and undo the ties at her hip and waist, the bodice falls into my hands.

She lifts my t-shirt, unzips my khakis, strokes my bulge. My manhood all excited in her palm, she's squeezing and stroking away my fuck-ups and misguided choices. This is virgin territory for me, in which I now want to walk as an erect man for her.

When I stand up, her dress drops. Kam kneels and pushes off my shorts.

I'm stunned as her fingers ascend the backs of my legs, caressing my thighs. Her moist mouth skates along my shin, traces the muscles of my hamstring with her dripping tongue, and her face smacks my dick when she sucks my balls.

Kam gazes up at me with real joy shining through her that… shines through me. "I have a surprise for you."

"This is surprise enough, baby."

She shakes her head. "No."

Standing, she takes my hand and *thinks* she's going to lead me the rest of the way. I scoop her up again, because I yearn like hell to be her knight in shining armor. French Fry's arms link around my neck like she might want me to be.

"Where to?" I ask her.

"The bedroom."

Inside, it's high afternoon, with the sun streaming through every room. The jacuzzi is full.

A pleased smile spreads across her whole face at seeing my confusion.

"What's popping here?" That liquid is not water. With small green plants and buds floating on its surface, I wonder. No, she couldn't have.

"Come find out."

Once I set her inside it, I step in behind her.

The cereal scent, of grains, barley, and malt engulfs me. I inspect the dried plants that afloat atop the liquid. The fact that she did it awes me. "A beer bath?"

The mixture is warm. She's kept it heated all day.

Well, mash me up in a damn tun.

Kam grins. "Somebody with a nose for these things told me this was… therapeutic… homeopathic… curative… erotic," she spouts off while wading in foam and plant buds.

"You mean you planned for us to… before the whole Duncan thing?" The sun streams through me also while I'm realizing this.

Kam tugs me down, into warm beer that encircles us. "Yes. I was planning to tell you today, so we could move on and do us. It's not cool that you found out like that."

This is new—a woman gazing at me, and me staring back and seeing the future. "It doesn't matter how."

I hold her face in my hands, and she dips beneath the surface. Her hair floats up, and her mouth drops down, attaches to my dick in beer, plays with my nuts while drinking and sucking.

Karate Kam bobs her head and gnaws, her tongue going to town, brewing my shaft until *I'm* the fucking pulp. Shit feels so good I can no longer see the lake and trees ahead when my head careens back.

Every bit of that energy she threw into her intense slap a few weeks ago, she now throws into her stroke.

"Kam, slow..."

She comes up from the beer, soaking, takes a few breaths. Dives back in. Goes back to milling my wood.

Slurping beer and deep-throating me until no liquid or space flows between her mouth muscles and my erection.

The way her head pulls, I'm thankful she's no virgin. Those years she spent in bars and clubs are coming in handy as hell, each time she nearly twists my shit off.

"Mmmph."

Thunder cracks from my dick, up through my core, in the middle of the daytime. Kam sucks me so hard in her throat I might be seeing stars and stripes. This woman can slap me as many times as she wants if it means I'm getting this at sunrise *and* sunset.

Kamilah pleasures this hardheaded Negro until he touches those eastern red cedars out there.

"Shit!"

THE FIRE THIS TIME

KAMILAH

KAMILAH

Today, on Fourth of July, American Freedom Day, Lion and I head to our families' houses, after we woke up together.

That'll take some getting used to.

Not that I don't immensely enjoy waking up to those big horse legs wrapped around me. But when you spend as many years as I have mentally bolstering yourself for the likelihood you'll never have morning cuddles, and then must reprogram your thinking to receive that, coupling up requires some adjustment.

I'll need to relax from the awkwardness of not knowing what to do with myself around him. I'm practicing how to let my smile come forward and not suppress it as a defense mechanism so somebody doesn't mistake my joy as weakness. Being guarded is still second nature. The fear still hovers over me, of someone attempting to take advantage. But I'm working on my defensiveness.

Like, who is Kamilah really, when she lets love in?

First, we're visiting my family.

Once we arrive, there's no light between them and me when my siblings swarm me.

"You and me, we were both at Brown together," Jerrell points out, flummoxed. "How did I not know all that?"

"Boy, you were two years behind me, and we ran in different social circles on different ends of campus. You had Raychelle, and when you weren't with her, you were with your boys or some other females. It's fine. I'm good now." I try to reassure him and hug the guilt from him.

The judgment and scrutiny our parents have always dispensed, which I so feared all these years, is not there now. I regret the sad tears pouring from Mama.

"It's okay, Mama, don't cry. You'll make me cry, and I'm happy now."

"I'm so sorry you didn't feel this was something you could come to me about."

I do remember hers and Daddy's strict lessons. *I didn't give birth to any fools,* she always said. And though I could have gone to her, and she would have stood by me, I still would have had to bear the unspoken disappointment in her eyes that I was that one fool.

Sheldon and Chrissy take turns kissing on me.

"You two, quit it."

My big brother's tears say all the things he can't fix his mouth to. "You know we would have beat the daylights out of him."

I shake my head. "That's why I didn't tell you. And it wouldn't have helped anything."

"But you should have told *me,*" Roland interjects. "I would have worked out the job so you didn't have to be around here, Kam. I'm… damn, I'm sorry. You were trying to tell me in your own words, without putting yourself out there, and I… I wasn't paying attention."

In my flurry of emotions, I connect with Lion's gaze where he watches across the room. "If you had listened to me, Ro, I wouldn't have started up with Lumberjack over there. So, I guess I had to get through that little storm to reach my rainbow."

Ro shoots back, "Well, I sure as hell wouldn't have given money to Milsap's damn Senate campaign."

"Right!" my other brothers chime in.

"I've already told Maddy we want the money back," Jerrell says. "Everybody was really disgusted yesterday after you left. Her parents won't allow anymore campaign fundraisers at their home. And—"

"And I'm going to stop working on his campaign and step down." Maddy hugs me in the formal way that Maddy expresses affection. "There's no way I'll teach my son that it's okay for his aunt to be treated so disrespectfully, or any woman."

I'm surprised when our hug extends a little longer. Not that there's tension between us. But for both of us, long hugs are just not our way. "Thanks, Maddy."

She redirects her attention to Lion. "Besides, there are other worthy endeavors that might require my time these next few months, if they'll have me."

There's a Fourth of July parade later on Eastville Avenue. But first, Lion and I stop by Slurp and Taste, to check in and make sure Miracle and Desmond are flowing smoothly.

"So you and The Lion are moving in sync now, huh?" Desmond teases.

I cut my eyes at him.

"All right then, I see you, Ms. I Don't Need a Man and I'm Never Having Kids."

Hand in hand, a while later, Lion and I ride through the

streets of Montauk to his folks' crib in Southampton. I'm gazing out the window at breezy families, his fingers occasionally playing with mine, bringing my hand to his lips to kiss as he drives. It's… a different kind of excitement. These sprawling emerald trees, humming sidewalks, peaceful beaches, high grasses on the marshes, lemonade on patios, is all a soothing escape. He turns up a narrow, paved road to his family's house.

Although I've met his parents before, this is the first "official" house visit.

I've never done one, so…

… massive inhale.

"Kamilah," his mother says in what I'm learning is her breathy way of talking. Her words are more like vocal sighs.

I've entered a modern museum. Over my head, hanging from the ceiling is the skeletal frame of what looks like a giant fish. I struggle not to stare too long, but I do take mental notes for when Mama, Princess, and Etta all interrogate me later.

"Hi, Mrs. Middleton, it's so good to see you again."

I'm nervous as hell shaking his father's hand. He seems amiable, but his eyes are stern, like even though he smiles, he's privately writing a list of concerns in his head that he'll review with Lion later.

"I've heard nothing but awesome things about you, and I know you come from good stock, Kamilah," the senior Middleton says. "They tell me you're kicking asses and taking names over there at Explore."

The humble me now shuts down cocky me. "I get the job done. Let's put it that way."

"I like it that way. That's the only way," he replies, warming up. "And I'm sure it's necessary with all these here knuckleheads you've got on your hands." He pushes his thumb toward Lion.

Lion and I—

Damn.

Lion and I. We swap bashful glances from where we stand on opposite sides of his father.

"Your son never ceases to surprise me." And because a large part of me senses this is important to both of them, I add this next truth. "You really raised him well. Not only is he a sharp leader and businessmen, but he's a damn fine gentleman when he wants to be."

The sunlight flickering in the trees outside also scatters bits of light on what may have been the shadows of Mr. Middleton's face. "Thank you, young lady."

"Come on, girl, let's chat, and I can give you some pointers on the Hamptons." His mother breaks in and ushers me toward a separate room.

Lion follows until Mrs. Middleton stops him at the door.

"All right then, baby, you can excuse her and me for a while."

She shuts the door in the face of a stunned Lion.

"Now," she starts and clasps her hands together. "How's he treating you?"

I can't help laughing. "A little rocky at first, but things are going all right, and we're on the same page. He's been a…" My voice trails off while I stare out the window at those sleepy, relaxing trees, and think of Lion's pretty teeth every time I miscalculated what was behind them. "He's been awesome."

Mrs. Middleton gazes into me on the couch and then pours us sweet tea. "He'd better be. And how do you like it around here?"

I shrug and dart my eyes round this immaculate piano room that smells of lemon pine polish. Large portraits line the walls, of well-dressed men and women, dating back hundreds of years, peering squarely at me. "At times, the

Hamptons, all these 'uppity' folk, as my grandmother likes to call them, can be overwhelming. It's an acquired taste, but I am beginning to appreciate it more."

"Don't let any of this intimidate you, and certainly not when it comes to Lion. By all means, you stand firm on what you know to be right, in Explore or with my sons, or anywhere else in these neighborhoods. Hold their feet to the fire. No matter what." Her brilliantly green eyes flare, as if their only job is to emphasize her points. "You make my son prove himself to you, you hear me?" Her finger taps my knee while she talks.

I'm smiling inside before I feel it emerging outside. "Yes, ma'am."

"Don't you go easy on him for anything. Lion is quite capable, but he is also spoiled. He usually needs a kick in his butt to get him right. And then he can literally do anything." She squeezes my hand. "But, honey, let me tell you, I've never seen my boy with this kind of energy. Always gone and trying so hard. You're already doing something right."

That warms Karate Kam.

And frightens her.

"Thank you. I think he's working me over also."

"That's good, but listen, these Middleton men can be a lot to handle. He will probably test you, so if you have any problems out of him at all, don't hesitate to come to me and I'll get him."

Kevin, Cher, Brendan, and his family come through, and we all chat for a while.

Observing the vibe among the brothers and their father, the respect and acknowledgment are there. But love and camaraderie… I wonder. I also can't help noticing how their conversations are a smidge terse, like the men suspect one another of having committed serious crimes.

"Come on," Lion whispers to me and leads me out.

He disappeared outside for a for a few minutes while I chatted with his family, and now I follow him through his backyard, to the boating dock. Several boats of differing sizes are tied to the posts. Instead of taking the handsome one I almost crashed the other day, imagine my astonishment when we approach a plain, simple canoe. It resembles the small boats in romance movies like *The Notebook*.

"What are we doing with this? Is this thing sturdy enough? Don't people drown in these?"

"You do remember who you're with, right? I've got a few surprises of my own," he replies and taps my hip. He drops a couple of large, woven baskets inside and hands me a big one that's kind of heavy.

A couple of minutes later, he takes the oars and rows us away from civilization. The sun begins its descent over the rooftops.

"Where are we going?"

The tree branches that are his arms paddle us over water.

"One of my favorite places around here. It might even be my favorite spot. Called Gardiner's Island."

"I've heard of that. Isn't it private, though? The biggest private island in America?"

"Second biggest. And you can keep this to yourself, but I might know the folks who own it."

"Of course you do. Why am I not surprised?"

"Be honest." Between deep breaths, he rows. "You don't like it? Hm?" Deep inhale and deeper exhale. "The nice mansion with heated floors and the latest technology, jacuzzi overlooking the lake, VIP treatment at the dress boutiques, excursions to a private island, French Fry? You scoff and roll your eyes, but…" More deep breaths. "You would give it up?"

I thumb the straps of my dress and think. "I didn't say all that."

We both crack up.

It's erotic watching his chest muscles expand and contract as he takes us over the bay waters. Lion rows down the river of my affection when he's gazing at me and ferrying us.

He stops after rowing what might have been a few miles, removes blankets and towels from the woven baskets, and spreads them around us for padding. He kicks off his summer loafers and unstraps my wedges.

"What are we doing here, in the middle of this water?"

Along the wooden slats, he tugs me against him. "Good things come to those who wait, baby."

So I lay in the crook of his arm, tucked under a pensive, thoughtful Lion. He is not exactly melancholy, but quiet, maybe reflective.

"Why did you take this boat and not the other?"

"I'm closer to the water in one of these. I love the big ones, too, but these leave little space between me and what God made. I don't take these boats very often. This one has personal meaning for me though."

"Why is this one special?"

"I tried to run away in it one time." Lion's face is unsettled, and those beautiful teeth he so easily displays are hard-pressed to appear now.

On these blankets and wooden boards, I shift for a better view of him.

"I packed food and everything and called myself never going to return. I rowed as hard as I could and flamed out about fifteen miles from here." Softly, his chest shakes next to me from his chuckles. "I stayed there all night and ate my sandwiches. I still had more food left, but my folks called and reported me missing. The coast guard caught up with me."

Now it's me who chuckles, though it feels like a thread of sadness lingers in here somewhere. "What were you trying to get away from?"

His focus ventures further out.

"My mom and I, we'd had a big disagreement. I was only about eight, and…" He wipes his face and stares at nothing. "I was heartbroken. I could tell she was, too. And at age eight, you don't know how to be mad when you still love them." He rubs his chest, as if pain lies underneath it that he's trying to massage out.

I take over that job—of massaging him. I'm not crazy enough to think I can remove this conflict gripping him now that has been there thirty years, but he can at least feel supported. He's not wading through that darkness alone.

"Things change is all. Seasons change. At some point, I suppose we've got to let go of that hurt kid. But this boat," he says, gripping the sideboard, "will always be my getaway vehicle."

I run my fingers along his jaw. "Maybe when I learn how to transport you over places that God made, I can also be your getaway vehicle."

That must trigger some seismic shift in him. He takes my fingers and sucks them. And I won't say I don't appreciate his tongue gliding over each of them like candy until the sensations get my pussy to skipping. I pull his beard to me, so he can do that in my mouth.

Lumberjack doesn't disappoint. Kissing and rolling his tongue, not just on my flesh, but all over my emotional desert. My fingers still on his face, the tension of his jaws ripple under my fingertips. He inches up my dress and rests his hand on my abdomen, thumbing and fingering my flesh. And my cervix responds, shifting and contracting like he's opening up some portal at the peak of my womanhood.

A cannonball-like blare scares the spine out of me, and I leap off him in a near escape from this boat. The sky explodes behind me!

Lion breaks into gut-splitting guffaws.

My heart clamoring, I stare behind me and up at the sky.

Sprays of fireworks paint a canvas the color of fiery sunset.

Lion still finds this humorous. Once my heart stops galloping and I'm back to breathing normally, I join his laughter and shove him.

"You could have warned me."

"Where's the fun in that? It's called surprise for a reason." Encircling me in his arms, he nibbles on my ear while the fireworks continue, squeezes my titties.

My inner canal creams into my panties, and my erogenous zones start to beg. And we're back to kissing and necking.

Against the blankets, we fall, and I straddle him. Up the skirts of my dress, his fingers explore my thighs, in the lead-up to my pussy. With his teeth, he peels down the straps and frees my breasts, sucking and slurping on each one. The sloppy wetness of his mouth munching on my titties sends me into a soft, moist abyss. I wrangle with his zipper to get it over his boat-sized erection.

"Oh, shit, get on him, girl. He is ready for your ass." Anticipation lights up Lion's face more than those fireworks as he scoots down his pants.

I sit my fireworks down on his raw dick and Lion's girth fills me up, reminding me this is my first time being on top of him.

"Fffuck."

Things were a little easier yesterday in the tub when I had beer. And I didn't have to get *all* of him in my throat, just enough of him. Now my reproductive organs need to adjust.

"Mmhm..." he murmurs. "A lot of fireworks right there, ain't it, girl?" He clasps my hips to his so I can't flee.

When I say he takes up the whole of me, up to my ribs... and I'm no spring chicken.

Lion smiles with amusement, pulling me to him. "Come here."

"Wait…let me…."

"Mm mm…"

We're slapping hands and fighting, and I'm whimpering and he's laughing softly.

In his smooth, rich bourbon voice, he instructs, "Move your hands. Move 'em."

Our foreheads kiss. He guides my hips, and my canal adapts to his full size. Now I start to pop on him. Tongues collide while we rock the boat.

I'm lost in him. Lost in his love of life and culture, the protectiveness of his family, his love of sea and nature, his desire to leave his mark on the world, his deceptive intellectual prowess that he strategically deploys to trip people up, and yes, his goofy-ass shenanigans.

In the motions of my hips, I adjust to his length and fatness and throw my head back to ride his intense thrust.

"That's right, French Fry, put your name on it," he mutters.

"Aah…"

His dick strikes a match on the nerves along my uterus, lighting me up in flames. Cannonballs blare in our humping, in my thighs beating on his, in the sparks blasting through me and balling up my feet behind me. Under my nails, his ass and back compress with each thrust, with each punch of his manhood into my existence. Our explosions squeeze my pussy walls, my juices bathing him, I give Lion all of me. And he holds me to him like he wants every drop.

I wish I could describe how the fireworks reflect off the pretty waters and how poetic it is but… I *am* the fireworks show right now.

BETTER MEN

LION

LION

Trust me, it's poetic.

Kam makes love to me like it's Juneteenth and Independence Day and Christmas.

Riding and bouncing on me until her pussy burns up and contracts on my every centimeter.

Ooh, and I love how she loses herself on my shit and her head tilts back. All that goddamn moaning and whining…

The rockets' red blare is bursting inside her, all over me, and through me. She strokes the nerves in my dick and my nut pops into her soft dome. Nerves I didn't know I had crackle up my groin and stomach. Inside her, I unleash my seeds, hold her, rock with her in this fireworks spray. Until we're breathless and spent, cradling one another.

I've been watching fireworks since I was a kid, and they've *never* been this sensational.

A couple of weeks later, not a day has gone by that we haven't connected sexually and mentally. I arrived here in the

Hamptons with selfish goals and priorities—revenge, self-preservation, longtime vendettas.

Strange how love—yes, that's crazy… I haven't said it yet but… *love*—realigns our priorities.

It impacts how we view the world and choose to operate in it. I'm finally getting around to what I've put off the past few weeks, the commitment I've put over a fourth of my life into.

My career.

And the conflict with which I've grappled even longer. Standing in the back office of Slurp, I address my younger brother.

The distrusting glare on his face indicates he is parsing my every word.

"Explore and MoneyCruncher don't have a choice. Just so you understand, Kevin, Houston PetroChem funds the supplies and inventory Explore relies on. I'm the primary contact with the distributors for Slurp's malt and hops and for Taste's chocolate. All of it, HP pays for, man. Your stress tests for Juneteenth and Fourth of July have gone well, without a hitch, because of me. Your restaurants exceeded expectations. You didn't just receive increased traffic from Black folks on your premises, I also increased sponsorships and sales from other racial demographics interested in products you can now sell nationwide."

I turn my back on him and his stoic face and stare out the little window to the taproom.

"Explore's products were made with ingredients you wouldn't have but for Houston PetroChem. And you need more of it, leading up to your big concert next month. You know what all this means."

Outside on the floor, Kamilah and Laney share a laugh with Desmond. All of them crack jokes with Virgil while sampling his latest menu additions. They must be taste-testing some octopus, the way Kam holds it. She hates that.

Her gaze darts up to meet mine. On that face—on all their faces—is the camaraderie and closeness of more than a business enterprise, but a community, and a family.

But it's still business, nevertheless.

I navigate my attention away from them and back to my brother.

"Lion, let me get this straight. You mean you're squeezing Explore to get access to MoneyCruncher?" Irritated, Kevin rolls his anger into his lips, and he clenches the table. He understands the stakes. "After I'm the one who brought you in here. To a growing enterprise where you'd have a platform beyond the oil industry. You and Dad and the whole 'reputation' thing," he says, swirling his finger around him, "you used Explore's holiday celebrations for the family history. No objections from any of us. And *now* you're trying to fuck us."

"Don't say it that way, man. We're all mutually benefitting from each other, my guy. You benefited off the Middleton name. Explore has benefited from me. Stop acting like the favors ran just one way."

Kevin squints. "But I trusted that you knew better."

"I do. Stop lamenting."

He stares at me. I stare back.

"What do they want?"

"Not just access, dude. Sell."

He scoffs and twiddles his thumbs, his options churning in his mind about how to counter this. He's not going to screw up the Sasha Static performance, possibly the biggest event that will ever happen to him in his life. "How much?"

"Six hundred."

"I can get seven-fifty elsewhere."

"Elsewhere doesn't have your shit locked up," I clap back, hands on hips.

I know my brother.

He knows I know him and what he's capable of.

Kevin nods.

At this point in our lives, I've gotten too old to fight. Not over our longstanding rivalry or our unsettled disputes about whose vision is best to carry on the Middleton legacy.

"They want an answer today on whether you'll sell, or if we're shutting all this down. I've put this off long enough. So, time is kind of tight. What'll it be?"

"Shutting all this down? What are you doing?" Kamilah demands, pushing open the crack of the door. Eyes wild and upset, fists curled like she's about to clock me. "Are you trying to play *your own* goddamn brother?"

"Ohh, shit," Kevin's friend, Brett, scoffs into his mouth.

"Baby." I terminate the phone call where Gavin from my job was listening on the other end.

"Don't 'baby' me, Lion!" Anger flares in her nostrils. "What *is* this? It sounds to me like smoke between you and him, and you're taking advantage."

Every time I think my heart couldn't be more smitten...

Quickly, before she can react and punch me, I grab her, spin her, and lock her in my arms.

"Li—"

"It's a ploy, baby," I whisper in her ear, once I see the call with Gavin has truly ended and he is no longer on the phone to overhear me. "It's a ploy. We're working together, sweetheart."

Kam's muscles relax against me. I start laughing and spin her toward the others so she can see Kevin and his colleagues working up a gameplay against Houston PetroChem.

"Really?" she asks me.

"Yes, really."

"But for a minute there, bruh, you were about to catch that beat down," Brett points out.

I look down at her. "Is that what you were about to do to me, baby?"

Kamilah's little fighter energy injects rocket fuel into my dick nerves, and her eyebrow shoots up. "Damn right. That's what I was about to do to you, Lion. You don't hurt your own flesh and blood."

I mutter through clenched teeth, "But you're not my flesh and blood, girl, so you can hurt me any time you want. You know I like that rough shit." I squeeze the giggles out of her. "Tell me how you were going to kick my ass. Hm? Here, put it in my ear." I place my ear next to Kam's mouth. "And don't leave out no details neither, girl."

"Negro." She bites my earlobe and pulls.

"Lion, he's calling back," Kevin says.

I say to Kam, "I've got to take this. Once I finish, I want a play-by-play."

Staring at her, at my future, I remember why I'm doing this and take the call.

"Gavin, my bad, dude. I got interrupted there with a small situation."

Actually, Kam popping up when she did was perfect. Me getting caught by a loved one who's upset I'm scheming lends authenticity to the lie that I'm feeding my job.

"Ha ha! Lion, Lion, Lion," Gavin cows on the other end. It's obvious he enjoyed every second. Dude loves backstabbing and drama. "Hope you didn't get chewed out there too bad there, bud. So, uh, you got your brother there with you?"

I nod at Kevin. "Yes, he's here with me. And he says he's ready to deal."

Setting the phone on the table, I now count on what I've always known Kevin to do—hack conversations.

"Ron, Gavin, my brother informs me you want something from me." Kevin stares at me.

"Kevin! We've wanted to talk to you for the longest time. Congratulations on building such a powerful platform." Ron kisses his ass.

As I sit here now, listening to Ron bend over and contort himself to appease my younger brother, I know I'm not making a wrong decision.

Dad was wrong. Corporate executives and financiers don't rule the world anymore. Innovation does. Innovation like that of my brothers—Brendan's and, yes, Kevin's.

Dad always felt the real power lay in major corporations, where we needed to prove ourselves for validation. Kevin set out to prove that innovation and technology didn't require a big company and could open a whole new realm of power for Black people, separate from behemoths of the old days.

"So, Ron, if I understand this correctly, you want me to open up MoneyCruncher to you," Kevin asserts.

"Oh, Kevin, think of it as more of a collaboration. Where we work together, you know. We've got a few challenges with our competitors, and we believe your apparatus can help us solve them. It's an incredible interface you've built, and this will benefit us both."

In the twist of Kevin's hands around one another, he must also be turning over his words. "Your company purchased a lot of supplies and inventory for Explore and distributed the goods through Allan Stafford and Sons. And you've worked with Aragon food distributor concerning the chocolate for one of our restaurants."

Ron replies from the other end. "Just helping out. Contributing to your cause. We'd like to help Explore succeed where we can, and in exchange, MoneyCruncher can scratch our backs, too."

Kevin and I stare across the table, in that way only

brothers can converse and expect one another to know what the other is thinking when no one else does.

"Ron, you are aware that the companies you paid employ discriminatory distribution tactics against minority businesses of color, right?"

Ron stalls. "Uh, well, Lion picked those distributors, you see. Now, Kevin—"

"But HP's company name is on those checks as the payor. And the same is true for Aragon and the chocolate. It comes from the Ivory Coast of Africa, where slave labor and child labor are used to produce that cocoa paste and powder. Houston PetroChem paid out checks to the companies engaged in that, too. And whenever Lion didn't respond to you soon enough, didn't you flex your muscle to hold up the shipments from being delivered to Explore's locations? So you were the ultimate party exercising control to hold back inventory from Explore. No?"

Ron chokes on his surprise, apparently realizing that I've set him up to look like he's in bed with dirty distributors.

"Kevin, friend, listen—"

"You're using strong-arm tactics to pressure me into selling. And in a conversation with my brother, your subordinate, Gavin, was just listening as you used Lion to pressure me."

The helpless sigh drifts through the phone. The tables are turned.

"You sure you still want to deal with MoneyCruncher?" A pissed off Kevin asks. "I've got a whole stable of investors on my platform, and press reporters in my pocket, who would *love* to see all that information I just shared with you."

There was never a moment when I didn't know this little runt had hacked my phone and was eavesdropping. As a result, he would have learned Allan Stafford was bilking

Black business owners and that Aragon is bleeding Black farmers in Africa dry.

And I'm certain hacking my phone and, maybe even my laptop, is also how Kevin knew my job didn't give me the promotion, that when I arrived in the Hamptons I likely needed a new job. Duncan would be no help, and many of my other friends wouldn't be either. With our family name sitting in the mud, I expected a lot of folks to leave me in the cold.

Rather than trying to shut Kevin down, the best move was to let him eavesdrop and play this to my advantage.

Now I lean against the table. "So, Ron, in light of all Kevin just noted, let's discuss my retirement package."

No matter what I did, or even if I could have convinced Kevin to sell in some alternate reality, Houston PetroChem was never going to make me CEO. Not in that racist part of the country.

But I now have leverage, in case they try anything foul.

Once the call ends, Kevin and I stand on opposite ends of the table from one another. It's not clear how an accord will play out for him and me. Maybe it's already happening, like Mom hopes.

At my side, Kamilah has been listening and she beams. The woman who makes sure she receives nothing less from me than a better man. Very much like my mother. And I don't want to be anything less than a better man for either of them. Especially as it concerns letting go of that seven-year-old boy and moving on.

Also in the room with us is Toni, our family's reputation management consultant, and a very pregnant Tosca Jessup, Brett's wife and Kevin's personal press manager.

"As far as the liquor and food distributors, let's make sure that part gets leaked to the press," I say. "And how the

Middleton family is taking the lead on anti-competition and discriminatory business practices."

Kevin eyes me. "Be careful what you leak. It could always come back to bite you."

I know he's referencing what I did in the oil industry, paying off injured workers and the families of dead workers so they wouldn't go public. If I disclose bad deeds of these liquor distributors, they will surely repay the favor and disclose mine.

"I'll think about it." My truth will come out eventually anyway, just as Dad's did. Calculating a strategy for exterminating those fools is now one of my top priorities.

Out in the taproom is the community of aspiring Black minds for whom Kevin helped provide a foundation. They've grown on me, and they are worth my effort as well.

Once the others leave us alone, he stares at me. "You knew I had hacked you and you didn't say shit."

"I put you onto a group that's pursuing your company."

"So you want something in exchange for that," he concludes.

"Of course I do. I just did you a favor." I think for a moment. "Dad. Work with him. It doesn't have to be real estate or an investment. In fact, it should be more personal than that. And mean it when you do it."

Dad has lots of friends, and a hell of a lot of money. If he truly wanted to build his beachfront resort in Florida, he's got enough history, connections and assets that he would have done it by now. So it's not Kevin's money that Dad needs, or even Kev's technology. Dad wants what every man wants in his household—Kevin's love and loyalty.

He must be realizing this in his slow nod to me.

Other than my brother's arrogance, I can tolerate him sometimes.

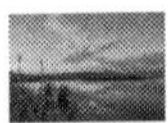

A FEW WEEKS LATER, at the old fire house, the cultural gathering center for the Black community in Sag Harbor, we've arrived for a special meeting of the old families.

Opening the door for my mom, I escort her and Dad into the facility.

Before we enter the doors, I check in with Dad a final time. All over the lines in his face, it's apparent this is hard for him. But necessary.

I squeeze his shoulder. "You good, Old Man?"

"Always. I've got to be." He shifts focus to Mom. "It's for the best if we're moving past it."

The two of them take one another's hand. In the closeness of their bodies and the matrimony of their shared gazes, they lock together in what finally seems to be more of a bond than a burden.

Seeing that for the two of them soothes the betrayed seven-year-old kid.

Kevin, Brendan, and their wives meet us inside.

Pastor Arnold enters to assist with keeping the peace.

Maddy and her parents, the Pages, are waiting, along with the children and grandchildren of Francis Manuel.

I'm well aware that not everybody knows the entire story, so when I start the greetings, I don't touch my father and Kevin's father.

"So, we're all here because of events that took place late last year which threw our community into a snare. But today, hopefully, we can free ourselves of hard feelings and return to the business of building the Black Hamptons. Especially because there is much money for all our various companies and businesses to make next month. Not only is it high traffic season, but of course, Ms. Static's trail-blazing performance could shore up our bank accounts and sales for years. We all stand to benefit. But first, working together requires that we cross some bridges. So, I'll begin."

I turn to Adella, Solomon, and their relatives.

Dad comes to stand at my side. "I'll do it, son." He stops a moment, takes a beat, and then wills his body to face Kevin.

Who might be battling his own internal storm where he stands and waits for what we've decided.

As is Mom.

"A few years ago, on a personal level, I had a dispute with somebody who..." Dad clears his throat. "Had a family of his own." He chooses his words carefully, just as we practiced with Toni and the lawyers. Yes, it's orchestrated, but the statement is no less true, and it still protects him legally.

"Two wrongs don't make a right. As for me and my house, we are working out our differences. I wish nothing but peace and prosperity for the family of Francis Manuel. In that regard, the Middleton family will return one half of the Smeralda Costa property to the heirs and assigns of Mr. Francis Manuel, minus the purchase price. Please be aware that this is not a settlement offer or some concession in exchange for court action. If you wish to continue the litigation, that is you all's decision. But as for us, the partial return of this property is a purely goodwill gesture. In the name of my son, Kevin, and my wife, Roberta. And for the peace and healing of my own family."

A breath. A lifetime of breaths.

Dad continues, "If you wish to discuss details such as interest accumulated over the period of time we held it, loans, liens and what have you, we can sit with our representatives and work it out. As for the Middleton half of that property, it will be donated to the Middleton Family Trust and designated for charitable uses. Primarily, taking high-achieving inner-city youth to Europe during the summers, who otherwise would not have the opportunity. Facilitated by Explore Adventures."

Audible gasps flow around the room.

Pastor Arnold claps and smiles until all his pearly whites wave at the world, the way he does during his sermons.

Adella steps forward and offers her hand to Dad. "Thank you."

The two of them embrace. Along with Solomon and Lonnie, with whom I once played as kids, before our families split.

Maddy, Chrissy, Adella, and Cher step forward.

"For our part, we apologize to the Middletons," Maddy begins. "What we did, what I orchestrated, was selfish and mean. Motivated by a longstanding feud between us and Kevin. I, in particular, should have used better judgment and grace." She faces my parents. "Mr. Middleton, Mrs. Middleton, I will do everything I can to help right the ship. I'm already working with Lion to ensure your family's awesome story receives the acclaim and honor it deserves. We're helping interview the top publishing houses for your book and are in talks with three major streaming services for the documentary."

Chenera comes over to my father. "Mr. Middleton, Mrs. Middleton, I'm so terribly sorry I had a hand in that. As much as I love your son." She glances at Kevin, and the expression he gives her seems reassuring. "There is no excuse. But I was putting my family first, concerning how they felt about Kevin. The whole act was vindictive and jealous. I'll do whatever you need to make up for it. And I hope one day, you can forgive us."

The unity and forgiveness continue to circulate, with all of us watching her and Dad hug it out.

"Thank you for that, Cher," Dad says.

She comes to me, and I sense genuine regret and conflict as she wipes tears. "Lion, I hope you won't always hate me."

"This is a good beginning to 'not always.'" It won't be easy, but I'll put in effort not to cringe whenever I see her.

My brothers and I share our own moment, one that might bridge our feuds, in which we understand perfectly where the other is coming from, while the rest of the world has no idea.

Brendan chastises me through his glare.

Kevin puts up a hard front. But his face is still asking, still expecting from his big brother.

WHAT COMES NEXT

LION

LION

This August East Coast humidity is cooking us aboard our yacht. On the water for one of our weekend outings, the summer heat has turned way up, and the ocean doesn't necessarily offer a reprieve. At least there's swimming to cool us somewhat.

Two weeks before the big Sasha Static concert, we've practically transformed the Hamptons with a huge performance stage, security barricades, large advertising banners, and marquees. Hordes of celebrities and tourists have made reservations in advance.

In the lead-up to one of the largest events of the year in the East, we haven't had too many breaks, so I'm taking full advantage of these few precious hours when I'm not training Explore's yacht crew or finding some boating violation that makes me want to throw somebody.

"You paid the lawyers, right?" Dad asks while we check the navigation lights.

"Yes, Dad."

"And when are we supposed to sign the agreement again?"

"Wednesday morning, Dad," I answer, preoccupied. But not too preoccupied I don't notice what's going on. "What are you nervous about, Old Man?" We've reached an agreement with the City of Boston for him to pay a voluntary fine in the equivalent of the bribe, and with the IRS for tax remittance, but I'm sure he won't trust that he's not going to jail until all this is long behind us.

"I got your damn old man."

"Uh-huh. So what's wrong?"

He rubs his chest. "You think, uh… you think your mama still… still loves me?"

Now I certainly wasn't expecting *that*. I recall my conversation with her, in which I specifically asked her the same thing.

Did you love Dad?

Yes. With everything in me. Still do. It's why I was so hu—

"Well, I would like to think so. She hasn't gone anywhere, Dad. Why don't you know that for yourself?" I venture to check him out when I ask this.

A bewildered, battered man stares around us. "Going to her is… so much has happened. A lot of time is gone."

They are at that point in their marriage where two people live under the same roof but not in matrimony. Ignoring one another, or finding other things to do, is easier than overcoming the fear of all the devastation you put on them. If Ash and I went through it in a couple of years, I can't imagine the gulf of separation spanning thirty years.

"But not so much time you can't show her what you're feeling today, Old Man." I pat his arm and make my way back to the deck.

Grabbing some champagne for Kamilah and me, I take her a glass because I notice she hasn't had any.

"Thanks, babe," she says. But she doesn't sip. Instead, she holds it politely while listening to Cher explain something.

Now that's strange. Since when does Karate Kam ignore alcohol?

Five minutes later, I'm still loosely observing her from where I sit with my brothers.

She still hasn't sipped.

"How's the book deal coming?" Kevin breaks into my thoughts.

"It's all right. Dad's received several offers for a few million. With book tours. But we'll have to hammer out those optics so he doesn't wind up talking to a bunch of soccer moms in the suburbs. I'm making sure we include our own folks, kids, schools, and churches as well."

"Word. So how do you feel about being one of the execs at Explore? Or even… MoneyCruncher?" Kev hesitates and sizes me up. "Desmond really didn't know what to expect when we brought you on, with the beef between you and Solomon and Del. Now he can't stop singing your praises. Neither can Solomon. Neither can Adella."

That's funny. No, really, I'm laughing, because this is a dynamic I wouldn't have expected ten years ago—my younger brother offering me a job.

After all the shit I gave him. "Kevin, it's my bad, man, for what went down when you were a kid. Shit was un… my conduct was excessive. I was pissed at Mom and jealous, and I took it out on you. It was uncalled for. I apologize." This wasn't something that could be said in front of all of Sag Harbor. Our family struggles are just that—ours.

He shakes his head. "I'm kind of glad you did it. My biggest motivation for succeeding was taking down you and Dad."

"I know. But pain shouldn't be what motivates a kid. It should be love and inspiration, not vengeance. I'm sorry for leading you to that place. And I *am* proud of you, despite what drove you to get there."

If I'm insisting that Kevin treat Dad better, then the example for that has to jump off with me.

He sticks out his fist for a pound.

Hugging and mushy expressions of affection have never been what we do.

And if you really want to help your family, do something useful! Kam's words echo in my head from that day she smacked me.

Feeling as awkward as an alien on a strange new planet, I get up and force myself to where Kevin sits. Shocking the hell out of him, Brendan, and everybody, I tap his shoulder.

"Get up, dude."

In a sort of stupor himself, Kevin rises from his seat. We throw our arms around one another. And squeeze.

"I love you, man."

He mutters in my ear, "I know, dude. I know you do."

The boat breaks out laughing. We certainly aren't lacking on humor around here.

"Nah, for real, I love you, too, dude."

I have no idea what I will do as far as taking his offer. I've been entertaining thoughts of my own sea and air cargo company, with large shipping containers traversing the high seas in the way of my ancestors.

But I'm not too worried about it. For now, there's only one priority.

Checking her full glass again, I pry Kamilah away from my mother and sisters-in-law, walk her over to the bow, and pin her between my arms on the railing. Warm summer ocean winds blow her hair in my face.

"What's up, Lumberjack?"

"So what is your plan for telling me you're pregnant?"

Her jaw drops in surprise. "Who told you? Your dad or your mom?"

Now *this* Negro damn near drops. "Wh-*who*? There are *multiple* people who know before me?"

She laughs, patting my chest. "Nooo. Just our folks."

"That's multiple!"

Her rows of teeth cheesing, she's kee-keeing, but I don't find it funny.

"I've been planning a dinner for us all at the house so I could surprise you. Your mom suggested it."

I scratch my head, fussing but happy as hell. "You and me… we're going to talk about communication. Because this secrecy shit better not happen with our next damn kid."

"Our next kid?"

I kiss her lips holding the sunshine.

"Yeah, our next kid. And the one after that. I'm putting a lot of 'em in there. That's the price you pay for me loving you. It's having your legs open as much as possible, no questions asked."

"You can have as many as you want up to three, *maybe*."

"I'll have to be smart about these three pregnancies then, and Imma have to make the most of them all." I lean toward her ear. "The way I did when I worked to get you pregnant."

"Ha!" Kam laughs. "No, you didn't!"

I bite her cheek, and with my hand over her abdomen, I murmur so the others can't hear me. "Remember your first night staying at Cyrus's house, and we sat on the bed? And I told you there was something else I wanted from you? But I wouldn't tell you right then."

Now it's Karate Kam's jaw that falls from her astonishment. There was no way I was telling her that night she would have my kids.

"You slick ass Negro." At the base of my neck, her fingers

play in my fine curls. "And what's the price you'll pay for your scheming ass ways?"

"Getting slapped and cussed out and bossed around and told what I can and can't do with my dick."

With her in my arms, the ocean breeze kisses on both of us.

"So that means you love me?" she asks. "For you to try and brand me *permanently* with your seed, you must think I'm incredible, and amazing, smart, beautiful, damn good sex. And you're not going to just run away like some coward?"

On her cheek, I caress her with my nose. "It means you're feisty, a headache, a pain in the ass, a know-it-all, a mean drunk. And I love you. If I ever show you anything different, all of your brothers have permission to come jump me at the same time."

Her fingers strumming my whiskers give life. "Good, Mr. Middleton, because I love you to the point that I *might* consider your offer of keeping my legs open as much as you want."

MY LIFE

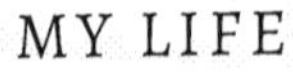

KAMILAH & LION

KAMILAH

"So what are you going to do? Oh my God, I'm so excited for you. And to think, you didn't even want to come to the Hamptons!" Princess gushes a few days later.

We're brunching on my family's portico, and I invited Chaitra since she's moving in with Solomon and she doesn't really know anybody around here.

"Why weren't you interested?" Shay asks.

I shrug. "Quiet and too slow. I like the bright lights and noise of the city, or at least I did back then. Turns out I needed this peace of mind more than I thought I did. It's tranquil, sinks into my bones like steam, and purges me of all the stress I don't know I was carrying. So yes, I suppose this sleepy kind of beauty is growing on me." I sip some orange juice. "As far as what Lion and I do next, we're looking for a place of our own. He wants this big spread because he's flashy. I don't. That is too much house to be cleaning."

"Hello?" Princess cuts in. "Cleaning staff! Ro and I have people come in twice a month, becaaaa...aggghhh..." She breaks into another coughing fit.

I grab water for her to drink and rush over to her side. "P! P!"

My fingers shake hard while pushing the water to her lips. She takes a sip.

"I'm sorry. Don't mean to wor... worry you."

"What have you and Roland been hiding?" I insist now. I gave them their privacy before and held off nosying in their business, but P doesn't look any better than two months ago.

"It's..." She starts coughing and gagging again.

As I tend to her and question if I should drive her to the emergency room, somebody steps out of our house and onto the porch.

The question leaves my head before I think. "What the hell is she doing here?"

This woman lowers to one knee and holds out her arms toward the backyard. Her son and my nephew, Hadar, comes running from where he plays with his cousins. "Mama!"

"There he is! God, you've grown in just a few weeks," Eugenia, my ex sister-in-law, marvels aloud. "You look like a grown man now. What are they feeding you around here?"

I roll my eyes. She may have a son in our family, but Genie's got a lot of nerve showing up around here after how she abandoned Sheldon.

"Ooh wee, chile," Shay starts. "You might want to fix your face. You look like you trying to jump somebody out here."

Scoffing and unable to fake a smile, I turn my head.

"Good afternoon, everybody," Eugenia says as she makes her way to us. Her eyes focus in on Princess. "Hey, P. Are you all right? What do you need me to do?"

I object, "She doesn't need you to—"

"Genie," P greets her with a weak voice. But even in her

apparent fragile state, P's inner angel warms us all. "I'm glad you could make it. You've been a godsend to me in the city. Come here, have a seat and join us."

But Hadar tugs on his mom. "Mama, come on. I want to show you my space inventions."

"All right," Genie replies. "Princess, you don't look too good. I'll be right back."

"Helpful in the city? You've been hanging out with her?" I ask Princess, as Genie follows Hadar into the backyard so he can show her what he's been "inventing."

My de facto big sister gazes at me. "Girl, I know there's..." Her lungs wheeze and whistle as she struggles.

"Don't worry about it," I tell her. "Stop talking. I need you to feel better."

P surprises me when she finds enough strength to grab my wrist. Her gaze toughens. "Sheldon is a good man, Kam, I know. You're justified in your feelings. But she and I are still friends. We're not enemies. We all have flawwwww..." Coughs wrack her body again.

Shay whispers, "Am I being too nosy for asking who's that?"

"My brother's ex-wife," I report. "And word on the street is she might be linking up with *your* brother. You didn't know?"

Chaitra's face registers that information. "Her? The one who's got Keenan wide open?"

"Yes," I reply. "And if you love your brother at all, you'll get him the hell away from her. She took my brother through so much heartache. Not to mention she's batshit crazy, tried to kill herself last summer."

Taking my mind off Genie, I shift back to Princess. "P, I think we should get you to an emergency room."

She hacks more.

Chaitra helps me pull up Princess. "That sounds bad. I can drive while you sit in the back seat with her. Let me get the door."

"What's going on out here?" my mother demands, bursting out of the house.

I almost give up my own innards at seeing P's eyes roll into the back of her head. "Princess! Oh, my God! Princess!" Furiously, I pat on her. "Mama, call 911!"

"Lay her out on the floor and let's open up her airway," Genie suggests.

"P!" I cry aloud.

"Don't shake her," Genie warns.

"Get off me!" I snap back. "P, wake up."

Eyes still at the top of her head, Princess convulses, breaking into seizures.

"Oh, my God! Princess!"

Roland is nowhere around. The ambulance arrives minutes later, which feels like an eternity in which I must watch the woman suffer who guided me through my suffering. Only, I'm helpless to give her the strength she's given me. I jump in the ambulance as the medics push her gurney in. Wails from her kids are our last sounds before paramedics close the door shut.

My parents tail us in their car, most likely calling her family down in Louisiana. A feeble Princess drifts in and out of consciousness.

"We love you, Princess, please don't leave us. You're so strong, the best part of our family." My lips tremble while I do the best I can to keep her here with us. To tell her all the things I know Roland would want her to hear. And especially to pour out how much of a joy she is in our family. After she left her own and became part of us.

Her eyelids flutter.

"Come on, P. The Rouse family isn't the same without you, girl. You're ours now. One of us, with your beautiful heart that my brother needs, and your children, and I need. Who's going to put up with our rowdy tails and be the calm one?"

Her eyelids crack open, and I leap with joy.

"P!"

A dazed, lopsided smile is the hug my heart needs.

"Don't try too hard to talk. You're on the way to see doctors who'll help."

"Kam," she croaks. So peaceful, like she already arrived some place in her mind I don't know about. "Be k-kind. You've found beauti… beautiful love…" Hacking and gagging. "… from somebody who accepts all of you. Give the l-love you've… found, Kam. And forgiveness. And grace."

My tears land on her shirt while the medics check her vitals.

"Girl, stop talking like you won't be here to give love yourself. You're going to do it. Forget me." Rubbing her hair, kissing her hand, I squeeze her with hopes the affection will keep life from trickling out of her.

The solemness on her is a chastisement to me. "Wheth…" Hacking and coughing. "Whether I'm h… here or not, be kind. Genie's been through a…" Her lungs torture her.

Arriving at the hospital, I race in behind the medics. The nurses ask me all kinds of questions for which I don't have answers. Roland and Sheldon come storming around the corner.

"What happened?" he bellows at me. "What—"

"I don't know! She started coughing really bad. Then her eyes rolled into the back of her head. Then she started seizing. She woke up a little in the ambulance, started talk—"

Roland throws his hands in front of him. "What did she say?"

"It…"

He pivots and goes to the nurses, and they take him to another waiting area.

"Ro!"

"What?" he yells at me, frantic and devastated.

Now I'm the one shaking my hands. "What do you want me to do? About the job? What do I *do*?"

He follows P's gurney through the double doors leading to another wing. "Shit, I don't know, Kam! Why are you asking me… You've been doing this long enough. Figure it out. Just handle it!" And he disappears.

LION

"Lion!"

"Hey, buddy, how did you get way out here to New York? Did you fly here on a big bird?" I ask Cedric.

The boy gives me a wide, snaggletoothed grin. "No! I flew on a plane. It was fun, and I had pizza and watched movies!"

'Yeah, and you must've had so much fun you lost a tooth, huh?" I check out Ashlyn's overly excited son who stands in my doorway.

"See! The tooth fairy came and gave me a whole ten dollars. Me and King spent it on ice cream."

Behind him trots in my lazy dog, King. The aging dog's mood changes at the sight of me, and I squat to hug him. "Awww, Kiiing, I missed you, fam."

The kisses he gives me on my arms and neck tell me the sentiment is mutual.

"Oh, look! It's King!" Braelan screams and comes running in from the pool.

Right along with him comes Chrissy Rouse's kids, Kara and Blake, and Sheldon's son, Hadar.

"A dog!" Kara yells.

Ashlyn steps into the temporary home I'm sharing with Kam. "Well, well, how things change. We've gone from keg and foam parties, topless dancers and nude poker, to kids, water guns, and rubber duckies."

"Cedric, you remember my nephew, Braelan, right?" I ask her boy.

"Hi, B!" Cedric waves.

"Hey, Ced! You want to come swim with us?" B asks.

The two boys know each other from Brendan's visits to my house in Houston, and I invite Cedric so he has somebody to play with.

Ashlyn's instant panic is a Kodak moment. "Actually, we can't, Ced. We're only in New York for a day before we're off to France. We just stopped by to drop off King, remember? We have to go see other people."

With disappointment, her son's shoulders sink. "Okay."

"Maybe next time, Ced, but even if you don't have time to swim, why don't you grab a hamburger or something. Hang out a minute," I suggest.

"So," Ashlyn says while eying me, "this is not the same Lion who left Houston all dejected and worked up a couple months ago." She doesn't just inspect me once. Those sharp blue eyes of hers are scrutinizing.

"I guess you could say New York's been good to me." My heart is full as hell and that's an understatement, but I have to downplay this new era for her sake. This version of me is what she had wanted back then.

"I'll say. You and Kevin haven't killed each other. I've seen you in some of the photos of the Black History celebrations, Lionel's book deal, a tour, charity work… you've come here and done a lot. And you're a whole vibe now. I'm glad to see it. Kudos, Lion. So when might you be returning to Houston?"

I walk alongside her, so I can keep an eye on the kids in the back. The past affection for her dives through my chest. "Yeah, I was going to tell you. I'm leaving Houston Petro-Chem. I've started figuring things out here in New York."

The tiny flicker of her eye pains me. That ever-so-slight swell of emotion in her, swells up in me. Though she's married now, we stayed friends. Okay, so, more than friends.

Even after she married Lamar, she and I shared the occasional romp in the sheets. He doesn't exactly have big dick energy. In the beginning, I'm certain she started dating Lamar to make me jealous, then accepted his offer of marriage to show me she was "serious" about having a man who'll be good to her, in hopes I would stop her and change my ways.

But Ash could never tame me. I'm not a complacent kind of man.

I *like* power, prestige, money, and thrills.

There were times Ash resented it and wanted me to "just be normal."

"Right," she replies from inside a dry throat. "And I suppose the… drop-dead gorgeous chick you were kissing on Instagram at some brewery wouldn't have anything to do with it?"

Kamilah knows what to do with me. Ashlyn's not visionary enough to fuck me in a fermentation room of Brite tanks, or jump behind a bar and whip up her own drink, or put on a helmet to disguise herself and grab my ass in touch football, suck my dick in a jacuzzi full of beer or to simply keep me guessing. My wealth and family lineage might scare Kam somewhat, but she doesn't detest it.

Ashlyn needed to be free of me.

My shoulders rise and fall in answer. "She does."

Truth is, Kamilah has a lot to do with me returning to New York, with me not punishing my younger brother, with me listening to my mom and forgiving her, with me thinking out my life beyond chasing power. And pussy.

My ex-wife continues what I'm sure is her mental trip down memory lane. "I'm happy for you, Lion. For b… for both of you." She steers her gaze from my face, and scans the house. "This is Cyrus's house, no?"

"Yeah, he's letting me borrow it while I put things in order."

She doesn't need to know I'm already having Kamilah's engagement ring designed by Tiffany, with a blue diamond from the Cullinan mine in South Africa, and several of my family's heirloom diamonds, or that I've already bought Kam a house in the city. And my parents will likely gift us another one here in the Hamptons, so Mom can pretty much make it her second home.

"I know Roberta is over the moon about having one of her sons home in New York full time."

The thought of Mom draws my hand to my chest where I rub over the area of my heart. She and Dad are now in marriage therapy. Our family is joining Kevin for family therapy.

"Hell, the moon? She's over the galaxy."

"And the kids out there?" she asks, checking out all the activity in the backyard, where the Rouse children play with my nephew.

"Yeah, Kam's got a family member who fell ill suddenly. Most of the Rouses are at the hospital, and a few of us are taking turns with the kids."

My new moves crash land on her face.

"You're babysitting a house full of *kids.*"

I wish I could shrink the size of Ash's awestruck eyes. Or at least make all this make sense for her so she doesn't walk out of here feeling a way. I reach for her arm, partly to comfort her, partly to steady her.

"Ash, I wish I could have gotten there faster for you."

"Babe! Did you say you brought extra chips? I can't find —" Kamilah bursts into the room as I'm squeezing Ash's arm. Kam's eyes focus on that physical, personal connection.

"Kam." I clear my throat. "Kamilah, baby, this is Ashlyn. My—"

Recognition crosses Kam's face because I've already discussed my marital screw-ups with her. "Oh, Ashlyn! Welcome. Nice to meet you."

Still pulling herself together, Ashlyn offers a handshake. "H-hi, Kamilah. It's a pleasure to meet someone who's finally reeling him in."

"Oh, Lion is nobody. More like a kitten." Kam throws her arms open. "I'm originally from Louisiana, and we give hugs where I come from."

Taken aback, Ashlyn goes into Kamilah's embrace. Over Kam's shoulder, a stunned Ash blinks at me. "Well, uh, thanks."

"Thank you for bringing the dog. Hi, King." Kamilah stoops to pet him. "Kids, don't smother him. He just got here. Let's see if he's hungry or thirsty." She reaches out to her oldest nephew, the son of Princess and Roland, who's lagging on the porch by himself. Clearly upset and worried about his mother. "Rome? Jerome. You see the dog? Why don't you come take care of him?"

The downtrodden boy's spirit drags toward her. "Yes, ma'am."

"I should go. He's having a hard time right now," Kam

explains. "But, Ashlyn, you're welcome to stay and eat with us. We have plenty."

"Oh, no, we have other stops to make." Ash still grapples with a sort of fight-or-flight reactive mode. "Cedric, honey, come on. Maybe we'll stop through on our way back from Europe so you all can have a sleepover."

"You're welcome to visit us any time." Kamilah also squeezes Ash's arm. As if Kamilah well knows what it's like to be "the ex" and refuses to inflict on another woman the coldness Tanja dispensed to her. "We'd love to have you and your family."

"Auntie Kam! The dog is eating all Hadar's chips!" Halle yelps excitedly and bangs her little hand against Kam's abdomen.

Instantly, Kam covers her barely existent baby bump. "Excuse us," she says to Ash and me, before following her niece and slipping a hand over her belly protectively. "Girl, why are you running through the house?"

"She's pregnant." In disbelief, Ash ambles toward the door, wide-eyed once again. "Kids."

I refused to give Ash any. Not while I was still "in the streets." I didn't want a repeat of my parents and their mistakes.

Slipping my arm around Ash, I bring her to me in a half-hug, while walking her out to the car.

"You've got a phenomenal life of your own. You're on your way to Europe for Heaven's sake." I'm trying to give the consolation talk.

She side-eyes me, her voice shaky. "So Lion is a 'kitten' now, huh?"

For Kam, yes.

"Ash, if you ever need anything, we're always here for you." Though Ash and I haven't messed around so much since she had Cedric, I still place my support for her in terms of "we"—for Kamilah and me—as a message that there will be no more romps.

I hold the car door open for her as she swipes at tears. I give Cedric a fist pound. And close that chapter of my life.

Back in the house, I embrace my future. "Thanks for being nice."

Now it's the doubt in Kam's side-eye that I face. Her features are pregnant with questions of her own. "Seems like she needed it."

"Kam..."

Her gaze drops to her belly, so all I see are her blinking eyelids and how, underneath them, she may be second-guessing her decision to trust me.

"Lion, I'm happy about our child, but don't think that me carrying your baby means I'm trapped. Or that I'll tolerate you—"

"Stop. You're going into stress mode, baby, and it's not necessary. I knew the moment I walked in that brewery you were my wife."

The windows to Kamilah face me.

"And my life."

Kam's wall of skepticism holds steady. "Our first day at the brewery, you said you preferred 'no strings.'" Those eyes scrutinize me.

"What was I supposed to say to a woman who destroys Negroes for fun? That you fascinated me? That you packed enough power in those beer shots for me to want all that energy on top of me? No." I circle my arms around her waist. "I just bided my time."

Even while she smiles, my French Fry is still on the fence, staring between me and the door Ashlyn just walked out of. "She seems like a decent lady, Lion. Bringing you your dog and everything."

"She is. It's one of the reasons I married her. But I wasn't ready. I mostly wanted a hot white girl on my arm at the company events, not the sacrifices or the commitment."

May as well 'fess up. The only way this can ever work between Kam and me is if I give her what my mother apparently never had. And what I am willing to learn. Accountability.

Mortified and hopeful, Kam stares at me from behind her windows. "And you're ready now?"

I place my hands on the most solid proof I can give her. "I'm trying my best to be. I want to be. I never put my seed in Ash, never thought to do it until you."

The metal armor loosens around my tough little warrior who always gives me shit. "You've never gotten anybody pregnant? Not even your own wife?"

"No. That's the hurt you saw on her. I've never looked at a woman and thought, 'If I do nothing else in life but breathe the same air as her, I'm good.' I'm an ambitious Negro, and that's just not how I think. But it's what's going on in me when I'm with you."

Watching the windows open in her eyes, I whisper so the kids don't hear.

"I never drank *any*thing from the crack of *any*body's ass. And I've never let *any*-damn-body call me a kitten." My one arm under her butt is all I need to hoist her from the ground, until her head is over mine. I speak through her windows, into her being. "I gave all of Lion August Middleton to you that night. So, let me show you you're changing this man before you start convicting me with my past. Okay, French Fry?"

Leveling me with one more threatening stare, Kam clutches my beard. "If you mess up, I won't need my brothers to jump you. Pregnant or not pregnant."

"You know when you talk like that, all you're doing is

setting yourself up for trouble. And we've got all these kids. So just tell me you love me and get on out there."

Still gripping my beard, the mischievous excitement returning to her eye, she sucks my lips and my heart. "I love you, Lumberjack."

"I love you, too, baby."

EPILOGUE

LION

It's hot as hell out here and I've been running around all day, but I don't give a damn if my skin melts off. Before I head home to Kam, this final stop is the most critical.

"Lion, dude, I'm pleading with you, buddy. I could have done this without you. Actually, Lion," my attorney, Percell, says to me, "I really wish you wouldn't do this. The situation with your dad is finally cooling off, and we don't need bad press on our hands right now. This is my job. I'm the one who should take care of it." He's damn near begging me on my way across the dock and I almost expect him to grab my arm and pull.

But I discussed this move with Kam last night, and she was totally on board. She even wanted to be here, but hell no. With her being older and at risk, I won't bring her into a stressful situation while she's carrying my seed.

Not even my mother had objections.

"Mr. Middleton! Wow, twice in one summer. I'm gonna have to hire me a welcoming committee, just for you." Allen

Stafford's beet red face is the last thing I want to see today. "To what do I owe this pleasure?"

"I'm coming to renegotiate the terms of our arrangement."

"Really now? Oh, don't tell me. Let me guess. Since Ms. Static's concert is right around the corner, you boys are flush with more money than you know what to do with, and you can't find a better place to park it than in my pocket. You'd like to increase your monthly payments."

Holding my damn hands right on my hip, I remember what I promised Kam and Mom. No violence. "I'd like the price to be placed at fair market rates that are comparable with all the other distributors in New York and New Jersey. In fact, whatever you're charging your predominantly white business buddies, that's what I'm insisting on for the black business owners."

Through his half-cocked smile, he snickers. "Ha. Insisting? You're *insisting* on what I should do here on my property."

"No." I've waited on this for months. "I'm insisting on what you should do on mine."

With the beads of sweat that roll down those cheeks, the cock rolls off his mouth. "What'd you say there, son?"

"You heard me...*boy*. This is my goddamn property you're standing on now. That there is my establishment, and if I say the prices will be fair market for *everyone*, then that's what they'll be. *Boy.*"

Recognition strikes the fear in his eyes that every white man must spend his entire life dreading. "I haven't sold to any Middletons. I cut a deal with a company named—"

"La Société Césaire."

Was that a scoff or a "whoof"...like a dog? It doesn't matter. His face is on the verge of eruption. "Get the hell out of here, and don't ever come back."

While Percell digs for the registration and transfer papers, I continue.

"Mr. Stafford, have you wondered why these past few weeks, you're not receiving as many calls and your shipments have gotten lighter? You're probably having a hard time finding your friends. They've dropped you for your competitors who offer dirt cheap distribution."

I sent middlemen to pay his competitors so they'd drop their prices. Local businesses now transport their products through Stafford's rivals, who still don't know they're in my pocket. That's an expense I'm willing to pay for.

"You all right there, Allen?" I ask.

"No way in hell—"

"It does kind of feel like that's where we are today, doesn't it? It's likely where you've been the past month while your business has fallen off. So you likely got a call from a man named Serge Césaire."

I definitely think he's having a health scare, but still, he manages to speak. "He was a damn Frenchman."

"Yeah, well, attention avec qui tu baises la prochaine fois ici en Amérique."

Percell hands him the papers, and now Stafford's sons are at his side, all of them scanning the papers together.

Inappropriate as hell, but I hold up my camera phone and snap a picture. After their disgusting tactics, I feel zero shame. They don't deserve decorum.

I took a page out of Brendan Middleton's playbook. Césaire is our mother's maiden name. Serge is my distant relative in France.

"You bastard." Stafford spits.

I screwed his business up bad enough that he couldn't pay bills and needed a buyer who would let him keep running the place.

"Not a nice way for you to talk to your new boss, Allen.

So as I was saying, you're going to adjust the practices accordingly, and if you've got a problem with your new marching orders, you can march your ass off my property now." Not later. For shits and giggles, I step forward, and hold out my hand. "Now that, I'll shake to."

There's no way I'll trust him to work for me. A locksmith is on the way to change the locks, and a new all-black crew will be starting here tomorrow.

THE END

HEY FROM LULA

Hey Fam, thanks so much for being patient with me while I got *Drink You* ready. These last few months have been trying, and I've pressed on. I've had Covid, plus a big personal setback, and those circumstances caused my projects and delayed deadlines to snowball. I'm still playing catchup but I'm determined to get it done. Your support has been amazing, and I can't express enough how you motivate me.

I do want to address this storyline. I usually don't talk about them, because once it's done, it's done. But this is important.

As for Kevin's "big secret" and whether it "comes out," his secret is not for the world. His identity or genealogy is not the business of Sag Harbor residents or outsiders, beyond the English and Middleton families. Other than the parties involved, there is no reason that non-relatives need to know his business. But there seems to be anticipation that Kevin's secret will "come out."

To whom? And why?

This is a fact of life for him. Kevin's secret is not a tactic or a gimmick I used as a means of suspense for the series. It was a disclosure of his circumstances that define and shape who he is. Just as so many of us carry our private burdens through life.

While I acknowledge my plots usually contain a bit of sensationalism and high drama (LOL), I also try to balance that with just "hard knocks" we deal with throughout life.

That said, there is no big "surprise!" moment where all the world learns his truth in some big twist. While I could have gone that route, Kevin has already been through enough.

This was Lion's story, and more important here was *Lion's, Lionel's,* and *Roberta's* growth in accepting the secret, acknowledging their mistakes in how they handled it, and them taking the lead in bridging the divide.

Thank you all again for sticking with me through the multiple delays of this release. On the web site and on Patreon, I will be talking more about my plans for the next series, and how I will likely move different in my future releases. These last few months of pressure really required my big girl panties.

Finally, if you enjoyed *Drink You* and it spoke to you in some way, please do share it with your book club, reading friends, and on social media. I have not had time to promote it or make the social media rounds!

For now, I've got to go. But I will likely host a Live chat and will announce that on the site. Also, shoot me an email lula@lulawhitebooks.com! I love hearing from you!

xo, Lula

LULA'S OTHER WORKS

Thank you for reading *Explore Men of the Hamptons*! If you enjoyed this story, please leave a review.

The remaining books of the series will all be released month by month. Ignore the Amazon publication date; I've pushed it out far so that Amazon won't bother me. But the books will come out sooner than listed on the site.

You can find me on my web site where I drop short stories once or twice a month. I will also be making books, videos and content available early as I write the books on my Patreon. Come hang out on my writing journey. Much love! 🖤

If you want to stay updated on when you'll see more series of class, distinction and growth among the black elite, here's how you can stay connected.

Web site: www.lulawhitebooks.com

Email: lula@lulawhitebooks.com

Join Lula's Luxe Suite Reading Group:
Facebook Reader Group

Read the stories before they go on sale:
Patreon

You can find me on my web site where I drop short stories once or twice a month. I will also be making books, videos and content available early as I write the books on my Patreon. Come hang out on my writing journey. Much love! 🩶

The *Sag Harbor Black Romances*

Brown Sugar This Christmas - Maddy & Jerrell
Hot Chocolate This Winter - Chrissy & Sheldon Part 1
Flinging All Spring - Adella & Desmond
Overheated for Summer - Chrissy & Sheldon Part 2
Rouse Family Christmas - All Couples

The Sag Harbor spin-off *Explore Men of the Hamptons* series

One Tasty Night FREE Novella - Solomon & Chaitra
Explore You - Kevin & Cher
Christmas Down Under Novella - Keenan & Eugenia - (FREE Download on website only)
Taste You - Solomon & Chaitra
Drink You - Lion & Kamila
See Through You - Keenan & Eugenia
Find You - Roland & Neeraja

Stand-Alone Related to Sag Harbor

A New Life for Christmas - Tazima & Odell

The Young & Luxurious

Love & Fire - Korienne & Easton

www.lulawhitebooks.com
Email: lula@lulawhitebooks.com
www.blackluxuryromances.com

Made in the USA
Middletown, DE
02 July 2023